THE
DEALERSHIP

To Rich,
Best wishes always !

THE
DEALERSHIP

A STORY OF UNCONTROLLED GREED AND CORRUPTION

ALAN WOLFORD

TATE PUBLISHING
AND ENTERPRISES, LLC

Published by Tate Publishing & Enterprises, LLC
127 E. Trade Center Terrace | Mustang, Oklahoma 73064 USA
1.888.361.9473 | www.tatepublishing.com

Tate Publishing is committed to excellence in the publishing industry. The company reflects the philosophy established by the founders, based on Psalm 68:11,
"The Lord gave the word and great was the company of those who published it."

Book design copyright © 2015 by Tate Publishing, LLC. All rights reserved.
Cover design by Ivan Charlem Igot
Interior design by Joana Quilantang

Published in the United States of America

ISBN: 978-1-63306-777-6
Fiction / Thrillers / Crime
14.10.30

ONE

She called herself Shari, and along with Amber, they were the two most common stage names among strippers and escorts available from Club Liquid in downtown Gainesville. Her head popped up from between the pillows when his phone rang. Groggy from the drinks and cocaine, she reached over and grabbed Larry's cell phone from the nightstand and pushed the talk button.

"Larry's maid service, Shari speaking." Completely naked, she sat up in bed, her blonde hair spilling over her breasts as she wiped cocaine residue from her nose and waited for the caller to respond.

"Hey, Shari. It's Tony, Larry's friend from last night. How you doing, darlin'? You guys tear it up?" She remembered Tony slobbering all over her last night at the strip club. She recalled what a pervert he was, and she imagined him probably touching himself as they spoke.

"What time is it, Tony?" Shari studied the welt on her wrist from last night's rough love play, trying to remember where she laid her watch.

"It's about seven o'clock, darlin'. Let me talk to Larry."

"He's in the shower. I'll see if he can talk, Tony. Hang on a second." She slipped out of bed and carried the phone a few feet into the tiny hotel bathroom where Larry was now busy brushing his teeth. "It's Tony, your bodyguard," she said, handing him the phone. Turning off the faucet, he cast a leery eye and admired her perfect body as she jumped back into bed.

"What's up, Tony? Did he pony up the cash?" asked Larry. He stood in the doorway with the towel wrapped around his waist, unable to take his eyes off Shari's heart-shaped derriere as she lay bottom up on top of the sheets, doing her best to lure him back into bed.

"Yeah, we got the other six grand, but Kirk and I had to beat it out of him. That piece of crap was trying to tell us we sold him bootleg dope and over-cut coke." Tony Grimes did double duty as Larry's debt collector and used car manager. Good with his fists and able to press four hundred pounds, he would clean anybody's clock at his boss's command. "So you convinced him otherwise," said Larry. "You sound out of breath, bro. What were you, playin' with yourself on the phone with Shari?"

"No, boss. I ran inside when I heard the screamin' cop cars. I'm at Kirk's condo downtown. You didn't hear them about a half hour ago?"

"Too far away. We wound up out west on 34th Street. Shari wanted to stay at the Hilton. You covered your tracks, right?"

"Yeah, boss. No way they track me here. I made sure there were no witnesses."

"Please tell me you took the guy's cell phone off him, right?" Larry wanted no record of the many calls to their ex-con drug dealers.

"Sure did. Got it right here." Tony sounded sure of himself, but Larry knew he wasn't always the sharpest tool in the shed. Last time he disfigured a business rival for trying to welch on drug money, Tony dropped his cell phone at the scene. If the bartender at Club Mystique hadn't found it before the cops did, they'd all be in jail doing ten-to-twenty.

"Tony, listen to me. On your way in to the dealership, wipe his cell phone down, pull the battery and SIM card out. Throw it into that big lake over at Kirk's condo. Stay inside until the cops leave and drop the six grand into the safe under my desk. Got it?"

"Got it. We got a little blood on a few of the Ben Franklins. Sorry, boss."

"Burn 'em. You'd be stupid to pass those bills with Tyrone's DNA on them. They could put you at the scene. I'll see you in two hours. Shari and I aren't quite finished with our morning workout."

"You bad boy. I hope you're wearing protection."

Detective Sergeant Gronske had been on the scene since six thirty in the morning, arriving twelve minutes after the custodian from Club Liquid found the victim unconscious and slumped against the dumpster. He had pulled up just as the ambulance arrived. Fifteen minutes after he called in for the lab techs, the forensics team arrived behind the nightclub. After forensics photographed the crime scene, the detective watched the paramedics load the unconscious victim inside the ambulance. The legs of the gurney folded under, and the medical tech locked it into place. As he sipped on his expresso, Gronske watched the paramedic adjust the IV and check the electrodes, making sure they were adhered to the victim and connected to the monitor. Then he watched the paramedic fit an oxygen mask over the patient's airway.

"How's he doing, Vince? You think he might be able to give us a statement?" Preoccupied with his patient, the paramedic glanced up briefly but was unable to give Gronsky his full attention.

"Well, detective, we've got him stabilized, but he's got a weak pulse and he's lost a lot of blood. He's got serious head trauma. Probably fifty-fifty he regains consciousness anytime soon. We need to get him to the hospital STAT. Do we have a name yet?"

"Yeah. Tyrone Davis. Forensics found his wallet in the dumpster he was leaning against. Tyrone's a known drug dealer. Looks like he pissed somebody off." Detective Gronske handed him his card. "Call me on my cell as soon as he regains consciousness. We need a statement."

Vince glanced at the detective's card and stuck it in his pocket. "Will do, Gary." In a louder voice, he said, "Andrea, let's roll!"

Gronske watched Andrea walk to the back of the ambulance and shut the back doors. She hopped into the driver's seat, slammed the door and hit the lights and siren. The ambulance lurched forward and rolled south down the alleyway with the siren blaring, on its way to Shands Emergency.

Matt Tyler, Forensics Technician, was busy thirty feet away, bagging the wallet, credit cards and drugs found on the victim. Detective Gronske put a hand on his shoulder and said, "Thanks for the coffee, Matt."

Matt looked up at the detective. "No problem, Gary. Got a question for you. If this was a robbery, why'd they take just the cash and leave the jewelry, drugs, and credit cards? The victim had a solid gold necklace and rings worth at least three or four grand."

"Maybe it wasn't a robbery," said Gronske. "I'm thinking maybe a drug deal gone bad. Maybe the vic owed money and knew the perp, which might explain the minimal defensive wounds. You took close-up photos of the vic's hands and head, right?"

"Of course. Ain't my first rodeo, ya know." Matt pointed at the clear plastic bag laying on the hood of his forensics truck. The bag contained the dope, HGH vials, and the cocaine rock that they found in Tyrone's pocket. "They're all in the bag, there. We've got all our photos and evidence, tagged and bagged. I'll call you if we get any hits on the prints or other stuff. We're going to wrap it up here, Gary." Matt placed all the plastic bags inside the evidence compartments on the truck, locking them both, and prepared to head for the GPD crime lab to finish processing the evidence.

Detective Gronske looked up and noticed a few onlookers gathering at the entrance to the alley. He set his empty Starbucks cup carefully on the hood of his cruiser, keeping it separate from the crime scene. As he approached the group, he asked, "Anybody here see or hear anything last night?" He studied their faces for a response, but all three shook their heads. *Just gawkers*, he thought. Then, he walked over to talk again with the young Latino student who was still standing at the back door to the club. He was his best source of information so far. Working part-time at Club Liquid as a custodian, Orlando was the one who had found the victim thirty minutes earlier.

"I appreciate your cooperation earlier, Orlando," said Gronske. "I just have a few more questions for you." He looked expectantly at his witness.

"Okay, but I'm not sure if I'm gonna be much help," said Orlando. "You think the guy's gonna be okay?"

"We're not sure yet," said Gronske. He paged through his notepad and found the notes he wanted to reference as a food service van pulled into the far end of the alley. He watched as the driver got out and unlocked the back door to the van, ignoring the crime scene and prepared to make a delivery to the rear of the restaurant on the opposite side of the alley.

From his earlier questions, Gronske knew that Orlando was in his third year at the University of Florida studying business marketing and worked part-time at the club. He called 911 at a little after six o'clock when he found the victim in the alley. He had patiently answered a litany of questions from the detective, but Gronske's probing had produced no solid leads.

"I know I may have asked you this earlier, Orlando, but I need you to think real hard," said Gronske. "When you came out back to empty your mop bucket, did you see or hear anything, or anyone at all? Anything you can remember would be helpful." In his twelve years as a detective working robbery/homicide at GPD, he could tell when a witness wanted to help. He decided to spend a little extra time with this one.

"Nope. Nobody." Orlando touched his fingers to his temple as if to trigger his memory. "Oh, wait. This might sound weird, but I thought I heard snoring when I first came out the back door. I'm not sure." He stared blankly at Gronske, waiting for a response.

"Snoring? In the alley?" Detective Gronske glanced up at the brick facades that enclosed the alley on either side. Squinting into the morning sky, he studied the buildings for more clues. He could see a couple of air vents near the roofs of the two older buildings, but no windows that would indicate living quarters.

"Yes, sir. But when I found that dude laying against the dumpster, I yelled for help. I never heard it after that." Orlando shrugged sheepishly, waiting for the next question.

"Okay. Anything else?" Gronsky's eyes narrowed and brow furrowed as he worked to extract every last detail he could from his sole witness. "No, sir. I got a marketing class starting at eight o'clock. It's a mid-term test, so I can't be late. I hope I've been some help to you." He was thinking that this had been the most time spent talking to a cop since he got caught with a beer at his high school prom five years ago.

"You have been very helpful, Orlando. You need a ride?"

"Thanks, but I got my bike out in front of the club." Orlando held up the detective's card. "If I think of anything else, I'll call you, okay?"

"Thanks, Orlando. I appreciate your help. Call me on my cell if you can remember anything at all." They shook hands, and Gronske headed toward the dumpsters at the north end of the alley to scour the area for more clues. As he searched for clues he may have overlooked earlier, Gronske sidestepped a dead rat, convinced there had to be more evidence. Something else caught his attention. Wedged into the corner behind the dumpster was a large cardboard box with MAYTAG printed on the side. Taking a closer look inside with his flashlight, he pulled away one corner to reveal a sleeping bag, unopened bottles of water, a half-burned candle, and several snack-size bags of potato chips. His nostrils flared as the strong stench of urine hit him and he closed the box back up. He made a mental note to stop by the makeshift home again later that night, hoping to find the occupant in residence. Intent on finding the second witness, he was determined to identify the perpetrator of the brutal assault.

TWO

It was Friday, April 17th. The warm weather and sunshine were a welcome change from his drenching the day before. Mark McAllister shaded his eyes from the bright reflection from the two-story glass building that sprawled on two acres. He could see smart, energy efficient features all over the building, including adjustable solar panels and a low-maintenance exterior—innovations that reflected Toyota's commitment to energy-efficient technology. This was the new breed of environmentally-friendly structures that Toyota was building in the US market.

Built to impress and the largest auto dealership in the Gainesville area, Brandson Toyota was a state-of-the-art sales and service facility that was inviting and new. It was visible from a half mile away in either direction up and down Main Street. The customer service lounge was second to none in comfort and amenities, offering luxuries like leather recliners, complimentary snacks, three HD big-screen TVs to watch the Gator games, complimentary beverages, wi-fi, car wash, and shuttle service to and from locations all over Gainesville. Local customers were in no hurry to rush out to save a couple of bucks elsewhere on servicing their Lexus and Toyotas when they could be pampered at the newest dealership in the county.

When the land use plans were first drawn-up, local politicians and developers in Gainesville had questioned whether or not it was too ambitious for a small-to-midsize college town in North Florida. Critics claimed it would put the local dealerships out of business and wreck the ecosystem it was built on. Toyota and the franchise partners did a good job of selling the elected officials on the project's value in providing a needed source of new employment and tax revenue for a city whose primary business—the University of Florida—was property tax exempt. With such an effective lobbying effort, the project was eventually approved by the local "good ole boy" politicians who were under constant pressure to control the burgeoning property taxes that gave Alachua County the dubious distinction of having the highest *ad valorem* property taxes in the state.

Mark's first visit to the new dealership took place about six months ago when he was on the hunt for the newly-designed Prius. After learning about the hybrid's upgrades and new body style, he had decided to postpone buying until the new model was introduced. His sales rep, Ramone, made several attempts to persuade him to drop a thousand dollar deposit on the new model Prius as a "refundable reservation agreement," but Mark was reluctant to do it without knowing the total costs.

Ramone had offered Mark some interesting facts about Brandson's recent sale. According to Ramone, the original owner, Red Rollman, had nearly been driven into bankruptcy by the unfortunate combination of expanding at the onset of a recession while being saddled with the new dealership's high operational expenses. Rollman and his partners lacked the deep pockets needed to weather the recession and were forced to sell it only six months after completion.

Brandson had also assumed responsibility for the dealership's huge mortgage payment and related franchise fees. The property taxes alone were over $1.6 million a year. With that kind of over-head, Mark figured they needed someone who could sell big-ticket items. Someone who believed in the product and could help them make a go of it. Brandson Toyota seemed like a good fit for a man with Mark's background.

He learned from the website that the new Prius would be partially solar-powered and offer significant advances in fuel economy and hybrid technology, including a new, more aerodynamic body style with lower coefficient of drag ratio and regenerative braking. The site also revealed that Toyota was the world leader in fuel-efficient cars at a time when the price of gas was approaching four bucks a gallon.

According to Consumer Reports, Toyota Motors was at or near the top in having the lowest cost of ownership, lowest incidence of service and repairs, and had received high marks from IHS and IntelliChoice in resale value and safety. Toyota's models were priced in the sweet spot of consumer value preferences as the recession forced consumers to become more value conscious.

Mark took a moment for reflection. Following his thirty-two days in county lock-up, he was glad to be out in one piece, unmo-lested, and nobody's bitch. He was leaner than he'd been for most of his years, except for those when cocaine ran his life. Vulnerable to the world, a little beat up but still in the game, he had become cautious with his causes and careful with his caps, never donning one whose logo he could not champion.

He prayed on his knees like an altar boy, but cursed like a stable boy. Raised in a Christian family, he often felt rebellious, sometimes even conscious of the bruises left by an abusive father, leading him to question authority, unwilling to always take things at face value. As a result, he'd taken more than a few walks on the wild side. There were three years sailing party animals around the Caribbean on his two sailboats, and a couple of years making runs to Denver with attache cases full of party favors.

His forties brought the trauma and chaos he experienced in the loss of five friends on 9/11 when the World Trade Center tower housing the investment firm Cantor Fitzgerald exploded and later collapsed. This was the catalyst for questioning his commitment to money management after twenty years of gathering financial assets the world over. So, he had foundered on the stormy seas of Wall Street and almost drowned in the aftermath. Weary from those harrowing adventures, he took a sabbatical and circumnavigated the globe, only to encounter two typhoons and a hurricane on his twenty-seven month journey. The closer to death he got, the more alive he felt.

Today, he parked his loaner BMW far away from the front entrance, giving him an opportunity to walk and study the lot. He checked out all the Camrys, Corollas, Avalons, and SUVs without the interference of an overzealous sales rep who might be more interested in a commission than in finding him a great deal on the right car. He decided to ask for Ramone inside, hoping that his sales rep would remember him to be a well-informed buyer with environmental concerns.

His lease was up in May on his 335i, which would be ready to pick up from the body shop in a few days following his drunken— now infamous—encounter with the truckload of live chickens. Mark was intrigued with hybrid technology, and two years ago, he helped convince his shapely ex-girlfriend Laura that the Prius was the car of the future that she could buy today. So she did, eventually saving thousands on gas, and wound up loving the car but hating him for not wanting to marry her. His reluctance was a hangover from his last three marriages, smoking train wrecks so crazy that a Hollywood producer had offered Mark a cash deal in a bar in Vegas for the screenplay rights to the stories. Later, he realized it was probably the martinis talking.

So, Laura left him and moved to St. Augustine with her actress daughter, but not before screwing the salesman in the front seat of her new Prius in broad daylight at the dealership, much to the delight of a small select crowd of miscreants. The absence of a center console, the quiet battery-powered air-conditioning, the window tinting—and the fact that Laura never wore panties—all worked together to make such lascivious liaisons all too leisurely for her.

These were his thoughts as he approached the main entrance of Brandson Toyota, this time as a prospective employee, not just a customer. He was amazed by the huge forty-foot high entry way with its thirty-by-thirty-foot section of open roof that exposed the sky above. Eyeing the open roof section, he wondered if they'd run short of funds, were drinking on the job that day, or had actually planned this odd missing roof section. Odd because this design flaw failed to offer customers any protection from the weather. Admiring the bright blue sky through the odd roof opening, he reflected on his drenching the day before during his long walk home from the county jail.

"Hi! Welcome to Brandson Toyota. I'm Ronnie. Can I help you?" He appeared out of nowhere, catching Mark by surprise.

Ronnie was a stocky salesman with a big grin from ear to ear. He extended his hand to Mark as he opened the front door. His teeth looked as though they hadn't come into close proximity with a dentist in decades. A patch of grey hair combed forward was cut straight across his forehead to form bangs. He wore khaki Dockers two sizes too small that displayed more anatomy that even his proctologist would have wanted to see.

Mark could hear the imaginary announcer's voice in his head continue, "And completing Ronnie's ensemble on the fashion runway into the dealership today, we have a wrinkled blue dress shirt, yellow tie, complete with pizza stain, and scuffed brown dress shoes. The shoes are a stark contrast to his white patent-leather belt, and in his haste to dress, fresh from a likely court appearance for indecent exposure, he sports a missed belt loop, which speaks volumes of his complete and utter surrender to detail."

Ronnie looked exactly like the kind of salesman that his mother had warned him of. He had a limited amount of time before his four o'clock appointment at the Nissan dealership and wasn't too keen on wasting much of it with Ronnie. He did have to give Ronnie a couple of extra points for matching his white belt with the white athletic socks, two inches of which were clearly visible by pants that were, coincidentally, two inches too short.

Mark approached and shook his hand cautiously. "Hi, I'm looking for Ramone. Is he here today?"

"Ramone? I think today's his day off. Can I help you with something?"

"Well, uh . . . are you guys hiring?" asked Mark. As he stepped inside the showroom with Ronnie, he admired the forty foot ceilings and curved reception counter with granite top. There was a Prius, Camry, and a Tacoma sitting inside on display, buffed to a high-gloss sheen and carefully positioned behind the reception counter. A young boy leaning inside the open window of the Prius with a Fudgesicle was dangerously close to dropping his frozen confection onto the leather driver's seat. An attractive middle-aged woman at the reception desk wearing a headset smiled at him from behind a bank of phones and electronics.

"Jo'll help ya," said Ronnie as he pointed toward the woman behind the counter. Ronnie had lost interest in him and walked back to the front of the dealership to look for his next victim.

"Hi, I'm Jo. Welcome to Brandson Toyota. Did I hear you say you want to apply for a job?" she asked. Jo was all smiles.

"Yes, ma'am, are they hiring salesmen?" Mark acted cool, not wanting to sound too eager. "Well, the guy to talk to is over there." She pointed to a glassed-in area further inside the showroom. "See that guy with the Mohawk with his back to you? That's Larry. He's the guy you need to talk to."

"Thanks, Jo."

He looked across the showroom and stepped around the end of the counter, working his way toward Larry. An obese, middle-eastern-looking guy with wide squinty eyes, fat head, and shirt hanging out intercepted him. "Hi, I'm Raj Patel. Are you being helped, sir?"

"Well, I was on my way over to meet that guy with the Mohawk."

"You're here to see Larry?" Raj took a step back.

"Yeah. I wanted to talk with him about a job."

"Ooohhhh . . . ," said Raj as he looked him up and down like the new kid on the block. Raj looked a little like Jabba the Hutt, not appearing to have missed too many meals. "You have any sales experience?" Raj asked, sizing him up, pained by the idea by the idea of having another competitor on the sales floor.

"Some. Stocks, bonds, financial services, real estate. A little action as a male escort, anything to pay the bills," he said, grinning. "How 'bout you? You been here long, Raj?" Friendly and disarming, Mark was doing some recon with Raj before hooking up with Larry.

"Ha! Male escort! Right! You and me both!" said Raj. Mark was amused at the thought as he tried to picture Raj pandering to the whims of a woman paying to play. "You'll fit right in here!" I've been here about five years now. Got this job right out of college. Gonna retire before fifty. You know much about investing?"

"A bit," Mark said, not wanting to reveal that he had $950 million in assets under management when 9/11 burst his bubble. He was still picking out the concrete dust from the Brioni suit he was wearing that day, even after dry cleanings.

"We'll have to compare notes sometime." Raj seemed to sense that Mark was holding something back.

"I hear someone asking for me?" Larry was eager to meet the new guest.

"Hey . . . yeah . . . I'm Mark McAllister and I heard you're the guy to see to get directions on the road to fame and fortune." They shook hands enthusiastically.

"That's what ya heard, huh? Larry Wells, General Sales Manager! You lookin' for a job here?" Now it was Larry's turn to size him up.

"Yessir, like to talk with you about that. You have a minute?"

"For you, sure," said Larry. A little puzzled by his appearance, Mark couldn't help wondering where he shopped. He was completely entertained by the combination of tan and beige ostrich-skin shoes and matching Louis Vuitton belt that Larry wore. Very expensive, but Mark had never seen anyone wear this particular designer's apparel with straight-leg Levis, black short-sleeve Toyota polo shirt two sizes too small, and a Mohawk. *Looked a little 'Redneck Riviera',* Mark thought.

The thick, ebony-framed designer glasses looked out of place on his face. Mark guessed he couldn't have been more than thirty. When he spoke, Larry had a habit of cocking his head and getting right in your face when he emphasized a point. When he was excited, his eyes would bulge and the veins in his forehead would protrude. "Let's sit down for a minute, talk a bit." Larry motioned toward one of the sixteen desks with computers, phones, and privacy partitions. Pulling out two chairs, he added, "I am looking for talented, motivated sales reps right now, so your timing's pretty good, Mark. Take a seat here. You have any sales experience?"

"Well, let's see," said Mark. "Twenty years on Wall Street, managing $950 million when 9/11 came along. Sold eighteen million in real estate last year, some of that to Red Rollman. After I retired, I did some sailing . . . "

Larry was trying hard not to be impressed, but Mark could tell that he was. "Red Rollman, huh?"

"Yup."

"So, is that why he had to give this place up? Cause he bought real estate from you?" He seemed to have some hard bark on him.

"Actually, maybe that's why he *doesn't* need this place as much. He has other sources of income. So, maybe, that's why he's now the general manager and co-owner of the new Mercedes Benz dealership. But, I'm sure you knew that already 'cause you strike me as the kind of guy who likes to do his homework. Am I right in assuming that, Larry?"

"All right, all right. You don't need to show off. You're talkin' to the 'closer of closers' here. You know that, right?" Larry enjoyed controlling the conversation by asking the last question.

"Now, about this other stuff you mentioned. Any hobbies?"

"Charity events."

"Why?"

"Free hors-d'oeuvres."

"Anything else?"

"Art auctions."

"Why?"

"Free champagne."

"Really? I'm sensing a pattern, here." Larry cocked his head and smiled, guessing that Mark was testing his gullibility.

"Any other hobbies? What are you afraid of?" Larry was fishing for something. Mark was trying to figure out what it was.

"Well, I used to be afraid of heights."

"Okay, so what happened to that?"

"Vanquished by parachuting from thirteen thousand feet."

"Okay, interesting. You like sports? You a Gator fan?"

"Absolutely. Went to school here."

"So, football, parachuting and . . . what else?"

"*Scuba* diving."

"So, football, parachuting, and *scuba* diving for hobbies?" Larry was taking inventory.

"Yup. And gas grilling, but only if there is a possibility of setting myself on fire. I'm thinking I might be an adrenaline junky . . . kind of . . . uh . . . seem to prefer activities that lead to paralysis and serious back and neck injuries."

Larry laughed. "Yeah, I got that." Entertained, he was enjoying taking a break from his paperwork. "You married? Got a girl friend? Family? Pets? Goldfish? Anything like that?"

"Well . . . kind of seeing someone. Her philosophy is, 'Find your spirit animal then ride him 'til his dick falls off.' So far, so good." Mark was trying hard to keep a straight face. Larry was amused by the imagery.

"Okay. Yeah, that's good. You mentioned sailing. You like sailing?"

"Yeah."

"How far did you get?"

"All the way."

"All the way where?"

"Around the world."

Larry leaned forward. This really had his attention. "You sailed all the way around the world? In what?" A redneck from Palatka, Larry was incredulous.

"Sixty-foot Cheoy Lee custom motor-sailor. Ran into a little bad weather here and there, and actually managed to avoid being eaten in Bora-Bora . . . "

Larry was laughing and his eyes and veins on his forehead bulged. "*Wwwhhaatt?* You managed to avoid being eaten? In Bora-Bora? Really? Well . . . should I congratulate you or feel sorry for you?"

Leaning closer with his elbows on the desk, Mark grinned. "I'm gonna feel like a starving, quadrapalegic Ethiopian watching a fresh-glazed donut rolling down the hill if I don't have your sympathy on this issue."

Larry broke into a belly laugh, removed his glasses, and wiped them off with the front of his shirt. After composing himself, he continued. "That's a great story. Is it true?"

"Bring you the photos tomorrow, if you like."

"Well, hell, yeah! So, Mark, what the hell else ya got to tell me?"

Mark reached into the back pocket of his dockers, pulled out his Alachua County Bail Bond Agreement, and slid it across the desk to Larry. He eyed it cautiously.

"What's this?" He unfolded it and began to read.

"I'm out on bail."

"What the F——are you talk . . . wait a minute. Are you that guy who crashed into all those damn chickens? That was you on YouTube? It got over a million hits in twenty-four hours!" Larry turned around, calling across the dealership, "Hey, guys, we got us a celebrity here today!" A group of salesmen in the sales tower looked up from their computers. A few of the guys on the sales floor glanced over at them, trying to figure out who their mystery guest was.

"Damn, man! They take your license?" Larry asked, concerned.

"Yup."

"Well, you do need a valid license to sell cars here."

"I have another one."

"Another license? From where? Bora-Bora?"

"New York."

"Well, hell, Mark. Ya got anymore surprises for me today? I mean Jeez . . . you're out on bail, and now I suppose you want me to offer you a job?"

"Yup."

"Can you say anything besides 'yup'?"

"Yup." Mark was grinning ear-to-ear.

Larry laughed again. He stood up, strode over to the front desk and grabbed a job application from the stack on the counter.

"Fill this out and bring it with you Monday morning with your license and insurance card. New class starts at nine o'clock sharp. Jo will have your name badge ready, subject to your background check, which I'll tell her to skip. Don't be late or you'll have to sing a song in front of the class. Got it?"

Larry extended his hand out, Mark shook it enthusiastically. "Welcome to Brandson Toyota. See ya Monday morning. Oh, and Mark . . . "

"Yeah?"

"Drive safely."

"Okay."

Mark gave a courtesy wave to a few onlookers in the glassed-in area they called the sales tower. They knew Mark looked familiar but couldn't quite place him.

"Congratulations!" A portly sales rep in his forties approached him, hand extended. "I'm Paul McCreedy. I heard that Larry just hired you. You should feel lucky. He doesn't usually hire reps that fast. Where ya from?" They shook hands as he eyed Mark intently.

"From here. While it's not my nature to be mysterious, I really can't tell you too much."

Puzzled, McCreedy took a few steps back and leaned his huge belly up against the passenger door of the dark blue Prius in the showroom, stretching his arms out over the car like he was about to hump it. Mark thought this looked more like foreplay than conversation, guessing that this strange behavior was some kind of prelude to a redneck conversation.

Mark continued. "I went to UF and lived in Boca, New York, and San Francisco since then. How 'bout you? Are you related to Paul McCreedy, Sr., the homebuilder here in town?"

"He's my dad."

"Thought I noticed a resemblance." Mark remembered trying to buy a house from his dad years ago. The deal fell through because McCreedy had been totally inflexible on all the major issues, unwilling to negotiate even the slightest detail to keep the deal together.

"Came to work here a coupla years ago when my dad had to lay everyone off when the real estate market took a dump," explained McCreedy. "Why would you want to come back to little ole Gainesville after the places you've been? Those sound like some pretty nice places." McCreedy looked for an angle.

"Guess after twenty-five years on the beaches, I was ready for some shade," said Mark, grinning. McCreedy wasn't grinning back.

"You graduated from University of Florida?" asked Mark. He was struggling to find some common ground with McCreedy, but not having much luck.

"Nope. Just high school and my dad's business. Now I'm here," he said smugly. It all seemed pretty simple to him.

"Well, you chose a real nice place to hole up. You could've done a lot worse." Mark smiled, trying to be gracious. Their conversation was interrupted by his cell phone. "Nice meeting you, Paul. Look forward to working with you." He glanced at his caller ID. "Gotta take this call," he said apologetically.

Mark walked out the main entrance, hitting the talk button. It was Ricky from the Nissan dealership, wondering if he was still coming in for an interview. He decided to relegate the less popular brand to being his back-up plan for several reasons. According to Mark's sources in the community, the managers at this dealership had garnered an unsavory reputation as practicing extreme favoritism and nepotism among their sales staff, resulting in a turnover rate of over ninety percent last year. He put the meeting on the back burner.

As he strolled along the front of the sprawling dealership under the covered pad, he could see row after row of Camrys, Tundras, Prius, Scions, Highlanders, Rav4s, Sequoias, 4Runners, and Corollas on display, gleaming in the sun. Including the new car inventory floor-planned on the lot, Mark estimated about two hundred new Toyotas waited for customers on fifteen acres of asphalt, complete with concrete curbing and attractive landscaping. He estimated about a hundred tall, high-efficiency sodium light arrays to turn the darkness into daylight for nighttime customers.

Mark had a good feeling about the last hour that he'd spent at Brandson, pleased that the interview with Larry had gone so well. The exhaustion that he felt yesterday after leaving lock-up began to fade. He was relieved to have left behind the biggest bunch of psychos he'd ever encountered and now felt invigorated by the idea of selling a product that he could get behind and believe in.

As Mark exited the front of the dealership, his thoughts were interrupted by a familiar voice. "Hey, thanks for stopping by," said Ronnie, waving at him as he stepped from behind one of the huge metal columns in front. Ronnie had managed to surprise him a second time with his odd appearance, and Mark made a mental note to stand out in the open when greeting a customer so they would feel a little less stalked.

"Nice meeting you, Ronnie." In Ronnie's case, the entertainment factor alone had been worth the price of admission. His strange appearance and odd manner made Mark wonder how long he would last at the dealership.

As he walked toward his loaner BMW and planned his strategy, he was thinking that money seemed to solve so many problems. But only by diverting attention away from the old problems and re-focusing it onto a whole new set of problems created by having more money. He thought about what he used to tell his clients when he worked on Wall Street. Money can't buy happiness, but we all have the right to find that out.

THREE

Following the five days of training that stretched from Monday through Friday, Mark earned his Certificate of Completion and was cleared to begin selling Toyotas at Brandson by the end of the week. By the end of the third day, the remaining classmates had shrunk to eleven after they learned more about the thirteen-hour days, the eighty percent employee turnover rate, and the factory course certifications required on every new Toyota model. The sales process at Brandson was brisk and complicated, and new recruits faced high expectations with no guarantees of success.

As the difficulty of the job became more apparent to the trainees, there was less enthusiasm for the two thousand dollar monthly draw and the inevitable attrition of the ranks began. New reps were required to sell a minimum of eight cars at Brandson in their first month on the sales floor. This intimidated many of the new recruits, especially the students who would occasionally wander into the sales arena whenever their funds ran low.

In Gainesville, there was a river of cash that came from the students who meandered through town in pursuit of their education and entertainment at UF. The locals would do their best to snag as much of the cash flow as they could as the students rambled through town, spending their parents' money like drunken sailors on cars, apartments, pizzas, beer and drugs. Brandson was all in on the grab for cash.

With gas selling for over four dollars a gallon, there was more pain at the pump, and Mark was convinced that the hybrid share of the market would continue to grow faster than sales of conventional gas-powered cars. Customers who pulled in to the dealership driving the gas guzzlers—vehicles that got between nine and sixteen miles per gallon—were keenly interested in fuel efficiency. If he could save a customer between a hundred and two hundred a month in gas expenses, there would be more room in their budgets for a larger car payment and greater profits for the dealership.

On his first day at work, he mounted his Certificate of Achievement from his training course on the privacy partition above his desk, right where customers could best see it. It took him about thirty minutes to set up his phone, voicemail, thin client, and monitor.

"So, ya made it through your clash, huh?" McCreedy was leaning over his desk with his immense belly partially supported by the edge of the desk that Mark had just sanitized with the disinfectant wipes. His shirt was soiled and wrinkled. He studied McCreedy as he rubbed his hands together to absorb the sanitizer, estimating his co-worker's weight at about three hundred pounds. A lot of it was now resting, uninvited, on the customer side of his desk.

"Sup, man?" said Mark. He knew it was McCreedy's favorite intro. Mark looked up at him and smiled. McCreedy looked disoriented as he steadied himself at the edge of the desk.

McGreedy squinted at Mark. "Afraid of germs, huh? You're gonna fit right in here. We got hand shanitizers about every ten feet!" Mark had noticed the many dispensers of hand "shanitizers" mounted on the walls. He was guessing he'd be using them a lot more often when McCreedy was around.

McCreedy's breath reeked of alcohol and pizza, and his eyes were bloodshot as he whirred his slurds. It was still early, a little after ten on Monday morning, and Mark continued wiping down the phone with the disinfectant wipes while he kept one eye on McCreedy.

"Late night at church, Paul?" asked Mark.

Frowning, McCreedy asked, "What meksh ya say that?" he asked indignantly.

Mark reached into his attaché case he kept under his desk, rummaged through it and found his breath mints. He peeled off two mints, handing them to McCreedy.

"Here, take these. My hands are clean. Just don't want to see you get in trouble. One for now, one for later." McCreedy wobbled as he studied the contents of Mark's hand, trying to focus on the mints.

"Trouble? Bryan'll take care of me, don't you worry 'bout that. He alwaysh takes care'a me. You meet Bryan yet?" He took the mints, popping them both into his mouth. "Thanks, Mac!" His eyes narrowed and his brow furrowed as he chewed, trying to identify the flavor.

"Sure. Uh . . . no, I haven't met Bryan yet. Bryan Pfister, right? Is he that big guy with the real short haircut sitting behind the manager's desk right now?"

"Yup, that's my bud. Known him since I was shix years old." McCreedy looked up and waved at Bryan, who was on the phone arranging a new car trade with a manager from a nearby dealership.

"He's the new car manager, right?" asked Mark. "Looks about six feet six or so . . . ," Mark turned around to see if Bryan had waved back. He was still on the phone, his eyes fixed to his computer.

"Six feet, seven . . . " McCreedy corrected him. "Don't bet on hoops if you play him. He's a good shoo . . . shooter. A regular Lebrown James." McCreedy motioned like he just fired off a jump shot, slipped, and almost fell down in front of the desk. He steadied himself by grabbing the partition, knocking Mark's certificate on the floor. "Oops. Here . . . " McCreedy reached down and handed it back, now complete with fingerprint smudges.

"Don't worry, I got it," said Mark. "Needs a frame to do it up right, anyway." Mark tucked it behind his PC to protect it from future drunks.

Now it was Raj's turn to join the conversation, unable to resist an opportunity to mess with the new guy. "Sup, guys?"

Word was that Raj, though he claimed on his name badge to have been born in Palm Beach, was actually born in Pakistan. He was the only rep at Brandson who got away with displaying no last name on his badge, and it made Mark wonder what else about Raj Patel wasn't quite right.

"Hey, just wanted to let you know that I'm available for training newbies on a split deal," said Raj. "I'm pretty good. You know I'm making six figures?" Eating with his shirt out, Raj was badly in need of a clothes iron and some deodorant.

"Good to know," said Mark. "Thanks. I thought that the managers helped you with training."

"Good luck with that," McCreedy chimed in, looking for his half deal.

"So, Mark . . . how many cars ya got out this month?" Raj asked, smirking at him expectantly, waiting for the obvious answer that would automatically elevate Raj to "salesman of the day" status.

"Dude, it's ten thirty on my first day here. Can you give me at least 'til noon?" Mark asked with a hint of sarcasm.

He'd heard from some of the other guys that Raj liked to stir up trouble and always steered the conversation to make himself look good. Mark overheard Bryan say that Raj's biggest accomplishment was graduating from UF after six years of study with a four-year degree in Middle Eastern culture, and that he had a great face for radio. The degree seemed pretty close to home, and he could only wonder at how much effort Raj's diploma had actually required.

"Hey, who's that guy over there with the shaved head and red face who's glaring at me? He always acts like he's mad at everyone." Mark was creeped out by the dark looks he was getting. McCreedy and Raj looked at each other, trying to think of an accurate description.

"He's one of our resident alcoholics." Raj was casual with his response, as if Brandson didn't really need a reason to justify employing multiple alcoholics.

"You mean there's more than one?" asked Mark.

"Yup. I don't think he likes anyone, especially newbies, and sometimes he's actually nice to customers." Raj leaned closer to Mark to avoid being overheard, whispering, "He got busted a few years ago for running a meth lab from a hotel room in Houston. We heard he got off light 'cause he threw his partner under the bus and turned state's evidence against him. They put his partner away for fifteen years." Raj tilted his head and smirked.

"Wow. We have some pretty colorful people here," said Mark, now feeling like Captain Obvious. "How do these guys get hired here?"

"Well, Larry hired you, didn't he, 'Killer!'?" Raj grinned. Mark supposed he was referring to the dead chickens from his car accident. "He likes guys that push the envelope. Claims they make better car salesmen." Raj shrugged. When he shrugged, his shoulders rounded, and he looked even more like Jabba the Hutt.

"They were chickens, man, not people! So, what about you. What do you do in the danger zone, besides working here?" Mark wondered if Raj had any hobbies other than eating. "You like to grill out or something? Wait. Let me guess. You drink milk a *whole* day beyond the expiration date, right?"

"Ha! Yeah right." Raj laughed. "You know I don't drink, right?"

"Milk?" Mark was curious about this. The idea of Raj adhering to any actual disciplines or principles intrigued him.

"No, alcohol. Strict Islamic rule." he said solemnly. Mark couldn't pass up the opportunity to mess with him.

"Okay, so you don't drink. Does that also mean you refrain from the use of C-4?" asked Mark as he waited for the lecture on profiling based on religious beliefs. Raj just glared at him, clearly annoyed with his teasing. He made a fist, depressed his thumb like he was pressing a detonator, made an exploding sound and turned away.

"Wait, Raj." Mark back pedaled and offered him a tongue-in-cheek explanation. "While it's not my nature to be mysterious, it's hard for me to talk about it."

"What are you talking about?" asked Raj.

"The truth is, I lost five friends on 9/11," Mark said.

Raj acted sympathetic, but Mark couldn't tell if he was being sincere or just patronizing him. Raj leaned forward on his desk, taking McCreedy's place who had wondered off toward the sales tower, probably hoping to find someone to give him a ride to the AA meeting tonight. He'd heard that McCreedy was so drunk yesterday that he'd actually bitten his hand eating a sandwich in the cafeteria.

"So, you were there? What was it like?" Raj was interested in hearing a firsthand account of the events on the infamous day.

"Lotta smoke and noise, crashing buildings, breaking glass, people screaming," said Mark. "Concrete dust so thick you couldn't breathe. We all thought that World War III had started. I quit Wall Street a week later. I was already tired of the smoke and mirrors, no pun intended." He could feel himself getting emotional about losing his five friends. One had jumped from the burning 103rd floor of the World Trade Center, the other four burned to death in the inferno created by the Boeing 767 that had obliterated floors 101 through 105 at Cantor Fitzgerald. He missed his friends and usually avoided talking about the terrorist attacks that destroyed the iconic American landmarks.

"What did you do after that?" Raj was curious how a man with Mark's background had wound up selling cars in Gainesville. He sat down at Mark's desk, respectfully folding his hands, anticipating more entertainment from the newbie.

"I went sailing. Had to get away for awhile. Clear my head."

"What do you mean?" Raj's eyes darted around the showroom like he had the attention span of a monkey on speed chewing on a fly swatter.

"I hopped on my boat and went sailing. Had to get some things sorted out. Started out being a month-long trip. I just kept on sailing."

"Really? For how long? Where'd you go?" Raj was having a hard time wrapping his head around this. He was watching Ryan over at McCreedy's desk, putting a heavy close on a man who was old enough to have been one of the original investors in apple, the fruit. He was leaning on one of those walkers on wheels. Mark found out early on that Patel and McCreedy were ready to pounce on any easy deal with older, heavily-medicated Q-tips on walkers.

"Wound up circumnavigating the globe. Took me two years."

"Cool. What kinda boat was it?" asked Raj.

"Sixty-foot Cheoy Lee Custom motor sailor. So, now here I am at the Brandson Toyota, Tire and Hair Care Center in beautiful downtown Gainesburg, right where I started college thirty years ago," said Mark.

Raj laughed. "Yeah, Tire and Hair Care Center. I got an app for that. You know, they do manicures and massages for service customers while they wait, right? Right down that hallway there." He pointed to his left toward the service area.

"Really? What do they say down there? Toyota, love what you do for me? Hey, thanks for the tip on the manicures." Mark was thinking if he was ever invited to dinner at Raj's place, he'd probably have to stop off at a store that sold wine in boxes and offered aerosol cheese. "So, where do I sign up for the manicures?" asked Mark.

"Gotta have a Toyota in service," said Raj.

"All righty then," said Mark in a lame imitation of Jim Carey. "I'm heading outside to find a customer with a checkbook in one hand, and a pen in the other."

"Oh, what a feeling . . . right?" Raj imitated the TV ad. He seemed nice for their first conversation, but Mark had been warned by the other guys about Raj's crazy-maker antics.

Mark headed outside to watch customers coming and going on the four service lanes. Paved in stamped concrete, they stretched over a hundred feet in both directions. Large LED green and red computer-controlled directional lights were mounted above the lane entrances facing both ways, governing the flow of traffic. As he stood looking out the glass door to the service lanes, he checked out the twenty or so customers waiting in the service lounge area who were busy watching CNBC, knitting, working on their laptops or reading the local mullet-wrapper, the *Gainesville Banner*. He noticed a very attractive woman in her thirties sitting in the service lounge, smiling at him. She wore a low-cut blouse, a black and tan suede skirt, and had a Jack Russell terrier sitting up in her lap. In need of a sale and a sucker for beautiful legs, he decided to try his luck with her.

Mark walked over and gave her his best Hollywood-style smile. "Hi, ma'am. You have your Toyota serviced here on a regular basis?"

She leaned forward on the leather sofa, smiled and put her magazine aside. "It's a Lexus. Could you check to see if it's ready for me? I've been here since ten o'clock." Mark checked his watch. It was almost eleven thirty. He smiled reassuringly at her.

"Sure. I'll check. Cute dog. Is he friendly?" Mark extended his hand cautiously and petted the dog's head. The Jack Russell's tail wagged furiously as he anticipated making a new friend.

"Yes, he is. I'm Sandra. Sandra MacGowan. Nice to meet you, uh . . . " She leaned forward to read his name badge. "Mark."

"It's a pleasure, Sandra," shaking her hand. She had a French manicure and a large diamond ring on her right hand, her strawberry-blond hair was well-cut and styled in a page-boy. Mark was admiring her green eyes and full, sensuous lips. Trying not to be too obvious, he shifted his attention to her Jack Russell. "What's your dog's name?"

"Fluffy," she said. Mark looked at her, perplexed, then back at the short-haired Jack Russell. Fluffy was licking and sniffing Mark's hand, pawing in the air like he wanted a high-five. Mark high-fived him and Fluffy barked in approval, holding up his paw again.

"Cute," said Mark as he obliged Fluffy with an encore.

"He'll do that all day. My boyfriend named him. He always wanted a dog named 'Fluffy,' so that's what we named him. He's very friendly."

"So I see." She leaned forward to kiss Fluffy on his head, giving Mark a nice view of her cleavage, which Mark found difficult to ignore.

"Wanna hold 'em?" she asked, as she looked up at him expectantly. She was still smiling as she caught him admiring her breasts. Mark's next thought could have gotten him fired on the spot as he tried to avert his gaze from the view she'd presented to him.

"You mean Fluffy? Oh sure." He grinned and noticed some pink coming into her complexion as she blushed at the double entendre. He was taking her in, enjoying the flirtatious behavior. Mark had always been a sucker for strawberry blondes with green eyes. She moved with effortless, feminine grace. He thought about Laura, his last girlfriend with strawberry blonde hair and green eyes. Then he remembered why they broke up. Laura was encumbered with so much baggage that twenty skycaps couldn't get her off the curb.

A loud, ghetto-type voice behind him broke the mood. "Sorry for the wait, Sandra. Can I go over a few things with you that our technician found on your ES-450?" Gene Haile was standing behind him, all six feet six inches, looking like Wilt Chamberlain. Gene was in a hurry with his clipboard, invoices and mechanic's notes, anxious to score a big commission on a fat service sale. The other service writers often called Brandson Toyota's service department "Haile's Toyota," a nod to Gene's position as their top service writer. The volume of business he wrote was double that of the number two guy, and some of the more experienced service writers often questioned how he was able to do it. Mark sat down beside Sandra and moved the *Southern Living* magazines out of the way. He held Fluffy's leash while Gene took a seat on the other side. Fluffy growled at Gene as he sat down, and Gene slid forward on the couch to get closer to her. Clipboard in hand, Gene glanced up and looked at Fluffy like he wanted to shoot him.

"Its okay, Fluffy. I'm sure Gene has some good news for us," said Mark. He smiled at Sandra, feeling protective of his new acquaintance. She turned to Gene, anticipating bad news as she checked out all the notes attached to his clipboard. She looked nervous, like an oncology patient bracing for her doctor's prognosis.

According to another servicewriter, Gene had a pretty checkered past before coming to Brandson two years ago. His rap sheet was filled with convictions for drug use, dealing, and possession. He had lost his license three times for drugs, preventing him from becoming a sales rep. Sandra kept looking back and forth between the notes in his lap and Gene's gleaming gold tooth that flashed every time he smiled. Following his list of recommendations, he handed her the pen and said, "Now, just need to have your okay right here, so we can get you out of here and on your way." He handed her the clipboard, pointing to the "X" on the customer authorization line.

"What was the total on that again?" she asked, taking the clipboard in both her hands. She squinted at it like it was written in Sanskrit, furrowing her brow in mild disapproval at the total.

"Eight hundred twenty-one dollars, ma'am, including the wash." Gene was doing his best to appear confident and assume the sale.

Sandra uncrossed her gorgeous legs and caught Mark's gaze as she did. She leaned forward on the sofa, and it was obvious that she wasn't buying Gene's pitch.

"Gene, are you sure the battery and air filter need replacing? I just had them replaced at the Lexus dealership in Atlanta last summer. I can see the tune-up and oil change, but this other stuff, uh, I don't know. Doesn't make sense. Can you check with your mechanic to make sure he didn't get my car mixed up with another one?" Skepticism had crept into her voice, and she looked at him expectantly. She studied the three gold rings and two gold bracelets on his wrists, and matching gold tooth, waiting patiently for him to respond. She was offering him a gracious way out. An older man sitting across from her wearing a Hard Rock Café T-shirt looked up at them, taking an obvious interest in their conversation that now centered on questionable charges.

"Uh . . . sure, ma'am, I can do that." said Gene, lowering his voice. "My technicians are usually pretty accurate with their recommendations. Are you sure that the Lexus dealer in Atlanta actually replaced those parts for you and didn't just charge you for them?"

Gene was fishing for weakness, testing her willpower, hoping Mark would stay quiet.

"Well, I guess I could call the dealership right now and double check. I know the mechanic that did the work, and Phil knows that my family owns the dealership, so I doubt if he'd try to put one over on me. I've known Phil for over twenty years. We went to high school together."

Gene looked embarrassed by her answer. "Let me double check with the technician," he said. "Maybe he got your car mixed up with another one on a different service lift. Sometimes that happens, especially when we get busy like this. Be right back." Sheepishly, Gene headed back to his service techs to try and save some face.

Mark had purposely stayed silent during Gene's presentation, waiting to see if he was going to do the right thing for Sandra. Some of his questions about Gene's sales practices were being answered, and it was obvious that Gene was looking to fatten up his payday.

Mark reassured Sandra with a pat on her hand and said, "Don't worry. We want you to come back for your next service, so I'm sure Gene will get everything worked out to your satisfaction. By the way, when you're ready to trade your three year old Lexus, I hope you'll give me a call." He handed her his business card. "I'll make sure you get a great deal. We'll get this service bill straightened out for you, Sandra. I promise."

"Sounds good, Mark. I appreciate what you're doing for me today. I'll be sure and ask for you when I'm ready to trade. It was really nice meeting you." She reminded him of the knockout blonde dancer in Rod Stewart's video "This Old Heart of Mine." He was impressed with how cool she was with the deception on the repair order, and how effectively and effortlessly she had dispatched Gene back to his desk to get it right.

Mark smiled at her, petted Fluffy one last time, and headed off toward the back, making a mental note to check with Sandra before she left to make sure everything was okay. After checking on a few customer emails, he spotted Gene sitting with Sandra again. He casually cruised over so he could overhear their conversation.

"And so that brings the new total down to four hundred twenty-six dollars. Sorry about the mix-up today, Sandra. Are we good to go here?" Gene asked her.

"I think that works. Appreciate you working with me on this. I feel a lot better about this now. Thanks, Gene."

"You got it." Mark watched Gene take a deep breath. He looked relieved that he'd escaped a potential disaster that could have been a major embarrassment for him.

"How much longer you think it'll be?" she asked him.

"We should have you out of here in about thirty-five minutes. Okay?"

"Sounds good." She watched him as he walked back to his desk to finish with the paperwork and turned her attention back to the news story on TV. Mark glanced over his shoulder to check on Sandra. Seeing that she was done with Gene, he walked back toward the service lounge area to check on her.

"How's my favorite customer doing?" he asked.

"Better now. Oh . . . .by the way, I wanted to give you my card with my cell phone number." She reached into her Coach purse, removed her wallet, and pulled out a business card.

"Thanks." Mark read the card to himself. Sandra MacGowan, MD.

"So, Sandra, you gave up a promising career in modeling to become an MD, huh?" Sandra chuckled, pleased with his remark. "Fluffy, take good care of her, okay, pal?" he said, petting him again.

"Thanks again, Mark. Appreciate you're watching out for me. My sister may be in the market in a month when her lease is up," she said.

"Love to help her when she's ready. Here, let me offer you a card for her, so you can keep one for yourself." She was the highlight of his day, and her scent was driving him nuts.

Mark made his way outside. Standing on the concrete drive, he was taking in all the activity, cars driving in and out, customers talking with their service rep. Some waited in their cars, some hanging out, a few walking inside to find their service writer. He was amazed at the bustle of activity outside. Pretty noisy out here, he thought. There must have been twelve to fifteen cars lined up outside, while wall-mounted big screen TVs were blaring ads for batteries, tires, shocks and oil change specials.

He wondered what percentage of the service customers were being approached with padded or unnecessary repair orders on any given day. He knew they called it "upselling," and situations like the one with Gene were tricky. The service writers were excellent sources of referral business, and alienating them would not be good for Mark's business.

"Hey, look who it is, our newest newbie. Sup, Mark?" Bryan Pfister was walking up. He looked every bit of six foot seven, wearing his black Toyota manager's shirt, size XXXL, and tan Dockers. His head was shaved so close it might as well have been bald. Bryan had a thing for expensive shoes. Today, they were the expensive crocodile slip-ons he wore with his signature argyle socks. Mark thought the argyle socks were a hoot. "Sup, Bryan?" They did the fist bump. "Hey, big guy, you know when my Toyota polo shirts are coming in?"

"Joe's bringing in a box of them on Friday. Red for salesmen and black for managers. Then you can quit with those dress shirts and ties. You look like an old man in those. So, hey old man, ya got a customer yet?" Bryan was grinning from ear to ear, as he typically did. "You know, we're expecting great things from you, right? Don't forget to get with Tommy to sign up for that new Prius roll out course in Jacksonville next week. I want you onboard with all the new specs on the new model Prius. I know that's one of the reasons you signed up with us, right?" Bryan was standing in front of him, checking off items on his clipboard.

"You know it, big guy," Mark responded. Bryan seemed to have a pleasant personality, and Mark was starting to trust him. Getting the masters of the trade to share their secrets was part of his plan.

"You know about the Friday morning sales meeting at nine o'clock sharp, right?" Bryan reminded him. "Newbies hafta sing a song. Have a song ready to go. No exceptions."

"What kind of song?" asked Mark.

"Surprise us," Bryan grinned. "Maybe a jingle about that new hemorrhoid cream they call Fire In The Hole—I don't care, as long as it's funny."

"Prepare to be entertained." Mark had heard about this tradition at Brandson, and he had a song already in mind for his first sales meeting. He just knew it was going to get raucous. He enjoyed being in a constant state of comedic relief. His naturally-dry sense of humor often kept his audience on the edge of their seats, and the ambiguity often led to wildly entertaining situations.

Bryan was the most positive manager there and a good closer, but he was still second to Larry in closing ability. Larry, the "Louis Vuitton Redneck," was closing car deals since he was eighteen and had talent. There wasn't really much that he was good at except being a fashionable redneck and selling cars. He got himself out of the trailer park fast. Now, he lived in a five-thousand-square-foot mansion on St. Augustine Beach with his wife and two kids. He didn't seem to mind the daily ninety-minute commute each way to and from St. Augustine in one of the nine luxury cars he owned. Three of them were worth over a quarter of a million dollars each. Larry led the lifestyle of a billionaire hip-hop recording artist, and Mark couldn't figure out how he did it.

The truth was that Larry had gotten far too attached to those beautiful coastal beaches to move to Gainesville-not to mention the bikini-clad women roaming them. When he wanted to party in Gainesville and skip the drive home, he'd just have his buddies line up some hot college girls and stay over for a few days, directing his own crazy episodes of *Girls Gone Wild*. There were entire weekends of drugs, fights, and debauchery, as well as drunk, under-aged girls at Jake's or Ricky's that Mark had heard about from his co-workers.

In contrast to his boss Larry, Bryan drove a huge late-model Sequoia, Toyota's largest SUV. He was married to a nurse, no kids, hated driving, even from his nearby home in northwest Gainesville that was only seven miles from the dealership. Bryan was all about selling new Toyotas, and he'd been doing it the longest of anyone on the sales floor at Brandson. He had started in sales ten years ago when they were still headquartered in the old building further north on Main Street, before Brandson had bought the Kia and Acura dealerships. After many years of sales success, they promoted Bryan to sales manager when the new building was finished.

All the sales reps wanted to know what Paul McCreedy was holding over Bryan's head, but McCreedy wasn't talking. McCreedy had some serious dirt on his buddy Bryan and didn't hesitate to lord it over his manager. This helped explain why McCreedy was shoveled deal after deal from Bryan, who rarely dished out any of those "cheese deals" to anyone else. Mark figured that with Bryan handing his buddy an extra twelve to fifteen deals a month, McCreedy had to be making an extra ten to fifteen thousand a month in commissions that weren't available to other reps. Most of them worked harder than McGreedy, as they all called him. And, there was no lack of speculation among the sales reps about the likelihood of untaxed cash kickbacks that were being paid to the managers for these "cheese deals."

With no cheese deals to fall back on, Mark had still managed to chalk up his first two sales by Thursday afternoon. The first deal was a sale to a blueberry farmer who had bought a new Tundra XSP double cab with four wheel drive and custom rims to tend to his 360-acre expansion in Newberry. That deal had earned Mark a twelve hundred dollar commission, a quart of fresh-picked blueberries, and a lecture on the evils of Catholicism. They had talked at length about all the health benefits of blueberries, high in anti-oxidants, vitamins, and complex sugars. What he had not expected to hear about was the oak tree that his younger brother had tragically impacted at sixty mph on his Harley one afternoon.

Mark's second sale had been on a clearance-priced Prius to a young premed student who was intent on saving the planet from the oil companies. Her dad had co-signed for her to secure the special incentive financing from Toyota. That deal had wound up being a "flat," a one hundred dollar minimum commission, owing to the price mark down. Even so, Mark was pleased to have sold his first Prius.

He was satisfied with his baptism-by-fire in the first few days of selling cars, and he felt ready to face the firing squad Friday morning. He hoped to entertain this wild bunch of brigands and wondered what else was in store for him at his first sales meeting at Brandson.

FOUR

The light morning rain had stopped in time for the rush of the thirty-three salesmen, managers, and F&I personnel who were filing into Brandson's meeting room. Each one was in a different state of readiness on this Friday morning. The meeting room consisted of tile floors and seventy-two seats separated by a center aisle. At the front were two large erasable boards, and another one to the left that looked like a giant spreadsheet that listed the sales staff. On the side roster, the managers kept a running total of cars sold by each sales rep and was updated at each sales meeting. There were two ceiling-mounted projectors up front that housed PowerPoint and CRM software programs for training purposes. To the right was a huge forty-foot window that overlooked the rear parking lot where no one was allowed to park. Late arrivals parked there anyway to try and avoid Larry's five dollar late fine.

All the new Toyotas that arrived overnight from the Port of Jacksonville were unloaded from the huge carriers in the two-acre assembly area that was viewable from the forty-foot window in the meeting room. There, new cars awaited the addition of Brandson's addendum that had become so notorious with their customers. The addendum was an add-on sticker that Brandson placed next to the federally-required Monroney sticker on the passenger side window of all new models prior to being displayed on the lots. This sticker itemized important information like factory options, MSRP, EPA-estimated fuel mileage and NHTSA crash ratings.

Mark learned that the special addendum was unique to Brandson and listed all the "dealer fluff" at inflated prices which added more profit to the dealership's bottom line. This special addendum included a Market Value Adjustment figure that could range up to ten thousand dollars of added profits. It was the presence of this addendum on Brandson's cars that caused so much controversy during price negotiations, often resulting in the loss of the customer's business to competing dealers who had no addendums.

This morning, Mark followed the trail of footprints that started in the hallway and led into the meeting room. He scanned the seats for the best vantage point and picked out a spot, one seat over and behind Brent Bell, so that he could see around Brent's shiny bald head, polished so shiny it reminded him of a giant cue ball.

As he took a seat, he leaned forward. "Hey Brent, you buff your head this morning? Looks great, man!" Mark gave him a cordial pat on his head.

Brent turned to see who was messing with him. "Yeah, with Meguire's Top Shine. The reflection makes it easier for my customers to find me on the lot. You should try it," he said, running his hand over his head.

Mark laughed. He touched Brent's head again and added, "Feels a lot like my girlfriend's ass!"

Not to be outdone, Brent thoughtfully ran his hand over his head again. "Damn! I think you're right, Mark. It kinda does . . . kinda does . . . " grinning back at Mark. He turned his attention back to his phone to check for incoming customer calls and text messages.

At a few minutes before nine, Raj took a seat near Mark. He was holding a half-eaten donut wrapped in a napkin with one hand, and a huge thirty-two ounce Starbuck's café latte in the other.

He glanced at Mark, sat down heavily, and took a big bite out of his donut.

"So Raj, you leave anything at Starbuck's for the rest of us?" Mark was enjoying the fact that Raj, with his mouth full of donut, was unable to speak momentarily. He looked blankly at Mark while he chewed on his donut and thought about an appropriate response. After a moment, he pointed at Mark and said, "Oh, that's right! We got a singerrrrr today." Mark shrugged. He was ready with his song.

The meeting room began to fill up. Scott Pruden, who took a seat behind him, was a former hedge fund manager and mortgage broker until the financial crisis took him down. As Mark scanned the room, he spotted Paul "McGreedy", sitting across the aisle with his best bud Bryan Pfister. Next to him was the duo from F&I, "Tricky" Ricky Gonzalez and Jake "The Chef" Sheahan, the latter so nicknamed for his insatiable appetite and culinary skills.

"Tricky" Ricky Gonzalez was their sleazy, forty-five-year-old, slick-talking transplant from Honda dealerships in Puerto Rico and Jacksonville Beach. "Tricky" Ricky had a thing for wining and dining underage girls and there were a lot of stories about what Tricky Ricky did with those drunk—and sometimes drugged—girls behind closed doors. Ricky had succeeded in bribing his way out of a rape charge in Jacksonville Beach six months ago, managing to keep it all quiet with a thirty-five thousand dollar "campaign contribution" to the State Attorney's re-election fund. This story had come courtesy of his buddy Jake, who'd been in attendance at the underaged sex fest on that day.

"All right ladies, listen up!" Known for making his Friday morning entrance at exactly nine o'clock, Larry's voice boomed from the back of room.

He marched up the aisle to the front of the room, taking command of the meeting. His black Toyota polo looked about two sizes too small for his six foot torso; and the tan Dockers, Bruno Magli ostrich loafers and monogrammed silk socks were pretty consistent with the "Redneck Riviera" signature wardrobe that he was famous for.

"Tony, let's update the board," said Larry. He was busy scanning the room from behind his brown-rimmed Ed Hardy designer glasses, picking out his newbies, preparing to ask them up one at a time to come up front for their singing debuts. Mark felt ready after practicing his act in the mirror this morning.

Tony Grimes stood up, a big, burly used car manager with short grey hair, who always had kind of a bewildered look on his face, like he wasn't quite sure what day it was. To protect his eyes from flying fists, he preferred the shatterproof frameless Oakley glasses. According to the scuttlebutt, Tony doubled as Larry's bodyguard when they went out on their drunken escapades. The second-in-command of the used car desk behind Kirk Shifter, big Tony stepped up to the sales roster board and started calling out the names listed on the board.

"Brent, how many cars ya got out?" Tony glanced at Brent playing with his cell phone in the first row, five feet away.

"I have one used, and one with a deposit, financing pending." Brent hadn't bothered to look up from his phone.

"All right! Good!" said Tony, adding two Xs in the blank squares next to his name.

"Paul, how 'bout you, bro?" He looked across the room toward McGreedy.

"So far, none, but got a couple coming in tonight after work that should be a deal." He seemed surprisingly sober this morning, but most knew that was likely to change as the day progressed. He was often heard saying that being sober made him feel "really weird."

"Paul, where's your name badge?" Larry was clearly annoyed at this lax behavior from one of his top producers.

"In my truck. Want me to get it?" asked McGreedy. They all knew it was never too early for McGreedy's brown-nosing.

"Too late. Five dollar fine. Cough it up," said Larry, stepping toward McGreedy with his hand out to retrieve the money.

"My wallet's in my truck, too . . . "

"And, let me guess. It's empty, like your gas tank. Right?" Larry's sarcasm had a ring of truth for McGreedy. His 5.6 liter V-8 Tundra was rated for only eleven MPG in town, and the way he drove it, he was likely getting closer to seven.

"Oh, I got it, but . . . "

"All right, but you better get it to me right after the meeting. Got it?"

"Yes, sir!" McGreedy already looked like he was ready for a drink.

Larry stepped back to the front, watching Tommy Catatonia standing in the back of the room. He had his chin in his hand, always carefully calculating everything. He nodded approvingly at Larry to continue with his agenda.

Tony turned back to the board. "Raj?"

"One."

"Counting the donut?"

"Well, that would make it . . . "

"Never mind. Bill? Bill Boyer? Where's Bill?" Tony scoured the room, looking for a sign from Bill.

"He's running late," Kirk chimed in. "He texted me. Something about a stuck garage door . . . or something." Kirk had a habit of covering for his top used car salesman.

"Again?" Larry wasn't happy. He knew Bill liked his liquor, loved to stay up and drink the night away with his trailer park tarts. "Call him again, after the meeting's over. We need everyone here today!"

"Rrrroger that, boss," said Kirk. Most of the sales reps tagged Kirk with the nickname Kirk the Jerk for his disagreeable personality. He liked his drinking so much that he had moved into a downtown condo so he could be closer to his watering holes. Only blocks from all the bars, he could stumble home on foot every night without risking another DUI. With three DUI convictions already under his size fifty-two belt, another conviction and he'd probably be doing some hard time.

After Tony finished updating the board, Larry spoke again. "All right, who's gonna be our first singer? Mark, you wanna come up, give it a shot?" Larry looked like he wasn't going to take no for an answer.

"Okay. Sure." Mark stood up, emptying his pockets onto the desk in front of him, taking his phone and keys out and pulling his pants pockets inside out so that they hung at his sides.

"Part of my act," he explained to Raj, who was trying to figure out what Mark was doing as he munched on his last bite of donut.

Mark made his way to the front, cleared his throat, and introduced himself to the room full of spectators quietly waiting in suspense. They were all anticipating some raucous entertainment.

"Hi, I'm Mark McAllister, originally from Detroit, hometown of American car manufacturing. So now here I am selling Japanese imports made in the USA. Go figure, right?" There was a twitter from the group as they waited, expecting more.

"I have a song for you, from when you were a kid. Ian, for you, that means last week." There was another twitter of laughter. Ian was the youngest rep there. Thin, and a little effeminate, Ian looked like he was about twelve.

"Okay. Here goes," He cleared his throat. Marching in place, he began to sing. "I owe, I owe, [grasping pockets pulled inside out], it's off to work we go . . . [arms outstretched in marching motion], with a Hummer here . . . [hand over groin], a 'Too High' there [dragging two fingers across face] I owe, I owe, I owe I owe I owe, it's off to work we go, got a 440 score, [checking his open palm], lookin' for the door, [squinting, hand shading his eyes], I owe . . . I owe . . . I owe, I owe, I owe . . . [voice trailing off] . . . It's off to work we go . . . "

There was laughter, followed by applause. Mark was relieved that they liked his song. He took his seat and Raj reached over to pat him on the shoulder. "Good one, Mark . . . good one. Want a donut?" Before he could answer, Larry chimed in again.

"Okay, so who else *owes*? Who's next? Brad? Come on up."

Brad reluctantly ambled his way up to the front of the room, head down, acting a little sheepish. "I'm Brad from Palatka. I know Larry's kid brother. Got a rap tune from 50 Cent, goes like this," then, as he mouthed the percussion background, five seconds into his show, he dropped two "F-bombs" in a row.

"Stop!" It was Tommy from the back of the room. "No F-bombs, guys! Brad, go sit down. Get some cleaner material for next week's meeting. Let's use some common sense here, guys! Jeez. Especially in mixed company. C'mon!" They all nodded in agreement. Mark was thinking you gotta go with the boss on this one. The singers that followed included Clay Leeson, who sang "Happy Birthday," followed by Jason Duquette's big blockbuster, "Jingle Bells." Then Larry retook the stage with a loud voice, saying, "You guys may know about Bill's crusher of a deal on Wednesday. A little ole lady came in and we *crushed* her for a twenty pounder! C-R-U-S-H-E-D her!!" Larry spelled it out, yelling so loud the veins in his forehead were popping out.

At first, Mark thought he was kidding. Crushing a little ole lady? Was he serious? He studied Larry, looking for signs that he was kidding, but he was dead serious.

Larry continued yelling, "This is the kind of deal I want *all* of you to do today! Got it? We *crush everybody*!" Larry was getting really worked up. Mark was thinking it was the steroids kicking in. "We gotta make some money here, guys! No mercy! I am the Devil! As far as y'all are concerned, I AM Lucifer!" Larry's veins were popping out as he made an impassioned plea for all of his staff to be "crushers" and "followers." The rest of the guys looked at each other, seriously wondering if he was possessed and what he was going to say next.

Mark was beginning to think that his general sales manager was likely a mental case. Larry was doing his best to convince everyone in the room that he had all the supernatural powers of Satan, and he was dead serious. He'd only known his GSM two weeks. Today, he was starting to think he didn't know him at all. Now, he was asking himself why he had to be a crusher of old ladies and a follower of Satan to sell cars.

"And you!" Larry got right up in Brent's face in the front row. "You gotta stop with the loser deals. I know internet is competitive, but we need high gross deals, guys, not *losers*!" He took a step back and addressed the room. "I'm not approving any deals less than one thousand bucks in gross until further notice! Guys, we got bills to pay here! No negative deals! Got it?"

"Another thing, guys. When you bluesheet 'em, if they ask you how much they're paying for the car, what do we say? Let me hear it. C'mon. Say it. Don't worry, I'm going to get you a great deal! If I can make the monthly payment and interest rate agreeable, are you ready to buy today? It's all about the payment. Close them on payment. I promise, you'll make a lot more money! That's where using the bluesheet will help you." Larry was on a roll now, and nothing was going to stand in his way. Not even little old ladies living on social security disability checks who rolled in on their walkers.

Mark had never heard of a "bluesheet" before. In training, he had been taught that it was a tool, a questionnaire disguised to look like a survey that gathered information that would later be used against the customer to get him to pay as much as they could squeeze out of him. That was the whole deal at Brandson-turn the customer upside down and shake as much money out of their pockets as possible.

The sales plan called for using this bluesheet to engage the customer in a seemingly innocent, helpful conversation while noting all the buyer's hot buttons, including credit information, social security, date of birth, and "deal-breaking" features and preferences. This process was designed to steer the customer into making as large of a down payment and as high of a monthly payment as they would agree to. Larry taught them to keep the customer focused on monthly payment and side-step questions about the total price and avoid the Buyer's Order. The Buyers' Order disclosed too much information in summary form and exposed parts of the deal where the dealer's profit was more visible.

Larry's sales process required the reps to bring the bluesheet to the sales manager's desk, where it was reviewed by either a new or used car manager. While the bluesheet was reviewed by the manager, the rep put the customer's name, trade-in, and desired car on "the glass." The huge eight by twenty-foot glass partition separating the sales tower from the showroom was known as "the glass." Depending on the customer's stated preference, the rep was given instructions on what car to show them, using a specific stock number, only after a manager had reviewed the customer's credit rating and matched their maximum monthly payment with a car from the inventory intended to maximize Brandson's profit. The sales rep would then use the stock number to retrieve the keys to the car by entering it into the ComputaKey machine. Then they would head outside, find the car, and drive it to the front to do the walk around presentation. And, of course, crush them.

"Jason. I see you with your hand up. Got a question?" As a rule, Larry had little patience with newbies, but today he seemed eager to get the new recruits onboard with the most profitable techniques that he had in his arsenal. Complete and total conversion for all non-believers is what he was thinking. Nothing less.

"Do we have to bluesheet them?" Jason asked. "Sometimes they don't want to come inside. Can we just show them around on the lot to make them happy and come back later if they don't buy?" On Jason's first day on the job, he was laughed out of the sales tower when he brought in a bluesheet that identified his customers as "Holden McGroin and his wife Pat." The customers had vanished before Jason could return to his desk.

"Did you see their ID? Make a copy of their license, Jason?" Kirk had asked, laughing at him that day. By the time Jason finally figured it out, his face was beet red in embarrassment. This morning, Larry was trying hard to hold it together. He was clearly pissed off. This guy just didn't get it, he thought. "Our job is not so much to be nice, Jason. If you want to be nice, get a dog! Our job is to sell cars and crush our customer for as much profit as possible. And we don't care what we have to do to sell cars. Anyone that does not fol- low these rules is history. Understood?" Jason nodded in agreement.

"Okay guys, what else we got? Tommy, you got anything?" Larry was looking to wrap it up and start crushing people immediately. Just then, Ricky's phone rang. "Guys, can we turn the phones off? Ricky? Thanks, man." Larry tried unsuccessfully to hide his annoyance.

"Yeah, I got something." Tommy walked up to the front to address the meeting. He liked wearing nice, expensive Italian silk suits to work. Today, he wore a light green-patterned sport coat with black slacks, a black dress shirt, and a tie that was so abstract that Mark thought it might have come from the Guggenheim Museum's gift shop. Sometimes he'd wear dress shirts with real pointed collars like Joe Pesci and Ray Liotta wore in *Goodfellas*.

"Guys, when you've got as much money as Jim Brandson, there's not too many things that you can't buy. So, this year's President's Award for Toyota Excellence is real important to him, and we're gonna do everything we can do to bring it home for him." Tommy was looking around the room to make sure that everyone was pay- ing attention and not on their cell phones.

"Now, you know that for a dealership, a green CSI rating of ninety-five percent or better is required in order to qualify for President's Award. That, and ten percent over last year's sales figures, is what we need every month." Tommy paused, looking around again to make sure everyone was paying attention.

"Year-to-date, our CSI—that's Customer Service Index for you new guys—is yellow at ninety percent. Now, many of you haven't paid enough attention to this, even though I've mentioned this many times, and that's gonna change." *Uh-oh, here it comes*, Mark thought. "So, as of right now, anyone that is rated under ninety-five percent will be fined five hundred bucks per CSI. We are going to get this thing turned around, guys, starting right now. I'm done talking about this." Tommy was being uncharacteristically stern with his new rules. Reading from a stack of printed CSIs he held, he read the top copy and continued.

"Brent. Good job. One hundred percent," handing Brent the document. "Bill. Where's Bill?" he asked, looking around the room.

"He's having trouble with his garage door today, Tommy." Once again, Kirk covered for his best used car guy.

"Having trouble with his CSIs, too. Fifty-nine percent! Unacceptable! Five hundred dollar fine! Larry, you're in charge of collecting this money."

"You got it, boss!" Larry didn't have to be coaxed. He knew that all those fines taken from the sales reps would drop right to the bottom line and be distributed as bonus money to the dealership's owners and managers.

"Dennis Testi, sixty-three percent. Five hundred dollar fine!" Tommy stepped to his left to hand the CSI to Testi.

"But Tommy, that guy lied to . . . " Tommy cut him off. "No excuses! Do whatever you have to from now on. We want to see ninety-five percent or better. Got it?" Tommy turned back around to read the next one.

Dennis Testi was a former black "male model" from Ethiopia. Rumor had it that he was actually a porn star over there, though he never owned up to it. They had heard stories about Dennis and Tricky Ricky sharing underaged girls during their now famous "Gainesville Girls Gone Wild" escapades.

"Can't read the name . . . "—Tony was squinting at the last CSI—"oh, Raj, ninety-six percent. Good job!" Raj got up and puffed out his chest as Tommy handed him the CSI. Mark was noticing the donut crumbs all over his shirt as he sat back down next to him. He leaned over, pointing at the pieces of donut on Raj's shirt.

"Hey, Raj, you saving that for a snack later on?" Mark was grinning from ear to ear. Raj glared at him in his fleeting moment of glory, refusing to buy in to Mark's teasing.

"Okay, guys, let's go sell some cars! Crush 'em!" Larry turned them all loose on a search and destroy mission. They headed out to find some customers they could crush.

FIVE

The room was dark because the brown silhouette shades were pulled down on the windows on either side of his bed. It was seven o'clock, Sunday morning, Mark's only day off this week. He couldn't make up his mind about whether he should go in or take the day off. As he opened his eyes, he watched the palm-frond ceiling fan slowly rotate, relishing the gentle breeze on his face.

He was exhausted from his first two-car sale yesterday. He'd worked until nine o'clock to deliver the new Camry XLE to a nice couple from church. Staying late last night, he patiently walked them through the deal and made sure they were happy with the price and the delivery. He felt good about their deal, successfully resisting the pressure that Bryan and Larry had put on him to "crush" them on the price.

Grabbing his favorite Picasso coffee cup from the kitchen cup-board, he poured himself a fresh cup of Starbuck's Verona creme from the automatic brewer and added a splash of hazelnut creamer. The cup depicting Picasso's most famous examples of cubism had been a gift from a female New York artist a few years back. This morning, he paused to admire the cubist figures on the cup and took a sip. It was perfect.

In the mood to sell some cars, he decided to go in to work today. He created a mental checklist. First, he would check his stocks for news, then he would do his morning 5-K run, weight training, home inspection, and church service. The digital clock on the microwave read a few minutes after seven—plenty of time for what he had planned. Brandson opened at noon on Sundays, and he wanted to be ready for the after-church crowd. He liked dealing with the faithful, feeling an obligation to protect his brothers and sisters, making sure they got a fair and honest deal.

He enjoyed jamming to 18th century classical tunes when doing his stock research, sourced from the internet or the cable channels connected to his Bose surround sound. This morning's composition *du jour* was Dvorak's New World Symphony.

He reflected on the market bottom several years ago, punctuated with the collapse of Lehman Brothers on September 15. With the market still fragile and in the early stages of recovery, he was being cautious with his picks and nimble with his trading. He hit a lot of singles and doubles, preferring not to marry his stocks. He reflected on the money he had pissed away while he paid his own tuition at the school of hard knocks over the years. Too many traders and money managers were focused on bending over to pick up a dime in front of a steam roller. One of the keys to making money was to apply an algorithm that worked, and adhering to the basic market disciplines to ensure success. With some high-yield energy royalty trusts and MLPs, some Apple, Tesla, Micron, Netflix, Ambarella and Wells Fargo, he was ready for the volatility he was expecting in tomorrow's global markets and headed outside for his run.

Sprinting through the woods, his strides were even and light as he darted in and out of the tree-shaded jogging path. His neighbor, Dr. Fontana, was busy with yard work. He thought it was odd for a plastic surgeon to do his own yard work. A hawk glided above him, screeching and circling her nest at the top of a tall pine tree. He would have missed out on these sights and sounds if he used earbuds like his friends who listened to iPod tunes during their workouts. Mark enjoyed the therapeutic sounds of wildlife in their natural habitat.

After thirty years of running on Florida and California coasts, he'd traded the sun and heat of the beaches for the shade of the forest. The woods had become the terrestrial version of the oceanic reefs that he had spent so many years exploring. He thought about the many forms of colorful reef life and the thousands of vibrant corals he'd encountered, some even possessing both male and female genitalia. Entertained by the idea of being so equipped, for a moment he thought about the money he could save on dates. The further he ran, the deeper he went into his trance-like state of subconscious thought. He often imagined himself floating in silence on the reef, twenty meters down and neutrally-buoyant, as if suspended in prenatal amniotic fluid.

Five thousand meters later and out of breath, he entered the side garage door to begin his search for renegade rodents. From the wall-mounted tool cabinet, Mark grabbed a flashlight. Starting with the garage, he did a thorough inspection of the exterior fascia and eaves, working toward the rear of the five thousand square foot house. He inspected all the hedges, the screened patio and pool area, guest quarters, mother-in-law suite, winding up back at the front. Nothing looked out of place.

Then he started his inspection of the interior, methodically inspecting the garage, closets, bedrooms, every nook and cranny that his flashlight could reach. After inspecting bedrooms one through four, he worked his way to the fifth on the east end of the house. When he opened the closet doors, he stopped. On the carpet in front of him was a pile of chewed up wallboard. Aiming his light into the corner of the ceiling, he could see the hole, about three inches in diameter, right where the CATV cable came down. It looked like he had uninvited guests.

The dealership was half-staffed on Sundays, which improved his odds of snagging an "up," and Mark enjoyed the relaxed feel of customers shopping during the abbreviated Sunday hours. The red, white and blue sale flags were flying freely in the wind as he drove up. He opened the car door halfway and reached down to retrieve the Sunday paper still lying on the driveway, stashing it in his attaché case.

As he walked from the employee parking lot, he noticed a young couple on the used lot and headed over to introduce himself.

"Hi, welcome to Brandson Toyota. My name's Mark. What information can I help you with today?"

"Mike Burton, this is my wife Judy." Smiling, they shook hands. Mark was doing his best to get them to relax and open up. Mike was tall, with grey hair, and his neatly-trimmed beard seemed to match the weathered crow's feet around his eyes. Judy was an attractive blue-eyed brunette dressed in tight-fitting jeans, white blouse, and a Miami Dolphins visor, which she had a habit of adjusting whenever she spoke. They were friendly and Mark was able to build good rapport with them right away.

"We're looking for a certified late-model Prius with low miles," said Mike. "We don't need a lot of gadgets, maybe a base model. We thought we'd start here at the Toyota dealership. We're not in any hurry, probably won't buy today, just started shopping."

"I'm happy to help you today, Mike and Judy. Are you here for the big sale?" There was always a sale at Brandson.

"Didn't know there was a sale. How much off the sale prices are we talking?" Judy clung to her husband's arm, content with letting him take the lead.

"Kinda depends on what model we land on. So, if I can find you the right car, tell me, what are two or three of the most important things about the car you're looking for?" Mark already had a car in mind. He wanted them to confirm their priorities to make sure he had it right.

"Well, obviously, great gas mileage, low miles, good warranty . . . really don't need a lot of extras. Just your basic Prius, I guess."

"So, if I can find you a certified, low mileage, like-new Prius, and the price was right, could you make a decision to own it today?" Judy got a little fidgety waiting for her husband's answer, clinging closer to her husband.

"Well, we wanted to shop around first. But yeah . . . if we like it, and the price was low enough, we could, maybe. What do you think, honey?" he asked.

Judy looked up, smiled at Mark and adjusted her visor. "Well, let's see what you've got."

"I have the latest list of certified inventory, with sale prices, right inside. Follow me." Mark turned, began walking toward the front door, but Mike and Judy hesitated, and Mike asked, "Can we look around first?"

Mark turned to them and asked "You want to save time and money?"

"Well, sure. Who wouldn't?"

"Then follow me." Mark smiled, and this time, they followed him.

"Do you live in the area?" asked Mark, looking to build some rapport as they headed for the front door.

"Over in Quail Hollow, northwest Gainesville," Mike replied.

"Nice area. Will you be keeping your new Prius in your garage there?" Mark liked using a trial close to gauge the buyer's motivation.

"Probably. We like taking care of our cars. We're giving Judy's ten year old Camry to our daughter. It's been a good car. She's turning seventeen and needs her own car. What's that car?" asked Mike. He pointed at a four door Yaris that Judy had stopped to look at.

"The Yaris is Toyota's most affordable model. It gets about the same mileage as a Corolla, mid-to-high-thirties, and priced a few grand less. The Prius would get you almost double that gas mileage." Mark had a feeling they were set on driving out in a Prius.

"So, what kind of work do you guys do?" Mark asked.

"Mike's a professor in environmental engineering and religion at UF, and I'm the office manager for an oncologist in Ocala, so I do a lot of commuting. That's why gas mileage is important to us," said Judy.

"Understood," said Mark. "That's an interesting combination, religion and ecology. I've had a few adventures on the high seas that took on a religious, sort of spiritual feel."

"Have you heard of a book called *Dark Green Theology*?" Judy asked.

"Yes, I have. I remember it got a nice write-up in the *New York Times* several months ago. Was it written by someone from your department at the University of Florida?" he asked.

"I wrote it under my pen name Brad Taylor. Have you read it?"

"A few parts that were quoted here and there, and some from the internet. Fascinating book. Congratulations!" Mark made a mental note to get his celebrity author to share some tips on how to write a best seller.

As he opened the front door for them, he asked, "Would you guys like a cold drink while we make a list of your preferences and I make a photocopy of your driver's licenses?"

They pulled out their licenses. "That does sound good. Honey, would you like a cold drink?" Mike asked. She had stopped for a moment to check out the late-model Prius Model V in the showroom.

"What's the difference between this one and a Prius a few years older?" asked Judy, weighing the pros and cons of new versus used.

Mark knew the correct answer would steer them further toward the certified pre-owned Prius. "This model V has all the upgrades and equipment you can get, some of which you may not want, including seventeen-inch alloy wheels, leather, upgraded stereo, navigation, back-up camera, and a price tag about ten to thirteen thousand higher than a late model, pre-owned Prius model II that has a better warranty. Plus, the biggest chunk of the new car depreciation has been paid for by someone else when you buy a certified pre-owned Toyota. Does that make sense?"

"What do you mean better warranty?" Mike was reading the Monroney sticker, and it was obvious that he was one of the many customers who were under the mistaken impression that new car warranties had to be better than used car warranties.

"The new Toyota factory warranty gives the owner three years and thirty six thousand miles bumper-to-bumper coverage, and five year, sixty thousand mile engine/drive train coverage. By comparison, certified pre-owned Toyotas that have gone through an inspection carry a one hundred thousand mile drive train warranty for seven years, one year of comprehensive warranty, with a one year roadside assistance program." Mark was wishing he had ten bucks for every time he'd quoted these figures.

"So, the certified car has a longer warranty then?" Mike asked.

"That's right." Mark could tell they were ready to sit down and move forward with a deal. "Why don't we sit down at my desk, let me get a little more information and check on a late-model Prius that is just now coming out of detail. It was certified today." As he led them to his desk, he said, "I'll show you where we can save you some money."

They all sat down at Mark's desk and opened their chilled bottles of water. Judy was entertaining herself by reading his certifications and letters of recommendation displayed on the partition above her head. Mike asked him, "What's a Market Value Adjustment?"

"Something you won't have to pay if you buy certified, Mike. Basically, its additional dealer profit added to the new car price, in this case because of the pent-up demand for the Prius."

"Well, I'm not paying that!" Mike was emphatic, and Judy nodded in agreement. "Doesn't Brandson make enough profit when they sell a car at MSRP?"

"Don't worry, I'm going to get you a great deal for you. That's my promise, Okay?" Mike and Judy were smiling again as Mark handed them back their licenses, and they started the bluesheet.

"That address, 10219 SW Cemetery Road, is it current?" Mark asked as he filled in the information.

"Yes, we've been there about six years, now."

"Sounds kinda quiet out there."

"Ha! Yeah. Very quiet." Judy drained her bottle of water, and Mark offered her another. "I'm good," she said, as she adjusted her visor.

"Now, do you like to finance your cars, or pay cash?"

"Depends on the interest rate," said Mike.

"With your credit score in the seven hundreds, you're sure to get the lowest rate available from any one of our thirty-five lenders. So, what kind of a monthly payment are we trying to get to?" Mark asked.

"Like to keep it around two-fifty a month. Isn't that what we talked about, honey?" asked Mike.

"Up to . . . what?" Mark gestured with his hand, looking to see how flexible they could be.

"I'm thinking two-fifty, maybe two-seventy max." Mike winced as if he was already writing the check. Mark needed to know what their maximum was, in case the target car was a little more than what they had in mind.

"You must be putting a lot down to get to such a low payment. How much down are we working with here?" Mark knew the answer was the key to both profitability and meeting their budget.

"We can put three to four thousand down," said Mike. Mark made a final notation on the blue sheet.

"Wait right here. I'm going to check with my manager to see if we have a Prius that fits your needs. I'll be right back."

Mark grabbed the blue sheet and headed to see Kirk Shifter in the sales tower.

"Gimme your bluesheet, put 'em on the board, Mark," Kirk barked. Unfortunately, it was Kirk the Jerk who was on the job. To add emphasis, Kirk farted loudly. Mark did his best to ignore the rude noises and finished putting all his customer's information on the glass. He turned around, facing his used car manager again. Suffering from a serious case of flatulence, Kirk let another one rip. All three hundred pounds of him was resting on a chair that looked too fragile to handle the load. Larry and Bryan sat at the desk beside

Kirk, suffering in silence, apparently too preoccupied with another deal to comment on the foul air.

Mark was planning his escape to clean air. "There's a certified three-year old silver Prius with only nineteen thousand miles on it in detail. Can I show them that one, Kirk?" Trying to stay on his good side, he made a special effort to be as polite as he could. Kirk had a reputation for an abusive demeanor and foul language, quite capable of flying off the handle at any moment. Mark noticed a red welt below Kirk's eye. He'd heard the stories of the drinking and brawling and decided he wasn't even going to ask. He just wanted to exit the sales tower as fast as he could, certain that the atmosphere on Mars was better than what he was being forced to breathe in the tower.

"It's priced three grand above their max. You think you can bump them?" Kirk stared at him like he had three heads.

"I think it's the perfect car for them. I'm thinking, if they like it, they could be flexible. What's the stock number, so I can grab the keys and show it to them?"

"You better hurry. Brent's got someone on it also, comin' in around three today. Stock number's 6P45701. Here's a copy of the certification." Kirk handed it to him, adding, "Let's move!"

"Thanks, boss." Mark snagged the keys and headed out to find the car in the detail area, stopping at his desk to brief his customers.

"Wait right here, Mike and Judy. I'm going to pull your car around to the front. I'll come get you when I've had a chance to check and make sure everything on the car is right and get the A/C running for you, okay?" He never had anyone turn him down on this offer during the summer months, especially since it was ninety-five degrees outside.

He walked quickly toward the rear of the dealership, passing by Gene Haile who did his best to ignore him. Mark guessed he was still embarrassed by his attempted overcharge of Sandra MacGowan a few days earlier.

Making his way past the rows of service lifts, past all the mechanics busy with their air hammers, ratchets, and computer screens, he found his way into the detail area. He spotted Marvin, one of the most cantankerous men to never grace the cover of *Auto Detailer Today*, polishing up the late model silver Prius that he was going to sell to the Burtons. The detail area was pretty busy, with eleven cars being prepped for delivery. Some were for the used lot. The guys in the back loved to blare their hip-hop and rap, and they loved their weed too, sometimes getting stoned inside the cars they were supposed to be cleaning. Sales reps would find everything from fresh burgers to joints stashed in the ashtrays and armrests of cars coming out of detail.

"Hi, Marvin. That Prius ready? I've got a customer waiting if it is." Marvin was playing Rick Ross so loud on his headphones they could probably hear it in Utah. Mark was thinking this was normal behavior for a mutant. Marvin wiped off one last smudge on the windshield then gave Mark the finger. It was always nice to feel appreciated.

After a quick inspection, Mark hopped in the Prius, surveying the interior carefully for rotting cheeseburgers or half-smoked joints. Finding none this time, he drove it up to the front of the dealership for his rendezvous with the Burtons. When he found them, Mike and Judy were back inspecting the new Prius Model V.

"You guys are gonna love this car!" he said to them. Mark's passion for the Prius was unmistakable. "The car of the future that you can own today, and the number one selling hybrid on the planet by a wide margin," he added. Mike smiled, amused by Mark's enthusiasm.

In the next ten minutes, Mark performed one of the best walk-around presentations and test drives of his nascent career, answering all their questions to their satisfaction. He covered the technical aspects of the Prius, including explanations of the regenerative braking, the electro/mechanical generators, the special ULEV Atkins-cycle gas engine that was married to the electric motor through the Hybrid Synergy Drive System. The car was a perfect fit for the Burton's green lifestyle, wish list and budget.

As Judy drove back up to the dealership, Mark said "Let's park it over there in the sold lane," flashing his best Hollywood-style smile.

As the Prius rolled to a stop, Mike got out and shut the passenger door. He said "Whoa, hold on there, partner, we have a lot of ground to cover before we're sold. What kinda deal you think we can get us here?" Mike posed with his chin in his hand, pretending that he wasn't excited by the car.

Mark took a step back, sizing up the situation, watching Judy inside the car. She was still pushing buttons, fascinated by the advanced, multi-colored laser displays and the ergonomic design of the interior.

Mark asked Mike, "If the price and terms are agreeable, is there any reason that you wouldn't want to own this car today?" He watched his customer's reaction carefully.

"Tell you what. If the price is right, we'll drive her home, but the price has to be right." He could tell Mike wasn't going to be a lay down.

"Okay then, let's go inside, sit down, and work this out the way you want. Judy, will you join us?" She was still fiddling with the Smart Key and interior features.

"Okay, let's see whatcha got," she said, as she exited the Prius, adjusted her visor and followed them inside.

Mike sat down at his desk while Judy paid a visit to the powder room and Mark inputted all the deal information into their customer computer file in the contact management system. He printed up the standard credit report and a worksheet for Kirk to pencil the figures in anticipation of a deal. "Mike, I'll be right back with the figures," said Mark. He snatched the prints off the printer and presented them to Kirk sitting at the manager's desk.

"What do we have, Mark?" Kirk still looked hungover, with the welt sticking out on his face. Mark was thankful that the air in the sales tower was, once again, safe to breathe.

"We have a nice couple, the Burtons, with four thousand down, up to two-seventy a month, credit in the seven hundreds. They're on the certified three-year old silver Prius II with nineteen thousand miles. My suggestion would be to pencil them at three hundred a month, and forty-five hundred down and let them work me down."

"Sounds like a plan. That's what you get, then." As he began working the figures and penciling the deal, Kirk added, "And you can have this as a bonus." Then, he farted again.

"Damn, bro, what did you have for lunch, four pounds of chili and beans?" asked Mark. Disgusted, he thought it was time to mess with him a little. "So, Kirk, what did you do with the money?"

"Okay, Marky-Mark, I'll play." He looked up at Mark, sliding the penciled worksheet across the desk to him, and asked, "What money?"

"The money your mom gave you for Betty Ford's School of Flatulence?" Kirk's face turned puppy-dog sad as he looked up at Mark.

"That's not funny, Mark. My mom's a regular patient at the Betty Ford Clinic. She even has a couch named after her there," said Kirk. At first, he looked serious then he broke into a grin. "Now go sell a car."

Mark laughed and grabbed the penciled presentation. He sat down again with Mike and Judy. "I have some really great news for you guys. Let me show you the figures my boss put together for you." Mark flipped the page over and showed him the figures.

After reviewing the numbers, Mike shook his head. "No, we can't do that." He leaned closer to Mark, saying, "Look, Mark, you seem like a nice guy, but we told you what we're willing to do. That's too high."

"I understand you want a better deal. You've both said that this is the right car for you. Low miles, like-new condition, certified to one hundred thousand miles, priced way under a new one. You seem like a reasonable couple." Mark shifted gears and lowered his voice. "I have an idea. Can you meet my boss halfway on the monthly payment if I could talk him into reducing the down payment to four thousand and include a Platinum Certification?" Mark picked up the pen, not waiting for his answer, writing down the "offer."

"What's a Platinum Certification?" asked Mike.

"A one hundred thousand mile bumper-to-bumper warranty, not just engine and drive train. Comprehensive, even bulbs and wipers."

"That part sounds good. And the payment? Can we do two seventy a month, including everything?" asked Mike, pushing hard to get the deal he wanted.

Mark responded with a compromise idea. "If we were to meet him halfway, that would be two seventy-five a month. My suggestion would be to give him the five bucks a month, meeting him halfway, and then you get twenty-three hundred dollars worth of Platinum Certification thrown in if he agrees. Now, I don't know if I can talk him into this, but I'm willing to try for you guys 'cause I want you to have this car, okay?"

Mark slid the offer in front of him, holding out the pen. Mike looked at Judy, asked her, "You okay with this, honey?"

"Yeah, I think it's a good deal. I like the Platinum Warranty idea. We wouldn't have to worry about repairs for a long time." She adjusted her visor again, and a pregnant pause followed.

"Okay, sign your counter offer right here." Mike took the pen and signed. Mark said, "Thanks for your offer. I'll do my best to convince him to give you this deal, but I can't make any guarantees." After Mark did the take-away, they both nodded in agreement.

Mark shook hands with his customer, saying, "Wish me luck." He walked back to Kirk and presented the counter offer. "Okay, here's what we got. Four grand down, they'll go two seventy-five a month, and we do a Platinum Certification. Can we do it?"

"It's a twenty-two hundred dollar front. Go write it up, Mark." This time Kirk didn't fart.

Returning to Mike and Judy at his desk, he acted very subdued, a little sad at first. He placed the worksheet face down on his desk, saying, "I did my best . . . and . . . I didn't think he'd go for it, at first, but I got you the deal you wanted. Congratulations!" He turned the signed offer over, and they shook hands enthusiastically.

"Now, I need to make a copy of your current proof of insurance, have you sign the Buyer's Guide and insurance affidavit, privacy policy, credit application then I'll go gas up your new car while you meet with our finance and insurance guy who will complete your paperwork. Are you excited?" asked Mark.

"Yeah . . . we are." Mike smiled and handed Mark his insurance card. He leaned over and put his hand reassuringly on his wife's shoulder. Judy drained the last few gulps from her water bottle, held it out, and asked, "Do you recycle?"

"We sure do," said Mark. He took the empty bottles over to the recycle bin a few steps from his desk and dropped them in.

"Good job, baby," Judy said to Mike, giving him a big kiss. She couldn't contain her excitement, relieved at successfully completing the negotiations for their new Prius. Now, they looked forward to driving it home to show her daughter.

"You guys have been fun to work with. I want to clarify something with you." Mark liked them and wanted to protect their deal, as well as any referrals he might get.

"Okay, sure. What?"

"Our deal that we just agreed to, four thousand down and two seventy-five a month for sixty months, covers everything, including all applicable taxes, title fees, dealer fees, and the Platinum Certification. That's solid and not going to change. When you meet with the finance and insurance manager in the next few minutes, please understand that his job is to create all the necessary documents, complete the title work and registration, but also show you, uh . . . various insurance and warranty products that you may, or may *not* need. If you choose to add any of those products to your deal, you will be changing your payment. You do understand, right?"

"Yeah, we understand, Mark. With the Platinum Plan, what else do we need?"

"I would say, maybe nothing. But that's your call, not mine." Mike nodded like he understood what Mark was trying to warn him about.

Mark checked and placed all the signed paperwork into the deal jacket. "Okay, then." He hit the print button for the gas voucher that printed in the sales tower. "Let me take you over to the customer finance lounge while I go gas up your car. Right this way," said Mark, leading them across the showroom to the finance lounge area as a few of the other reps looked on in envy.

After he'd sat them down and turned on the big screen TV, he walked the deal jacket back to Kirk in the sales tower. As he approached the doorway, he hesitated as he listened to Kirk speak, realizing he was hearing something he wasn't supposed to hear.

Kirk was on the phone. "Doesn't matter. Just have the porter drive it in one end of the garage, out the other, and then sign the certification. No, skip the inspection, we're going to pocket the four hundred bucks and add it to our profit. Don't give me a hard time about it, Jon. Larry says to skip all the inspections on used Toyotas with less than thirty thousand miles. Yes, I'll take responsibility." Kirk hung up. Mark felt uncomfortable, just having overheard something that nauseated him. He proceeded into the tower and placed his deal jacket on the counter in front of Kirk, who snatched it up, pulled out the documents inside, scanning each one for errors.

"Everything in here, Mark?"

"Yes, I think so . . . "

"You forgot to put the mileage on the jacket." Kirk looked smug in finding something he had missed. He handed him back the jacket.

"Got it right here. Nineteen thousand five hundred sixty miles." Mark was reading it from the back of a business card. A conservationist all the way, he used old business cards to make his notes. He wrote the mileage down on the deal jacket in the space provided, thinking about the conversation he just overheard. That conversation bothered him, especially since he just sold a certified used car. He wondered if the Burton's certification had been faked. He decided to pose the question to his used car manager.

"So, Kirk, on these certifications, we *are* doing the hundred and sixty-point check on them, right?" Kirk looked up, glaring angrily.

"Mark, let's get something straight here. We don't care how we sell cars here, *as long as we sell cars. Got it?* "You got a problem with that?" Kirk was really in his face.

"Well, I just—"

"Now, get the hell out of here and go gas up the Prius before I give this deal to someone else!" Kirk was ready to come unglued. Mark grabbed the gas voucher from the printer and quickly walked out the door, heading for the Prius still parked out front. He had a bad feeling about the conversation with Kirk.

McGreedy had been watching the drama unfold, and Mark passed him on the way outside. "What the hell did you say to set him off?" asked McGreedy. He was always looking for dirt. He was a lot like Raj, continually looking for ways to ingratiate himself with the managers, usually at someone else's expense.

"Never mind. Gotta run." Mark was blacked out about it, ironically at a time when he should be the most happy—the moment of his newest sale. As he rode up to the Kangaroo station to gas up the Prius, he promised himself he was going to figure this out. Ten minutes later, he backed the spotless Prius into position for delivery.

It had been forty minutes since the Burtons entered 'Tricky Ricky' Gonzalez's office to complete the paperwork. Mark was at his desk catching up on service order follow-ups and possible referrals when they returned. He was disappointed to see them with a very unhappy look on their faces.

"Everything go okay?" They weren't acting like the happy couple he'd taken over to F&I earlier.

"Well, yeah, I guess so," said Mike. Judy was looking down at the floor, holding something back. "He talked us into paying another sixty dollars a month for a pre-paid service plan that he said wasn't covered anywhere else. He said our bank required the extra plan to get the lower interest rate. We just wanna get our car and get going. We've got company coming in about twenty minutes. Appreciate your help, Mark. You have our keys?" Mike wasn't nearly as cordial as he'd been before he'd met with Tricky Ricky.

Mark handed them two keys to their new Prius. "Let me do a quick inspection of the car with you before you take off to make sure everything is to your liking, okay?"

They walked out onto the delivery pad together. The couple were still in a sour mood. Mark was doing his best to cheer them up. "She's all gassed up and ready to go."

They did a fast final inspection. Mark attached the temporary tag, and as Judy climbed in her new Prius, he added, "I really do appreciate your business, Mike and Judy. Thank you for the opportunity to be of service. I'm hoping your best-selling book gets made into a top-grossing movie."

They both smiled politely, waving as if they had just been condemned to the gas chamber. They said no more, and they drove off together with the windows down. As he walked toward the front door, he couldn't shake the feeling that he'd just lost a friend, but he couldn't figure out why. Then, as they rounded the corner of the building ten feet from him, Mark overheard Mike from inside the car.

"After that deal, honey, about the only thing they *didn't* take from me are my kidneys."

SIX

After a walk through the woods on the morning of his fifty-fifth birthday, he was amazed at the abundance of wildlife that was living, hunting, and mating in such close proximity to his bedroom. It was ironic, given the extended period of celibacy that he was experiencing himself.

The aroma of fresh-perked coffee greeted him from the kitchen after his unexpected encounter with his wild neighbors in the forest. He poured himself a large cup and turned back to the Family Historical Registry lying on the onyx countertop. His mom had prepared and sent the research file for his birthday, along with a check for two thousand dollars. Knowing that her son was a workaholic, in the memo section of the check she'd written "for something fun."

He interpreted her gift of The Family Registry as yet another reminder from his mom that it wasn't too late to pass on the family heritage that was his to squander, or to share. He had come close a few times to becoming a dad, but always right at the most critical time, his love relationships seemed to fall apart as soon as the intensity of the romance subsided. From what he remembered from his college psychology classes, he recognized that he was addicted to pair formation sex and would likely never be happy with the less-intensive level of pair maintenance sex that normally followed in most relationships.

As his mother so often pointed out, their lineage was uncommon. His great, great, great, great grandfather was a gentleman named William Brewster, who was born near Scrooby, Nottinghamshire, England and came to Massachusetts in the Mayflower in 1620. Mr. Brewster was the spiritual leader of the Mayflower, and of the Plymouth Colony. He was also one of the founders of the Congregational Church in America. As a true blue blood and direct descendant of the founding fathers, Mark had some big shoes to fill, as his mother was so fond of reminding him.

As he arrived at the dealership that morning, he had told no one that it was his birthday. Birthdays made him feel old, and for that reason he preferred the anonymity of a normal day. There was an outside chance that he might tell someone if the situation felt right.

As he sat at his desk and prepared for his day, he reflected back on his first two years as a sales rep at Brandson. It made him feel successful to know he'd averaged eighteen sales a month, putting him in the top quartile of reps at the dealership. As the dog days of summer had wore on last year, Mark had cut his deal for a new Prius with its solar-powered roof. The other three newbies who were in his training class had either quit or were fired during his first few months at the dealership. There were five other sales reps fired for poor performance, including Bill Boyer, who had offended one too many customers with his drunken rants and temper tantrums. One less horsefly to deal with was okay with him.

Placing in the top sales quartile at Brandson was no small feat, since many in the top tier were being handed eight to twelve cheese deals a month. But not Mark. These unearned deals were worth an extra five to ten thousand dollars in additional monthly commissions.

Whenever the coveted "point position" was occupied, he hopped on the phone and brought customers into the dealership, making an additional couple of sales each week from the appointments he made. He knew he just didn't fit the good ole boy profile required to be on the cheese deal gravy train with his managers. Nor did he have any desire to be included in the ranks of drunks, brawlers, coke heads, and party animals just so he could be on the list for extra house deals.

Over the course of his first two years at Brandson, he'd watched quite a bit of schmoozing and brown nosing by the guys he called "The Redneck Mafia." At first, he was mildly entertained by the antics, but lately he'd become more cautious of the group of misfits that included McGreedy, Dennis Testi, Raj Patel, and now another of Larry's drinking buddies hired last week, Jack Gates. Mr. Gates, a/k/a "Juicifer", had a checkered past and a reputation for running quite a few scams at his last few jobs. He found out that Juicifer was arrested in Seminole County last year for fraud, and Mark began to have serious concerns about the direction where things were going at the dealership.

"What are you so smug about?" Bryan had caught him daydreaming as he walked into the showroom from the side entrance. He was carrying a large plastic bag of food with him, not unusual when you ate as much as Bryan did trying to keep his six foot seven inch frame fueled up.

"Just thinking about how to double my new car deals before the end of the month." He pointed at the bag full of food, "I see you're still feeding that tapeworm you got, huh?" Bryan stopped at Mark's desk. "Hey, I thought about a way you can get rid of it. You could sit behind your desk, very still, mouth open, with a hunk of pate resting on your tongue. When he crawls up to get it, we could grab him. Whad'ya think?" Mark was grinning.

"I think you're retarded, bro." Bryan laughed at the imagery. "Besides, you know I can't stand pate. Hey, I want you to do me a favor." Bryan leaned on his desk.

Feigning a lisp, Mark said, "I'm sorry, Bryan, but I'm not that kinda guy."

"Get real. Neither am I. We just hired a guy from AT&T Cellular. His name is Rich. I want you to train him, show him the ropes, okay?" Mark could tell it wasn't really a request. Bryan stooped down to pick something off the top of one of his crocodile shoes.

"Will I get the half deals when he and I do a sale?" He knew that during the first month of training, newbies were paid a two thousand dollar monthly salary and put their training partner's name on the first few deals.

"You'll have to work it out with Rich, but, yeah, it's okay with me. He's a nice guy, you two should hit it off. He'll be at AT&T for another few weeks. He wants to make sure they pay him his last paycheck before he starts with us. You up for this?" Whenever Bryan pointed his finger in your direction, Mark knew to pay attention.

"Absolutely. I'll make him a top producer by the end of the month." Bryan gave him a fist bump on the note of confidence. Mark was looking forward to his first training assignment. He thought it odd that the managers at Brandson generally avoided any formal training, preferring to hand it off to top producers who were compensated from the deals they generated during the training process.

Bored with his phone calling, he decided to head over to the service lounge a hundred feet away and meet some customers who might be interested in trading up. He noticed a blonde woman wearing jeans and a teal colored blouse sitting by herself who was pretending to read a book. She had her legs crossed and was undulating her foot up and down expectantly, almost like she was pumping something with her pent-up energy.

"Hi. Are they taking good care of you in service today?" asked Mark, giving her his warmest smile.

"Oh, sure. Lenny is having my oil changed and tires rotated. Are you one of the managers?" she asked, putting her book down on the empty seat beside her.

"Just a customer service rep. I'm Mark, and you are?" he asked, grasping her hand and leaning forward to hear her name.

"Norma. Norma Daniels. Nice to meet you," she said, smiling, looking up at him. She seemed excited to be the focus of his attention.

"A pleasure to meet you, Norma. I see you're reading Sarah Palin's best seller there. What's it called? *Going Rogue?*" Mark took the empty seat next to her.

"Yeah, I really like it," said Norma. "She's a very independent lady, very forward thinking, ahead of her time. Always been an admirer." Norma was waiting for a reaction from Mark.

"I agree. I actually voted for her and Senator McCain when she ran for VP on his ticket. Really wanted them to win." He could tell she was waiting to see if their politics were going to match, and seemed pleased that they did. Steering her more toward business at hand, Mark asked, "So, what model of Toyota do you drive, Norma?"

"It's a three-year-old Rav 4. I like it a lot. My sister's always borrowing it. Obviously, she likes it too. Her partner is always borrowing her car, so she likes to borrow my Rav. One of the reasons I came here today was to help her find someone to help her get a good deal on a new one. She'll be here in about twenty minutes. Would you have time to meet her?"

"I'd be delighted to help her, Norma. What's her name?"

"Sarah."

"We have a sheriff named Sarah Daniels. Is that who we're talking about, Sheriff Daniels?" Mark was excited at the prospect of making a sale to a well-known elected official, but kept his emotions in check.

"Yes, she's my sister." Norma lowered her voice to a whisper. "Can we keep this to ourselves? Sarah is very private and low-key about her public dealings, and keeps a low profile, mmm . . . for obvious reasons." Mark thought of all the criminals she'd put away, and immediately understood the importance of her sister's request.

"I understand one hundred percent. I'll do my best to keep it quiet. You know, Norma, since we have a few minutes before she arrives, if you know what her preferences are as far as color and features, maybe we could look around, do some homework and save her some time. Let me take you over to my desk so we can talk more privately."

"Sure. I think my sister would appreciate whatever time we can save her today. I know she has a meeting with the County Commission later. Where's your desk?" Norma gathered up her things and followed Mark.

They spent the next ten minutes completing the blue sheet for her sister Sarah. To speed things up, she called Sarah and gave her a progress report on the Rav 4 deal. Mark heard that Sheriff Daniels was en route to Brandson and learned that she wanted a cash deal on a new silver, two wheel drive Rav 4 Limited. In order to help keep a low profile for the Sheriff, Mark had substituted Norma's name on the glass in the sales tower. He had located and retrieved the desired Rav 4 Limited Model and he was in the process of parking it at the front entrance when the sheriff pulled up in her cruiser.

The sheriff's big Crown Victoria arrived with it's collection of three rooftop antennas, and Norma joined Mark outside to wait for her sister. A fierce-looking officer in his thirties emerged from the passenger side of the police cruiser, and as he stood beside the car in the parking lot, he did a stationary three hundred sixty degree recon of the area. He walked to the driver's side door and opened it for his boss. She exited the cruiser, waved to Norma and Mark and headed toward the entrance with the tough-looking officer escorting her.

The sheriff proved to be remarkably unpretentious, introducing herself as Sheriff Daniels as she shook hands with Mark and hugged her sister. She asked that everyone call her Sarah. The long-sleeved green uniform couldn't hide the obvious fact that she stayed in shape, and her brown eyes were warm and friendly, framed by crow's-feet from years of making difficult decisions as the chief law enforcement officer of Alachua County. She was of medium build, her brown hair was well-cut and styled to shoulder length, and she had an attractive, slightly masculine appearance.

"Norma and Mark, this is Sergeant Davis," said the sheriff. She was direct, but not heavy-handed. They all nodded at Sergeant Davis who smiled, but said nothing, the outline of his bullet-proof vest clearly visible under his tight-fitting uniform and duty belt that was saddled with his forty caliber Glock. The sergeant had the face of a professional boxer and the demeanor of a seasoned linebacker, completely devoid of personality.

"Sergeant Davis will accompany me today. I have a County Commission meeting in an hour. Do you think we can test drive, work out the price, and finish all the paperwork in an hour?" Obviously familiar with what was required in the sales process, she was courteous in the way she had asked him. Coming from her, Mark understood that it really wasn't a question and knew it would be a challenge to finish within her time constraints.

"Absolutely, yes ma'am, Norma has shared your preferences with me, and I will do everything in my power to find the right car today. Shall we start with this Rav 4 Limited? It's got all the features that are important to you."

Larry unexpectedly emerged from the front entrance, cell phone to his ear. Spotting the two police officers standing with Mark, Larry walked up to the group and quipped, "All right—fess up, Mark. Whad'ya do now? You in trouble again? You run over more chickens?"

"No, sir, she won't need her cuffs today. Our sheriff is here to buy a car," said Mark. He proceeded to make the introductions to his GSM.

"Welcome to Brandson Toyota, ma'am, pleasure to meet you," said Larry as he shook their hands. "If I can give you a ridiculously-good deal, ya think ya might throw in a couple of get out of jail free cards?" asked Larry with a big grin. "My guys can get kinda rowdy."

Sheriff Daniels smiled politely at Larry. "How 'bout a reduced sentence?" she answered without skipping a beat.

Her response caught Larry off guard, and he pointed at his cell phone. "Gotta finish this call. Mark will take good care of you today." He disappeared around the corner, still yelling into his phone at someone in finance and insurance.

Sarah had turned her attention back to the Rav 4 Limited sitting in front of her. "I think I like this color better than the silver I had in mind, and I really like these alloy wheels. Let's take it for a quick test drive, can we?" She was already sitting in the driver's seat, checking out all the controls, pushing buttons, noticing the upgrades from Norma's older model. Mark stood on the passenger side with the door open, and had just begun to show her the navigation, Bluetooth, smart air bags, leather, power seats and safety features. Norma and Sgt. Davis quickly slipped into the back seat and fastened their seat belts, waiting quietly for Sarah to start the car.

As he slid into the front seat, he asked, "Okay, Sarah, you have your Florida driver's license with you? Wouldn't want us to get pulled over, right?" Sarah did a mock check on all the weaponry on her duty belt, laughed, and said, "Got it, and don't worry. I'll handle it if we do get pulled over."

Mark was about halfway through his presentation of the interior safety and convenience features when he heard the police siren. They had traveled a few miles when he looked over the top of the seat to see that the deputy's cruiser behind them had his lights on and looked intent on pulling them over. At first, he thought it had something to do with his high-profile customer, but when he saw the surprised look on her face, he knew that this wasn't planned. He could hear Sgt. Davis unbuckle his seat belt in the back seat. "Shall I handle this, ma'am?"

"That's okay, Dave, I'll handle it," said the sheriff.

As both vehicles came to a stop in the right access lane, Sarah unbuckled her seat belt and opened the door. "I'm sure this is a mistake. I'll be right back," she said.

Mark adjusted the rearview mirror, not wanting to miss the surprised look on the deputy's face as the sheriff of Alachua County emerged from the Rav 4. He knew it couldn't be for speeding. Sarah had been careful to not exceed the posted limit of forty-five mph.

He rolled down his window so he could hear as much of the conversation as possible, now keenly interested in knowing why they were being pulled over.

Mark listened to the conversation. "Yes, ma'am, sorry for stopping you, couldn't see the window stickers from behind . . . please continue with your test drive. I agree, I'm sure it was only an oversight on his part." The officer tipped his hat, got back into his cruiser, turned off the flashing lights, and pulled onto the highway. The deputy looked embarrassed as he hit the gas and headed east.

As Sarah climbed back into the driver's seat, she turned to Mark. "I've got some good and some bad news. The bad news is that we forgot to display a dealer tag on our vehicle," She looked at Mark sternly, then smiled. "Good news is that I talked him into letting us off with a warning." She put the Rav 4 in gear, pulling out smartly, and added, "I like this car. How 'bout we write it up for two thousand under the sticker price and Brandson pays for upgraded rubber floor mats, a cargo net for the back, and the first tank of gas?" She looked at him expectantly.

"Hmm . . . " he said. He thought for a few moments. A woman who knows what she wants. He noticed Norma shifting her position in the back seat, uncomfortable with the silence. The taciturn seageant seemed ambivalent to the conversation and continued with his imitation of Mt. Rushmore.

"And you want Brandson to include upgraded floor mats?" asked Mark. He couldn't make it look too easy for her.

"Can you do it?" asked Sarah.

As Mark weighed her offer, Sarah completed a U-turn at an opening in the median, and was now heading back to the dealership at flank speed while she waited for his answer.

He decided to mess with her just a little. "And you want a full tank of gas, not a half tank?" asked Mark with a straight face.

The sheriff looked at him. "Are you messin' with me, mister?" She was smiling, so he felt pretty good about avoiding the possibility of being handcuffed. Wanting to win her business, and the valuable referrals that were sure to follow, Mark prepared his curve ball.

"To make this work, I think we need to do better. How about this, Sarah. Rubber mats, full tank of gas, wash, wax and detail, cargo net, and only five hundred over invoice? That would save you another twelve hundred bucks."

"You can do that?"

"Pretty sure we can for our Sheriff, yes ma'am. If I can talk my manager into it, do we have a deal?" Mark smiled and extended his hand, knowing that his managers would go for it once he told them who the buyer was.

Sarah shook his hand, saying, "Okay, partner, you got yourself a deal. You always drive such a hard bargain?"

"No ma'am. Only when it's my birthday."

SEVEN

Rich Deveraux was born in Canada, and during his childhood, moved to a coastal area on Sydney Harbour, Australia, where his family bought a large tract of land squarely in the path of progress. Just about the time he was old enough to attend high school, his family sold the acreage to a hotel developer for a small fortune, which they used to buy a forty room motel in Seattle. They moved to Seattle twenty years ago to manage their new income property. Years later, after receiving an MS degree in computer sciences from the University of Florida, he went to work for the Gainesville Police Department and was eventually promoted to lieutenant. As head of computer forensics, he was responsible for solving more than five hundred crimes involving the use of computers. By the time he left GPD, he had run their computer forensics unit for seven years before being forced out on a bogus charge involving a young lady that, ironically, he was currently married to.

Now, in his late thirties, he had tired of his dead end job at AT&T and put it in his rearview mirror. As he drove to the dealership, he was preoccupied by his marital problems, worried that he wouldn't be able to afford his wife's runaway legal expenses. His beautiful, sex-crazed Asian wife was addicted to drugs and had already logged six trips through rehab. He sipped his can of Monster Energy as he zipped along in his seven-year old Honda Civic coupe doing fifteen over the posted limit of forty-five, confident he knew just about every traffic cop in the city.

Relying on his background as a former cop to get him out of speeding tickets had always worked for him in the past, but this new problem with Carla being arrested for breaking and entering, grand theft, and possession with intent to sell was vexing him. He had to lean heavily on a high-priced defense attorney who was on the phone with him now, calming him and reassuring his friend that he would handle it.

Rich pulled into the employee parking space at Brandson, hoping he could double, maybe even triple, his income. The three thousand a month from AT&T wasn't cutting it. He felt better after his conversation with his attorney who had succeeded in arranging bail for his wife. He presented himself at the Brandson front desk with measurably more confidence than he had twenty minutes ago. Rich had helped his attorney out of a tight spot with a warrant six years ago, and they'd been friends ever since.

He spotted a familiar face as he entered the showroom. "Hi, Jo. I'm Rich, I met you a few days ago," he said. He wore a new blue dress shirt and yellow tie he just bought yesterday, wanting to look sharp for his first day at the dealership.

"Hold on." Jo was holding up a finger, finishing up with a customer on the phone. As she hung up, she said, "Hey, Rich, 'course I remember you. Are you here to start your training?" Jo appreciated well-built, hunky men, and she could tell Rich worked out.

"That's why I'm here. Which one is Mark? He's supposed to handle my training. I was told he's good. Is he?" he asked, inviting her to assess his new trainer's abilities.

"I like Mark. He's honest, nice, smart, and one of our best sales reps. He's right over there." She pointed to her left. "Short brown hair, red polo, tan Dockers. See him? You're lucky. He's usually too busy to train anyone."

"Thanks Jo." Rich turned to meet his trainer.

"Good luck today," said Jo.

Mark was on the phone when he walked up. He offered his new trainee a chair, holding up his index finger to let him know he was about to finish his conversation. Rich sat down, looking at all the certificates, awards, and letters of recommendation mounted on his partition wall.

Mark hung up the phone, extended his hand, and said, "You must be Rich. Welcome aboard."

"Nice to meet you, Mark. Like all your letters there."

"Well, thanks. I just wish my mom hadn't charged me twenty bucks apiece to write them for me," Mark said wryly.

"Ha! Yeah, well, Bryan said you can turn me into a top producer before the end of the month."

"Any computer skills?" Mark asked.

"Only a master's degree in computer sciences. I ran the computer forensics unit for seven years at GPD. Does that count?" Rich cocked his head and smiled confidently.

"Might prove somewhat helpful, yeah, maybe," said Mark dryly, nodding approvingly, trying to disguise the fact that he was impressed with Rich's credentials.

They hit it off right away, and Mark spent the next two hours showing him the ropes. They covered Contact Management, meeting and greeting procedures, blue sheeting, creating customer files, credit applications, disclosures, file jackets, and accessing keys from the ComputaKey machine. Mark showed him how to protect his customers from vultures and snakes like McGreedy, Testi, Patel, and the newest member of the Redneck Mafia, Jack Gates, who they nicknamed "Juicifer."

Mark had a pet name for just about everyone at Brandson. "Juicifer" was the combination of Jack's given name, and Lucifer, in view of Juicifer's favorite pet phrase for excusing himself from all manner of decorum; "the Devil made me do it." Juicifer invoked the phrase whenever he was caught red-handed screwing someone over, now a daily event.

McGreedy suddenly appeared at Rich's desk. "Lemme show ya how to do this, guys." Mark and Rich exchanged knowing glances as they both smelled liquor on his breath.

"Thanks, but I think we got this, Paul." At first, Mark was content to let McGreedy dig his own hole in front of his new recruit but grew impatient with the stench of alcohol. McGreedy made a face and sauntered off to brown nose the managers in the tower.

Then it was Raj's turn to take a shot at the newbie. "If you want to learn from a pro, you should talk to me," he said, smirking. "I'm makin' six figures, guys!"

"Okay, thanks, Jabba," said Mark as he wondered how many more members of the Redneck Mafia he'd have to deflect in order to defend his training turf.

After Raj had left, Mark continued with Rich's training program. "Never turn your back on those four guys"—pointing at their names on a roster—"and always put notes in the customer's file to document your contact if you want to protect your customer." Larry uses a "three-day contact rule" when it comes to claiming ownership of a customer file. If you don't have notes in the system within that three day time frame, you'll lose your claim to any deal created. Also, review your customer files to check for snakes trying to circumvent you. If you don't do this everyday, it could cost you thousands of dollars in lost commissions." Mark paused, adding, "Also, when you greet customers, Rich, you'd be better off without those 'Terminator' sunglasses. Making good eye contact with your customer will help build trust. Any questions?"

"Think I got it. So, now that I know who the snakes are, can you tell me who I can trust? I mean, besides you of course." Rich smiled. Mark wasn't sure he was completely convinced.

Palms up, Mark added, "I can only relate my own experiences. I've found Brent, Dave, Travis, Binh, Scott, and sometimes Buck are fairly honest. The rest of them, better watch'em like a hawk." Scanning the list of names again, Rich added, "Roger that."

Mark straightened up in his chair. "Okay, tiger. Let's go up your first customer. I'll show you what to say and what to do the first time you bring in a customer. After that, you're on your own. I'm always available to help with questions if I'm not with a customer."

"I'm ready. Let's do it." In spite of his trainer's advice on making eye contact, Rich put his cop sunglasses back on. With his blonde crew cut, military-style black boots, and stocky build, Mark thought he looked more like a cop than ever, but he could still see some talent in the guy.

They walked out the front entrance to work their first deal. Juicifer had just upped an old man in a battery-powered wheelchair, and his wife was pushing a walker on wheels. The old man had to be in his nineties and looked ready to expire on the spot. He had a plastic nose tube hooked up to an oxygen tank that rode with him in his wheel chair, and they were both moving at the speed of molasses in winter. Rich opened the front door for them, and they could hear Juicifer mutter, "while we're still young . . . " under his breath, flashing a smile and winking at Rich and Mark as the group entered the dealership.

Once they were outside and out of earshot, Mark nodded toward Juicifer's customers. "I weep for the future of those Q-tips. Probably going to be a twelve to fifteen pounder."

"What's a twelve to fifteen pounder?" asked Rich.

"Twelve to fifteen thousand dollar front-end commission."

"You think he'll screw them over that bad?" Rich asked.

"We'll see." Mark had heard that Juicifer liked to target older handicapped couples, and those deals usually had a staggering amount of profit.

Just then, a beat up Chrysler Town & Country mini-van riding on the donut spare tire pulled up in front. They watched a middle-aged couple exiting the rusted van.

Mark looked at Rich. "All you there, partner. That's a really good up. Let them get out first, then walk toward them with your best smile. Remember to say what we talked about."

Mark withdrew a safe distance so he could overhear Rich introduce himself and take control of his customers. The customers were both slim, in their sixties, and wore jeans, T-shirts, and deck shoes. As Rich led them in the front door, he looked over his shoulder at Mark and gestured for him to join them inside.

"Hi, I'm Mark McAllister, Rich's training partner. Welcome to Brandson Toyota." As they shook, Mark noticed their hands were rough and calloused.

The old man spoke first. "Bill Franklin and this is my wife Sharon. We're here to look at some mini-vans."

Mark smiled reassuringly. "We can certainly help you with that. Are you looking for new or used?"

"We're thinkin' used, but with a good warranty and low miles. Your website said you had something like that here. We're on a tight budget." He noticed his wife had wandered over to check out the new Prius in the showroom.

"Sure. Please, have a seat and make yourselves comfortable. Would you like some cool, bottled water?" Bill took a chair and looked over his shoulder at his wife a few steps away. "Honey, you want some water?"

"Sure. Sounds good. Really warmed up today." She was fanning herself with a brochure she'd picked up, pushing her graying hair back from around her face. Bill looked up at Mark. "You still have this silver late model certified Sienna here with thirty-two thousand miles?" Bill was leaning forward, showing him the Brandson certified pre-owned van from yesterday's web page.

"We'll check on that right away. Let me get a little information from you, Bill, and make a copy of your driver's license." Mark proceeded to fill in the blue sheet and qualify his buyers. After completing the questionnaire, Mark took it to the sales tower, with Rich in tow, and wrote their customer's name, trade in, and target vehicle on the glass.

"You guys know where Kirk is?" asked Mark.

Larry looked up. "Not our week to watch him. Might be out front. Show me what ya got, there, Marky-Mark."

"You got a used deal there?" Kirk asked as he entered the tower. Sweaty from running around outside and smelling like Chinese food, he sat down at his desk to study the blue sheet.

"Think so," said Mark. "Customer's on this late model silver Sienna LE, stock number 6P80853. He has two to three thousand down, can go up to four hundred a month, credit of six fifty or better. Is the van still here?"

Kirk was checking his computer screen. "Yup. Go grab the key. Rich, you go do that while Mark sits with them and keeps them company." Kirk was actually being nice today, probably a show for the new guy.

"So, ya got yourself a bitch there, huh, Mark?" Larry was grinning.

"I guess. Rich, you remember your password and code for the ComputaKey machine, right?" Rich nodded, and Mark returned to their customers at his desk.

"Okay, folks. Good news! That certified, low-mileage silver Sienna that you like is still available. Rich's going to bring it around to show you." He noticed they didn't seem excited by the news. Mark wanted to find out why and used a a trial close to dig deeper.

"If you like this two year old certified Sienna, and we could make the price and terms agreeable, are you ready to drive it home today?" Mark asked.

"We'll take a look at it, but we need to talk to Sharon's mom to see if she can still lend us the down payment," said Bill. "We'll be seeing her tonight for dinner. We didn't want to go over four hundred a month. That down payment money is important for our budget."

"I understand. I think I see Rich bringing around your Sienna right now. Let's go take a look at it," said Mark.

"Sure," said Bill. They seemed hesitant as they headed outside, whispering back and forth.

"Do I know everything there is to know, Bill and Sharon?" asked Mark, wanting to remove any other obstacles they may be hiding.

"We also need to check to see if the other Sienna that we found is still available," Sharon explained. The road blocks were piling up, but Mark was unphased. His instincts told him this was the right van for them if his managers could make the price work.

"Okay, I understand." As he opened the front door for them, Mark said, "Rich is going to show you the Sienna while I check on any other models that might fit your needs. I'll see you after your test drive, okay?" He smiled, passed them on to Rich, and walked back inside to talk with Kirk. Earlier, Kirk assured him that he would do whatever was necessary to make their deal on the Sienna.

When their customers returned from their test drive, they decided to make an offer. Huddling together, they hammered out a deal for three thousand down and three hundred eighty dollars a month, including a Platinum Certified Warranty.

Although the Franklins really liked the Sienna, they stuck to their guns and refused to sign until they could consult with their mother over dinner later. Leaving the dealership on friendly terms, they promised Mark and Rich that they would return tomorrow and ask for them by name. The price was right, and the Franklins saw the value in the Platinum Certified Warranty. Mark knew that the other late model Sienna they were considering wasn't certified and didn't offer a one hundred thousand mile warranty. The Franklins had been the best up of the day, and Mark was impressed with the progress Rich was making.

It was after six o'clock when Rich approached him as he stood at the reception desk. "Mark, you were right," he said. "I found out that Juicifer's deal with that older, handicapped couple was a twenty-six thousand dollar commission! Can you believe that? How the hell do you do that?"

Frowning at this, Mark said, "That can't be legal." His mind rebelled at how twisted it seemed to overcharge a handicapped couple that kind of money. "Wait 'til their family finds out about their new car deal. They're gonna go ballistic."

As they tried to make sense of Juicifer's egregious commission on the Q-tip deal, Jo offered her two cents. "Someday this rodeo's gonna come to an end," she said. "They always do."

At seven o'clock, Mark was back at his desk and surprised to see Mike and Judy Burton in the dealership. He walked up to check on his certified Prius customers from a few days ago. They looked upset. Mark was hoping everything was okay with their car, but he had a bad feeling. Recalling that the Prius had been a perfect match for them, he remembered they were unhappy when they left.

"I got this, Jo. Well, hey there, Mike and Judy. How're things going with your new Prius? Everything okay?" He extended his hand, and Mike shook it reluctantly.

"That's what we need to talk with you about, Mark. You've been good to us, but we want out of our deal." Mike looked upset, and he noticed Judy was looking at the floor as she reached into her purse and pulled out their closing documents. They were crumpled, and it was obvious that the documents had been getting a lot of scrutiny.

They seated themselves at Mark's desk. "We've got some issues with the car and the payment," said Mike. "The Prius wouldn't crank yesterday, so we had our family master mechanic look at the car. He tells us that almost none of the items checked off on the inspection list have actually been inspected. He's been our family mechanic for over fifteen years, so we trust him a hundred percent. We feel we got ripped off."

"I'm shocked to hear this, Mike and Judy."

"We appreciate everything you did for us, Mark, but the other issue we have with Brandson is that when we did our deal here at your desk, we agreed to two hundred seventy five a month. Instead, we're paying three hundred fifty-five a month. That's another eighty dollars a month, times sixty months, is an additional forty-eight hundred dollars that we didn't agree to pay. You told us that our payment included taxes and the cost of the certification, but Mr. Gonzalez told us otherwise and charged us an extra forty-eight hundred dollars. We've left several messages for Mr. Gonzalez, but he hasn't returned any of our calls. We want to cancel our deal. We're tired of getting the runaround. Car's outside. Here are the keys." He held up the keys with a determined look on his face. "Who do we talk to about getting our money back?"

"Uh, wow . . . I'm so sorry you feel this way. Give me a minute. I want to help you. I'll be right back." Mark headed into the sales tower to find Larry who had already left. He explained to Kirk what had happened with his customer. Kirk got angry and picked up the phone to dial Ricky Gonzalez. After yelling a few profanities at Ricky, he slammed the phone down. "Take them over to Rick's office now!"

Mark escorted the Burton's over to Tricky Ricky's office. Gonzalez was waiting at his office door. "Hey, guys. I can't believe you want to cancel your deal. C'mon in, let's talk about this." He grimaced at Mark and said, "Thanks, Mark. I'll handle it." On his way back to his desk, Mark was intercepted by Brent Bell.

"So, Marky-Mark, what's up with your customer?"

"Tricky Ricky reamed them for forty-eight hundred dollars more than what they agreed to pay for their Prius. They claim he lied to them and changed the deal. On top of that, he and Kirk apparently sold them a Platinum Certified Warranty without any inspection on the car. Hell, I'd be upset too!" Mark watched Brent's face carefully to see where his allegiances lay. Several other reps who overheard were now drifting over to find out how it was all going to shake out.

"Yeah, Ricky's gotta stop with this overcharging stuff," said Brent. Mark was relieved to hear what he said. "He's gonna get us all in trouble," Brent said in a subdued voice. His eyes were darting nervously back and forth to see who else might be listening. Ian and Scott nodded in sympathy but said nothing.

"What about the fake certification, Brent. Have you heard about any fake inspections?" Mark asked in a conspirational whisper. Brent nodded his head and walked away, confirming Mark's worst fears.

He looked at Scott and Ian standing there, afraid to say anything. With everyone so stressed, Mark broke the tension. "Guys, if things keep going like this for me, I may get a chance to sign up for that pottery course I've been putting off."

Ian rolled his eyes, and Scott chuckled in amusement. "Yeah, wonder how they handle this one."

Ten minutes had ticked by since the Burtons entered Tricky Ricky's office. Watching a very animated conversation through the glass partition from his desk a hundred feet away, Mark yearned to be a fly on the wall and hear what smoke and mirrors were spewing from Ricky.

After what seemed like an eternity, Mark saw his customer exiting the front door of the dealership. They looked angry. He'd never expected to hear profanity coming from them, but that's what he heard. Everyone in the dealership was watching. Ricky Gonzalez had left his office and now stood at the front desk trying to explain all the yelling and screaming. Mark walked to the front desk to confront Tricky Ricky over the deceit.

"So, Ricky, what are we going to do to fix this for the Burtons?" He smelled like cigarette smoke, and his black eyes reminded him of a shark's, lifeless and cold. Everyone knew that money was all he cared about. And underaged girls.

"We're not doin' anything," said Ricky. "They own the car. It's theirs. What did you tell them?" Ricky scowled, angry that Mark wasn't backing him up.

"Only the truth and what I'm supposed to tell them. I think it's pretty obvious that you changed their deal. Wasn't three grand enough of a profit for the dealership that we don't have to fake certifications? What if they sue us? Where does that leave us?" Mark was upset and tired of cleaning up Tricky Ricky's deceptions. The confrontation with Gonzalez had been brewing for some time. All the sales reps knew Tricky Ricky been taking front-end commissions that belonged to the sales reps and pushing it to the back of the deal where he used it to buy insurance products so he could make more money for himself.

Ricky laid into him, oblivious to the fact that they stood in the middle of the dealership and could be overheard by everyone. He wanted a show, to make a mockery of Mark so he could reassert his control, no matter how dishonest the deal.

Ricky stepped forward and got right in Mark's face. "You need to be very careful about what you're saying right now, Mark. They can't prove anything. And if they sue us, it's their word against ours. We are in business here to make money, pal, and *you* are not in a position to tell anyone here how to run their business. Or to take sides with a customer! Do you understand? You want to get fired? I'll fire your ass right now!" Ricky was nose-to-nose with Mark, and they were quickly losing control. Mark felt like he was being forced to choose between backing off, or knocking Tricky Ricky on his butt.

"Alright you two, break it up!" Kirk got between them. "Mark, get back to your desk! I ought to fire you right here! You never take sides with a customer against the dealership! The next time you do, you are history! Understood?" Kirk was in his face and on his case, and all three hundred pounds of him was behind the finger stuck in his chest right now. Now, there were four sales reps watching the show, not believing what they were hearing. His new trainee was one of them.

"I want to go on record in with you both and ask for fair and honest treatment of my customers," said Mark. "Is that too much to ask for, Kirk?"

Kirk pressed his finger into Mark's chest. "Is there a name for this fantasy land you live in, Mark?"

Still upset, Mark continued, ignoring Kirk's finger. "I work hard to earn their business and their future referrals, but I can't do that unless we treat them fairly. We can still make a profit." Mark didn't care if he got fired. He had little desire to work in a place that lied and deceived his customers as badly as the Burtons had been.

"You got a problem with any of this, you can talk to Larry tomorrow," yelled Kirk. "This isn't some sensitivity training class. Welcome to the car business, Mark. Now get back to work! I'm done with this crap!"

As Kirk finished his tirade, Tricky Ricky was back in his office fuming over the confrontation, shooting sinister looks at Mark.

Mark walked back outside to calm down and get some fresh air. He began to question how long he could survive at the dealership with so many crooks running the show.

EIGHT

Traffic on SR 222 was lighter after eight o'clock, and Mark was making good time on his morning commute in to the dealership. Always on the prowl for new stock ideas, he sipped his Verona Crème café and listened to the Bloomberg Surveillance show on XM Sirius satellite radio.

The stock analyst was talking about the illegal practice of trading on inside information. It took him back to his rookie year on Wall Street when his desk mate was escorted out of the office in handcuffs by police for participating in a group of shysters who were trading off inside information. They'd caught up with him because he was leveraging his cash by putting on large option positions that were being tracked by the SEC. Mark learned, up close and personal, that if you ever want to go to prison, just buy large option positions in a stock that you have private information about. The SEC will find you and send you to prison to get butt raped by Neanderthals.

As he reflected on the dishonesty he'd witnessed on Wall Street, he couldn't avoid the comparison with the blatantly deceptive sales practices that were becoming more common at the dealership. He wanted to figure out a way to encourage more honesty and fair play at Brandson without putting himself on a collision course with his managers. It seemed like the collective consciences of his managers were buried deep beneath a quagmire of greed, alcohol, and drugs.

After a brisk ride in, he sat down at his desk and checked to see who was in the sales tower. Larry had come in early, and Mark couldn't help noticing that he'd gotten his haircut in a super Mohawk. It looked bizzare. Mark had just set his attaché case down when he heard Larry call him in to the tower. Knowing he was about to get reamed, he took a deep breath and stepped toward Larry's desk to face the music from last night's confrontation with Tricky Ricky. He knew Larry's personality was becoming more volatile from the steroids, HGH, and cocaine that he was taking throughout the day. He'd heard the stories that all the managers were even injecting themselves while sitting in the sales tower, in full view of customers. More and more, reality was taking a back seat to the grotesque.

"Close the door, Mark." Larry only made this request before a serious reprimand.

"What's up?" Mark was apprehensive.

"Heard about your little spat with Ricky Gonzalez. We're not going to have anymore melt downs in the showroom like that again, right?"

Mark was doing his best to be conciliatory and non-confrontational. "No sir, didn't mean for that to happen." Mark disliked the butt kissing, but he knew he had a dance to perform if he wanted to keep his job.

"You better believe it. Next time you have any pangs of conscience about what you think our profits should or shouldn't be, you come and talk to me about it. Got it?" Larry slowly raised his voice from behind the Louis Vuitton designer glasses, which looked strange with his new Mohawk. "Larry, the Burtons got totally screwed over. Rick changed their—"

"Our F&I guys are going to sell their products. They gotta make a living, too. Your customers signed the contract, right?"

"Yeah, but they were lied—"

"Get over it, and don't forget who signs your checks." As usual, Larry wasn't going to let him speak. "Another thing. We have outside mechanics dispute our work all the time. If I hear one more word from you about fake certifications, you're outa here. Got it?" Larry's veins were popping out on his forehead. "Now, go get on the phone and make some appointments," he yelled, pointing at the door. "Go!"

As he logged back onto his PC, Mark realized that Larry had rejected any responsibility for defrauding his customers on both the price and the certification. Neither had he acknowledged charging his customers twice for taxes, dealer fees, and add-ons. The dishonesty was becoming a matter of routine now, and it was beginning to undermine his morale as he watched Larry grabbing a piece of everything, front, back, or outside the deal. It didn't matter. Everyone's pocket was being picked, with the proceeds going toward the "The Redneck Mafia Retirement Fund."

"Hey, what's up with Larry?" Arriving early, Rich dropped his lunch on his desk, and logged onto his work PC. He turned to study his trainer, concerned that Mark was in hot water again.

"Don't ask. They just aren't interested in playing nice. I'm starting to wonder if they even have a conscience." Mark was disgusted with the conversation. He knew he had to step up and work on getting his head right if he was going to sell anything today.

"Hey, can I show you something here?" Rich was on his computer, looking over his customer files. Mark sat down at Rich's desk, so they could both view the same screen.

"Hey, Marky-Mark, gotta go with the flow, man. Don't you know Larry's always right?" Raj was walking by their desk, stuffing a donut in his mouth. His squinty eyes looked sinister.

"Just ignore him. What's your question?" asked Mark.

"Look. This is the customer file that we set up yesterday for our customers. Then, there's this new file right underneath, but all the contact information is the same as our file, so it's gotta be the same customer," said Rich.

"Yeah, you're right. Looks like our pal Dennis Testi has made a duplicate file on our customer from yesterday. There he is, up front, talking to Jo."

Mark shouted across the showroom. "Hey, Dennis, can we talk to your for a second?" Dennis nodded and walked over to Rich's desk where they had his bogus file displayed.

"What's up, guys?" Dennis was out of uniform, wearing a black manager's polo today. As one of Larry's Redneck Mafia, he knew he could get away with just about anything. "Rich upped this customer yesterday," said Mark as he pointed at the customer file on the screen. "We spent two hours with them, test drove 'em, blue sheeted 'em, and ran a credit check. We're ready to close their deal today on the silver Sienna LE. What's with this new file you created here on our customer?"

"Yeah, well they were my customers from a month ago, and he called in last night to get a better deal on that Sienna. That's going to be my deal. Sorry, guys." It annoyed Mark to see Testi act so arrogant with his planned theft of their customer.

"Hang on there, partner. When we upped him yesterday, there was no file on him, no notes in CM, and no mention of you by the customer."

Dennis got right in Mark's face. "Ya think?" he asked rudely.

"All the time," said Mark. "You should try it."

Angrily, Dennis stepped back and said," You don't like my explanation, go talk to Larry." Dennis spun around, turning his back on them, already heading to the sales tower to poison the well.

"We will. How about right now? Rich, print our file with our notes. Let's go talk to Larry about this. This is our customer."

Dennis was already in the tower and pleading with Larry when Mark and Rich walked in to defend their deal. Mark grabbed the printed customer activity page from the printer and placed it in front of Larry.

"This is our customer, Larry. Check out our notes from yesterday. They're coming back today to do this deal with us. There was never any mention of Dennis."

Rich stepped up. "He's telling the truth, Larry. We both worked hard for this deal, and now that we're in scoring position, Dennis is trying to snake us."

Larry scanned the printed customer file from contact management, then studied all three of the men standing before him. "Dennis says they called him last night on this deal," said Larry.

"Well, even if that were true, which I have serious doubts about . . . " Mark paused to allow his comment to take effect, "our notes and activity protect us for three days, according to the rules that you taught me two years ago, boss." Mark knew to play to Larry's power-hungry ego when pleading a case of customer ownership, and the customer file documents supported their right to the business based on Larry's own rules.

Larry thought for a moment. "Dennis, they're right. They've already done a lot here, and they have a lot of notes. This is their deal. Let them follow up. I have a referral customer to give you instead. Mark, you and Rich better man up and close this deal today." Larry handed the print out back to Mark and took an incoming call on his cell phone, ending the session of "Court Diablo." Testi was fuming.

As they exited the tower, Testi lost his temper and flew into a rage. He pointed at Mark and Rich yelling, "You're a couple of faggots! You guys will never close this deal!" Then, he flipped them off and stalked away.

Rich commented, "He looks madder than a one-legged man in an ass-kicking contest."

Mark said, "We'll see who closes this deal." They walked back to Rich's desk where they sat down to plan their strategy. Mark hadn't expected Larry to support them, but figured that he'd done so in order to make things look good for their newbie. Rich looked at the print-out and shook his head.

"That guy's a lunatic," said Rich. "You were right about him, Marky-Mark."

Mark nodded. "Sometimes I wish I wasn't. Okay, time to call our customers. Let's get them back in here today and wrap this deal up. Whad'ya say, partner?" Rich got their customers on the phone. Mark coached him on getting a credit card deposit of five hundred dollars, and they set an afternoon appointment. Ten minutes had gone by since the confrontation with Testi in the tower, and they both were wondering what the Ethiopian porn star was up to.

"Good job, Rich. Now, go give the card information to one of the F&I guys to run, and put it on the glass as a *sold* deal, okay?" When Rich returned, Mark continued with his suggestions. "Now, let's grab that Sienna and put it into detail so it'll be spotless when they get here. You know how to do a detail and gas ticket, right?"

"Yup. You showed me yesterday."

Keys in hand, they headed out to the used lot to retrieve the silver Sienna that sat a hundred yards out. As they walked up to the Sienna, Rich whistled as he did a quick inspection. "Hey! This wasn't here earlier today. Check this out, bro!"

Mark walked around to the driver's side, and there was a four foot scratch along the side of the van that looked like it had been keyed. "Look—this is fresh. You can still see the little flakes of paint along the scratch. This was done today. The rain from last night would have washed off these little flakes if it was from yesterday."

Rich squatted down to study the scratch along the side of the Sienna. He'd seen plenty of these in his eight years as a cop and he knew what to look for. "I think you're right. This is fresh. I'd say, within the past hour." He looked up at Mark, asking "You thinking what I'm thinking?" asked Rich.

"I think our pal Testi is mad enough to do almost anything to kill our deal," said Mark. "Bet you a thousand bucks he's the culprit." He scanned the lot in all directions. "You see how it's scratched on the side away from the building's security cameras? Looks like our perp knew exactly where they were located."

Mark continued, "Okay. We've got our customers coming back to take delivery in about three hours. Let's gas her up then get the van back to detail right away so they'll have time to paint and buff it out."

"This guy's a wacko. No way that this was a random vandalism. I'm totally convinced Dennis Testi did it." Rich had to be wondering what kind of psycho program he'd just signed up with at Brandson as they both climbed into the Sienna to gas it up.

Five minutes later, they pulled back onto the lot with a full tank of gas. Mark said, "Drop me in front. I gotta go talk to Kirk or Larry about this. They're going to want to see this." Mark paused with his hand on the door handle. "You realize that whatever it costs to fix this will probably come off of our commission, right?"

Rich nodded that he understood. He put the gear shift back into drive. "When you told me this guy's a snake, I had no idea he was sick enough to vandalize a car to try to kill our deal. Unbelievable. And this guy's best buddies with Larry? Does that make any sense?"

"Birds of a certain feather . . . " said Mark.

Back inside the sales tower, Mark told Kirk about the vandalism. Kirk went ballistic when he heard about it. He spewed out a string of profanities, then bolted toward the back of the dealership to inspect the van.

Returning a few minutes later, Kirk said, "Bad news is your deal with Rich just went from a twenty-two hundred front to nineteen," he said with a smirk. "Good news is Jon thinks he can make the scratch disappear. When Jon's done with it in about an hour, park it in the far corner of the delivery pad with the damaged passenger side facing the glass wall. That's the darkest spot out there. Maybe they won't notice anything. What time are they coming in?"

"One o'clock," said Mark, as he scanned the showroom for Dennis. He was nowhere to be found.

Kirk slipped back behind his desk, dropping heavily into his manager's chair. He picked up his phone to dial Jon in detail to make sure they would have it ready on time.

Mark spent the next hour showing Rich how to do service follow-up calls. They managed to set an appointment with a melon farmer from Bronson with credit issues. "What's our famer's name, Rich?"

"Slim Pickins."

"Yeah, right. It's twelve thirty You want to check on our van? You know where to park it, right? Jon's got the key."

"I'm on it," said Rich. He grabbed the last donut from the box at the reception desk, eating it on the way out the door. A few minutes later, he returned from parking the freshly-detailed Sienna. "They did a good job on the scratch. One of us should be near the front door in case they come in early. We don't want our customers winding up with our favorite snake when they return in a few minutes."

Mark nodded and said, "I'll start on the file jacket." After assembling the necessary documents, he went out to the delivery pad to inspect the Sienna repair. He was impressed with the job their paint specialist had done. The scratch was almost invisible. After a few minutes working on the file, he looked up to see Rich walking in the door with their customers, and walked up to meet them in the middle of the showroom. From the corner of his eye, he noticed Dennis Testi back at his desk, trying hard to look disinterested. Mark new better.

"Hi, good to see you again, Bill and Sharon." He shook their hands enthusiastically. "We got most of the paperwork done already to save time. Just need your signatures on a few things. Right this way."

"Can we see the van again before we sign everything?" asked Bill.

"Sure. Follow me. It's on the delivery pad, gassed up and fully detailed. I think you'll be impressed." Mark was keeping his fingers crossed for the inspection. "Rich, can you get me the odometer reading on their Town & Country. We'll need it for the deal jacket." The couple did a full walk around inspection of the Sienna and liked what they saw. Now, they were ready for the documents and the contract signing. Mark was hoping that the F&I manager would be Jake and not Tricky Ricky. As if on cue, Jake emerged from his office to introduce himself and took them into his office.

Mark looked up to see Dennis having an animated conversation with Kirk in the sales tower. Everyone in the showroom could all hear Dennis yelling that the deal was his. Mark couldn't believe his ears. A moment later, they all stood together at Kirk's desk, preparing for yet another confrontation with Dennis over ownership of their Sienna deal.

Mark was pleading his case again. "Kirk, Larry has already confirmed that this is our deal from start to finish. I know he's not here, but you can call him if you like. Here are the notes, deal jacket and blue sheet. Dennis just needs to stop snaking his co-workers and get his own customers." He looked accusingly at Dennis.

Hearing Mark's comment, Dennis flew into an uncontrolled rage, lunging forward at him, grabbing Mark's shirt collar with his right hand. He screamed in his face, "*You damn son of a b——! I'm going to slit your throat!*"

Stunned by Dennis's violent tantrum, Rich and Kirk froze. Screaming profanities, Dennis picked up Larry's desk phone, ready to smash it against Mark's head. Mark blocked Dennis's arm while Rich jumped in and grabbed the phone from behind.

"Put it down, Dennis, or I'll break your arm!" yelled Rich.

Inches from Dennis's face, Mark yelled, "You want to go to jail? I'm ready to dial 911 right now! I'm done with your crap!"

Kirk stepped forward, yelling, "Dennis, put the phone down! Let go of Mark!! Back off, or by God I'll fire you right now!!"

Seeing he was outnumbered three-to-one, Dennis dropped the phone on the desk and let go of Mark's shirt. He stuck his finger into Mark's face and screamed, "I'll kick your ass if it's the last thing I do!" He stormed out of the sales tower, grabbed his car keys from his desk, and disappeared outside.

"Can you believe that?" asked Mark. His ex-cop trainee stood in the doorway in disbelief, while Kirk headed out the door to find Dennis. By then, there was a crowd of four reps and two customers who gathered in front of the sales tower.

Mark was visibly shaken. As he exited the sales tower, Rich said. "You know, you could have him arrested for felony assault and battery, right? Up to you, if you want to be rid of him for good. As a cop for eight years, I will say that what Dennis did could put him in jail tonight. If you pressed charges." Mark worked to compose himself as he tucked his shirt back into his Dockers.

"I need to calm down and figure this out. I don't want Larry teeing off on me for having his boy arrested, but I know one thing. I'm not putting up with this BS! Where's Kirk?" Mark scanned the dealership for the used car manager. Kirk was nowhere to be seen. He peeked over the top of the partition toward Jake's office. Their customers were still sitting with him, signing documents, unaware of the violent confrontation that just took place in the sales tower over their Sienna deal.

Then he saw Kirk walk in the front door with a disgusted look on his face, crooking his finger and gesturing for them to join him in the tower. "Mark, Rich, inside."

As they both entered the sales office, he said, "Close the door." Rich complied. "I sent Dennis home for a few days to cool off. Mark, management appreciates you not bringing the cops into this. You need to be less confrontational. We need Dennis for the Toyotathon starting Friday."

"Whoa, hang on," said Rich, stepping in for his trainer. "We were only protecting our deal. Larry already gave us the green light to move forward, so that's what we did. In spite of the fact that he keyed our Sienna."

"You're gonna have to talk to Larry about this. I'm done here." Kirk brushed his hands together as if he was clearing his conscience. He added, "Mark, your customers are coming over."

Regaining his composure, Mark stepped up and extended his hand to their new customers. "Congratulations!" he said. "I know you're going to enjoy your new Sienna. Rich, you have their keys?"

"Right here," said Rich, handing them the keys to the Sienna. "Thanks for your business." He was amazed that he and Mark had managed to complete the delivery, given Dennis's totally insane efforts to kill their deal.

"Oh . . . you know what? Almost forgot. We need to switch your tags over. Let me grab my screwdriver. I'll meet you at your new van," said Mark.

Their customers headed to the delivery pad. After removing the plate on the Chysler van, Mark brought it over and attached it to their Sienna. Two minutes later, they rolled off the lot, and Mark breathed a sigh of relief as he watched them drive away. Rich walked over and joined him on the delivery pad. They did a fist bump to celebrate their deal.

"Seemed like we'd never get that deal finished," said Rich. "Dennis should fry for threatening to slit your throat, bro. He tried just about everything to kill our deal. You gonna let him get away with it?" he asked. He cocked his head, waiting for Mark's reaction. It was the cop in him talking now.

"I'm going to think and pray on it tonight," said Mark. "I appreciate all your help, especially with grabbing the phone. This could have turned out a lot different. I could be in the ER with a concussion."

"Yeah, well, sometimes you gotta stand up to the dark side. I appreciate you showing how to keep the snakes off my deals!" said Rich. "You know that Dennis belongs in jail. Right?"

"I agree, but I have to weigh Larry's reaction to putting his best bud in the slammer. This is a hard lesson," said Mark. "The Redneck Mafia are a devious bunch." He paused. "I'm curious. How long of a legal window do I have before deciding on whether I report this to the cops?" Mark asked as he ran his hand through his hair, exhausted from the ordeal.

"In this situation, GPD would probably say no more than seventy-two hours." Rich looked at him, asking, "What's with you two. Why does he dislike you so much that he's wanting to 'slit your throat'? Damn! I mean . . . I know he's a scumbag, but that's pretty radical."

"You mean aside from the fact that we're dealing with a complete psycho? Gee, I don't know. He's from Ethiopia. I have no idea how they think. What options do you think I really have here? I'm going back inside. It's too hot out here." As he sat down at his desk, his cell phone rang. It was Larry. Mark answered, certain that he'd heard about the violence, dying to hear what he would have to say about it.

Larry sounded like he was in a bar. His voice was measured and subdued. "I spoke to Kirk about your run-in with Dennis," he said. "Dennis is gonna be taking a few days off, get his head straightened out. You need to understand a few things." Mark could hear the sound of hip hop, women laughing, and glasses clinking in the background.

"Where are you, Larry?" Mark asked.

"I'm at my attorney's office, dealing with this IRS stuff."

"Larry, Dennis tried to snake us again, threatened to slit my throat and clobber me with your phone—"

"Listen to me now." Mark should have known better than to try to have a real discussion with Larry. He resigned himself to a listening only mode. Larry continued. "Dennis is important to me and to the dealership. I'm not going to let anything happen to him. Now, it may seem like you have some options here, but if you want to stay in my good graces, you'll do as I say. Otherwise, I'll make your life at Brandson miserable. Or fire you. Got it?"

A long pause followed. Larry wanted his threats to sink in. "You're a good worker, Mark. You're making good money. You've gotta ask yourself if you want that to continue." He paused again, waiting for agreement.

"Doesn't sound like I have much of a choice," said Mark quietly. Larry's blunt-force coercion made him feel like his head was in a vise.

"No, you don't. Not if you want to continue working at my dealership. Now, you are going to let go of this. No cops. And you're going to have to start doing business my way. No more of your nonsense, asking if we can be more honest, or crap like that. Got it? We don't care how we sell cars, as long as we sell them. We are in business to make money. Period. Do I make myself clear?"

"I understand but I can't function when my life is being threat—"

"Listen to me. Dennis's super pissed off at you. When he's like this, bad things happen. I've made myself clear on what I expect from you, Mark. I got court tomorrow, so I won't be in. I'll see you at Friday's meeting. Don't do anything stupid. Gotta go." With that, Larry had hung up. The Devil had spoken, and the Devil's apprentice was at large.

Mark sat at his desk and thought about this conversation for a few minutes in complete silence. He was seriously blacked out. Six o'clock couldn't seem to come soon enough. He was still so upset on his drive home that he forgot to stop by Vahn Thai's to pick up his dinner.

NINE

The patter of light rain on the roof grew stronger as he gathered his foul weather gear together. Mark enjoyed working out for an hour each morning, forty minutes running and twenty minutes with his in-home gym. It was seven o'clock as he finished his last set of chest presses. His inner drug dealer was calling him, and he needed his endorphin fix. Running in light rain kept him cooler and the air always seemed sweeter and cleaner. The stress at Brandson was getting to him, and running everyday not only kept him in shape, it produced the pain-killing endorphins that gave him the patience he needed to get through the increasingly surreal workdays.

As he put his running shoes on, he made a mental note to call a pest control company about the rodents still running amuck in his attic. The warmer July weather was making them more active. He hadn't slept well. A loud bang had awakened him around two in the morning, and he tried to recall what was stored in his attic that could have fallen over. He decided to delay that investigation until the pest control guy could get up there with a flashlight.

He closed the door to the garage and pulled the hood on his foul weather gear over his head. After stretching for a few minutes, he headed down the long driveway in the light drizzle to start his run.

He was greeted by the sight of pieces of his mailbox strewn over the front lawn and in the road in front of his house. There was even a piece in the tree. Only the post remained, leaning to the side. It was obvious that some kind of explosive device had demolished his mailbox during the night. Now, he knew where the loud bang had come from, and it wasn't from his attic.

Overcome with fear, he cautiously stepped up to take a closer look at the largest chunk of debris. Laying across the street, it used to be the bottom portion of his mailbox. Part of the PVC top was still attached. Mark rolled it over with his foot in the drizzle, turning it upright and peering inside at what remained, careful not to touch it or smudge any fingerprints that might still be present. He could see two short pieces of unexploded dynamite lying inside, with the fuses still twisted together. He imagined what the damage would have been like if all of the dynamite had exploded. Mark surveyed the rest of the debris field, pulling his hood down lower over his head to keep the rain out and peered out for any other telltale signs of what had happened to his mailbox. There was only the soft sound of rain falling lightly as he stood in the middle of the debris field.

He heard a car pull up behind him, and as he turned to see who it was, the black BMW stopped and the driver's window rolled down.

"Hey, Mark, what happened to your mailbox? You forget to send your mailman a Christmas card or something?" Dr. Fontana was the cosmetic surgeon who lived around the corner on the "back nine," as he called the row of houses in the rear of the subdivision. He usually left for work about the same time that Mark went on his morning run. Puzzled by all the pieces of what used to be Mark's mailbox, he sat behind the wheel of his 750 iL, rubber-necking at the strange sight.

"Yeah, well, it was old, I was ready for a new one. Nice, quiet, family neighborhood we got here, right Al?" Mark had occasionally traded stock tips with Dr. Fontana when they passed each other in the neighborhood. "Hey, you didn't happen to notice any other mailboxes that were damaged, did you?" Disgusted with the mess, he began to assemble a short list of suspects in his head.

"No, didn't notice any others. Just yours, looks like. You think it was kids?" Dr. Fontana ignored the rain and leaned out the driver's window, craning his neck to get a better view of the destruction.

"Not sure. I can tell you one thing, it wasn't any kind of fireworks. I think it was real dynamite," said Mark.

"Really? What kind of a maniac does this sort of thing?" asked Dr. Fontana rhetorically. He looked sympathetic. "Well, I'll try not to run over any evidence. You ought to call the police and let them deal with it. That's why we've got the big property tax bills out here, right? Hey, by the way, you still own your shares of Tesla and Apple?"

"Sure do. Two thousand shares of Tesla, looking for a hundred fifty dollars a share or more, and five hundred Apple, looking for seven hundred a share."

"Tell ya what. I'll spring for a coupla boxes of Cohibas and a case of Remy XO if you're right, partner. Good luck with your mailbox." The tinted window rolled back up as Dr. Fontana headed off to resurrect his next set of breasts. It wasn't just a job. It was definitely an adventure.

Mark ran inside, retrieved his digital camera, and returned to the scene of the crime. Using his hand to shield the camera from the rain, he took over thirty photos, including close-ups of the unexploded dynamite using the macro setting. After stashing his camera in his attaché case, he went on his 5K run. Mark made a mental note to call his friend Andrea Mitchell at Alachua County Forensics, sure that she'd be interested to hear about the bomb.

By the time he'd arrived at the dealership, the rain had stopped. Ian Pritzker was walking toward him, looking like he wanted to talk. Mark rolled his window down.

"Hey, Marky-Mark, 'sup with you and Dennis? Raj was telling me what happened yesterday." He couldn't make his mind up whether Ian was a closet case or just a little on the effeminate side, his thin light frame flitting around with his odd "grandpa" walk.

"Apparently, I'm throat-slitting material," said Mark. "I think Testi's off his meds again. So, what's up with you, you still on that web site 'Men with Hairy Chests?' You getting any good dates off that site? C'mon, fess up." He knew he could mess with Ian. He was good natured and took the ribbing in stride.

"Get outa here . . . " Ian waved him off with a mock bitch slap. "So, are you going to have Dennis arrested? You know, he's Larry's boy. Larry'll make your life miserable if you do," he said, leaning on the door with his arms folded.

"I know. Larry already makes my life miserable, screaming profanities, flashing gay porn at me on his cell phone all the time, steering my deals to his drinking buddies. C'est la vie. Hey, I'll catch ya later." He headed to employee parking, while Ian headed inside to see what damage he could do on Ebay.

Mark dropped his attaché case on his desk and headed over to talk with his training buddy who had just hung up the phone. "Hey, bro. What's up? You look kinda depressed. Everything okay?" asked Mark. He sat down with his buddy. Rich was frowning and rubbing his temples.

"It's my crazy wife, Carla." He lowered his voice so no one could overhear their conversation. "She hasn't been home for two days, and I just found out why. She was arrested two days ago for drug possession and child endangerment by the Marion County Sheriff's Office. The whole house full of nine people where she's been staying was busted, too. She had our daughter with her when she was all doped up."

"Does she have a history of substance abuse?" Mark knew his new recruit had a lot on his plate. He was reluctant to pile on more drama right away with news of the bombing. The last thing he wanted was to overload his trainee with his problems, but Mark figured his background as a cop made him a good candidate to confide in.

"Yeah, she's been arrested before. She's been in rehab six times. I have to go down to DCF and pick up my daughter. They put her in protective custody. Debbie's only six, so I have to hire a sitter before I can come back here. I doubt they'll let me have the day off to deal with this crap." Rich rubbed his forehead. He looked worried. "I'm heading to Daytona Saturday, take in some strip clubs, get my mind off this. Maybe drive my car off a pier."

"That's the spirit. Death by lap dance," said Mark. "Look, I'm sure Bryan will work with you on this stuff. Just be up front with him. Larry won't be in today. He's in court with the IRS with that tax evasion thing he's fighting." He paused, then added, "Wait 'til you hear what happened at my house last night."

"What?"

"Someone blew up my mailbox with an IED."

"Are you serious?" Rich's eyes got big. He leaned forward, wanting to hear the story.

"Wait." Mark reached into his attaché case and pulled his digital camera out, powered it up, and displayed the color images for Rich to see.

"What the-? You don't think . . . "

"You see these photos of unexploded material. That's dynamite, bro. That's not the work of kids or pranksters with fireworks. This psycho has access to high explosives, and I think someone is sending me a message. I mean, you can't make this stuff up! First, these death threats from Dennis, and now someone blows up my—"

"Keep your voice down. You call the cops?" Rich was rubbing his forehead again, paranoid that someone was going to overhear them.

Lowering his voice, he answered. "Not yet. I just took these photos about an hour-and-a-half ago. I'm going to call my friends over at Alachua County Forensics. I need to do this while the evidence is still fresh." He looked up to see Bryan watching them from the tower.

"I agree. Who else knows about this?" asked Rich in a whisper.

"You're the only one who knows," said Mark. "You and the perp. I'm not mentioning it to anyone else. I want to have my ears up, hear what the buzz is. This is serious. I entered the sheriff's office number into my cell and I'm heading outside to call them and file a police report. I'm certain they'll do a full investigation."

"Yeah, okay, and while you're cleaning up your mess, I've got one of my own," said Rich. "I'm gonna let Bryan know I'm heading over the DCF to pick up my kid. Let me know what they find, okay?" Rich put his cop sunglasses on and turned toward the door.

"I will. I'll be on my cell if you need me. You have any customers coming in today?" Mark asked.

"None confirmed, but if I do, can you cover for me?"

"You got it." Mark headed out the side door to call ACSO Forensics. He could see Raj trying to intercept him on the service drive. As usual, he was eating something and his shirt was hanging out.

"Hey, Marky-Mark, you gonna put Dennis away? Heard he wants to cut you up. Said you tried to snake him on a deal. Is that true?" He was cruising through the service area carrying a plastic bag full of tortilla chips. With his bag of snacks and slovenly appearance, by comparison, he made Jabba the Hutt look like he just stepped out of GQ magazine.

"Not right now, Raj, I have to take care of something." Mark kept walking, heading out to the proverbial grassy knoll for a private conversation with his friends at forensics.

When he called ACSO, he asked for Officer Andrea Mitchell. He was told she was working a case and unavailable. The sergeant on duty took down all his information and gave him a case number, telling him that they'd be sending out a unit to investigate the crime immediately. They asked him if anyone was injured or at home, possible suspects, and bomb materials, if known. He provided the officer at the desk with all the information that he had.

Mark made it clear that if they could figure out who was behind it, he would have no problem prosecuting the perp. The officer asked to see the photos he'd taken at the crime scene earlier, so Mark agreed to email them to the sheriff's office when he got home. He also contacted the post office, told them about the IED, and requested they hold his mail until he could put up a new mailbox. The clerk at the post office sounded incredulous when he heard the reason for the request.

After turning over the investigation to the ACSO, he headed back inside to make some sales calls, trying to get his mind back on work. As soon as he'd settled into his chair, McGreedy came over, holding up his wash-out pay sheet and sporting a new, ultra-short haircut, amazingly similar in appearance to his buddy Bryan's buzz cut.

"So, how'd you do last month? Betcha I got ya beat on gross." McGreedy liked to brag about his paycheck, ignoring the fact that more than half his income came from Bryan's cheese deals. Mark was surprised to see that he appeared sober, but it was still early in the day.

Mark humored him. "I stumbled through seventeen car deals last month. How 'bout you? Did you get to twenty-five, there, cowboy?"

"Twenty seven," he said, displaying his pay sheet like it was a PhD in nuclear physics.

"Hey, that's great, Paul. Congratulations." He reached for the phone, adding, "Let me make some calls, here, see if I can catch up this month."

Mark spent the next half hour making sales and service calls, looking to nail down some of those elusive deals that seemed just out of reach. Not having too much luck with calling, he began reviewing older blue sheets on customer deals that looked promising. The crime scene at home gnawed on him, interfering with his ability to concentrate on work.

"Hey, dude. You selling your way into the history books?" As a former hedge fund manager, Scott Pruden enjoyed swapping investment ideas with Mark. They also shared a thirst for adventure on the high seas. Scott preferred his motor yachts, and Mark was a rag bagger, but they managed to find enough common ground on nautical adventures to talk about.

"Let me show you the boat I just put an offer on." Without waiting for an answer, Scott sat down and showed him some photos on his cell phone of a twenty meter custom Sea Ray. "This one's loaded up, they're asking nine hundred grand. I offered them eight hundred grand cash, closing one week, with no survey." Scott was excited about upgrading from the fifteen meter Sea Ray he'd just sold last month.

"Could I hook up with you later? Got some stuff I gotta take care of." Mark was focused like a laser beam on finding out who the perp was on his mailbox IED.

"Sure, man." Scott stood up, then remembered something.

"By the way, I have a buddy who just got popped for DUI," said Scott. "What kind of hoops did you have to jump through a few years ago with your DUI?"

"I feel for him already," said Mark. "They gave me a three month license suspension, thirty days in jail, two years probation, a hundred hours of community service, and a two-thousand-dollar fine. It would have been a lot worse if it hadn't been my first offense. Thank God I'm done with that. The attorney fees were over four grand."

"Those were some expensive chickens!" Now Scott had a better idea of what kind of trouble his buddy was in.

Bryan interrupted them. "Marky-Mark, here's your washout sheet," he said. "Scott, did you make those calls like I asked you to?" Bryan stood beside Mark's desk, annoyed with their personal chit-chat.

"I'm on it, boss," said Scott. He stood up and headed back to his desk on the far side of the showroom.

"Thanks, big guy," said Mark. As he reviewed his wash-out, he remembered he had opted for Brandson to set up a direct deposit pay program with his bank account. The wash-out sheet was the summary of all the deals for the June sales month, including net payable commissions, splits, customer names, deal and stock numbers, and amounts paid on the back end of the deals to F&I. A flash of anger swept over him as he studied the figures more closely. It looked almost three thousand dollars short. Instead of the six thousand dollars he expected, the net was just under thirty-two hundred.

Trying to contain his anger, he pulled his calculator out. With a forty-six percent short fall in net payable income, he intended to find out what caused the shortfall and began a deal-by-deal accounting of his sales last month. After a thorough examination of all seventeen deals in June, he had uncovered three short payments of almost one thousand dollars each. He decided to ask Bryan for an explanation.

"Hey, what's up?" asked Bryan as Mark walked in the tower. He'd managed to catch Bryan on the desk without a phone in his ear.

"My washout check looks short by about two thousand eight hundred dollars, and these deals I highlighted are the ones that I got shortchanged on." Mark laid his washout sheet on Bryan's desk, pointing at the three underpaid deals. Kirk was taking notice of his question on unpaid commissions and watched him carefully from the far end of the desk.

Bryan said, "Probably just an accounting error. I'll look them up in the system later when I have time. Right now, I've got three deals working. Check with me in a few hours." Bryan was not his usual friendly self, and Mark could tell something wasn't right, but he couldn't put his finger on it.

"Thanks for your help, Bryan," said Mark. "I've got bills that need to be paid, and I'd be grateful if we could fix this today." Mark was being as diplomatic as he could, given the fact that he was unhappy about missing almost half of his paycheck. Mark's attempt at a smile turned into more of a pained wince.

He walked back to the cafeteria to see if there were some leftover egg McMuffins from the sixty or so delivered yesterday by one of their lenders. Danziger was seated by himself, eating something that looked like it was part of someone's science project. He was sporting a new, shorter haircut and beard, and his bright red hair had earned him the nickname "Shock Top."

"Hey, Shock Top. Where you been? Haven't seen you for a couple of weeks. Everything okay?" Mark could see a shaved area on the right side of his head about the size of a golf ball covered with round bandage.

"Brain surgery," he said, calmly pointing at his bandage.

"What? Seriously?" Mark sat down with him at the table, wanting to hear his story.

"No, really man. They had to cut a hole in my skull, go in, and take out a tumor the size of a grape." As he described his ordeal at Shands Hospital, he appeared detached and unemotional. Almost like it was an everyday event. Danziger was an odd but intelligent kid who'd been kicked out of med school at UF for selling drugs to students in his dorm.

"So, is that why you're talking like you're in dreamland? They got you on some pain meds?" As soon as he'd asked the question, Mark regretted it, feeling like Captain Obvious.

"Dilaudid four milligrams, four times a day; plus ten milligrams oxycodone, six times a day. I'm out-there, bro." His eyes were completely expressionless, his words were slurred and uneven, apparently feeling no pain at all in his euphoric stupor.

"I can't believe that they made you come back to work so soon after your surgery. How long ago was it?" Mark asked.

"Five days ago," answered Danziger from dreamland.

"Five days? Are you kidding? You should be home resting up, man. Do the managers know that you're heavily medicated?" Concerned that Danziger was being forced to work in a heavily medicated state, Mark concluded that allowing him to drive a car seemed risky.

"Yeah, I guess so. I told them what I'm taking, but they said I had to be here for the Toyotathon this month. Hey, I heard about Dennis threatening to . . . slit your throat, was it? What are you going to do?"

"Haven't decided yet. They want me to just let it go, but with a psycho like him, I'm not sure I can. The maniac almost took my head off with Larry's phone," said Mark. "What's that you're eating?"

"These are goose eggs . . . from the geese I'm raising . . . in my backyard. They're really good. A lot more . . . protein and vitamins than chicken eggs. Here, try one. I have . . . six more in the fridge." Danziger stopped every few words to let his mouth catch up with his brain. Using a plastic spoon, he pushed half of an orange-looking goose egg on a napkin across the table for Mark, expecting him to join his exclusive wild game club. The eggs looked like they were right out of a sci-fi movie.

"Ah . . . no thanks, looks good, but I'm just not real hungry right now."

Raj made a grand entrance, completely destroying the *Doctor Who* patient environment that Mark had created with Danziger. "So, hey, Marky-Mark. What do ya like in the stock market right now? I just bought a couple hundred shares of Friend Finder on the IPO. You miss me yesterday?" asked Raj.

"Like my balls miss jock itch," said Mark.

"No, really, what do you like? Techs? Hey, I heard that Facebook's planning an IPO too. You like Facebook, right?" Raj relentlessly pursued Mark's stamp of approval.

"You buy Facebook, and your portfolio, or what's left of it, will be liquidated by lesbian margin clerks living on cocaine and Red Bull." He noticed Danziger was having trouble trying to keep up.

"If you buy Ball Mason jar . . . stock at the end of the summer . . . canning season, you'll always . . . make money," said Danziger. He was sharing his best stock idea. Not wanting to be feel left behind, Shock Top had emerged from a zone of narcotic euphoria that Mark couldn't even imagine with an idea on canning.

Ignoring Danziger's odd response, Raj asked, "How can you not like Facebook, man. They're huge! Facebook is everywhere!" Raj was clearly convinced his idea was superior and continued to push his "Smartest Guys in the Room" act.

"Think of it this way, Raj," said Mark. "This could be that one time our teachers told us about when math could save your life."

"Whaddya mean?" Raj was mystified by his reference.

Mark offered his last attempt at reason. "They're talking about pricing Facebook at two hundred sixty times next year's projected earnings, with the S&P market multiple at about eleven now. As usual, Raj, you've molded a reality to fit your premature conclusion."

Brent appeared in the doorway "Hey, guys." Brent had stopped by to grab his leftover lunch of General Tsao Chinese from the fridge.

"Hey, Brent, Mark's telling me that Facebook's a bad investment. What do you think?" Raj was getting a second opinion, unable to grasp why anyone would have a different opinion than his. The valuation metrics were beyond him.

Brent turned to Raj, holding his box of Chinese, and sat down at their table. Often at odds with each other, he would always take the man from Pakistan with a grain of salt. Raj was constantly campaigning for Brent's job, and Brent wasn't crazy about it. As he reached for the bottle of hot sauce, Brent answered. "I think you gotta go with the experts. Just out of curiosity, what kind of returns have you put up since you've been investing, Raj?" A touch of reality was exactly what Raj was looking to avoid.

Their debate was interrupted by Bryan's appearance in the doorway. "Mark, been looking for you. Thought you might be back here. Need to talk to you for a second." Bryan was waving him around the corner for a private conversation in the hallway.

Mark excused himself and met his boss in the hallway. "Sup, big guy? Were you able to fix those errors on my paycheck?"

"No, man. You're gonna have to talk with Larry about that tomorrow. Hey, I spoke to Dennis, and he wants to come and talk with you and maybe apologize tomorrow. You up for that?" He could tell Bryan was pushing for them to work things out and make up. Mark didn't have a good feeling about Dennis's motives. He was smelling a rat.

"Sure, I'm open to having a conversation, but given our history, Bryan, I can't say that I'm optimistic about anything. I just don't trust the guy. There are some new events that need to be explained." Mark waited for Bryan's reaction to his subtle reference to his mailbox bombing.

"What do you mean?" From Bryan's reaction, Mark could tell he was unaware of the mailbox IED, and decided to steer away from the topic.

"Look, honestly, bro, I think Dennis is a dirtbag, and I'm feeling a lot of pressure here from the managers. Maybe the guy deserves a second chance, but I don't trust him. He's screwed me over so many times, I can't even remember. Rich and I are pretty sure he keyed the Sienna the other day. Then you have the death threat issue," said Mark. "I'm not okay with this stuff."

"I know, I know, but Larry wants you guys to patch things up. Will you talk to him? For me?" Bryan was almost begging him, knowing that Mark would find it difficult to say no.

"Okay. I'll talk to him. What time tomorrow?" Mark was reluctant, but wanted to appear open minded and conciliatory to his bosses, especially if it meant keeping his job and actually getting paid a full paycheck.

"How about after the sales meeting, say ten o'clock?" he suggested.

"Okay, but if he so much as looks at me cross-eyed, or threatens me in any way, he's going down. I'm kinda at the end of my rope with him. Agreed?" Mark was not going to give Dennis anymore opportunities to mess him up. He was ready to move on. He wanted to be done with the whole thing as of tomorrow, one way or the other.

"Just talk to him, okay? Thanks man. We need you both." Bryan gave him a fist bump and headed back to the tower to make the call. He knew Bryan's interests were all about increasing sales. Preventing sales reps from slitting each other's throats was a little further down the list. After all, they were there to sell cars, and they didn't care how they did it. That's what he kept hearing.

TEN

Arriving to an empty meeting room early, Mark sat in his seat in the second row waiting for the rest of the staff to show up. Everyone began to dread Friday morning sales meetings. Managers were getting more greedy, and the paychecks for salesmen continued to shrink. He was dreading the meeting with Dennis later in the morning, convinced Dennis was only looking to avoid jail time for his felony assault a few days ago.

There were rumors about a consumer protection group that had taken up the fight against Brandson's overcharging and frauds against the elderly. Juicifer had been named the defendant in at least eight civil complaints brought by his own customers in the last two months. These had been highly lucrative deals for the dealership, and the word on the street was Brandson had paid out over seventy-eight thousand dollars in private settlements to keep them quiet. How they managed to keep the cases away from the courts and the press was a mystery.

Adding to the pressure he felt this morning was the fact that Larry threatened him with termination if he stood up to Dennis's threats, and he felt powerless to protect his customers against over-charging or fraud.

There was the scary issue of explosives being used at his home, and—as of yesterday—there were earned commissions that he wasn't being paid. There was a lot that weighed on him this morning as he wondered what else could possibly happen to make his job more difficult.

His reverie was interrupted by Scott's voice behind him. "Hey, Marky-Mark. After some hemming and hawing, the bank took my offer on the Sea Ray."

Mark turned around in his seat. "Congratulations!" he said. "When's the shakedown cruise?"

"Well, I've gotta decide if I want to hire a skipper to sail her from Miami up the west coast to Steinhatchee, or if I want sail her back myself."

"If it was me, I'd cough up the five hundred or so to have her brought here. That way, you don't tie yourself up for two days, missing sales you could make here, and you eliminate the possibility of damaging her on the trip." He thought of another reason to hire a captain. "I would offer your skipper a nice tip to put together a list of defects to present to Sea Ray for warranty work. You could probably cash in on some nice equipment upgrades under the warranty."

"Hey, I like that. That's a great idea, Mark. After I get her set up, I'm going to take you and a friend out for an all-expense paid trip. How 'bout that?" Scott was pleased with the advice, offering him a fist bump.

"All right, ladies, listen up!" Larry bellowed from the back. He strutted up the aisle to take center stage. "Anyone not here now will be fined twenty-five dollars this morning. You guys are going to learn to be on time!" Bewildered, Mark looked around trying to make sense of this pronouncement, as the offenders were clearly missing from the room.

He noticed that Larry had trimmed his crazy-looking Mohawk shorter on the sides to accentuate the hair sticking up in the center of his head. Together with his designer glasses, it made him look like a punk rocker on steroids wearing a black Toyota polo that was two sizes too small. Once again, the knuckles on his right hand were bruised and scraped. A cell phone rang in the front row.

"Jack, turn around and turn off your cell. I hear anyone else's phone go off, it's a ten-dollar fine. Got it?" On the warpath, Larry had a bug up his ass.

"Paul, where's your nametag?" McGreedy sat there and stared at Larry. He gave him a pained expression, but didn't offer him an explanation.

"Five-dollar fine. C'mon, pay up." He stepped forward, holding out his hand. This time, he collected the five dollar bill from McGreedy and stuck the bill in his pocket. "Guys, we have two more days left in the month, and we need to sell thirty-three more cars. Some of you are going to step up and get yourself a new Toyota this month, right Mark? Right Scott? Okay, Tony, let's update the board."

"Brent, how many ya got out?" Tony Grimes was looking bulked up, his two hundred ninety pounds looked leaner and beefier. It was rumored that he'd been shooting steroids with Bryan and Larry in the tower. From the scrapes on Tony's knuckles this morning, it looked like his services as his boss's bodyguard were in demand.

"I got eighteen." Brent continued to check his cell phone messages, not paying too much attention to Larry's drama.

Tony went down the list methodically, adding the Xs for a whole deal, hash marks for a half. "Ian? Ian?" Looking around the room, now. "Okay, anyone seen Ian?"

Juicifer chimed in. "Think he was lonely, headed to the men's room for a romantic encounter." A twitter of laughter swept the room as Juicifer looked on expectantly from his seat on the front row. He had a big grin on his face, ecstatic to entertain the masses.

After the update of the board for the eighteen sales reps, Larry continued with his agenda. "For those of you who don't know, a group called Consumers Against Crimes is on our case. We've had to settle eight civil suits brought by this group just this month alone, so you guys are gonna have to straighten up and fly right." Mark thought this was ironic, since it was Larry's Redneck Mafia who were responsible for the frauds and overcharging. Finally, the rumors were being confirmed by the Devil himself.

Larry continued. "Anyone responsible for screwing up and causing a civil suit to be brought against us, that sales rep will forfeit all of the commission in the deal. If there is a second time, they'll be fired." He paused and looked around the room to add emphasis. "Tommy and I are tired of writing checks to fake victims at CVC. So far, we've been lucky, kept it out of court, and no media coverage. Any questions?" He glared at everyone, daring someone to ask a question about this new policy. Tommy Catatonia stood in back with his arms folded like the head enforcer, not saying a word.

When the meeting had adjourned just before ten, Larry strode over to Mark. "Appreciate your meeting with Dennis. He's running a little late, a little hungover. He'll be here at ten thirty. I've got a manager's meeting now."

Mark blurted, "Wait. Larry, my paycheck's short—"

"Hafta' deal with it later." Larry cut him off and left the meeting room without giving Mark a chance to speak. For the next hour, Mark sat at his desk making sales calls. It wasn't until eleven o'clock that Dennis finally found his way to the dealership.

"Hey, Mark," said Dennis. "Wanted to apologize for the other day. You got a coupla minutes we can talk?" The man who threatened to slit his throat wasn't dressed for work. He wore a Hard Rock Café T-shirt with jeans and flip-flops, and his eyes were puffy like he'd been up all night partying.

"Sure. How 'bout we duck into the porter's office right behind us. That way we can have some privacy."

Dennis nodded, and they both took a seat in the porter's office. Mark closed the door and let Dennis take the lead in the conversation.

"Hey, I'm really sorry about the way I acted on Wednesday, but I can't afford to lose my job or get arrested. Especially right now."

He paused, getting emotional, some wetness appeared around his eyes. As he continued, it all seemed a little too rehearsed. "My fiancé's pregnant, and she's talking about breaking up with me. Says she's tired of being razzed about dating a black guy. Her parents are Southern Baptists." Dennis looked down at his lap, waiting for Mark to sympathize with him.

"Sherry's pregnant?" Mark was trying to be understanding. Sherry was the former receptionist at Brandson, a cute blonde who used to be Jake's girl until she met Dennis. A few weeks ago, there were rumors that they were doing threesomes with her—convenient because they all shared the same house.

"That's what she says. I've got a lot on my plate right now, and I know you're a Christian, and we've been talking about joining a church. We want you to be our spiritual leader." Mark watched Dennis's eyes well up in tears, still a little skeptical at seeing him portray the role of a born-again Christian. This certainly wasn't the Dennis that had openly professed to having no morals or ethics whatsoever only a few weeks ago. He knew this man was an accomplished actor with several commercials and porn movies under his belt. In spite of his lack of conviction, Mark relented. "I believe in forgiveness and second chances and I'd sure like to think that you're serious about this, Dennis. That you're not playing me, or just saying this to stay out of jail," said Mark.

"No, man, I'm serious. I want to change." Tears rolled down his cheeks. If Dennis was acting, he sure was doing a great job.

"All right, relax, man. I'm going to give you your second chance. Just don't make a fool out of me, right? I'll get upset—like a stick of dynamite going off," said Mark in a test of Dennis's reaction to the bombing. There was a brief flicker of recognition, and Mark saw him blink for just a second. Then he returned to his born-again act.

"I need to keep this job," said Dennis. "I need to provide for my baby coming. Thanks, man." He shook Dennis's hand firmly, but his gut told him he was getting played. After exiting the meeting, Dennis gave a thumbs up to the managers in the tower and hopped into a car outside with Sherry behind the wheel. Following Dennis Testi's dramatic performance, Mark decided it was time to track Larry down to find out about getting paid the other part of his paycheck. He was intercepted by Rich, who wanted to talk in private. Whenever they talked, he and Rich were cautious and met outside on the "grassy knoll" where no one could sneak up and overhear their conversations.

"So, what's up with Dennis. His eyes looked puffy. Did you hold the line with him, or are you going to let him off?" Rich had become his confidant. Mark knew that he could keep secrets.

"Yeah, gonna give him a second chance. Claims he wants me to be his spiritual leader. What do you think of that?"

"Get real. Leopards don't change their spots overnight. He's a psycho loony and you know it." His brow furrowed and eyes narrowed as he made his point. Now, Rich was talking like a cop.

"Gonna put this one in God's hands, bro. I will do what I can to bring a change in the man. No one gains by putting him in jail. It's all up to him," said Mark, acknowledging there were bigger forces in play than just his own personal feelings.

"You hear anything from forensics about your IED?" Rich knew when it was time to move on in a conversation.

"Nothing yet. Did you check your paycheck for errors? Mine was short forty-six percent. How 'bout them apples?" said Mark.

"No, haven't had time, but sounds like maybe I should. Kinda wrapped up in this stuff with Carla. She showed up at one this morning at my house, drunk on her ass, begging me to let her in."

"Did you?"

"Yeah, she had this really hot-looking blonde stripper friend with her, and I did them both 'til eight o'clock this morning," said Rich.

"You dog! And you didn't even call me."

"Should I have?" asked Rich.

"No, not really my style," said Mark, shrugging his shoulders.

"What is your style?"

"Been pretty celibate lately, clearing my head. Women sure can mess you up. Maybe I got low 'T' or something."

"Right. Next thing, you're gonna be shootin' 'roids with Larry."

"I wouldn't go that far. He is pressuring me to buy another new Camry," said Mark. "Has he said anything to you about buying one?"

"No. He knows I have bad credit. How's he pressuring you?"

"Keeps asking me if I like working here. You know, that kind of stuff."

"Well, he knows you have money, but that's illegal," said Rich. "I overheard him in a conversation last week where one of the guys, I think it was Raj, telling him that you don't even need to work. So, why do you put up with this crap?"

"My work ethic's killing me," said Mark. "I don't know how not to work. I mean, I don't know what I'd do with all my spare time. I need to be challenged."

"That's sad, man. If I had your money, hell, I'd be gone from here—that's for sure!"

Mark shifted gears. "I gotta go track down Larry to see about the rest of my paycheck so I can afford to buy a new Camry to keep Brandson in business. I mean, after all, aren't we here working our asses off to make them all millionaires?"

Rich cocked his head. "Yeah, well, seems like that's the program here. Got a customer coming in at two. Lend me a hand with her?"

"Unless I find the rest of my paycheck, a hand is all I can afford to lend ya, bro. Sure, if you need me, I'll handle it."

"Thanks." Rich spotted a customer out in used cars, and he bolted in his direction.

"Better hurry there, partner, I see McGreedy heading that way too." Mark headed inside to track down the Devil and see about a paycheck. He found Larry at his desk, off the phone, and hopefully available to explain his paycheck. Stopping by his desk to grab his visual aids, he entered the sales tower, ready to collect.

"Hey, boss, got a sec?" Larry looked up, saw the washout sheet in his hand and the determination on his face, and he knew Mark wasn't going to let go of this without a detailed explanation.

Larry slid back in his chair and laid his pen down. "Yeah, sure. Bryan told me you have some questions about your paycheck. Let's take a look, see what we got here . . . " As he examined Mark's wash-out, Bryan was on the phone, Tony was outside appraising a trade-in, and Kirk was probably out shopping for some Gas-X. Larry brought Mark's short deals up on his computer screen to double check the payout.

"This one, James Barton, new Corolla deal, we don't pay commissions on dealer cash, so that's why you were expecting an extra eleven hundred on this one." Mark looked on the computer screen with him.

"Wait," said Mark. "The dealer cash was only five hundred bucks here." He pointed to the figures on the screen. "See, right there. That would only reduce my payout by one hundred seventy five dollars. Isn't that how it works?"

"No, you're wrong about that. You don't understand. This deal's correct." Larry was very matter-of-fact and showed no sympathy for Mark's reduced payout. "Let's look at the next one . . . Arthur Willis . . . new Highlander deal, this one looks correct also. If you were expecting more, someone just plain told you wrong." Larry entered a few more keystrokes. "Now, this last one, Cassin, used Camry, let's see . . . looks like the lender required us to shift the front payable commission to the back to do the deal. Sorry, that reduced your payout by nine hundred eighty dollars." He looked up at Mark, expecting agreement.

"Whoa, wait, Larry, how come I go from a thousand dollar pay-out to a flat one hundred bucks while Tricky Ricky winds up with a six thousand dollar back-end commission payable to him? Does that seem fair? I feel like I'm getting screwed." Mark was preparing himself for screaming and profanity from Larry, but the GSM remained matter-of-fact.

"I checked 'em, Marky-Mark. You got paid what you were supposed to. That's just the way it goes sometimes. Welcome to the car business."

Hope for a fair paycheck evaporated, and Mark reluctantly resigned himself to to making four-figure monthly contributions to

'The Redneck Mafia Retirement Fund'. Larry pulled a prospect list from under his keyboard.

"Tell ya what, here's a list of fifty fresh leads. Just for you. Give them a call. I'm sure there's at least one good deal in there. It's my way of saying thanks for meeting with Dennis." Larry calmly handed him the lead sheets, fully expecting him to take them as a consolation prize instead of almost three grand that he'd been shortchanged.

Mark walked out of the tower speechless, completely blacked out, and seriously wondering what kind of psycho dog and pony show he signed up with at Brandson. He had met with Dennis and complied with Larry's demands to make peace and forego prosecution. He felt he had a right to expect better treatment, even from convicted felons. He stopped to think about his situation. As the dog days of summer loomed ahead, he was concerned not only with getting shortchanged, but also with the favoritism, fraud, and overcharging that was getting worse everyday. Though he enjoyed selling quality, fuel efficient cars and admired Toyota's dedication to customer service, he had not signed up to work in a crime scene. He knew that the daily conflicts he faced on these issues would wear on him, undermining his ability to perform at his best, and eventually causing him to reevaluate his commitment to Brandson. Unless things could dramatically improve.

ELEVEN

The January morning was a crisp forty-nine degrees, and the cool air swirled through the passenger compartment of his Camry, providing a refreshing change from the hot summer months that were behind him. He had spent Thanksgiving with his mother and her ninety-three year old boyfriend in Naples, and Christmas in Atlanta with his sister. Two days of running on the beach and body surfing had reminded him of how much he missed living on the Florida coast.

As he entered the showroom this morning, Tony Grimes stood beside his desk waiting for him. He was smiling and holding a stack of lead lists. Tony had become the latest member of the "Almost Bald Club," now sporting the ultra-close haircut that had become popular among the managers in the tower. His silver Transitions glasses fit him so tightly at his temples that they made his head look fat. Tony's blue eyes were dancing with joy about something he was waiting to share, like a big kid in class who just got a peek under his teacher's skirt. Tony was their in-house, hands-down "Village Idiot." No one else even came close.

"Marky-Mark, glad to see you come in on your day off. Let's sit down for a minute, take a look at your blue sheets. I've got some leads for you, and you gotta see these photos of my new squeeze."

Mark sat down with Tony who wasted no time in producing his iPhone. He scrolled to his X-rated photo gallery and turned the phone for Mark to see, first covering the screen with his hand to ask him a question. "You like girls, right?" This was Tony's way of disclosing to his reps that he was about to show them porn. He decided to have some fun with Tony.

"As opposed to . . . what?" Mark liked messing with him because it usually made him stutter.

"Ccchhheck this out!" He pulled his hand away, and there in front of him was a nude, derriere-first photo of a beautiful, young Latino girl on a bed on all fours, wearing only a pair of black high heels.

"Wow, Tony, you scored, man! That's your new squeeze?" he asked, a little incredulous. He studied the photo more closely and noticed the words "hot models.com" in small letters in the lower right corner, indicating the photos were pulled from a porn website.

"Yup. Who knows more about girls than your Uncle Tony?" he asked.

"Well, there's Warren Beatty, Bill Clinton, Rosie O'Donnell."

"Think she'll wind up being a one-night stand?" asked Tony.

"Who? Your date?" Only if she doesn't return for her handcuffs, right?" said Mark.

"Ha! Howd'ya know? What else you got going on today, Marky-Mark?" Mark wasn't sure if he and Tony were on the same planet, much less the same page.

"I have Dr. Palmer coming in at ten o'clock on that new black-on-black, all-wheel drive Highlander Sport. Should be a deal. He's been waiting for that model for over a month now."

"Better move on it," said Tony. "I heard Brent has a customer who might want it. Just get a deposit as fast as you can." Mark nodded in agreement, while Tony walked over to show McGreedy the borrowed images of his "new squeeze." Mark thought how pathetic this was. Not only did 'The Village Idiot' mislead his customers, Tony was even dishonest about the dishonesty of cheating on his wife.

Then Mark's cell phone rang. It was Dr. Palmer. "Hello, this is Mark."

"Hey, Mark, Dr. Palmer, just finishing up on my patient rounds, running a few minutes behind. I'm heading over to pick up my wife at Shands, so should be there in about twenty-five minutes, okay?"

"Sounds perfect, Dr. Palmer. I'll have your new Highlander out front, cleaned up and ready to test drive, okay? See you shortly."

When he found it, the black SUV was covered in a light layer of tree pollen. Mark wanted it to show better, so he drove it around back and took it through the car wash. Presentation was everything, and he planned to have every advantage under his control.

As he walked back inside the front door, McGreedy approached him, looking less than pleased. His instincts told him that McGreedy was ready to unload on him about something.

"Hey, could you move your Highlander?" asked McGreedy. "I have a customer that'll be here in half an hour." Mark could smell liquor on his breath and spotted barbeque sauce on his clothes. Their designated dealership drunk looked like he was intent on being ornery. McGreedy always had a problem with Mark taking center stage with a deal, wanting to push him out of the way whenever he could. It had to be jealousy, but who knew for sure with a guy that drank as much as Nicholas Cage in *Leaving Las Vegas*.

Mark squared off with McGreedy. "Well, sir, I have a doctor and his wife that will be here in five minutes and they'll be looking for that Highlander to be sitting right where it is now. As soon as I'm done with—"

"I need for you to move it right now!" McGreedy was getting down right belligerent with him. He could see a few of the managers watching from the tower to figure out what was going on.

"Excuse me for a second." Mark walked out to the car, locked it, and came back inside, walking right by McGreedy with the keys. As he passed him in the middle of the showroom, he turned and added, "As I was going to say, I'll move it after my customer's test drive is over." Mark was implacable, deciding he was not going to be bulldozed around the showroom by a drunk redneck today. Neither was he going to let McGreedy black him out right before a deal.

As McGreedy drew closer and prepared to tee off on him again, Dr. Palmer and his wife entered through the front door. They spotted Mark and met him in the middle of the showroom as McGreedy skulked back to his desk.

"Mark, this is my wife Sandy." Dr. Palmer had a blue sweater draped over his green scrubs, and he looked like a surgeon on vacation. His wife was pretty, with blue eyes, and blonde hair. "Pleasure to meet you, Sandy." After shaking hands, he said, "As you may have noticed, I have your brand new Highlander Sport right out front on the pad, ready to go."

Sandy said, "Yeah, we stopped to look at it as we came in. Beautiful." He could see that Sandy was onboard with the deal already, and he was banking on Dr. Palmer wanting to please his wife with the car they'd been waiting for.

Five minutes later, they were test driving it. Following their five mile cruise, they parked it in front and were sitting at Mark's desk, putting the deal together and signing documents, very happy with their new Highlander Sport. They had negotiated price and terms on the test drive and came to terms, agreeing to put ten grand down and finance thirty-two thousand dollars at the special incentive rate of zero percent interest. Mark quickly assembled the documents and placed them into the blue deal jacket. Next, he took it to Bryan's desk, placing it in front of him.

"So, how we doin'?" Bryan asked, anxious to pen a new deal.

"We're good, everything agreed to, ready for the box. Nice couple. Perfect car for them. We have to speed things up, though. Dr. Palmer needs to get back to the hospital by noon. Think we can keep him on schedule?" asked Mark.

Bryan looked at Mark. "Take the deal jacket over to Jake. Then, get the Highlander into detail as fast as you can. You gas it up yet?"

"Did that before they got here." Mark grabbed the keys, made a mental note to get the second set from Brent, and walked the deal jacket over to Jake's office. Then he hopped in the new Highlander and drove it to the back. The guys in detail were glad to see him. They were having a slow day with only two cars to work on. He ran into Rich coming back inside. Rich gestured that he needed to talk, so they walked to their secure spot on the grassy knoll for a private conversation.

"What's going on with Carla? She still giving you problems?" Mark did a quick survey of the area to make sure no one was eavesdropping on them. He noticed a couple of Swisher Sweet cigar wrappers left in the grass. Rich noticed them too.

"Those must be Ron's. He likes those cheap cigars." Rich kicked at them with the toe of his shoe, hesitant to offer Mark the update on his crazy wife's latest antics.

"Yeah, Swishy Sweets for gay caballeros. Right?" There had been lots of rumors about Ron's sexual preferences, and the fact that he liked gladiator movies and guys who wore cargo shorts.

Rich finally opened up. "Carla's stripping now at a club in Daytona. Says she needs the money to pay for her defense attorney's fees."

"Whoa. That's pretty hardcore, bro. If she's out on bail, isn't leaving the county a violation of her bail bond conditions?"

"Yeah, I told her that already. She doesn't care, says the money's so much better there than that redneck truck stop in MacIntosh. What's it called, Risque something or other? What's going on with your mailbox bomber? Forensics come up with any leads yet?"

"They said they haven't been able to lift any prints. They think the perp wore gloves. They even dusted the unexploded pieces of dynamite. Not one print."

"Still think someone's sending you a message?"

"For sure. I heard that Tommy Catatonia, Larry, and their buddy Rocky Gambrone have some hard core underworld connections who are very capable of handling something like this for them."

"Wouldn't it just be easier for them just to fire you, bro?"

"What, and give up all the money I'm making them? They probably think it's cheaper and more profitable to intimidate me like this to scare me and try to keep me in line."

"Are you scared?" asked Rich, testing him.

Mark cocked his head at his buddy and extended his left arm out, pointing at a four-inch scare on the inside of his forearm. "See this? A little momento from a ten foot bull shark when I was blue water hunting on the Great Barrier Reef a few years back. He was after my game bag full of snappers, lobsters, and groupers." Mark paused then added, "We met, up close and personal, and I went home with dinner."

"So, what happened with the shark?" Rich asked.

"He wasn't after me. When I spun around at seventy feet down, I didn't know he was there. I accidentally stuck my arm in his mouth. When he came back, I flipped my spear gun around and butted him in the nose with the rubber end. He took off. I never saw him again."

"And, so, that explains your scar. So, your point is?"

"I'm not a quitter, and I'm not easily intimidated," Mark said. "That's why Larry is playing a dangerous game of chess with me. I like challenges, and maybe I'm just too dumb to be scared. Chess is the only game I can think of that's one hundred percent skill. You play?"

"I used to. Not much now." Rich looked across the tarmac at a homeless guy passing through the used car lot. The sun popped out from behind the clouds and was warming things up. A nice breeze had begun to blow. There were a lot of cars coming and going from the service lanes, with service writers looking busy, escorting customers back and forth from the service desks inside.

"I'm going back to detail to check on my delivery. Good luck with Carla's stuff, bro. At least, with her exotic dancing skills, you'll have some entertainment if you both wind up in the same cell together."

"You're a funny guy. You couldn't get a hotty like her even if your semen cured cancer. Hey, what did you make on that deal, anyway?" asked Rich.

Mark stopped to answer him. "It was a two pounder. That's reasonable, right? These deals that Juicifer, Dennis, and McGreedy do where they totally put the screws to their customers and make twenty thousand, that's just wrong—especially when they're old and handicapped." Rich nodded in agreement.

"Later," said Mark, on his way to detail. As Mark turned the corner, he could see it was ready. He got the keys from Marvin, cranked it up and headed to the delivery pad on the other side of the dealership. As he passed by the main entrance, Ian was waving at Mark to stop and talk. He pulled up and rolled his window down. Ian had on his red Toyota shirt, khaki slacks, and the elfish suede shoes he liked to call his "driver" shoes.

"You got a deal?" Ian liked to lean on the car when he talked. He thought it made him look more like a player.

"Yup. What are you working on? Hey, I heard there's a new website that you might want to check out, called 'Men Wearing Cargo Shorts.' Have you heard about it?" As he watched Ian's reaction, Mark tried to keep a straight face, but couldn't suppress his grin.

"Get ouda here. Maybe you're the one that's gay." Ian was mock bitch-slapping him through the car window.

"Maybe . . . how bad you wanna know?" asked Mark. He liked messing with Ian, who was used to being ribbed about his effeminate nature. "I gotta go deliver this Highlander," said Mark. Ian headed onto the lot with his keys to find his customers the car they'd selected.

Mark backed the Highlander into the third of four spaces under the portico covering the delivery pad in preparation for the Palmer's final inspection. As he stepped out of the Highlander to do his own walk-around, he noticed Danziger sitting in the yellow Mazda two spaces over with an attractive female customer in space one. Their engine was running and, from Mark's line of sight, it looked like

Danziger had his hands under her dress in the front seat and they were kissing. He stepped back and walked to the front of the SUV, inspecting it again. Avoiding looking in their direction, he decided to give Danziger and his hottie a chance to compose themselves and skip the embarrassment of getting caught having sex in the car.

As he began to turn around to inspect the Highlander one last time, he only had a fraction of a second to react. Instinctively, he extended his left arm out to protect himself from the yellow blur coming straight at him. As the rear of the backing car struck him, the spoiler hit his right hand hard, knocking him backward onto the tarmac where he landed on his back. Dazed by the impact, he vaguely heard the screeching brakes. The wheels of the yellow Mazda stopped barely a foot from his head, almost crushing him as he lay semiconscious on the asphalt. The next thing he remembered was the sound of Jake's voice.

"Marky-Mark! Hey man, you all right? Can you get up?" He could feel someone's arm under his shoulder, trying to pick him up from the pavement. Then he heard someone yell, "Don't pick him up! He could have spinal injuries!"

He was surrounded by four or five people, all hovering over him as he regained his bearings, trying to focus. He could taste the blood in his mouth and feel the cut on his tongue where he had bit himself at the moment of impact. As he lay there, he could see the gorgeous brunette from the Mazda now squatting over him, her long brown hair falling forward in his face. From his angle on the tarmac, Mark could not help but notice that she was not wearing any panties. He was wondering if this was really happening or a hallucination.

Undecided about trying to sit up just yet, he couldn't take his eyes off the girl with no panties. He said, "Whoa. Didn't see that one coming. Who, ah . . . was driving?" He felt dazed and woozy, pain shooting through his body. He tried to sit up, holding his left hand to his head. His right arm was numb with pain.

The beautiful brunette now stood over him with the others. "Robert was driving," said the brunette. "We didn't realize it was in gear. We are so sorry! He's around here somewhere." As she spoke and looked around for Danziger, she held up her hand to shield her eyes from the sun, holding her dress down with her left hand, leaving the right side of her dress to blow freely in the wind and expose her perfect pantyless anatomy. Enjoying the show, Mark was still not ready to sit up yet, trying to imagine an encore.

"Can you stand up?" asked Dr. Palmer as he bent over his salesman who was now his patient. He checked Mark's arm for fractures. Mark was sorry to see the brunette stepping aside to let the doctor examine him. The show was over, so he stood up and stumbled forward a step, still woozy from the impact.

"Yeah, thanks, I'll be okay. I was just doing . . . an inspection . . . of your, ah . . . Highlander, Dr. Palmer. Hey, Ian, I might need some help installing Dr. Palmer's tag. I'm not sure I can, uh, handle a screwdriver right now."

"Sure, man," said Ian. "I can help with that. Dr. Palmer, I'll be right back and take care of your tag transfer. Take it easy, Mark. You should go sit down." Ian was concerned and wanted to help. Groggy from the impact, Mark walked back inside the building with Dr. Palmer's help.

Bryan met him inside. "Hey, take it easy, Mark," he said. "We saw the whole thing on the video security cameras from the sales tower. Why don't you sit down for a few minutes and get yourself together. I'm gonna have Ian handle the rest of your delivery for Dr. Palmer. He says he'll help, and you won't have to split the deal with him. Man, you really got smacked there! Gotta watch where you're walking! Hey, you want us to call an ambulance?" Bryan studied him as he took a moment to weigh the dealership's liability.

"No, that's okay. I don't think I can afford the two grand. I'm gonna sit down for a bit. Feel a little woozy. Everything go okay with my deal?"

"Everything's done. Ian will finish the delivery for you. Go sit down." Bryan had his hand on Mark's shoulder, trying to reassure him.

He made his way back to his desk and laid his right arm out in front of him. He looked at it intently, trying to figure out what was causing so much pain. His right wrist and hand were start-ing to swell, his right shoulder was throbbing with intense pain. If he hadn't stiff-armed the oncoming car, it would have hit him in the back and damaged his spinal column. He looked up and saw Danziger in the sales tower talking with Bryan. Mark couldn't figure out why Danziger hadn't come over to check on him. He caught Bryan's eye and gestured for him to come over.

"Hey, Marky-Mark, how you feeling?" Bryan stood over him. As he laid out his arm on his desk, he sensed that Bryan was conflicted over protecting the dealership or helping him with his injuries.

"I think I should get some X-rays. I've got severe pain and swelling in my hand, wrist, and shoulder. Is there a specific urgent care location that I need to go to, since this is likely a Workmen's Comp issue?"

"Not sure. Let me go check. I'll be right back." Bryan walked back to his desk and dialed up the Director of Human Resources of Brandson Enterprises in Sarasota. Then he rang Mark at his desk.

"You need to go to a place called Primary Care out on West University near the Gainesville Health and Fitness Center. You know where that's at, right? You want someone to drive you, or are you okay to drive?"

"I know where it is. I'm okay to drive. Thanks for your help, big guy." Mark hung up, logged off, and powered down his computer. He grabbed his keys and attaché case, heading for his car.

Fifteen minutes later, he slowed in front of the big three-story red brick building across from Gainesville Health and Fitness on University Avenue. The sign read "Primary Care," and Mark turned left onto the side street, then left again into their parking lot. He pulled into the spot closest to the main entrance, thinking that it couldn't be that busy at one thirty in the afternoon. He was wrong.

As he entered the large waiting room, he was greeted by a scene very similar to the bar scene in the first *Star Wars* episode. It was the

strangest assortment of weirdos he'd ever seen anywhere—except for
the drivers license bureau. As his arm hung in the temporary sling
he made from his belt, his eyes searched the room for the receptionist. He spotted a group of creepy-looking people standing up and
leaning on the wall like a group of bare trees on Halloween night.
They looked like they were waiting for food stamps, an unemploy-
ment check, or a methadone injection. Behind them he could see
the receptionist's window. He wound his way through the group
and knocked on the glass. There was no answer, so he knocked
again. This time, the glass slid open, revealing an obese woman who
looked about the size of Utah and had a huge, greasy Rasta hairdo.

"Sir, are you having an emergency?" Mark looked at her computer screen that displayed a game of solitaire in progress, then back
at the obese woman. She looked at Mark like he was an insect.

"No ma'am, I got hit by a car," was all he could say. There was
a scrawny man leaning on the wall next to the window, adjusting
his arm sling. He had nicotine-stained teeth, meth sores, and track
marks on his arms.

"Have you been here before, sir?" She leaned forward and
grabbed a clipboard with a multi-page questionnaire attached to it.

"No, ma'am. I would have remembered this place," he said, as
his eyes roamed the room in complete disbelief.

"Shirley, you got a pen?" asked the Rasta woman.

A female voice from behind the partition said, "Ya got three of
them stuck in your hair, Shanika. Why don't ya use one of those?
Ya always asking me for a pen when ya got two or three already,
woman."

"Oh! Yeah." Shanika reached into her Rasta do and pulled out a
Bic pen that was so greasy it looked like it had been dipped in Wesson
oil. "Here ya go, sir." She handed him the clipboard and pushed the
sign-in sheet under the glass. "Fill this out, and I'll call your name
when we have a doctor available," she said, holding the pen out.

Mark looked at the pen like she'd just pulled it out of her rectum. "Uh . . . Shanika, thanks, but I have my own pen."

She stuck the pen back into her Rasta do for another lube job, and Mark signed the registry, printed his name, and took the clipboard and questionnaire. Shanika slid the glass window closed and returned to her game of computer solitaire, fairly certain that management would not have a forklift large enough to remove her from her current position.

He surveyed the room, looking for a chair free from blood stains or bodily fluids. His most fervent hope was that he could eventually make his escape without contracting any STDs or terminal diseases. Making his way through the room, he tried not to touch anything. A woman on crutches had just vacated a chair in the far corner. He inspected it carefully before sitting down to fill out the questionnaire. A few minutes later, after completing all six pages, he made his way back to Shanika's window, knocking on the glass again.

The glass window slid open slowly. This time he was greeted by Shirley, a middle-aged woman with red hair that looked almost as big as Shanika. She had freckles and a missing front tooth. There was a box of half-eaten fried chicken sitting on the counter in front of her. Shirley was chewing away with a piece of chicken stuck to her cheek.

"Can I help you?" she asked. Her name tag was loose and dangled precariously, but her name was still readable.

"Hi, Shirley. I'm Mark McAllister. Here's my questionnaire. Do you know how long it will be before I can see a doctor?"

"Well, let's see." Shirley checked her clipboard. "You got five patients ahead of you. Probably be about an hour or so."

"Okay, thanks, Shirley." Mark went back to his chair, still available, and free from bodily fluids. He waited for the next hour and a half before hearing from anyone inside. He passed the time doing some market research on his cell phone, reading a tattered *Money* magazine from twelve years ago, and spoke with three people from work who had called to see how he was doing.

Then he heard his name ring out. "Mark McAllister." He checked his watch. Almost two hours had gone by. An Asian nurse in her thirties wearing green scrubs and a stethoscope greeted him at the door to patient care, holding his questionnaire. She made it obvious that she didn't want to be there.

"Are you Mark?" Mark nodded and tried to smile. She had a heavy Chinese accent, smelled like sweet-and-sour sauce, and wore horn-rimmed glasses. "Follow me." He followed her into an examination room where she closed the door, sat down, and reviewed his questionnaire.

"So, dis first time here, right?" He nodded his head yes. Seemed like this was an important question here. It made him wonder who in their right mind would ever want to return for a second visit.

"We take brud pesher now, right?" Mark nodded again. After she'd performed all the vital signs, she said, "Doctor be in bury soon, okay?" He could only guess as to how long "bury soon" would be. She left, and he waited another ten minutes before there was a knock on the door.

"Hi, I'm Dr. Newsome." When he saw the doctor, Mark felt like he was trapped inside the pages of a *Mad Magazine* comic book.

"Mark McAllister." Dr. Newsome was a middle-aged man with freckles, red curly hair, and plastic-framed glasses. Kind of goofy-looking, he looked exactly like Alfred E. Neumann from the comics.

"So, we had ourselves an auto accident, huh?" said the doctor.

"Not exactly. I was on foot when the car hit me. Backed into me at the dealership. It's all in the questionnaire that you're holding."

"I only scanned it. We don't usually have time to actually read everything. Let's take you out of that sling so we can get some X-rays."

After Mark had freed his arm, Dr. Newsome did a quick exam of his hand, arm and wrist. He began asking questions about the swelling. "So, you had this bad hand and wrist already, right? And, you have had a history of back problems, correct?"

"Uh, no. Why would you think that?" Mark was confused and uncomfortable with the questions, as if the doctor was looking to blame his injuries on pre-existing conditions.

Dr. Newsome said, "We get a lot of scam artists in here, wanting narcotic pain meds, faking accidents at work so they can go on Workmen's Comp, watch TV, and eat Cheetos." Mark was insulted, having no intentions of lying on the couch and collecting Workmen's Comp checks. Although he did like eating Cheetos. He'd never been treated like this by a doctor. He was already a little grumpy from the pain, and getting annoyed with this doctor's attitude.

"By the way, who pays your fees here for the medical care, Dr. Newsome?"

"Your employer does." Dr. Newsome treated the questions as routine, although he could see that his patient was clearly annoyed.

"Well, I hope that you don't let that influence the quality of care that I receive as your patient, because I do expect certain standards of medical care. This is my health we're talking about, Dr. Newsome. I'd like to be able to play horseshoes again." He winced from the pain, not sure of what he was saying. He knew that the medical industry was full of fraud, littered with degenerates who looked at medicine in terms of dollars, instead of providing quality medical care. Some of these guys were no more than OTB guys with medical licenses. He wasn't going to let this doctor deal him a bad hand, wrist, or shoulder.

"We have certain procedures and cost structures that we adhere to here at Primary Care," said Dr. Newsome. "Keep in mind that this is free medical care that your employer is providing to you. I'll have our radiologist take you to X-ray. I've authorized him to X-ray your hand, wrist, arm, back, and shoulder. Anything beyond that will have to be performed by your regular physician. Then, we'll have a second conference."

Dr. Newsome didn't seem to mind that he had established an adversarial relationship with his patient, who was now intent on questioning every diagnosis, medication, and recommendation that followed. Mark would likely seek a second opinion on anything Primary Care proposed, including the color of his penis.

He liked the radiologist. Dr. Waters was a nice, young family man in his thirties who was both professional and considerate with Mark's patient care. It took twenty minutes to perform all the

X-rays that Dr. Newsome had authorized. The X-rays showed that Mark had broken his wrist, right finger, tore his rotator cuff, and had a severely sprained hand.

A half-hour later, he met again with Dr. Newsome, who had an orthopedic nurse fit him with a splint for his hand, finger, and wrist. They also fitted him with a cheap, uncomfortable arm sling for his shoulder, and he was prescribed thirty of the ten-milligram Lortabs for the pain.

On the way out of the clinic, he noticed Shanika still playing her computer solitaire. He thought about the money that George Lucas could have saved by shooting the *Star Wars* bar scene in the lobby of this wacko clinic. It was no wonder that medical care expenses were skyrocketing and people were complaining about the quality of medical care. He made a mental note to call the Workmen's Comp insurer to arrange for a new team of physicians to take over his patient care.

After filling the prescription at the pharmacy downstairs, he popped two Lortabs as he sat in his Camry with the engine running. Desperate to stop the pain, he chewed them up and swallowed them without having anything to wash them down. He grimaced from the bitter taste and checked his watch, noting that four hours had elapsed since he entered the clinic at about one-thirty. On an empty stomach, he could feel the narcotic hit him. He was on his way to la-la land.

As the heavy narcotic took effect, he had a flashback from the seventies. The Forecast For Tonight: Alcohol, Low Standards, and Poor Decisions.

TWELVE

It was the first Friday morning meeting Mark missed in three years, and he couldn't help wondering what all the buzz was about on his accident yesterday. January 20th was another beautiful day, but the drug hangover from three Lortabs and the cabernet made him miss the first few hours of the day. He hurt everywhere. Even in places where he didn't know he had places. He thought about calling in, but decided to keep a low profile.

He heard his cell phone ringing from across the house. He stumbled out to the family room to see who it was. It was Rich. "So, how'd it go? Break anything?" asked Rich.

"Broken wrist, broken finger, sprained hand, torn rotator cuff. Painful, but the drugs are handling it," said Mark. "When they said not to drink and do narcotics, they were right. I got such a cloud over my head right now, I might as well be on Mars. What's up?"

"Oh, there's so much crap flying around about you that you wouldn't believe it," said Rich. "The reps have been laughing at the video footage of your accident at Bryan's desk. They're even talking about putting it on YouTube. Raj's telling everyone that you planned this accident so you could get time off and do drugs. It's a three-ring circus here."

"I swear as God is my witness, I'm going to punch him when I see him. A solid left hook with my good arm. Does he really think I wanted to get run over by a car to get out of work?"

"Who knows with Patel? He's always tryin' to make himself look good." Mark could hear Rich walk across the showroom as they spoke.

"Rich, was Danziger having sex with that hottie in the car that hit me? 'Cause it sure looked like it to me. Wonder if that had anything to do with the car jumping into gear. You know, when I was semiconscious and she was squatting over me, she wasn't wearing any panties."

"You dog, you. I'll bet you they were screwing around and knocked the gearshift into reverse. He said he had the engine running to keep the AC on. At least he fessed up to that when he was in the sales tower."

"I'd put money on it. I think she actually helped me regain consciousness by adding more adrenaline to my system. What's the deal with Danziger? Is she dating him?"

"That's his fiance."

"No way. For real?" asked Mark. This came as somewhat of a surprise. Danziger wasn't exactly a smokin' hot stud with the ladies. "C'mon, the guy's running around with a hole in his head for God's sake!"

"That's what he says," said Rich. Being married to Carla, a hot-looking stripper, even he was jealous of Danziger's fiance.

"Well, Danziger never even came over to me or called to see how I was doing. Can you believe that? If it was me driving the car, at the very least I would have walked over and apologized."

"Yeah, I don't get that either. Maybe he's afraid you'll sue him for your injuries," said Rich.

"Yeah, well, after sitting in that zoo they call a clinic for four hours, I did manage to talk with an attorney over at Havera and Smith. He said that the way Florida Workmen's Comp Law is written now, an employee injured on the job is prohibited from suing any fellow employees and prohibited from suing his employer, as long as the employer is taking care of the employee's medical care expenses."

"What about the money? When does that kick in?"

"The income portion in Workmen's Compensation starts after a thirty-day elimination period. It's limited to eighty percent of the average of your past thirteen months income, but only if your income after the injury is reduced by more than twenty percent as a direct result of your injury." Mark had done his homework. The state laws on Workmen's Comp were convoluted and full of bureaucratese.

"Jeez, you sound like a Philadelphia attorney," said Rich.

"Yeah, well, I didn't write the damn law, I only suffer under it. Listen, do me a favor?"

"Sure, what?" Rich was eager to help his injured buddy.

"Is that yellow Mazda 3 that Danziger hit me with still on the lot?"

"Yeah, it's kinda hard to miss. Sticks out like a sore thumb. Sorry, bro. Poor choice of words. Yeah, it's still here," said Rich.

"Okay. This is what I want you to do. Grab the keys and check the car for her panties. If they're still in the car, it would likely prove they were fooling around when he hit me. I have a hunch that she forgot to put them back on. We're going to get to the bottom of this."

"Badump-bump. Good one. You know what? I'll bet you're right. I'm on it! I've got a nose for panties!"

"Badump-bump right back at ya. Call me right back, will ya?" Mark was certain his theory was correct. He never envisioned that the training he provided would involve sending his trainee on a scavenger hunt for a pair of panties.

After they'd hung up, Mark began to think that maybe taking some paid time off was exactly what he needed with all of the crap he was dealing with. He planned to call AmericaSure and request a change of attending physicians. He'd had enough of the Doc-in-the-Box and that zoo they called a clinic.

He found out his case handler at AmericaSure was a girl named Ashley. They had a fifteen minute conversation about what to expect in the days ahead. She was adamant about Mark keeping his second scheduled exam with the zoo at Primary Care on Monday before she would even consider changing physicians. Right after his conversation with AmericaSure, his cell phone rang. It was Rich.

"Hey, I woulda called ya sooner, but I got tied up with a customer in the showroom. Guess what I found stuck in the storage pocket behind the passenger seat in the Mazda?" Rich sounded excited and a little out of breath.

"Uh, gee, let me think. A ham and Swiss on rye?"

"No, smart-ass. Woman's panties. Now, see if you can guess what color and brand." Rich was having fun with this.

"Knowing what I know about that girl . . . I would say . . . red lace Victoria's Secret."

"Close. Black lace, Frederick's of Hollywood. They're a silk thong. And they smell real nice."

"You're a pervert. Let me guess what they smell like. Liz Taylor's White Diamonds."

"How the hell did you know that?"

"When she was squatting over me, her hair was falling in my face, and that's the scent I remember. White Diamonds. Where are the panties now? Please tell me they're not wrapped around your head."

"I have them stashed in my bottom drawer," said Rich.

"Okay, good. I may need them for evidence. We'll get to the bottom of this, I promise. Keep her drawers in your drawer, okay? Gotta go." Mark was content with having that little piece of evidence, but he wasn't exactly sure how to play that card yet. He went on YouTube to see if they'd actually put his accident on the net. He couldn't find it, guessing that they'd run into some red tape on that one.

Sunday morning he went on his 5K run for the first time since the accident. The orthotics slowed him down, but he was missing his body's endorphins and compelled to run. He discovered that his body's endorphins were more effective at relieving the pain than the prescription narcotics. Gradually, the chronology of events floated up from his subconscious, and he began to remember all the details of his accident. Somewhere along the way, the pain from his fractured wrist triggered the frightful memories of the monster typhoon he sailed into halfway between Hawaii and French Polynesia eight years ago. Breaking something every now and then seemed useful in reminding him of his mortality.

Finally, Monday morning rolled around, and it was time to visit the *Star Wars* zoo again. This time, they tried to pawn him off on an ill-trained physician's assistant from Bangladesh named Rachel who smelled like curry. After Mark insisted on being treated by an orthopedic physician, they brought in Dr. Wilson, a short little rude fellow with a German accent, glasses, and bad acne.

The scene turned into a repeat of his first visit to the clinic on the day of his accident. Dr. Wilson was attempting to sidestep the responsibilities of Mark's medical care, still insinuating that most of them were due to pre-existing conditions. Once again, Mark was disappointed to see that the staff at Primary Care was more concerned with containing or eliminating medical costs than they were in providing the care that he needed to heal his injuries.

Deciding he'd had enough, Mark called Ashley at AmericaSure with Dr. Wilson still in the room.

Offended at hearing Mark's remarks to the AmericaSure case handler, Dr. Wilson huffed out of the exam room with Rachel right behind him. *Good*, Mark thought. Now, maybe they would agree to transfer his medical files without anymore of the dog and pony show. He continued with Ashley, who waited silently on the phone.

"Now, if we can't switch caregivers today, I'm going to get back into my car and drive over to see an attorney at Havera and Smith who specializes in Workmen's Comp cases. He has yet to lose a court case with a counter party. I'll sign a retainer agreement with him today, and then you can deal with him. I'm done with the zoo here." For a few moments, he could hear only silence on the phone. "Are you there, Ashley?"

"Yes, I'm listening. Please calm down, Mr. McAllister. There's no need for all that. I'll set you up with an appointment to see Dr. Pharr at The Orthotic Institute in the next few days. Would that be agreeable?" Mark was relieved to hear that she'd became more conciliatory.

"Sure. That works. I've heard good things about TOI. I'll look for a follow-up call in the next day or two. I appreciate your flexibility, and I'm glad that we could come to an agreement." Mark smiled to himself. No more *Star Wars* zoo.

With his call concluded, Mark walked out of the exam room and the doctor's office. He passed Rachel and Dr. Wilson without saying another word. He walked past Shanika, still playing her game of computer solitaire, oblivious to the needs of her patients in the waiting room. As he was about to leave the patient lobby at Primary Care, he turned to take one last look around at the biggest collection of lunatics he'd ever seen outside the driver's license bureau.

His parting thought was that the world needs to be warned of what goes on in this dungeon. He would start that ball rolling with his call to the dealership's personnel office tomorrow. As he climbed back in his car, his cell phone rang. He was surprised to see the call was from Tommy Catatonia, his general manager.

"Hey, Tommy. How are you?" asked Mark. He had enjoyed a good relationship with Tommy in the past, and his GM had even given him some charitable projects and market research to work on from time to time.

"The question is how're you doing, Mark?"

"A little banged up, but I think I'll live. Got a broken wrist and finger, torn rotator, and sprained hand. The orthopedic supports, arm sling, and splint make it hard to hold a pen or work a computer, and the pain meds make me a little woozy."

"Well, you can hold a phone and talk okay, right?" Mark wasn't expecting a callous response from his boss, and given the dealership's potential liabilities in the accident, he was expecting a little more understanding from Tommy.

"Yes, I guess so, if I dial it with my nose. I'm not trying to be a wise guy here, but I'm gonna need some time before I can come back in and be effective in selling cars for you. I'd like to be able to shake hands with my customer and make sales without feeling like they're buying from me because they feel sorry for me."

"Hey, what's wrong with that? When I was in sales in Cleveland and I had my hand in a cast when I broke it in a car accident, man, I played the sympathy card to make the extra sales, and it worked!" said Tommy. "You thought about that? I mean, we don't care how we sell cars, as long as we sell cars! You on board with this?" He could tell Tommy wanted him back pronto, regardless of his condition, and it was always the greed factor that seemed to outweigh any other considerations at Brandson. Sometimes, he just got plain sick of it.

"I have given some thought to this. Give me the rest of this week to recover a bit, and I'll call you sometime next week. Can we at least do that?" Did he honestly have to remind his boss that his injuries were the result of Danziger being under the influence of narcotic pain killers while being forced back to work prematurely?

"Well, all right. If you feel that way, let's talk again next week. But, we need ya here." Tommy's voice was firm and unsympathetic, and it bugged him.

"Sure, boss. I'm healing as fast as I can. See you soon." Mark hung up and thought more about his talk with his GM. Apart from his underworld connections, Tommy could appear to be a nice guy from time to time, but he had a habit of dropping the charities if they were not immediately profitable for the dealership. Deep down, he knew that his general manager was a greedy man, and dishonest when it suited him. With Tommy, it was always all about the money. The rest of the niceties were just for show.

Although it was in the back of his mind the whole time during his conversation with Tommy, Mark had purposely not brought up the fact that Danziger had been forced to return to work while still heavily medicated. Mark knew the managers were aware of the dangers that his condition posed. He kept turning over the irony of his situation in his head. It was also very likely that Tommy was aware of Danziger's sexual escapades with his fiance while driving under the influence of narcotics at the time of the accident. Allowing himself to be pressured into returning to work while *he* was still on narcotic medications would be very ironic, indeed.

He sat in the parking lot at Primary Care, his engine running and his mind whirling. He felt like he was being pushed into a mold that didn't fit him, forcing him to become someone he wasn't, someone he didn't want to be. He needed some time to think things through. And right now, he needed a pain killer.

THIRTEEN

The large, three-story brick building that housed the headquarters of The Orthotic Institute covered almost an entire block. Turning off University Avenue into the main entrance, Mark was impressed with the appearance. As soon as he stepped through the large automatic door into the main lobby, he was greeted by two attractive, young staff assistants dressed in blue scrubs standing behind a wide, marble-topped reception area. The brunette with the page-boy, brown eyes and dark-framed glasses standing nearest to him noticed his splints and sling.

"Good morning, sir, may I please have your name and the doctor you're here to see?" Her name tag said 'Stephanie'.

"Hi. Mark McAllister. I'm here to see Dr. Pharr."

"Great." A patient sign-in sheet spewed out from the printer in front of her, and she placed it on the counter between them. "Would you please sign here? I'll need to make a copy of your driver's license." He produced his ID and stood at the counter while Stephanie checked the computer to verify his appointment and made a copy of his license. He noticed a patient refreshment area to his right, furnished with several large stainless steel containers of coffee, hot chocolate, and fresh orange juice. Pointing to the bank of beverages and cups, he asked, "Stephanie, is that for your patients?"

"Of course. Feel free to help yourself. You can take it back with you to the waiting area around the corner. The second nurse's station you come to will be where you check in to see Dr. Pharr. He should be available in just a few minutes."

"Thank you, Stephanie." Mark smiled at her appreciatively. The professional atmosphere at TOI was a big step up from his experience at the *Star Wars* zoo.

Wanting to stay tuned in on the global financial news, he returned to his seat in front of the CNBC broadcast and found himself drifting into a review of the events of the past week. Six days had passed since his last conversation with the big boss, and in those six days he'd been busy in phone conversations with attorneys who specialized in Workmen's Comp litigation. He recalled that each of the attorney's expressed a strong interest in some of the other issues at Brandson, including fraud, theft of commissions, threats, coercion, and overcharging. Mark wasn't ready to throw in the towel, hoping there was an opportunity to turn things around at the dealership. He heard his name called, and looked up to see an attractive nurse in blue scrubs, long brown hair, and blue eyes smiling at him. He recognized her immediately.

"Laura! I had no idea you worked here. I thought you were over at North Florida Regional. How are you?" Mark was happy to see her, and when he walked up, she gave him a big hug. Her hair smelled like fresh coconuts, and the hug made him feel good.

"It's good to see you, Mark. I've been here for about a year now." She smiled and checked out the orthotics he was wearing. "So, what happened to you?" she asked. He'd met Laura on the beach in St. Augustine about eighteen months ago. They had played a competitive game of paddle ball and took a long run together.

"I got hit by a car a week ago. It looks worse than it is. So, what happened to that guy you were dating? What was his name? Randy?

He was a doctor, right?" Randy was the only reason that they hadn't taken it to the next level when they'd met on the beach.

"We got engaged about a month after I met you, and broke up about two months ago. We just weren't right for each other. It was a big mistake."

"I'm sorry," said Mark. Elated by the news, he did his best to hide it.

"Don't be. Are you running in your orthotics?"

"What, you think this gear's gonna slow me down. Get real, girl." He was grinning from ear to ear, knowing they both had a thing for extreme fitness. His mind drifted as he fantasized about whether her enjoyment of intense workouts extended to indoor sports.

She must have read his mind. She pulled out her card and wrote down a number. "Here's my cell. Call me sometime." She stuck the card in his arm sling. "Now, let me take you over to Dr. Pharr's nurse for vital signs, okay?" He tucked her card away in his back pocket, fully intending on following up with Laura as soon as he had time. She was a sweetie, and they had a lot in common. As he followed her down the hallway, she was enjoying teasing him with her walk and flounced her hips suggestively.

She stopped and opened the door to an exam room. Showing him inside, she said, "Hey, it's real nice to see you again, Mark. You're in good hands." Before she closed the door, she leaned in and whispered the words "call me." *Count on it, baby,* he thought.

He barely had time to sit down before a pudgy blonde nurse named Sally came in and introduced herself. She took his vital signs and entered some data into a computer. Sally was pleasant and professional, and it was obvious that she enjoyed her work.

"Laura said to take good care of you. Is that sling comfortable?" she asked.

"Not really. I think it's from China and has one of those all-day warranties. How'd you know to ask?" He was starting to feel like a guest at the Four Seasons in San Francisco.

"Experience. You get that at Primary Care?"

"Bingo again. I made my way over here after the staff at Primary Care tried to convince me that my injuries were the result of pre-existing conditions. It was unbelievable."

"I've heard similar stories about their operations and staff." Sally was writing something into his patient file. When she finished, she looked up. "I don't understand how they're still in business. I've heard they've had a lot of complaints. Dr. Pharr should be in shortly." She smiled as she quietly shut the door behind her.

A few minutes went by before Dr. Pharr entered. He was sixty-three, conservative, and a highly-respected orthopedic specialist who himself had hip and shoulder implants done at TOI several years earlier. As a former patient, it gave him some unique insights into how to provide better patient care. He examined Mark carefully, discarded the X-rays from Primary Care, and authorized new X-rays of his injuries after reading the description of his accident. He had the nurse fit him with new, more comfortable splints and a padded arm sling that was custom-fitted for him.

By the time he finished his appointment, it was almost noon. He was on his way home and his cell phone rang. It was Tommy. He didn't want to take the call, but knew he had no choice.

"Hey, Tommy. What's sup?"

"Are you coming in today? We need you here, Mark."

"I'm just now leaving my doctor's office. AmericaSure finally approved a change in doctors, and I've just been through a new exam and new X-rays." Mark was apprehensive about what he knew Tommy wanted.

"Hope they went well. Come on in. Let's meet in my office in a half hour. You can update me on your condition. Wear your work clothes. See you then." The conversation ended abruptly, and Tommy sounded firm. The conversation made Mark feel more like an indentured servant than a valued employee.

Obviously, there was going to be no discussion with the boss about staying out any longer on medical leave, and so he headed over to Brandson to meet with Tommy to discuss the terms of his servitude. It was his first day back since the accident eleven days ago. Bryan Pfister was at the side door when Mark walked in, and had a skeptical look on his face, standing with his hands on his hips and a confrontational posture.

"So, where's your neck brace?" Bryan asked with heavy sarcasm.

As he studied Bryan, Mark set his attaché case down and adjusted his arm sling. He felt defensive with Bryan's attitude, but answered him politely. "My neck's okay, Bryan. It's my finger, wrist, hand, and shoulder that's broken. Are you doubting my injuries? I know you watched the video from the security cameras." This didn't seem like the same Bryan that he'd left eleven days ago, and Mark was trying to figure out the reason for the change in his attitude.

"So, when's the big lawsuit?" Bryan wasn't smiling. Mark couldn't tell if he was trying to antagonize him or just messing with him.

Mark stayed calm. "I have no plans to sue anybody," he said. "Under Workmen's Comp, as long as the employer takes care of the employees injuries, we're good. But, you already know that, right? I know this isn't the first time you've seen an on-the-job injury. Are we still on the same team, big guy?"

"Depends. Tommy's waiting. Catch ya later." Bryan was acting like Mark had signed up with one of their competitors. He picked up his attaché case and crossed the showroom, asking himself how he could be at fault in any way. He felt like they'd pulled the welcome mat out from under him for his return to the dealership.

He could see Tommy on the phone and sitting at his huge, hand-carved teak desk. Mark knocked politely on Tommy's glass door, and he waved him in. As he sat down, Tommy hung up the phone. He normally dressed casual, but today he was wearing a grey sharkskin suit. Tommy eyed the orthotics he was wearing with skepticism. "Wow, that's some get-up you got there. That was Ashley from AmericaSure on the phone. She says you threatened her with a lawsuit, and your new doctor charges twice as much as Primary Care. Is this true?" asked Tommy in an accusatory tone. He had his elbows propped up on his desk and hands folded, his demeanor demanding an explanation.

"Yes, and I will explain that to you, boss, but first, here's the updated paperwork I'm supposed to give you from my doctor on my Workmen's Comp case." He handed Tommy the X-rays and medical opinion from Dr. Pharr's office, including his new work restrictions.

Mark took a seat and leaned back in his chair, wanting to create a more relaxed posture with Tommy and reduce the tension between them. He was feeling defensive. "My number one goal here is to heal and regain full use of my hand, fingers, wrist, and shoulder. While I enjoy selling cars here at Brandson, there is really nothing more important to me than my health. With all due respect, I'm sure you can understand that." He paused, letting that sink in a bit.

"Sure, makes sense. Go on." Tommy could tell he had more to say, so he gave him some latitude and gestured for him to continue.

"Did you know that Primary Care was claiming my injuries were pre-existing conditions and they were refusing to treat most of them? Also, Primary Care Group has been the target of one hundred and eighty-seven patient complaints just in the last year. Some complaints were about malpractice, and some similar to my situation where they refused proper treatment. They are genuinely lucky to still be in business, and may not be by the end of the year." After his first less-than-satisfactory visit, Mark had gone online and retrieved the information from the AMA, the County Health Department, and Florida Workmen's Comp Administrative website.

"No, I didn't know that. Does Human Resources know this?" Tommy knew Mark did his homework, which is why he liked to put him on special projects that required a certain level of initiative and creativity.

"Not yet. I wasn't sure if it was my place to tell them. What's even more interesting is that copies of these complaints were sent to all the insurance carriers in the State of Florida who are licensed Workmen's Comp providers, including our carrier, AmericaSure. So, our carrier was already notified of the many complaints filed against Primary Care. But they send our employees there anyway."

"Well, Mark, while I applaud your investigative work, I'm sure you understand it's my job to control costs and keep our overhead as low as I can, right?" Tommy leaned back on his chair, now, calculating a way to regain control without seeming too heavy-handed.

"And I've been happy to help you with that over the years, as you've asked," said Mark. "You need to know that my doctor at TOI has prescribed physical therapy twice a week, and I need to follow through with this if I want to avoid shoulder surgery. The surgery would cost AmericaSure and Brandson Automotive about eighty-five thousand dollars. Therapy's cheaper." Mark smiled, knowing Tommy wouldn't argue this point. He was all about the money.

"How long will that go on. The therapy?" Tommy was looking to get his arms around the total cost of care for his crippled employee.

"I think he said four to six months. Would you let Larry and Bryan know so I can do the therapy twice a week without getting a hard time? They've been razzing me about faking my accident and injuries. You saw the video of my accident, right boss?"

"Yeah, hey, don't worry about them. They're just messing with you." Tommy laughed nervously, but Mark wasn't sure how to take Tommy on this. He knew Tommy was likely behind all the pressure for a premature return to work. Tommy was a tournament-level poker player, and he didn't get to be the general manager at Brandson without knowing how to play his cards.

Mark decided it was time to be more direct with his boss and lay more cards on the table. "Tommy, let me ask you something. Do you think Larry was messing with me when he threatened to fire me if I prosecuted Dennis for threatening to slit my throat and bash my head in with a phone a few weeks ago?"

Tommy got upset. "What? Mark, I can't believe you're bringing that up. Don't take him seriously on this stuff, that's just Larry's way. I heard something about that. You gotta let go of that. You guys are both great salesmen. Are you and Dennis getting along better? I'd hate to lose either one of you." The thinly-veiled threat didn't deter him from wanting some answers, and Mark could tell that he'd caught Tommy off guard. He wanted to gauge his boss's reaction. Tommy shifted his weight nervously and took a sip from the bottle of water on his desk.

"Okay. Let's give it some time. In the meanwhile, let's get you back on the floor selling cars today. You've had a week off now, so you should be all rested up. You got anything else you want to bring up? I've got a lunch appointment with our CFO, Bob Gregory." Tommy stood up.

"Tommy, we've always had a good relationship. Can we keep a problem I'm having just between us if I share something with you? Larry will make my life miserable if he hears that we spoke about this."

"Sure. What is it?" Mark was still not sure if he was on solid ground with his boss, but decided to take a chance. Tommy had a good poker face, pretending he had no idea what Mark might be bringing up.

"Several of the guys, *and* myself, have had some irregularities with our paychecks in the last few months. I've been underpaid about eight thousand dollars in gross commissions just in the last three months and I know several of the others have too. When I try to talk to Larry about it, he says its dealer cash, or a lender re-fi, or a mistake someone else made. But his explanations never really make any sense. I know all the dealership's profits go to the managers, but I just want to make sure that I get paid the money I earn."

"You said Larry reviewed this?" asked Tommy.

"Yes sir, but the explanations don't add up," said Mark.

"Okay, I'll look into it, but right now, I gotta run." They shook hands, and Mark had this uneasy feeling that nothing was going to happen. He knew Larry did all of Tommy's heavy lifting and dirty work so Tommy could stay squeaky clean.

He sat down at his desk after the conference with Tommy, trying to figure out how to work his keyboard and phone with just his left hand. Booting up his computer, he forgot what his passwords were and had to look them up. He wondered if the meds were affecting his memory. He decided he would try and skip the painkillers during the day and take them only at night.

"Hey, look whose back. Enjoy your vacation?" Raj stood in front of him, grinning, holding a blue deal jacket in one hand and a half-eaten jar of peanuts in the other.

"Hey, Raj, will you come to the restroom and help me?" asked Mark. "I gotta take a piss, but my doctor said not I'm not supposed to lift anything heavy."

"Ha! You wish. So, what did you and Tommy talk about?" asked Raj.

"Have a seat and I'll tell you what's going on." He knew Raj wouldn't be able to resist hearing all the latest gossip. He grabbed one of the empty chairs and sat down, setting his jar of peanuts on Mark's desk.

"Want some?" Raj unscrewed the lid and tipped the jar toward him.

"No thanks. Trying to quit. Raj, your reputation as a behind-the-scenes crazy maker is catching up with you." Mark adjusted his arm sling and wrist splint while he waited for a reaction.

"What d'ya mean?" Raj's dumb blonde act needed some work, and Mark wasn't falling for it. He leaned forward, laying out his free arm on his desk for emphasis.

"Why are you going around telling everyone that I planned this accident and purposely stepped in front of Danziger's car? You really think I'd intentionally step in front of a moving car to injure myself to collect Workmen's Comp benefits? Really?" Mark was calm, expecting a straight answer, knowing he'd be lucky if he got one.

"I was joking around, that's all. Can I joke around a little?" Raj was popping peanuts into his mouth like he was sitting in a theater watching a movie, obviously entertained by the effects of his smoke-and-mirror antics. He loved stirring the honey pot so he could watch the bees fly around while everyone else got stung.

"Well, you've convinced some of the guys and our managers that I engineered this whole thing. Truth is, my right wrist and finger are broken, and I've got a torn rotator cuff. That sound like fun? It'll take six months to a year to heal."

Raj thought about this for a moment. "Well, guess you'll just have to jerk off with your left hand now, huh?" Raj laughed at his joke. McGreedy, who was walking by, overheard this and broke out laughing. Mark couldn't ignore the humor.

"Hey, Mark, welcome back." Brent was walking by, customer in tow, adding over his shoulder, "Hey, watch out for backing cars, man! Especially those hard-to-see bright yellow ones."

"Everyone's a wise guy," said Mark. He smiled at the humor, knowing he was unable to stem the flow of comedy at his expense. Apparently, his co-workers were glad to see him back. Maybe they were thinking that he'd be less competition now that he was on the injured list. Or maybe they were just sickos, he wasn't sure.

"Dude, what's up?" Now it was Scott's turn to razz him. "I see you got a new place to hide your oxycontin!"

"Yeah, you caught me. That's why I'm wearing all this crap. So I can stash my drugs. When do you take delivery of your new Sea Ray?"

"This weekend. The captain is sailing her here next week. Like you suggested, he's making a list of equipment that's gonna be replaced under the warranty." He checked out Mark's orthotics more closely, pulling on his sling. "Does that hurt? Looks like you may have to wait on your cruise, there, Captain. I've got a customer. I'll catch up with you later." He headed back to his desk to work his deal.

Mark turned his attention back to Raj, still seated at his desk. "Hey, I heard that Larry's running way behind this month on the new car sales target. Must be because he didn't have me here for the past two weeks, right?" Raj smirked, expressing his distaste at the idea that Mark could be responsible for any of the success that Brandson enjoyed.

Mark continued. "We have two more days to the end of January, counting what's left of today. Tomorrow's the thirty-first. How many cars does he need to get out?"

Raj looked at him askance. "As of right now, he has to sell fifty-two cars to get his hundred thousand dollar monthly bonus from Toyota." Raj raised his eyebrows, indicating his skepticism that Larry would be able to make it to the big money bonus.

"That's a big nut to meet for less than two days left." Mark didn't see how he could do it this time. He certainly wasn't going to buy another car just to help Larry get his bonus. Larry had already coerced him into buying three. He touched Raj's deal jacket. "At least you got one here, right?"

"Yeah, it's just a flat, though. But, they all add up." Raj shrugged and picked up his deal jacket, heading to his desk to finish his paperwork.

Mark busied himself with service follow-ups and phone calls on unsold "be-back" customers for the next hour. He set an appointment with Jack Shaw on a new Tundra. Later, when he came in at five o'clock with his wife, he sold him a new Tundra XSP. It was a flat, but it had put him back in the saddle and kept him busy until seven o'clock. It was his first sale since the accident with Danziger and his panty-less fiancée.

Expecting that Bryan would allow him to leave early under his new "light duty" hours, he got up to let them know he was leaving. He walked over to the drinking fountain and popped a pain pill, hoping it would kick in just as he got home. As he made his way down the hallway approaching the sales tower, he heard Bryan say to the used car manager, "Way to go, Tony. Our best customer of the day! Nineteen cars! You rock, man! Your part of that new car bonus is about eight grand!" Then he heard a loud high-five just as he walked past the sales tower. Wandering toward his desk, he blended in as if nothing happened.

Then he heard Bryan's voice. "Hey, Mark, need to talk to you for a second." Bryan looked serious, so Mark walked back into the tower to talk to his new car manager. Bryan didn't look very friendly.

"Hey, on that Moore deal two days ago, Paul says he's been talking to them for weeks about them buying a new Tundra, so that's going to be his deal." Bryan was pretty matter-of-fact about taking yet another hard-earned deal out of his dwindling paycheck.

Mark did not react well to this news. He tried to appeal to Bryan's sense of fair play. "Wait. Bryan, when they came in, they didn't ask for anyone, including Paul, and when I blue sheeted them and set their file up in the CM system, there were no notes and no file on either of them. Where's there any proof of McGreedy's claim on that deal?" He had spent four hours making that deal happen, and he didn't want to lose it to McGreedy's subterfuge.

"He showed me his cell phone where they called him. Sorry, but I'm giving that deal to him," Bryan said with an air of finality. "Just go find yourself another one." Bryan picked up the phone and ushered Mark out, but Mark wasn't done.

"Bryan, you know those aren't the rules. You've taught us for years that if there is no file in CM, and the customer doesn't ask for anyone, and no proof of prior contact, then the customer is ours to work and sell. Now, I followed your rules, and worked hard to sell that Tundra to the Moores, and I think I deserve their business. You can't keep taking deals away from me and giving them to Paul because he's your drinking buddy." Hearing this, Kirk's ears perked up, waiting to see how Bryan would react to Mark's challenge.

Bryan slammed his phone down and stood up, clearly annoyed. In an effort to intimidate him, he yelled, "I'm giving it to Paul. He's says he's known them for years, and I believe him. That's it. We're done here. Don't you have to go to rehab tonight?" Bryan was angry.

Without saying another word, Mark turned and walked out of the sales tower. He could see the dishonesty getting worse and worse, and the managers were becoming more blatant about steering deals to their friends instead of following the rules and giving the business to the reps who'd earned it.

As he walked back to his desk to log off, it dawned on him what that earlier high-five actually meant. They just talked Tony into faking the purchase of nineteen new cars so they could con Toyota out of their six-figure sales bonus. He tossed that around in his head as he walked out to employee parking, fairly certain of what he'd heard on the desk. There's no way this stuff could be legal. It was fraud, and he felt bad for Toyota.

The next morning, January 31st, was the last day of the commission month. Things were bound to get a little crazy. As he pulled in to Brandson, he thought he could see a long line of new Camrys, Corollas, and Avalons with a big yellow "Certified Used" sticker on the windshield parked out front at the main entrance and stretching in a long line along the front pad. This got Mark's attention. Instead of walking in the side door from the service lanes, he walked around to the front entrance to check this out.

These areas were typically reserved for the display of new cars. Sure enough, there were nineteen brand new "Certified Used" Toyotas that weren't there the night before, parked all around the front entrance to Brandson. Not one of them had more than thirty miles on their odometer. He jotted down the VIN numbers to three of them. He decided he would check and see if he could locate these vehicles in contact management to check on the document trail.

Once inside at his desk, he logged into the CM system just like he did everyday. He found the file he wanted. Anthony J. Grimes, their used car manager and part-time bodyguard. There, he found nineteen "new Toyota purchases" for a "sale price" that was exactly identical to the amount "financed" on each car. According to the file, the purchase price, trade-in value, and amount financed were all identical figures. He knew this was impossible, and that the figures had to be fabricated. The VIN numbers matched on three of the new cars, and he was sure that if he'd checked all nineteen, he'd find all nineteen cars parked right out front and inventoried into the floor plan as "certified used" cars. He was glad Larry's day off was Wednesday. If he'd been at work today, he may have noticed

Mark jotting down the VIN numbers. Thankfully, no one seemed to be aware of his covert investigation.

He had no idea that Anthony J. Grimes was so wealthy that he was approved by lenders to finance nineteen separate, brand new Toyotas, all within one hour. According to the time stamps on the deals, all of the "sales" had taken place within sixty minutes. Mark knew they would have had to commit bank fraud to get those deals approved. Now he knew that Toyota was probably being defrauded out of millions of dollars of faked bonuses, depending on how far back the frauds went.

Seeing his managers faking new car sales made his stomach churn. He had no desire to work in a crime scene and felt he had reached a turning point. Not feeling at all good about these developments, he was trying hard to remember the last time he felt good about anything at Brandson.

FOURTEEN

Brad Danley was a little OCD about what he allowed to stay on his desk at the FBI's office in Gainesville. He almost discarded the note written on the back of the Brandson Toyota business card that his assistant placed on his desk at eight o'clock this morning. He kept reading the note, trying to decide how much credibility he should give it. Deciding to hang onto it, his intuition told him this was not a prank and could be something serious. The block printing on the back of the card read: $70 MILLION FRAUD, MAILBOX BOMBED, CALL ME 352.231.2997.

As the highest-ranking FBI agent in the county, it was Advanced Officer Brad Danley's responsibility to prioritize how he used the modest resources he had at his disposal at the field office. With the government cutbacks, his staff had been reduced from seven to four, and he was hearing rumors that his current staff of three agents and one assistant might be cut back even more. Three years ago, budget considerations had forced the district office supervisor in Jacksonville to move them out of a three thousand square foot facility to their modest accommodations located downtown on the fourth floor of the bank building.

Much had changed since Danley graduated in the second quartile of his class at Quantico. Unafraid of hard work, he had attained six advancements in seventeen years of service with the Bureau. Although he was feeling a little burnt out at the age of forty-five, he held the rank of Advanced Officer III. Although he'd passed his last fitness test, he was losing the battle of the bulge, and what was left of his hair had turned solid grey. Working in jeans or Dockers helped him blend in when dealing with the "good ole boy network" that dominated local politics. The limp he carried was a reminder of a drug bust gone bad in New Orleans fourteen years ago when he was shot in the leg by a drug-crazed Cajun drug dealer who had committed suicide during his arrest. With a wife who taught college-level computer forensics and two teenage kids, he and his family were comfortable with the laid-back lifestyle of north Florida. Major crimes, high-level frauds and bombings were rare in this area, so this tip came as a surprise to him.

As he leaned forward to boot up the six computer monitors at his desk, he began his search for images of the person who left the note. Scanning through fourteen hours of time lapsed digital video in a matter of seconds, he found the images of his informant. He appeared at their outer security door at seven twenty-five last night wearing an arm sling, red Toyota shirt, and tan slacks. A nice-looking middle-aged white male who didn't look at all like a prankster. Using facial recognition software, Danley ran checks in NCIB data banks to find out more about his informant. He found a file that matched the name on the card.

"Fran, can you put a fresh pot of coffee on for me?" asked Danley.

"Sure, Brad. You going to be here a while?" she asked.

"Probably 'til noon," answered Danley.

"Where's Frank?" Special Agent Frank Moser was his senior agent. If he could get the informant to come in, he wanted Moser with him when he interviewed this McAllister guy. His other field agent, James Costello, was an economic crimes specialist who was out of town attending specialized training in Jacksonville.

"Said he was on his way fifteen minutes ago. Coffee should be ready in about five minutes." Fran dropped the court docket file on his desk and picked up his empty coffee cup.

"Thanks, Fran." He dialed Mark McAllister on the unlisted house phone, wondering what kind of far-fetched story he was going to hear from this guy. When it came to car salesmen, he trusted them about as far as he could throw them.

The cell phone rang three times before he heard a male voice. "Hello, this is Mark."

"Mr. McAllister, Agent Danley, FBI. Are you the one who left a note in our door last night?"

"Yes sir."

Danley paused to get his notepad ready. "So, what's going on at Brandson? I'm assuming the fraud you speak of is allegedly occurring at Brandson Toyota?"

"Yes, that's right. For several months now, I've been conflicted about what to do about all the fraud going on here. I've also witnessed what looks like money laundering, forgery, and income tax evasion." He paused, and hearing no response from Danley, continued. "My mailbox was blown up in an attempt to intimidate me. And, there's more you should know."

"Okay. Do you have any proof?" Agent Danley was a little skeptical of such allegations. In his experience, they often involved hidden agendas or petty personal issues.

"I sure do. I work at Brandson, so I have access to most of their customer files and a lot of the transaction documents."

"Are you involved in any of these frauds?" asked Agent Danley.

"No, sir," Mark said. "Typically, my customers were defrauded *after* we agreed to the price and terms of the deal. When they met with the F&I guys."

"F&I guys?"

"Finance and insurance, separate managers who close the title transfers and loan documents. They also sell extended warranties and service agreements to customers, sometimes without consent."

Danley had a light schedule, and the informant's information intrigued him. He was curious to see how deep the rabbit hole went. "When can you come in and talk to us?" asked Danley.

"This is my only day off of the week. I usually work on Thursdays, but I could come in and talk with you in about forty-five minutes. Can I remain anonymous? These guys are dangerous."

"C'mon in. We'll talk about it."

"You want to say, ten o'clock? Uh . . . what should I bring with me?"

"Bring everything you have. We'll figure out what we need after we meet." Danley was following the FBI playbook, step by step.

Mark was nervous about the meeting. He knew he'd opened Pandora's box. A little unsure of himself, he decided to move forward anyway. "Okay, Agent Danley. See you at ten."

The skies ahead were an ominous dark blue and the rain made the already chilly February day feel colder. The trip across town took a little longer than usual, with the local drivers ahead of him overreacting to the light rain. With these pokey drivers, Mark wondered if everyone in this town was either retired or getting paid by the hour. No one ever seemed to be in a hurry. He remembered what it was like driving in south Florida where they did fifty-five on their lawn mowers. Anyone driving the limit down there would wind up with tire tracks up their backs. Often impatient with the leisurely pace of local traffic, he did appreciate the fact that when drivers waved at you, at least they used all five fingers.

He parked in the parking garage on the west side of the four story bank building and walked to the bank of elevators. As he waited for the doors to open, he noticed the marquis on the wall next to the elevator with an entry that read "Federal Offices." There was no mention of the FBI's presence in the building. Stepping into the elevator, he could see the bank customers milling about in the lobby, likely unaware of the FBI offices upstairs. The arm sling was cumbersome, and he was still getting used to having his bulging attache case strapped over his left shoulder instead of his right. There were ultra HD facial recognition security cameras everywhere, two in the parking garage, two in the elevator lobby, and two more on the elevator ceiling. They were state-of-the-art and could be controlled remotely from the internet. The FBI was well-prepared to identify threats before they could pose a danger to their offices upstairs.

When he stepped off the elevator on the fourth floor, he noticed more security cameras and sensors located about every ten feet along the hallway leading to the main entry door. There were another three cameras focused on the door from different angles. Unsure of which camera was active, he smiled, waved at all of them and pressed the call button.

He heard a female voice answer. "Yes?"

"Mark McAllister, here to see Agent Danley."

"Be with you in a minute," said the woman's voice.

After a few moments, he heard a loud electronic buzzer go off, releasing the door. Mark pushed it open and stepped inside. There were more cameras and a scanning machine with a conveyor located just inside the small entry. A bald, beefy middle-aged FBI agent was watching the scanner screen and waved him through the detection device. Another grey-haired agent stood on the other side of the steel mesh divider that separated the entry area from the rest of the office. The grey-haired agent standing furthest from Mark was studying him.

"Mr. McAllister, will you put your attaché case down on the conveyor?" asked the tough-looking agent closest to him who directed his screening. Mark did as he was instructed. A moment later, a second electronic buzzer sounded, releasing a gate that opened into the office.

"You can pick up your attaché case and come on through." As he did so, the agent with the grey hair and blue jeans walked up and introduced himself.

"I'm Special Agent Danley. This is my associate, Agent Moser." With his right arm encumbered in the sling, Mark awkwardly shook his hand, and Agent Danley led him inside.

"You'll have to excuse all the security," said Danley. "We get threats and have to be prepared for anything. Have a seat." He was curious about Mark's orthotics. "Were you in an accident?" Mark took a chair and set his attaché case next to him on the floor.

"Yes sir, got hit by a car a few weeks ago," explained Mark. Agent Moser took a seat to his left, and Agent Danley leaned on the edge of the desk in front of them with a pad and pen. Moser looked like the tougher of the two. Danley seemed to have the people skills.

"Where'd that happen?" asked Agent Moser. He looked like a pro linebacker with deep-set brown eyes and a rugged face.

"One of my coworkers on pain meds backed a car into me a couple of weeks ago while he was having sex with his fiance in the front seat There's a rumor is he was paid to do it."

"Paid to have sex or paid to back into you?"

Amused by the unlikely scenario of Shock Top getting paid for sex, Mark smiled at Danley's question. "Uh, I meant paid to back into me."

"Really? That's interesting," said Danley. "Sounds like a fun place to work," he said dryly.

The stories Mark had heard about FBI agents lacking a sense of humor seemed to be accurate. Danley continued with no change in his expression. "Workmen's Comp taking care of it for you?" Mark nodded.

"So, besides people having sex in cars and running over employees, what else is going on at Brandson Toyota?" asked Danley. He held his pen, ready to jot down more juicy details.

Mark reached into his attaché case and pulled out four legal-sized file folders, placing them in his lap. The two agents looked at each other, curious about the files.

"Everything we talk about here is one hundred percent confidential, right? These guys at Brandson have underworld connections, and capable of turning violent at the drop of a hat."

"Of course. What do you mean by 'underworld connections'?" asked Danley.

"Tommy Catatonia's the general manager there, the general sales manager is Larry Wells, and the unofficial chief information officer and tech lackey is a guy named Rocky Gambrone. Word is that they all have connections with organized crime figures. They've got fully-auto assault rifles, including AR-15s and AK-47s. Theses guys brag about their weapons constantly, even showing photos of their guns to everyone at work. They actually brought in armor-piercing rounds to the dealership. They talk about having thousands of rounds of this type of ammo." Mark paused to adjust his sling.

"Do you know where they keep these weapons or what they're planning to do with them?" Moser looked concerned, and Danley was making notes as fast as he could.

"They've built concealed gun safes at their homes. Tommy lives here in town, and Rocky and Larry live in St. Augustine. They claim they only hunt with them, but-c'mon. Who needs armor-piercing rounds to hunt deer?" He waited for Danley to catch up with his notes before he continued.

"Guys, how 'bout some coffee?" Frances appeared from her office in the back holding three mugs in one hand and a freshly-brewed pot of coffee in the other. She set it down on the desk next to Danley.

"I'm a little concerned about the armor-piercing rounds, Mark. Okay if I call you Mark?" asked Danley.

"Sure, and the coffee sounds good. Cream and sugar, if you have it." He was starting to feel a little more relaxed with these guys, and felt relieved that they seemed interested in what he had to say. His first impressions about the agents had proven correct. Agent Moser seemed more like the enforcer, and Agent Danley had the better skills when more diplomacy or finesse was called for.

"Call me Brad. Frank's the musclehead. And this is Fran," said Agent Danley. Fran was pouring three cups of coffee on the desk next to Brad. "I'll be right back. Let me know if you need anything," she said. He did a double take on Fran because she looked so much like a thin version of Mrs. Doubtfire.

"So, what else we got here, Mark?" Danley was anxious to hear more.

"Well, there's a lot of criminal activities that you should be aware of. I'm not sure how much of it falls within your jurisdiction. They brag about their bank frauds, forgeries, and defrauding Toyota out of millions of dollars in bonus money. There's the tax evasion, fake warranties, price packing, misrepresentation. The list goes on. Also, they wire their illegal profits to overseas accounts. Isn't that money laundering?""

"How do you know they have overseas accounts?" asked Moser.

"I've overheard them talk about it. And, I made a copy of one." Mark pulled a copy of a wire transfer from his file and handed it to Danley. The agents took an immediate interest in the document.

"You might be right, but that's not my call. Sounds like you've done some homework here." Brad took a sip from his coffee, still wanting to be convinced. Mark knew they needed hard evidence.

"I've seen it go on everyday. Here's a summary I prepared of the crimes and who's responsible for them. I have a buddy who I trained there. He's former law enforcement. He may be willing to help us. Here's, ah . . . some supporting documentation . . . I printed up, ah . . . fifty-two fake car deals . . . from their internal files." He was fumbling through his files, but his arm sling got in the way. Ignoring the pain, he slipped his arm out of the sling.

"Here, let's lay your files out on the desk, make it easy," said Danley. Mark handed the documents to him, and Moser helped pick up the loose pages Mark had dropped. They squinted at the printed screen shots from the contact management software, asking questions to get a better understanding of what they were looking at.

Danley looked up from the screen shots. "We have a third agent assigned here. Special Agent Costello, our economic crimes specialist. He'll be back tomorrow. I'd like to share this information with him. Would you mind if we made copies?"

"Feel free to make copies of any of these documents, but I can't give you these. They're my only copies." Mark wasn't ready to mention the digital files stored on his computer.

"Fran, let's use the high-speed copier on these. Go ahead and copy all four files. Is that okay with you, Mark?" asked Danley.

"Sure." Mark nodded in agreement. He wanted to get them moving on the investigation. Relieved to see such civility from law enforcement officers, he felt like a crushing weight was being lifted off his shoulders.

They made duplicate files of all the documents that Mark had brought with him. The three men spent another hour huddled over the files he'd brought in. Mark answered a litany of specific questions about the significance of certain figures and the meanings of terms commonly used in the car business. Together, they reviewed more than two hundred documents covering thirty-eight months of criminal activity at Brandson. He was clear with the agents in explaining that he didn't have access to the AX Management and ERA Financing Systems at Brandson. These were the software programs that would give them more of the specific details in any individual transaction. The bank financing agreements in the ERA system identified who the bank lenders were on each deal, and he explained that he wasn't sure which of the lenders were participants in the frauds.

The FBI agents expressed their appreciation for the "Mob-style" pyramid diagram Mark had drawn up, a detailed illustration that laid out the various positions and functions of the entire Brandson organization.

"Where did you get the idea for the diagram, Mark?" asked Moser.

"Oh, some movie I saw. You know, the one with Denzel Washington and Russell Crowe. I'm trying to remember—"

"American Gangster," said Danley.

"That's it," said Mark. "You sound like a movie buff."

"Netflix member," said Danley. "Mostly for my kids."

"Do yourself a favor, Brad. Buy the stock."

After touching on the Netflix stock purchase idea, Mark took the time to update the agents with a summary of the nineteen civil complaints prepared by John Dunne, the local Director of the Consumers Against Crimes. He explained that CVC had settled twelve of the nineteen customer cases in out-of-court settlements totaling one hundred seventeen thousand dollars, all of which was returned to the victims. There were new cases cropping up every week at CVC, and Mark explained how Brandson was using bribes to suppress the news story with the local media.

Mark called the dealership and rescheduled his one o'clock appointment so he could finish his briefing with the FBI agents. They had a lunch of sub sandwiches, and after three hours, they concluded their initial meeting. Danley prepared a list of additional information that he needed from Mark and gave him an email address to send it to. The agents suggested certain security measures be taken, including his use of the code name "KG" to protect his identity.

The criminal investigation of Brandson had the potential to become one of the largest economic crime cases in the history of Alachua County.

FIFTEEN

At seven thirty the next morning, he headed for work. He wanted to get there before any of the managers arrived to print out some super-sensitive customer transaction files to scan and send over to CVC and his new friends at the top of the bank building downtown. With his new radical change in direction, Mark had turned a corner in his career at Brandson. He was sailing in uncharted waters. There was a storm brewing on the horizon, and the Friday morning sales meeting was scheduled to begin in an hour-and-a-half. He needed to finish this task before the sales staff started streaming in.

On his drive in to the dealership, Mark reflected on his new role as an informant for the FBI. He had spent month's weighing his choices as to how to deal with the daily corruption at Brandson and was left with only two viable options: quit, or try and change the way that Brandson does business. After more than three years of trying to right the ship, he was weary of watching his customers get defrauded.

Never in his life had he felt so compelled to become a whistle-blower. As he thought about his new responsibilities in taking on the role of confidential informant, his job situation began to have a surreal feel, almost like there was no longer any ground under his feet to support him.

He weighed Tommy and Larry's objections to his twice-a-week physical therapy. It was painfully obvious to him that none of the managers gave a rat's ass about his well being. The latest X-rays showed that therapy wasn't healing his torn rotator, and he had only partial use of his right arm and hand. As much as he tried to avoid it, he knew arthroscopic surgery was in his future. This morning, arriving early gave him the pick of the best parking spots, and he entered the dealership from a side entrance.

Once he was in front of his work station, he noticed Jo was the only employee present in the dealership. She would be busy with incoming service calls and the showroom was his alone for about forty minutes. He booted up his computer, logged on, and searched for the two customer files that he knew contained the fake car deals. He brought up the Grimes and McCombs files and hit the print button on each of the forty-eight fake deals. He could hear the printer in the sales tower whining as it powered up as he began making the trips in and out of the sales tower to snag his prints as soon as they were available. He could feel his heart racing as he double checked the paper tray to make sure the printer wasn't going to run out of paper and print his screen shots at an awkward time.

"Hey, Mark, whatcha printing up, there? Ya writing a book or something?" Jo had been watching him run back and forth into the sales tower, and now her curiosity was aroused. She also was not a fan of the corruption at Brandson and he often heard her say "someday this rodeo's going to end. They always do." Still, he wasn't willing to bet his life on her discretion.

"Lead lists and customer files for follow-up, Jo. Nothing as exciting as what you do up there at reception." He was hoping she would stay put at her desk until he could finish printing.

"An extra gold star for being in so early. Maybe they'll give you a raise." Amused by her own joke, she chuckled and turned her attention to her switchboard.

"When pigs fly," said Mark from across the showroom. He checked his watch. Forty-five minutes had gone by, and reps would be drifting in now. Almost finished, the last few prints were coming out. He grabbed them and quickly walked back to his desk, stuffing them into a special file with the others in his attaché case. As he did so, he felt the drops of perspiration rolling down his face and onto the prints. He switched computer screen images to display today's service ups so that his work would look routine to anyone walking by. Then he spotted Scott coming in the front door, checking out all the "certified" new cars out front.

"Hey Marky-Mark, you ever seen so many 'certified' used Toyotas before?" Standing in the middle of the showroom, he made the air quotes as he said the word 'certified'.

"Why, no Scott. What do you make of that?" said Mark, tongue firmly in cheek. While Scott was not a big fan of the rampant corruption at Brandson, Mark still didn't trust him. Scott was somewhat of an opportunist.

As he was on his way to his desk, Scott stepped closer to Mark and lowered his voice. "Looks to me like they'll do just about anything to get that big fat Toyota new car bonus. What do you think, Marky-Mark?"

In an equally-conspirational tone, Mark answered, "They think they're too pretty for jail." Then he reached into his pocket and held out a dollar bill, stretching it between his hands. "In God we trust, right Scott?"

He knew Scott was all about the money. From the far side of the showroom, Scott said, "You got that right! Hey, where's your sling?"

"Dumped it." Now he could see more sales reps streaming in from employee parking, walking across the service drive into the side doors. They walked quickly, hoping to avoid the late fines the "Devil" was likely to levy.

"Hey, you don't have your sling," said Rich. He had stepped over to Mark's desk wearing his famous black cop boots, Terminator sunglasses and short crew cut. He still looked like a cop, not always resembling the nice guy that he was. "Hey, you ever hear anything back from forensics on that mailbox bombing?"

"They're still clueless. No prints. Nothing." He wanted to tell him about his meeting with the FBI, but there were too many people around. Earlier in the week, they both agreed to use the code words "those guys" whenever they referred to the FBI and IRS.

It was five minutes before nine. Just as he was ready to walk toward the meeting room with Rich, he spotted a customer walking in the front door. He was Mark's be-back from last week, hot for a new 4WD Tundra double cab. Last week the customer wasn't ready to close the deal, claiming he wanted to do a little more research. Mark went up to greet him and gauge his motivation today, hoping that he could skip the brain damage from the sales meeting if he was with his customer.

"Hi, Doug. Good to see you. If I can get you the price and terms you want on that Tundra, are you ready to own it today?" They shook hands enthusiastically, and Mark could see his customer was in a more amiable mood than he was a few days ago.

"Yes sir, let's find out how close we can get to where I need to be," said Doug. "You ready to give me the deal I'm looking for?" In his eighties now, and wearing his trademark Farmer John denim overalls complete with red flannel shirt, Doug was a retired melon farmer with five hundred acres that had become too much work to farm himself. So, he leased all his property to his sons, content to collect his four thousand dollar monthly check so he could hang out with his grandkids in his retirement.

As he and Doug walked to his desk, they passed Rich on his way to the meeting. "I'll tell Larry you've got a customer," said Rich.

"Thanks." Mark couldn't think of a better way to skip all the garbage that Larry was sure to dump on them. Several reps now referred to it as the "Friday Morning Beating."

Forty minutes later, following a presentation and negotiation, he was sitting with Doug and completing the paperwork on his new 4WD Tundra double cab. Mark had reduced his commission to seven hundred dollars in order the make the deal work. He did some extra pleading with Bryan, reminding him that his customer was now a three-time buyer.

To show his appreciation for Mark's work in getting him a better deal, Doug referred him to his daughter-in-law who was in the market for a small economy car under twelve grand.

Later on, Rich had finished with his customer and made his way over to his desk again. "Larry was the Devil himself in the meeting this morning," he said. He sat down heavily at Mark's desk. His buddy looked tired.

"How bad was it?" Mark cocked his head, wanting to hear the details from the meeting that he'd missed. "What other really nasty stuff did Larry unload on the masses today?" He knew the managers were disgusted with his rehab and medical care.

Rich lowered his voice and leaned forward. "Just being his normal abusive self. I think McGreedy was drunk again. Larry was really on your case, too, making all these sarcastic comments about your pain meds and restricted hours because of your "fake accident." Rich smirked. He and Mark were getting fed up from all the lies and nonsense, but neither was ready to quit.

"Keep a secret?" Mark had to tell him about his meeting yesterday, knowing it would buoy his mood by showing him the light at the end of the tunnel. Rich leaned closer so they could keep their voices down low.

"I spent four hours yesterday with 'those guys.' They know everything I know." He sat back to study Rich's reaction.

"Wow. There's the tidbit of the day," said Rich. "Did they seem interested in investigating?" Rich's experiences with federal agents was a little checkered, having mixed results on sharing cases with Federal agents during his seven-year stretch as a GPD computer forensics officer.

"Well, I spent four hours with them. They're interested in the crimes going on here, and they did mention coordinating with other law enforcement agencies." He gestured at his surroundings, adding, "This place has got to change. Not to sound too judgmental, but I've never seen such a cesspool of dishonesty. That's including all the smoke and mirrors I dealt with in twenty years on Wall Street."

Rich nodded in agreement. "I can't believe some of the stuff they're doing here. When I was at GPD, we prosecuted crimes a *lot* less serious than what's going on here."

"Tell me about it. I didn't meet their economics crime specialist because he was on a training assignment. I'll hook up with him next week. C'mon and ride with me. I've got to gas up a Tundra. There's more."

Rich nodded, looking forward to hearing what else was in the works to clean up the cesspool they shared. "Meet you out front. I'm driving," he said.

"Sure, fine. I'll grab the gas ticket," said Mark as he hit the print button on his keyboard for the gas voucher. He disappeared into the tower to retrieve it.

Rich was already in the driver's seat by the time Mark came out and hopped in the Tundra. "By the way, no more Danziger," said Mark as he buckled his seatbelt.

Rich looked over at him. "What? Why? Because of the accident?" He hit the accelerator a little too hard and drove over the curb on the turn onto Main Street. The bounce was so jarring that Mark was checking his fillings with the tip of his tongue.

"Watch out, Mario. Let's keep the next pit stop on the pavement," said Mark. "The story I got from Tammie in accounting was, last night, Kelley was working late in her office and heard some noises in the back parking lot. She breaks out a flashlight, walks out there and catches Danziger pulling scrap metal out of the dealership's scrap pile and putting it in his trunk. So, she calls the cops on him."

"Jeez. Unbelievable. This place is like a bad soap opera. Who would believe this stuff? So, what was Danziger doing pulling out scrap metal from Brandson's supply at midnight?" asked Rich.

"Apparently, he was selling the special alloys along with the platinum from the catalytic converters for some pretty good money," said Mark. "Only this time he got caught. He tried telling Kelley that he had the boss's permission when the cops came. The cops called Tommy and woke him up. Tommy said he didn't have permission and they fired him last night."

"This place really is unbelievable. I mean, you can't make this stuff up. So, they fire Danziger for stealing scrap metal, but not for running over your ass while having sex with his fiance in the car while he was doped up? What the hell, man?" Rich was incredulous.

"Yup," said Mark. "Some pretty weird priorities there." Mark thought about what a strange bird Danziger was. "No more drilling for brains, goose eggs, or running over sales reps.There goes some of the strangest entertainment ever offered by mankind." Things had gotten awkward with Danziger, and Mark wasn't going to miss him, but he could never figure out why the guy couldn't at least offer him an apology for backing over him with a car. Or maybe a weekend alone with his fiancé.

"So, what kinda game book are 'those guys' putting together?" asked Rich.

"Well, they said they're sharing the investigation with other agencies. GPD has original jurisdiction, the FTC has the trade issues, the US Attorney General has jurisdiction over the corporate fraud, Florida Department of Revenue has the state sales tax violations, and the State Attorney is all over the consumer fraud. I found out GPD detectives already had open files on Juicifer and Dennis Testi. Also, the Florida Division of Banking and Finance has jurisdiction over the bank fraud. Let's not forget my pal John Dunne at Consumers Against Crimes, with the nineteen civil complaints filed on the customer overcharges. We're sharing data, too. Who'd I leave out?" asked Mark.

"The NSA, the CIA and the KGB." Rich grinned with the irony in having so many law enforcement agencies already involved.

"Yeah, well, give it some time. Maybe we have enough heavy boots on the ground already. Right?" Mark held up his fist for the bump as the Tundra cruised north on Main Street with the deep-throated roar of all 5.6 liters.

"Right," agreed Rich. "You know, I have *never* worked in a place as screwed up as Brandson, and I've worked in some pretty screwed up places." He swerved the Tundra just in time to miss a bagwoman on a bike who veered out of the bike lane. Rich swore under his breath at the near miss. Mark crossed himself.

Forty minutes later, he finished delivering his customer's new Tundra, and Mark thanked him for his business and for referring his daughter-in-law scheduled to come in next week.

As he sauntered back to his desk, his attention was captured by the attractive, well-dressed woman in her late thirties wearing a Cache suede skirt ensemble sitting with Rich. She wore her straw-berry blonde hair up in a French twist, nicely complementing the grey-blue suede suit. He discretely admired her poise, his eyes dart-ing away when she looked in his direction. From her posture, he was sure that she had studied ballet at some point. She had the air of an executive, and he was sure she was the Law School Dean that Rich mentioned earlier at the Kangaroo.

In the middle of Mark's fantasy, Rich turned around to face him from his desk ten feet away. He asked, "Hey, Marky-Mark, do you know if the Prius Model V comes with the solar roof option?"

Not one to miss an opportunity for an introduction to a beauti-ful woman, Mark stepped over to Rich's desk. He smiled and said, "The solar roof comes with the Models III and IV, but not the V." Addressing the attractive woman dressed in suede, he added, "Which features are most important to you, ma'am?"

She looked at Rich, then back at Mark, saying, "Uh . . . leather, the upgraded stereo, navigation, and well, the solar package . . . "

"By the way, I'm Mark McAllister, and you're . . . ?"

"Dean Ross, School of Law. Please call me Michelle," she said, smiling.

"Michelle, the pleasure is all mine." She offered her hand. She had a gentle touch and he noticed the French manicure. He turned to Rich, and asked him, "How come you get all the good-looking women, Rich?" Rich shrugged, and Michelle laughed politely, adding, "C'mon, now, you guys probably say that to all the deans."

"Oh, no m'am, not at all," said Rich. "Mark's kind of a Prius expert, and we both want to give you great service. Let's make a list of the top three or four features that are most important to you." Mark hoped for her sake, and for Rich's, that the managers treated her right on her deal if they wanted to avoid the wrath of the College of Law.

"Let me get a Prius brochure," Mark said. He rummaged through his drawer and pulled out the newest Prius brochure and handed it to Rich. "I'll be right over here if I can be of further help." He spotted an older couple approaching. The white haired woman and her elderly husband were barely moving. Rolling his walker slowly across the showroom floor, the elderly man looked unsteady as she supported him. It was obvious they were looking for someone. Mark walked over and introduced himself before Raj or McGreedy could react.

"Hi, can I help you find someone?" Her husband was bald and very gaunt, and Mark guessed he was undergoing chemo treatment. His wife spoke first.

"Are you a manager, sir?" They both looked to be in their eighties.

Mark had gotten used to being mistaken for a manager, and it was obvious that this couple was upset and wanted to speak to a manager right away.

"No m'am, but I can help you find one. Can I tell him your name and maybe what you'd like to see him about?" She seemed very upset. "We're Mr. and Mrs. Eastman, and we came back to return our car and cancel our deal. My son is a lawyer, and he's on his way here now. He says we overpaid by eighteen thousand dollars. We just want our money back."

"I'm very sorry to hear that, m'am. Who was your salesperson?" It was hard not to feel sorry for an elderly couple in their situation. She pulled her yellow contract copies from a Brandson Toyota envelope she had stuck in the side of her purse and held it up close to her eyes so she could read it.

"Ah . . . , it says Jack Gates. That man is a liar! You see this signature here," pointing at the bottom line on the contract, "isn't even
our signature! We told him we didn't need any warranty stuff, and
he put it in there anyway and signed our name to it without our
permission!" She was so distressed that her glasses were fogging up.
Her husband stood next to her, heavily medicated and leaning on
his walker. After a moment, he nodded in agreement.

"Yes, ma'am. Can you tell me who your finance manager was?"
Mark could tell Juicifer had put these Q-tips through the ringer. If
what she said about the signature was true, they had jacked their
deal and forged her name.

"Ricky something . . . Gonzalez. That's it. Ricky Gonzalez. He's
the one who signed our name."

"Yes, ma'am," said Mark. He looked up to see a man approaching from across the showroom.

"Hi. I'm Peter Eastman and these are my parents. Are you a
manager?" The bald, middle-aged man wearing a dress shirt and
tie joined their group in the middle of the showroom. He reached
inside the pocket of his shirt and extended a business card to Mark.
On it was printed 'Peter M. Eastman, Attorney at Law'.

"No, sir, but let me get you one right now. Please wait here."
Mark turned and walked over to the sales tower, where Bryan was
sitting and watching the entire episode unfold. He seemed completely unfazed.

"Hey, Bryan, we got a problem here. We have a couple claiming that Rick forged their signature and Juicifer overcharged them
eighteen thousand dollars. Do you know about this deal?" Mark
handed the business card to him, waiting for him to say something.
Bryan didn't seem too surprised, acting as though he was expecting this.

"Yeah, be real nice to them when you go back over. Take them
into Rick's office. He's going to take care of it."

"Okay." Mark went back out to the family standing in the showroom. His intuition told him that they were telling the truth about
their bad deal. He had witnessed so many of these deceptions before.

They all knew Ricky and Juicifer had teamed up to do this dozens of times, amazed that they hadn't been put behind bars months ago.

"Mr. and Mrs. Eastman, will you please come with me? I'm going to take you over to Rick Gonzalez's office. Peter, I'm sorry your parents had this experience," said Mark as he led them across the showroom floor.

"Yeah, me too," said Peter, adding, "I sure hope they don't try to give us the run around again, because I'll put this whole thing in front of a judge in a heartbeat." The Eastman's were really upset, and Mark couldn't wait to drop them off with Rick and step back to watch the fireworks that would follow.

He led them to the other side of the showroom and into Rick's office, where Tricky Ricky waited like a spider in a web of deceit. Ricky reeked of cigarettes and had a disgusted look on his face as he met Mark at the door. He said nothing to Mark as he held the door open and ushered the three into the office.

"Hi, Mr. and Mrs. Eastman, and you must be Peter. I'm Rick Gonzalez. We're going to get everything worked out for you today."

"Yeah, well, we've heard that line before," said Mrs. Eastman.

After dropping off the Eastmans, Mark made his way back to the cafeteria to grab his lunch. As he approached the cafeteria doorway, he could hear Dennis, Juicifer, and McGreedy arguing about the Eastman fiasco and the penalties for committing fraud against the elderly. They were seated at a table in the back of the room and suddenly grew quiet as Mark entered. Without saying a word, he grabbed his lunch from the fridge and walked back out of the cafeteria, not wanting to share the room with the men who were so intent on destroying the dealership's reputation. As he looked toward the F&I offices on his way back to his desk, he spotted Tommy Catatonia entering Tricky Ricky's office for the big showdown with the Eastmans. He would love to be a fly on the wall for that conversation.

Sitting at his desk now, he unwrapped his turkey sandwich and punched up the Eastman file on his computer. Before he printed the details of their deal and the rest of the file, he looked over his shoulder to see who was on the desk beside the printer. Kirk was busy with his lunch, Larry was away from the desk, and Bryan had just headed back to the cafeteria. He hit the print button, gathered some other printed files of service follow-ups off his desk and headed toward the printer to retrieve the Eastman documents. As he grabbed the Eastman files from the printer, he put the service prints on the top of his stack of papers.

"What ya got there, Marky-Mark?" Kirk had a mouthful of beef and bean burrito, and being the sole manager presently on the desk, offered a token interest in Mark's activities.

"Gonna make a few service calls here, see if I can put some deals together," he said as he held up the handful of documents showing Kirk the service prints on top. He wasn't a very good liar, but Kirk bought it.

"Carry on. Bring me some used car deals, how 'bout it?" As Kirk turned his attention back to his Mexican feast, Mark was thankful for escaping with more incriminating documents to fuel the fires of investigation.

Back at his desk, he reviewed his customer files, looking for possible new deals. As part of his preparation for what he was planning when he got home, he went into the printer drop-down menu and selected the "Off Site" choice as the default setting. This would ensure his being able to print any internal file of his choosing in contact management from home, far removed from the prying eyes of his managers. From home, he could scan the documents and email them to anybody. Even to "those guys."

His plan to place the evidence into the hands of those who could bring change to the dealership was unfolding. The eradication of the denizens of the sewer had begun.

SIXTEEN

Mark forgot all about the frozen peas therapy for his shoulder and focused on booting up his home PC to print and scan the files that the FBI needed to further their investigation. He checked the list of items that Agent Danley had given him. After a minute, he was at his computer and in the Brandson CM database, printing screenshots of all the fake car deals and scanning them into his C-drive.

In order to maintain his anonymous status, he used the new email address with code name "KG" that he set up two days ago specifically for this purpose. He didn't want to give anyone an easy path to track. Brandson's attorneys would be unable to initiate any legal retaliation against an anonymous source known only as "KG." Without a source to trace, the redacted files could still be introduced into evidence for a criminal investigation during the discovery process without sacrificing his anonymity.

Along with the Eastman fraud files, Mark also emailed CVC and the FBI information about two more victims of fraud and forgery from the week before. This was in addition to over nineteen cases that CVC was already handling, with Juicifer, Dennis, Tricky Ricky, Raj, and Larry still at the center of most of them. GPD had initiated active investigations on all five of them. The magnitude of the frauds and forgeries Mark was exposing was beyond belief.

Consumers Against Crimes was lucky to have John Dunne as their volunteer supervisor. Before retiring a few years ago, Dunne spent almost three decades on the New York City Police Department, seven years as a decorated patrol officer, and twenty-one years as a detective, retiring as a lieutenant in the homicide division. Methodical and unrelenting in his pursuit of criminals, he was one of those cops who was always out there, searching around for evidence in the pursuit of his prey, never giving up.

This evening, Dunne was exchanging emails with "KG," an anonymous source of sensitive documents and information about corruption at Brandson Toyota. He was finding that there was a whole slate of crimes that were about to shake up this quiet little college town. The information that was being passed on to him by KG had proven very useful. Although he had a few ideas of who the confidential informant might be, he had promised to respect the CI's desire to remain anonymous in his phone conversations with him and protect his anonymity.

In almost three decades at the NYPD, Dunne had seen inform-ants disappear for a lot less than the seventy-million-dollar value of these Brandson frauds. He knew there was a significant level of risk his informant was facing, and Dunne was taking a personal interest in protecting his CI by offering his own experience and strategies to KG in order to help protect his identity. No one at CVC or the FBI wanted their informant's blood on their hands.

The weather in May was fairly unpredictable in Florida, and today the sky was overcast. The dark grey cumulus clouds in the west were moving fast, indicating a weather change was underway. Saturday was always the busiest sales day of the week at the dealer-ship, and Mark had come in early, hoping to score a few deals before it got too hot. It felt strange to be working both for, and against, his dealership at the same time, but he was getting used to it.

He found out later in the morning that Tommy Catatonia had refused to cancel the Eastman's purchase, and that this decision had thrown the Eastman family into a whole new dimension of pissed off that promised to provide some real fireworks at the dealership. By emailing Dunne all of the Eastman's contact information last night, Mark knew the timing of his call to the victims would be perfect in ensuring the filing of yet another civil complaint that Brandson would try to settle out-of-court. By avoiding a court trial, Brandson could sidestep the process of evidentiary discovery and prevent the unsavory stories from ever becoming public. As a result, potential victims continued to trickle in to the dealership everyday, unaware of the skullduggery that awaited them.

His reverie ended when he heard Rich's voice. "Meet me outside. Gotta talk to ya." Rich had just gotten off the phone and stood, ashen faced, at Mark's desk.

On the way to their 'grassy knoll', Mark asked, "How's all that Carla stuff coming, bro?" He was concerned that Carla's drug-crazed crime sprees were going to bring his friend down. With his wife either in jail, court, or on probation from day-to-day, Rich was forced to bear all the expenses of caring for his six-year-old daughter.

"She's been arrested again, DCF won't even let her visit me now, but that's not what I need to talk to you about. C'mon." Rich walked toward their rendezvous point outside beyond the service drive. Minutes later, he met Rich beside an FJ Cruiser on display on the far side of the used car lot.

"Sup? You look upset." Mark could tell his buddy wasn't getting a lot of sleep these days. He looked tired.

"You're gonna love this. You need to know that our desk phones can be used as remote listening devices." Rich wore his reflective cop glasses, so his eyes were hidden. He was in full cop mode.

"What do you mean? They're bugging us?"

"I found this out last night. Anyone, including a manager, can pick up their phone, dial in anyone else's four digit extension, and it goes into intercom mode after giving you a beep at your desk. I tested it this morning by dialing up McGreedy at his desk, who was busy talking dirt to his new girlfriend in the accounting office."

"Wow. Did not know that. So, you get a beep, but if you're already in a conversation at your desk, I can see how you may not notice it. That is certainly good to know, bro." From now on, Mark was going to be a whole lot more careful about what he said inside the dealership, convinced that most of Brandson's employees and managers were not above eavesdropping on their private conversations.

"I don't trust 'em," said Rich. "I wonder how many times we've been eavesdropped on already? So, let's not talk at all about 'those guys,' or anything about that stuff inside, right?"

"Agreed. Only out here, where we can see anyone coming or going." Mark looked around, then back at Rich. They would both be subject to immediate termination, or even far worse, if the managers knew they were helping the authorities investigate the dealership. The intercom-turned-eavesdropper was a major risk to avoid.

"Also, Mark, are you ready for this?"

"What?"

"I called my Dean, Dr. Ross, this morning to see how she's liking her Prius, 'cause yesterday, right before she drove off in her new car, it seemed like she wasn't very happy. She wouldn't tell me what was bugging her when she left."

"She's smart and gorgeous," said Mark. "If there was anyone they shouldn't mess with, it would be the Dean of the Law School." He squinted at his buddy. "Why would you even consider defrauding a professor who taught courses on business law? Hello?"

"Ya think?" parroted Rich.

"So, what happened?" asked Mark.

"That scumbag Rick bumped her payment a-hundred-fifty dollars a month, telling her that Toyota wouldn't agree to the zero percent financing unless the car was sold with a pre-paid Platinum ten year warranty. What a liar that guy is." Rich threw a jab into the air in anger.

"You have to be kidding. And he knew she's the Dean?" Mark was incredulous. "And the car already comes with a factory-paid three year bumper-to-bumper warranty. You explained that to her, right?"

"Sure did!"

"So, what's she want us—"

"Nothing. She found out the truth from Toyota USA's website, and she's sending them a certified letter accusing Rick Gonzalez and Brandson of fraud. She says she's happy with me, so she's leaving my name out of it."

"I swear, as God is my witness, you can't make this stuff up! The greed at this place is just out of control," said Mark.

"Tell me about it. Watch. They'll probably blame me, take five hundred dollars out of my check for a bad CSI, and take my two pounder away." Having said this, Rich looked pretty disgusted. Mark had a feeling in the pit of his stomach he was probably right.

"Anything I can do?"

"No, not right now. She likes us. She mentioned you, but don't call her. She's super pissed at Brandson management."

"That sucks, bro. If they take your commission away because of what Rick did . . . man . . . promise me we take them down *all* the way. They deserve to be locked up." They did a fist bump on this.

Suddenly, there was loud shouting coming from one of the service writer's offices two hundred feet away. They could see Lenny through the glass partition in his office standing behind his desk screaming at a young, skinny ghetto-looking guy with his pants hanging halfway off. They stood face-to-face, screaming obscenities while the man threatened Lenny with his fists.

"What the?" Mark decided he better walk over and help his friend out, and Rich followed. Before he got to the glass door, the customer threw a powerful right hook that landed on Lenny's left ear as he tried to duck, and a fight ensued. Lenny jumped out from behind his desk, grabbed the guy by his shirt and lifted him straight up, pinning him up against the glass with his feet dangling inches off the floor. Mark expected the glass to shatter, but it stayed intact. The customer was swinging his fists, trying to punch him, scream-ing, *"You mo———— fu————, I got a gun in my car and I'm gonna put a bullet in your head! You a dead man!"*

Before they could get to Lenny, two service writers appeared and pulled Lenny off the customer. Lenny was screaming, "I'm not let-ting this dirtbag go so he can get his gun! You're not goin' anywhere 'til the cops come!"

It took the two service writers and the service manager to get Lenny to back off. Three other guys were holding the brawler down on the floor while they waited for GPD to show up. There were dozens of customers watching through the glass from the customer service lounge at the bizarre scene.

Mark stepped over the brawler who was still yelling obsceni-ties at the three service writers restraining him. He walked over to Lenny, now sitting in a leather chair in the service lounge, holding his bleeding head.

Mark took a look at his friend's wounds. "I'll be right back, bro. Gonna grab some paper towels to stop the bleeding." He remem-bered the first aid kit on the wall in Jon's office. He pulled the kit from its holder and ran back to Lenny, pulling the packages of gauze out of the first aid kit, tearing it open.

"Here, Lenny." Lenny pressed the gauze against the side of his head while Mark sat next to him with the first aid kit, rummag-ing through it to see what else there was that he could use to stop the bleeding.

"Yeah, thanks Mark. What the hell did he hit me with? Is that dirtbag still over there?" Lenny continued to press the gauze against his head. Mark peeked over the cabinets to see if the perp was still there. Customers were walking through the dealership in amaze-ment, talking about the fight.

"Yeah, but he's not going anywhere," said Mark. "They're hold-ing him for the cops. I heard somebody say they found a set of bloody brass knuckles behind your desk. What the hell happened?"

"I was just—"

Before Lenny could answer, two Gainesville PD squad cars pulled into the service drive, lights flashing, screeching to a halt. Four of Gainesville's finest quickly exited the two cars and entered the service area through Lenny's office. They surveyed the situation and started questioning the bystanders. Two police officers were speaking to the kid who punched Lenny, and two came over to talk to Lenny.

After taking statements from the witnesses and both of the combatants, two of the officers went into the service bay area to find the attacker's Corolla and conduct a weapons search. A few minutes later, they returned holding a black 9MM Beretta and an extra clip which they bagged for evidence and fingerprints. Mark overheard one of the officers say that the weapon they found escalated the charge from simple assault to aggravated assault with a deadly weapon. By now, many of the service customers had found their cars and left the dealership, fearful of having their names mentioned in the police report. After seeing that Lenny would live, Mark retreated across the showroom to Jo's desk.

"Can you believe this stuff?" he asked. He was standing with Rich at the receptionist's console trying to make sense of it all. "Just when you thought it was safe to go back in the dealership!"

"How's Lenny doing?" asked Jo. She was the mother hen at Brandson. Whenever any of her friends at the dealership were in danger, Jo would typically react like a protective mom.

"Well, he declined medical attention," said Rich, joining them. "The service manager said he could go home after he makes his statement to the cops. Who comes to a dealership with brass knuckles in their pocket? Seems like I've seen more psychos here than I did in my seven years at GPD."

"That's 'cause you attract them, bro. They're drawn to you." It was Mark's turn to mess with his buddy.

"Did you two see what happened?" Raj had snuck up on them, wanting to stir up the bees nest and inject his own share of malicious gossip into the mix.

"Yeah, well, apparently somebody didn't care for the punch," quipped Mark.

It was Juicifer's turn to grab the spotlight. "What the hell did you do to Lenny, Mark?" he asked. They were all noticing Juicifer's newly-shaved head. It looked as smooth and shiny as a baby's behind.

Mark gestured at Juicifer's head. "Nice buff job there, Juice. That glare'll get you noticed. You get detail to buff that up for you?"

Juicifer squeezed his crotch obscenely. "I got your buff job right here."

Larry stormed out of the tower. "All right, ladies, show's over. Break it up! Let's get back to work. We've got eighteen cars to sell today!"

As he headed back toward to his desk, Mark watched the brawler being led outside to the police cruiser in handcuffs. A few people were clapping. He'd found out the customer's name was Demetrius Brown, and Demetrius had a rap sheet four pages long, according to the service manager who looked him up on the internet. He scanned the dealership for Lenny, but he'd already left. Mark was certain he wasn't expecting to get punched in the head today by some punk kid with a set of brass knuckles.

Brent was crossing the showroom, curious about all the commotion. He stopped to talk with Mark, looking a little frazzled. "How's Lenny?" he asked.

"I think he's gonna be okay. He won't go to the hospital. Says he's all right, except for a headache. The guy hit him with a set of brass knuckles he had in his pocket. Can ya believe that? Another satisfied customer, right?"

"Yeah, wow, hope he's gonna be okay." Brent had his hand wrapped around the back of his neck trying to relieve some tension. Mark could tell he was stressed about something.

"Hey, I'm a little jammed up this afternoon," said Brent. "You want to work a deal with me?" The manager of the internet team was selective about who he split his business with, so Mark felt good about being asked.

"Sure. What time are they coming in?" Mark enjoyed working deals with straight-up guys who could be trusted. There just weren't that many of them left. He had his pen ready to put notes into his daily planner.

"I know you're good with doctors and professors. Dr. Beville and his wife should be here around one o'clock, looking for a silver Rav4 Limited that we have in stock. I'll put your name on the deal."

"Got it. Thanks, bro. I'll tell Jo to ask for me when they come in and make sure they leave here happy customers. Oh, by the way, nice buff job." Mark couldn't help but mess with him about his super-smooth bald head. "I'll bet it feels just like my girlfriend's ass," said Mark.

"What? Oh, um, thanks." He ran his hand over the top of his head and smiled. "You know, you're right. I think it does feel like your girlfriend's ass."

"I think I just made a glaring mistake." Mark was almost even on the puns. Brent headed back to his desk.

Mark looked over at Rich who had just slammed his hand down on his desk in anger. He was really pissed off about something.

"What's up, dude?" Mark got up and walked over to his buddy's desk.

"They did it again! Look at this on my washout check. They shorted me fourteen hundred dollars! Five hundred for a bad CSI that Rick screwed up for me, and nine hundred on another deal!" He rarely saw Rich raise his voice about anything.

"Here, let me see that." Mark studied it, saying, "Yeah, I see where they got ya. My contribution to the 'Redneck Mafia Retirement Fund' this month was only a thousand dollars. That was down seventeen hundred from the prior month." He looked over his shoulder at the sales tower. "Larry's there, now, go ask him about it. See if you can find out who the caterer is."

"What caterer?" Rich smelled a punch line.

"The caterer for the 'Redneck Mafia Retirement Dinner' that you're springing for this weekend." Rich wasn't amused. Mark could see that his buddy was still really upset. As Rich got up to see Larry about the rest of his money, he looked at his pay stub again. "I can't even pay my bills with this check."

"Tell it to da Devil. His name be Larry." Mark jerked his thumb over his shoulder at Larry sitting behind him in the sales tower. "Good luck," he added.

He spotted Ian walking in the side door coming his way. "Hey Marky-Mark, how's Lenny?" Ian was wearing his signature slip-on soft suede loafers that Mark called his 'elf shoes.' They looked suspiciously like moccasins.

"He's okay. He just didn't care for the punch."

"You're sick. You're a sick man, Marky-Mark." Ian stood at his desk, grinning.

"Hey, you still on that website, 'Men With Hairy Chests That Love Men With Cargo Shorts'?" Mark was having a hard time trying to keep a straight face.

Ian stared at him, then said, "I'm gonna' slap you," waving a mock backhand through the air in front of Mark's face.

"Hey, all kidding aside now, I have a serious question for you."

"What?"

Mark waited for the drama to build so he could make it look serious. "What's your favorite color of cargo shorts?" Mark asked.

"Okay, that's it. Now I am going to slap you!" said Ian as he waved his hand again.

Returning from the tower a few minutes later, Rich interrupted them. "He gave me three hundred bucks back, Mark." He looked disgusted and headed outside to cool off.

By the end of the day, Mark had succeeded in selling Dr. and Mrs. Beville a new silver Rav 4 Limited. The deal wound up being a flat, but he was prepared for that. He expected the minimal commission amount on internet transactions, where it's all about price. After upping two bogues with sub-five hundred credit scores and no cash later in the afternoon, the Beville sale wound up being his only deal of the day, and he was grateful to Brent for the split deal.

At five o'clock, the sales reps heard that the service manager made a decision to fire Lenny Costello. Lenny was popular with his customers and the Brandson staff, and they were shocked to hear the news. It didn't sit well with most of the reps. A few of those on the inside track knew the real reason for his dismissal. It wasn't about the confrontation with Demetrius Brown, but more about Lenny being an honest service writer who resisted the pressure to upsell his customers with parts and service they didn't need. Until today, he had survived several confrontations with management over his insistence on treating his customers honestly.

In Mark's little black book, this was yet another stain on the record of Brandson Toyota. It had become painfully clear to him that the more dishonest an employee was, and the more money he made, illegal or not, the more likely it was that the employee would be supported by the dishonest managers. One by one, the honest and truthful employees were being forced out. That evening, in his anonymous emails with John Dunne and Agent Danley, he updated CVC and the FBI on two new victims of Brandson frauds. He included detailed information on the up-selling of non-essential parts and services within the service department, as well as a description of the certification frauds. Mark included all the unsavory details of how Brandson defrauded the Dean of the Law School, Dr. Michelle Ross, who sent a certified letter to Toyota USA accusing Brandson of fraud. He knew he hadn't heard the end of that deal.

Also in the emails exchanged that night with John Dunne was a breakdown of the more blatant illegal activities at Brandson, complete with attached documents, to be forwarded by John Dunne to the State of Florida, Department of Revenue and included in their investigation of unpaid sales tax by Brandson. Mark made a point to document scores of violations of the Federal Trade Laws, the Federal Fair Labor Settlement Act, Florida Statutes, and the Monroney Act. After emailing for hours, he was starting to feel a little less like a one-legged man in an ass-kicking contest.

In his anonymous phone calls and emails exchanged with retired detective John Dunne, they began to organize the next phase of their investigation.

It was time to get the media involved.

SEVENTEEN

Doug Grayson studied the proposed layout. Two of the photos planned for the front page of Sunday's edition of the *Gainesville Banner* were lifted from Brandson's "Meet Our Employees" section on their website. The third photo of John Dunne was taken last week at his office in the sheriff's headquarters by a staff photographer at the paper. All three photos were good likenesses and positioned next to each other on the bottom right corner of the page. The accompanying text said Larry Wells, general sales manager, was thirty-five, Tommy Catatonia, general manager, was forty-four and John Dunne, SVC director, fifty-eight. To the left, near the bottom of the front page, were the opening paragraphs of a full-page article that continued on page three. It was written by the business editor, Andrew Tarr.

The story was about the nineteen civil complaints filed on behalf of the victims by Consumers Against Crimes that were being investigated by the Gainesville Police Department. The article described the alleged frauds and overpricing at Brandson Toyota over the last several years. It was a juicy story, and the editor-in-chief knew it would sell a lot of newspapers. The story could evolve into a series of articles as the details emerged, maybe becoming the catalyst for the paper regaining its lost luster as a community watchdog and a champion of investigative journalism.

As he proofed the article for factual accuracy and grammatical errors for a second time, Grayson thought about his first interview with the young reporter two years ago. He was hesitant to hire Andrew with his lack of experience, but with the salary limitations of twenty-four thousand a year, there had been only a handful of applicants with resumes worth reviewing. The former student reporter had demonstrated the highest level of ability among the small group of candidates interviewed. It was two years later, and he was glad he'd made the decision to hire Andrew Tarr. Grayson was proud of the story, ready to publish it in Sunday's edition.

At sixty-two, Grayson was a cancer survivor who'd given up smoking years ago. He was only a few years from enjoying a full retirement pension that he'd earned after forty years of dedication. He had no intention of jeopardizing it at this stage of his career by getting sued over shoddy journalism.

"I made you some fresh coffee." Marta stood beside him, hoping her boss would notice her new dress. Carefully, she set the Gator coffee cup down on the mahogany desk. She was one of the few luxuries that Grayson had managed to hang onto through the corporate downsizing. Widowed as a result of a tragic car accident eleven years ago, Marta was devoted to her boss, and the paper had become her life now. She could see her editor was busy and told herself not to be disappointed if more pressing issues prevented him from noticing her new outfit.

"Thanks, Marta. Is Andrew in yet this morning? I know it's early, but I want to go over this story with him and check his sources. What time do you have?" Sentimental about his watch, Grayson had worn the same black Movado wrist watch for twenty years, and after two decades of use, the watch was prone to running slow. He tapped on it again to see if the hands would move.

"I have seven fifty-nine. Do you know where your reporters are?" asked Marta. She smiled at her boss, looking to get him to lighten up a little.

In his conversations with Andrew, Grayson was acutely aware that James Brandson would do everything in his power to suppress the story that his reporter had been working on for the past month, included threatening litigation. With his deep pockets and a net worth well over a hundred million dollars, Brandson and his law-yers could be quite intimidating, especially to a small-town paper like the *Banner*. But Grayson saw himself as a champion of the truth, and he would do whatever it took to make sure the truth got printed.

Marta looked out the window into the parking lot from her boss's second floor corner office. "I think I see his car pulling in now. I'll tell him you'd like to see him."

"Thanks, Marta. Let him know I need fifteen minutes before he gets on the phones."

"Sure thing." She headed downstairs, while Grayson took a sip of his coffee and focused his attention on the three photos in the arti-cle. He wanted to include a portrait-type photo of James Brandson as the sole owner of Brandson Enterprises, but they'd had no luck in finding one anywhere on the net. He found it remarkable that someone of Brandson's wealth and fame was so successful at protect-ing his privacy and controlling his public relations image. He knew that Brandson was a man whose power and resources needed to be respected. In view of this, Grayson weighed his options carefully.

He looked up to see Andrew and waved him in. "There you are. C'mon in, Andrew, have a seat. I've got some good news for you."

"Thanks, boss. How are you this morning?" asked Andrew as he stepped into his editor's office.

"Just fine." Grayson gestured for his star reporter to take a seat.

Andrew chose one of the three overstuffed brown leather chairs, sitting his cup of Starbucks down on the coffee table next to him. At the age of twenty-six, he was one of the youngest business news editors in the country. Normally he dressed very casual, but today he wore a tie, dress shirt, and slacks to look sharp for the ten o'clock meeting scheduled with Brandson's attorney, Eric Berman.

"I like what I see with your story on Brandson Toyota, and I wanted you to know we're planning on running it on the front page of Sunday's paper."

"Fantastic! That's great, boss." Andrew was excited that this was the first time any of his business stories had ever made it to the front page. He leaned forward in the leather chair, brushed his thick black hair back and clasped his hands together like a choirboy, eager to hear what else his editor had to say about his story.

"Also, based on the response I'm expecting from our readership, we may decide to turn this into a series of articles as we anticipate this story developing further. I know you've worked hard on it over the past month. I've seen you here late at night. It's a fine story and should get us a lot of eyeballs. I just have a few things I wanted to cover with you." Grayson took a sip of his coffee and leaned forward, placing his elbows on the top of his desk and folding his hands together.

"Who have you spoken to at the FBI to confirm they've begun an active investigation?" It was clear to Andrew that his boss had shifted gears and now wore his editor-in-chief hat.

"I met with Agent Danley, who told me, off the record, there was an active investigation, but, on the record, could not comment on the existence of an active investigation at Brandson. He also asked me not to use his name." Andrew took a sip of his triple expresso, anticipating more questions from his boss on the article, knowing he was especially adroit at maneuvering through the intricate details of the cloak-and-dagger stuff.

"Okay. That's understandable. That's standard procedure for the FBI. Who did you speak with at Toyota USA?" His brown eyes narrowed, wanting more clarity on these specific details.

"I spoke with a guy named Richard Geller, a regional vice-president. Mr. Geller refused to comment, and would neither confirm nor deny the existence of an investigation at Brandson."

"Did you mention the alleged fake car sales?"

"Yes, and he refused to comment." Andrew knew that it would be unlikely that Toyota would declare themselves to be a victim of any frauds, knowing full well that such an event could lead to the story going global, and viral, severely damaging Toyota's coveted reputation. He knew enough about Toyota to predict that they would do everything in their power to avoid such a public relations catastrophe.

"Okay, good. I see you have that in your story. How much corroboration have you done with John Dunne's statements?" Grayson's cell phone rang, and he squinted at the number displayed on his caller ID. Not recognizing it, he hit the voice mail button and set the phone back on his desk.

"John has been golden with sharing details from documents filed at his group, Consumers Against Crimes, or CVC, and two of the victims who have filed their complaints with CVC and GPD have agreed to allow their names, but not their photos, to run in the article."

"Okay, so the door's not shut completely. Go on." Intrigued, Grayson took another sip of his coffee.

"I've corroborated all John's statements with a minimum of two additional sources. Also, these eighteen cases are from sworn statements, and I'm pretty sure I referenced this fact in the article."

"Yes, I read that. Good. Now, you're referencing 'an anonymous source' here. Who has spoken with this 'anonymous source'?" This was the part of the story the editor was most concerned with, how the information appeared, and the tricky part of verifying an anonymous source. From past experience, he knew that the wording on this was crucial to avoiding a lawsuit based on hearsay, rumor, or innuendo.

"The anonymous source calls himself KG," said Andrew. "I've checked it out, and there are no employees at Brandson that have those initials, so I have no idea what the initials stand for. I've spoken with him four or five times so far, and he always uses a pre-paid, untraceable throwaway cell phone when we talk. He also disguises his voice. KG seems determined to clean up the crimes and dishonesty at Brandson. I'm fairly certain that he's a current employee there, which makes him a valuable asset to us, and to the police." He paused to add some weight to his last statement.

Grayson thought about this as he tapped his finger on the edge of his cup. He was torn over allowing his newspaper to be the "community watchdog" by giving this whistle-blower some latitude. They were already pushing the envelope with source corroboration, and striking the statements would leave gaping holes in the story. Allowing the statements could leave the paper open to a suit for damages as a result of printing unproven allegations, so great care was need to successfully traverse these tricky slopes.

Andrew took another sip of his triple expresso and continued. "KG has access to internal documents that he's shared with CVC and the FBI. These internal files definitely point to fraud at Brandson. The documents have been redacted, but their authenticity has been confirmed by law enforcement forensics and Detective Matt Anderson at GPD as originating from Brandson Toyota." Andrew could tell his editor wasn't sold on the idea of quoting KG.

"Okay, go on, I want to hear everything you know about KG. We need to figure out how much of this part, if any, we can print." Grayson was not particularly fond of betting his retirement income on an outcome that seemed so uncertain.

"Okay, sure. Believe me, I understand how important that is. John Dunne has gone on record with stating that he's had many conversations with KG, and he's cross-checked KG's statements and documents himself with many sources, including the NCIB databank."

"How's he got access to the NCIB?"

"Well, since his office is at the sheriff's department, I figured—"

"Okay. Makes sense. What else we know about KG?"

"Well, as the area director of CVC, John is convinced the source is legit and the information that KG is supplying is one hundred percent accurate. As you know from the story, John is a retired New York City detective and a close friend with our sheriff. He says KG's witnessed unbelievable criminal activities inside Brandson. Having someone who works there is a huge help with giving us the inside track."

"What are KG's reasons for wanting to stay anonymous?" Doug wanted to dig deeper into KG's motives, wanting to make sure that all this wasn't part of some personal vendetta that they were getting wrapped up in. His desire to speak directly with this informant was growing stronger.

"Excellent question, boss. One that I did ask him. Two reasons. One, KG describes these managers at Brandson as drunks and drug users who not only brag about their use of automatic weapons, he says they hunt while they're drunk and doing cocaine. He also says he can prove they have connections with organized crime."

"And we thought this is such a quiet college town. So he's concerned for his safety."

"Exactly. Second reason is KG wants to continue to feed us information that he has access to, but he can do that only if he remains an employee there. If he quits or gets fired, obviously they will terminate his access to internal files."

"Makes sense. Is his access legal?"

"Well, the files he's sharing with us and law enforcement are documents that he has everyday access to, so he's not doing anything illegal. He's reporting criminal actions by his employer. I thought that maybe it was important to make that point."

"Okay. Absolutely. So, we have a confidential informant situation that could become a full-blown whistle-blower story with Toyota as one of the potential victims, with the perps having connections to organized crime. Wow." Grayson was becoming more impressed with his reporter's skills and the scope of the drama that was unfolding. As the two sat in Grayson's office, they began to realize that this story had the potential to become one of the biggest in the history of of their small town paper. They needed a hot story like this to help shake off their mundane image.

"Maybe we'll be doing fewer stories about eighty-six year old cheese slicers passing away," added Grayson with a note of sarcasm.

Andrew laughed. "Yes sir! I'd like that too, boss. From your lips to God's ears, right? No disrespect to cheese slicers of the world."

Grayson had another probing question. "Has KG given you any indication as to the economic value of the frauds being committed?" The editor was struggling to wrap his arms around the monetary value of the alleged crimes as a way to measure the importance of the story.

"Yessir, we discussed that also. He's been there four years, and he estimates the consumer frauds like fake certifications, overcharging, price packing, fraudulent warranties, that kind of stuff, has made them an extra ten to twenty million in illegal profits. He claims that the corporate fraud against Toyota with the fake car sales has made them thirty to forty million in unearned bonuses just in the last four years."

Grayson did the math. "So, if his figures are correct, he's saying that the amount of the frauds could top sixty million dollars? That's a lot of ill-gotten gains for a business in little ole Gainesville." Grayson stood up and walked over to the window. He stared outside, trying to weigh the enormity of the whole thing. This was a huge story.

Andrew drained the rest of the coffee from his Starbucks cup. "KG's done his homework, and he says it's likely that they're hiding even more criminal activity."

Grayson turned from the window. "Like what? What else could possibly be going on?"

Andrew leaned forward in the leather chair. "Money laundering, drugs, illegal wire transfers to offshore banks. That sort of thing. He says there's a major drug investigation going on at the dealership right now."

"Really? Does KG have any proof of these other crimes?" Grayson was kind of incredulous, trying to figure out just how deep this rabbit hole went.

"He says it's all happening right now," said Andrew. "He's heard the conversations and seen some of the wire receipts from offshore banks coming in on Brandson's own fax machines."

"Can he get us copies of the wires?"

"He might, but it's risky. If he gets caught, he's not sure what they might do to him. Also, the managers are buying high-end collectible cars with their illegal profits and driving them to work everyday. He says Rick Gonzalez, one of the crooked F&I guys, drives a rare Mercedes worth over a quarter million bucks, and he owns five cars. Can you believe that, boss? It's like they're flaunting it."

Grayson studied his reporter for a moment, then he said, "Yeah, if it's true, it seems that way." He paused a moment, rubbing his chin. "Okay, here's what we need to do now. Any alleged activities in the story that have not been confirmed by at least two other sources, we need to delete. So, get busy with that. We have got to be sure of our facts. If we can get it right, this is the kind of story that wins Pulitzers. You know that, right?"

"Yessir." Seemingly oblivious to the dangers of running the story, Andrew did his best to contain his giddiness over the possibility of winning a Pulitzer.

"Okay. Have you contacted their general manager, Tommy Catatonia, and general sales manager, Larry Wells, to give them an an opportunity to comment and respond?"

"Of course, boss. Their responses were confirmed by my assistant, Pam. She was on the phone with us." Andrew shifted his body in the chair, now wishing he'd bought the larger size cup of Starbucks.

Marta appeared outside Grayson's office and stuck her head in the door. "Sorry to interrupt, gentlemen. That was Eric Berman on the phone, Brandson's attorney. He said something's come up and he has to reschedule his appointment today. Said he tried to call you on your cell phone a few minutes ago but couldn't reach you."

"Okay, thanks Marta," said Grayson. "I'll call him later to reschedule our meeting." He turned to Andrew, adding, "Wonder what angle he's working on now. I figured the reason for the meeting today was to give their attorneys an opportunity to intimidate us and get us to back down and bury the story. Why don't you get busy with tying up your loose ends, re-confirming your sources where you have less than two, and I'll give Mr. Berman a call to find out what they have up their sleeve. We have three days before press time."

"You got it, boss." Andrew jumped up, eager to clear the way for his editor to print the story that was sure to turn so many heads. He wanted to wake up this quiet little college town with a bombshell. Like his boss, he was tired of the stupid, idiotic stories about eighty-six year old cheese slicers passing on, and kids roasting marshmallows at summer camp. He had three days to perfect his story, and he could almost see himself holding that Pulitzer.

Mark stood on the scale and weighed himself for a second time, questioning the accuracy of the the digital readout. Again, it flashed one hundred seventy-eight pounds. How could he lose eleven pounds in three days? Now, he was as concerned with his weight loss as he was with the non-stop pain, nausea and vomiting that had become part of his daily routine since his surgery on Monday. His vomiting had become so violent that he worried about tearing the stitches in his shoulder loose. This couldn't be normal. He'd been puking for three days straight, unable to keep anything down. Weak and sleep deprived from breakthrough pain, he decided he had to call Dr. Fiore's office again. Mark cleaned himself up, put his bathrobe back on, and got on the phone.

Settling back into his leather office chair, he got back on his computer, checking the last series of emails and attachments sent to the FBI and CVC using the anonymous email address. The heavy narcotics slowed his reflexes and made working on his PC feel like he was moving in slow motion, but he was still able to uncover another twelve fake car sales. They were structured just like the Grimes and McCombs deals and had the sales prices, trade in prices, and amounts financed expressed in identical amounts of money. The figures were not only highly suspicious, they were actually impossible to achieve in a real life deal. To a trained eye, these customer screen shots proved that the managers at Brandson were committing blatant fraud on a daily basis.

He picked up one of his prized documents from his desktop, one that had almost cost him his job. It was a copy of a wire transfer receipt showing a deposit of one million, five hundred thousand dollars to the Abu Dhabi Commercial Bank in the United Arab Emirates at 0937 hours on the morning of Friday, July twenty-seventh, account for the benefit of Kenneth Larry Wells. He found it that same morning lying in the FAX tray.

Realizing its importance, he copied it immediately only moments before Larry had walked back to retrieve it. That was the closest he'd gotten to getting caught with incriminating documents in his possession. Now, he scanned it into a new file, and attached it to an email he sent to CVC and the FBI, certain that it proved money laundering was now an integral part of the frauds. Five minutes later, Mark got a call on his throwaway cell phone from a number he immediately recognized as the office number at FBI's Gainesville branch. He answered the phone.

"KG."

"Special Agent James Costello, FBI. I received an emailed document a few minutes ago reflecting a wire transfer to the United Arab Emirates in the amount of one million, five hundred thousand dollars US. Got a question for you."

"Sure." He remembered that Agent Costello was their economic crimes specialist, the one he hadn't met yet.

"How did you come to possess this document?"

"Well, sir, it was laying in the FAX tray at Brandson Toyota on the morning of July twenty-seventh. I just happened to be in that office to send an outgoing FAX on a deal I was working on. I immediately made a copy of it and put it back in the tray. I passed the intended recipient in the hallway moments later. He has no idea I copied it." From Agent Costello's tone, Mark could tell that the agent understood the importance of the document.

"Okay. Did you in any way alter the original or photocopied document?"

"No, sir. It's exactly as it was transmitted from the bank. You should know that I've also overheard conversations about additional offshore wire transfers by Rick Gonzalez and Jake Sheahan. The copy I emailed you was the only one that actually documents the activity that I've been hearing about." Mark did his best to mirror the businesslike tone of the FBI agent on the phone with him.

"Okay, copy that. I'll check it out. Next question. I've also received documents of what appear to be internal customer transaction screens from Brandson Toyota's computer system. How did you come into possession of these files?"

"Well, I'm not sure if you're aware of my surgery, Agent Costello, but I'm home recuperating from arthroscopic surgery for the next two to three weeks."

"Yessir, I heard about it. Hope you're doing better." He wasn't expecting flowers from his buddies downtown, but he wouldn't mind putting a stop to the puking. This was probably about as much sympathy as he could expect from the FBI. Mark continued with his chain-of-custody explanation, trying to ignore the nausea that made conversation difficult.

"Agent Costello, you may find this ironic. I'm following my manager's instructions to search the system for sales opportunities from my remote PC access while I'm home recuperating. I came across these deals in contact management, and they definitely looked suspicious. The figures don't make sense. I'm certain they are additional fake deals. I scanned and emailed the files as attachments thinking you might want to take a look at them."

"Oh, absolutely, KG, and we really do appreciate your help with this. Anything else?" asked Costello.

"That's all I've got for now. I have a buddy on the inside over there who is former law enforcement helping me with this stuff."

"So, our CI has his own CI, huh?" Agent Costello got a chuckle over this, and added, "Okay, KG, feel better and keep up the good work."

"Copy that."

A few minutes after his conversation with Special Agent Costello, Mark's regular cell phone rang. It was Dr. Fiore's office at TOI. He grabbed the phone, eager to hear about some new meds that would actually relieve the extreme pain he was in. With all the money from Workmen's Comp that was being spent on his surgery and recovery, he didn't feel like he was asking for too much.

"This is Mark."

"Mr. McAllister, its Jamie from Dr. Fiore's office. Dr. Fiore has approved two new prescriptions for you. Dilaudid, eight milligram tablets and oxycodone, ten milligram tablets. Your meds will be ready to pick up at the pharmacy on 24th Avenue in about thirty minutes."

"Thank you, Jamie. Maybe now I can actually get some sleep." Mark continued to be impressed with the patient care he received from TOI.

"Okay, then. Feel better, and call us if we can help." She hung up, and his fair-haired angel of mercy was gone.

Twenty minutes later, Mark was in his car, finished with his emails and document scanning for the day, and on his way to the pharmacy. He drove like a little old lady in his heavily medicated state, knowing they'd nail him for DUI if he got pulled over—CI or no CI.

Doug closed the door behind him, sat down at his desk and prepared for the phone conversation with his boss, Harvey Morgan. Mr. Morgan was the chief financial officer of Media Springs Group, headquartered in Atlanta, owner of the *Gainesville Banner* and fourteen other newspapers in the southeast. A phone call from Harvey was rare, and Doug couldn't honestly remember the last time Harvey had actually called him. Their corporate communications and regular quarterly reports usually took the form of email.

"Harvey, this is a pleasant surprise. How are you and the family?"

"I'm good, Doug. How are things in Gatorland? Oh, and thanks for the birthday card." said Morgan. "You don't mind being on speaker phone, do you?"

"Speaker phone's fine. You're welcome for the card, Harvey. Things are going well. Workin' on some big stories. To what do I owe the honor of your call today? I don't think we've spoken since last Thanksgiving."

"That's one of the things I love about you, Doug. Right to the point. I have you on speaker with our lead counsel, Jim Douglas. Jim, say hi to the executive editor of our paper in Gainesville," prompted Morgan.

"Good afternoon, Doug. I've heard great things about you." Douglas sounded very somber.

"Doug, I know you're familiar with our papers in Ft. Myers, The *Press-Journal* and the *Sarasota News*. You may know we made those acquisitions a year or two before the *Gainesville Banner*. What you may not know is that they derive about ten percent of annual advertising revenues, about eleven million dollars, from Brandson Enterprises, parent company of seven area car dealerships in Sarasota, Naples, and Ft. Myers. These seven dealerships are some of our best customers in southwest Florida." Jim paused to let this sink in. Doug smelled a rat.

Doug said, "Uh, I think I see where this is going." His hopes for a real barn-burner of a story in Sunday's paper began to vaporize.

It was Harvey's turn to speak. "Doug, we got a call earlier today from Eric Berman, corporate counsel for Brandson Enterprises. As you know, Brandson Enterprises is parent to Brandson Toyota in Gainesville. I have some bad news for you. They've not only threatened to cancel all their ads with our four papers in southwest Florida, your sister publications, but all future advertising as well, if we allow you to print your negative story about Brandson Toyota. We simply can't afford to lose those revenues. I know you don't like—"

Upset by the turn of events, Doug interrupted him. "Excuse me, Harvey, but are you suggesting that we allow Brandson to suppress our story about rampant corruption at their Gainesville dealership so they don't cancel their advertising in newspapers printed in communities at the other end of the state? That's bribery! What about our responsibilities to report on corruption in Alachua County?" The editor was incensed by Brandson's subterfuge.

"Doug, listen—"

Harvey interrupted his boss again. "What about our readership in Gainesville?" Doug was angry beyond words, furious over Brandson's deception. He knew it would do no good to lose his temper. The guys at corporate wrote the checks and ran the show. It was all about the money.

Harvey continued. "Look, Doug, we don't appreciate their tactics anymore than you do, but eleven million a year in lost revenue is a lot of money. A lot more money than we would see as a result of the possible increased readership of our paper there in Gainesville if we were to run the story."

"But, Harvey, they're hundreds of miles—"

"Listen to me. We've already looked at all the figures, done the math, and we've determined that these revenues are vital to the financial health of Media Springs. You know how tough it is out there right now, competing with internet-based publishers. Our hands are tied. I don't want to have to make anymore cuts because of reductions in revenues at any of our papers. Now, I'm sorry, but we will not be printing that story. Are we clear?" Doug resigned himself to the likelihood that his boss wasn't going to budge an inch. Not with eleven million in annual revenues at stake.

There was a very long pause. Doug lowered his voice. "I understand the financial considerations. I'm just tired of watching the art of real investigative journalism take a back seat to corporate profits and ad revenue. I'm sorry, too. I'm going to have to try and explain this to one of our rising stars, Andrew Tarr. He's been working on this story for over two months now." He stopped for a moment, hoping they might relent and let him publish the story, but there was only silence on the line. Finally, he threw in the towel.

"Thank you both for the courtesy of an explanation," said Doug.

After sharing a bit of banter to smooth over the rough edges of their conversation, they all hung up. None of the news executives enjoyed being railroaded into suppressing an important news story, but the survival of the parent holding company was supreme to all other considerations, and Doug knew it.

Finding himself out maneuvered by Brandson's subterfuge, Doug was so enraged at having to bury his best story that he took aim at his plastic trash can and kicked it all the way across his office, shattering it into pieces against his office wall.

EIGHTEEN

His wildlife study was interrupted by the sound of his cell phone ringing. It was Rich. "Hey, bro, what's up?" Mark was expecting an update on some shared customers they were working.

"Hey, how you feeling? Did you get those heavier meds?" Rich was curious about his progress after six days of recuperation from shoulder surgery.

"Yup, sure did," said Mark. The heavier doses of synthetic morphine and oxycodone were taking his mind off the pain, and he was thankful now that he could actually get some sleep.

"Larry is off the chain. You won't believe this, but he punched Juicifer in the head when we were doing the walk-around on the used lot this morning. Right in front of Tommy, Bryan, and Kirk. Can you believe that? The guy is so trashed out from the night before that he's lost it." He sounded out of breath, and Mark remembered that Rich was taking medication to control his blood pressure.

"Why'd he punch our top producer?" asked Mark. "I thought they were best buds."

"He was showboating, not paying attention to Larry on the walk-around. Larry got pissed off. There's more."

"You sound out of breath. What else is going on there?"

"Hang on. I'm moving away from the building to get some privacy. I peeked inside the tower earlier this morning, before the walk around. There's Larry, Tony, and Bryan all shooting up testosterone in plain sight. There were empty vials of the stuff all over his desk, along with a half empty bottle of vodka. They had their arms tied off with those rubber tubes that junkies use."

"You mean syringes, injecting it? You're kidding me." Mark knew Larry and the other managers were injecting illegal drugs, but he didn't expect them to be stupid enough to do it in broad daylight in the sales tower where anyone could walk in.

"These guys are totally out of control," said Rich. "Raj let it slip out that Larry's been selling the stuff up and down the street. He asked *me* if I wanted to score some."

"I heard he was selling cocaine," said Mark. "You'd think with Larry raking in his sixty to eighty thousand a month from his extortions and fake bonus money, that would be enough. He's gotta sell drugs too?"

"Well, you know Larry. He's like an octopus. He's got his tentacles in everything. You know how they're always bragging about kicking someone's ass downtown?"

"Yeah, I've heard them bragging about their fights before."

"This morning, all three of them have bloody knuckles. Larry, Kirk, and Tony. Look's like they were up all night, drugging and brawling."

"I'm kinda glad I'm not there today," said Mark. "Where's Tommy Catatonia? Can't he see what's going on? It sounds like a scene from *Pulp Fiction* or something."

"He's gone. He doesn't care. They're making him too much money. The 'Redneck Mafia' is runnin' the show here. See what you're missing?" He listened as Rich quickened his pace, moving further away toward the outer parking lot.

"Yeah, I'm gone a week and the place goes to hell in a hand basket," Mark quipped. "Feels weird to be popping narcotics and collecting Workmen's Comp checks. Not exactly what I pictured myself doing."

"Oh, by the way, I sold that Camry last night for us to the McClellans. Thanks for the split deal. It was an easy two pounder. That's another half deal for both of us."

"Well, yeah, if only they would pay us what we actually earn." He knew Rich wasn't immune from Larry's pilferage. With twenty-two sales reps to steal from, there was another twenty-six grand a month going into the "Redneck Mafia Retirement Fund."

"I could get used to this," said Mark, referring to his current status on the injured list. "Maybe I'll just continue collecting pay on half deals, floating on clouds of painkillers all day, getting Workmen's Comp checks in the mail."

"Yeah, right. In spite of Larry's thievery, you could never stay away. You know you miss the action." Rich was right. Mark missed the action. "They're still cracking jokes about you planning the whole car accident thing."

"Yeah, whatever. Hey, what's going on with Carla? Someone said that you guys actually met when you found her in the woods humping a defrocked priest. Any truth to that?"

"Funny guy. Actually, it was two priests. Hang on, I gotta take a piss," said Rich.

"In the parking lot?" Mark asked. "Oh, I get it. You're not afraid of being arrested for indecent exposure 'cause they'd have to let you go for insufficient evidence." Mark was feeling a little chippy from the painkillers.

"Yeah, right. I do it all the time. Just go in between the cars when no one's lookin'." Mark was hearing a lot of background noise as Rich held his cell phone between his jaw and shoulder. "Hang on. It takes two hands to handle a whopper."

"Yeah, right. What else do you see there in fantasy land?"

"Aaahhhh . . . ohhhhh . . . that feels good. I don't like Chevys anyway."

"You're pissing on a Chevy?"

"Yeah, just the wheel. The rain'll wash it off." As an ex-cop, Rich didn't seem too bashful about exposing himself in public. After he zipped up, he continued. "Okay. Now, I can talk. You remember me telling you about my DCF hearing coming up next week, right?"

"DCF. That's Division of Children and Families?"

"Right. Well, this coke-crazed stripper that Carla's been shacking up with in Ocala calls me and tells me she's coming to the hearing with Carla, and how they're are going to take my daughter away from me."

"How are they planning to do that when Carla's been arrested three times in the past month for grand larceny, burglary, and drug possession?"

"She says she's going to testify that I did drugs when I was in college, fifteen years ago for God's sake. Says she sleeps with Carla and a nine millimeter under her pillow. I said that's my wife you're talking about. I told her you're messing with the wrong guy, and that's the second time I've warned her to stay out of my business."

"So, what are you going to do?" He could tell Rich had something up his sleeve. He knew just about every cop and probation officer in the county, and Mark knew you didn't threaten ex-cops.

"Already did it. Turns out this coked-up stripper that Carla's shacking up with is on parole after doing three years for felony assault with a deadly weapon and conspiracy to sell more than a pound of coke. You know that felons aren't allowed to have firearms, right?"

"Yeah, I think I can see where you're going with this."

"Right. So, I find out who the bitch's parole officer is yesterday, call him up, tell him there's drugs and weapons in the house. So he calls in two squad cars from Marion County Sheriff's office for backup, and they busted her at five o'clock this morning. Done deal."

"You sly dog, you. Congratulations on a real slice of police work, there Rich. Guess she won't be coming to your DCF hearing after all."

"Nope. Hey, I think I see a customer on the other end of the lot. Gotta roll."

"Go get'um, tiger. Just don't let them fall in love with that Chevy you just pissed all over."

Mark turned his attention back to the morning's market action as he checked his trading screens. He had scheduled a phone call with John Dunne at CVC later on. John had set up some possible media contacts who wanted to talk to KG with the idea of putting together a story.

John Dunne was planning on enlisting the help of local media to help in their fight to put an end to the fraud and corruption at Brandson. During the past few months, he was interviewed by WJXT-TV, the *Gainesville Banner*, and WUFZ/NPR radio. Jan Barnes, news editor for WXJT-TV, had already turned down his request to air a piece about the corruption, claiming a conflict of interest. The conflict of interest was really all about the million dollars spent by Brandson at her TV station each year for local advertising. With WXJT being bribed out of the picture, that left Andrew Tarr, business editor at the local paper, and Jennifer Treadstone at WUFZ radio as interested reporters that wanted to run stories about the corruption at Brandson.

At a little after eleven o'clock, he called John Dunne at CVC on his throwaway cell phone.

"John?"

"This is John."

"It's KG. Sorry about the code name. It was the FBI's idea. You have a minute?"

"Sure do. I heard about your accident and surgery from Agent Danley. Hope you're doing better." After exchanging forty or fifty emails with the director of CVC from his anonymous email address, this was Mark's first actual phone conversation with John.

"Appreciate your well wishes. The good news is that, even though I'm home recuperating from surgery, I still have access to lots of internal documents and other information at Brandson. We have two CIs on the inside right now. Myself and one other. Like you, he is a former law enforcement officer."

"The staff at CVC want to thank you for your participation in all this. Your, ah, information has been valuable in helping the victims we represent."

"You're welcome. There's a lot more coming, John. There are literally hundreds of victims."

"Preying on the elderly and handicapped on fixed incomes may open them up to additional felony charges," said John. "These fraudsters don't seem to realize that defrauding seniors is a felony."

"I don't think they care. They see the Q-tips as easy pickings," said Mark.

"Sad, isn't it? By the way, you do realize that Toyota may never come forward as a victim themselves, which is ironic because they are the biggest victim of all these frauds. In monetary value."

"I know."

"Also, I need to explain to you that, because of your anonymity, I may not be able to share information with you on day-to-day progress in the investigations, or the results." As a former lieutenant detective at NYPD, John knew the ropes. He was articulate, intelligent, and familiar with legal proceedings. Mark was expecting a man of lesser abilities, and he was relieved that his liaison was someone experienced in undercover work.

"Share what ya can, John. There could be a point in the future where I change my status, but for now, I need to stay completely anonymous. This way, I don't become a target myself, and I can continue to supply evidence of criminal activity right from their own internal systems. While I still have access."

"I understand," said John. "When I worked homicide cases at NYPD, I had a lot of experience working with anonymous sources that gave us valuable intel. Let me ask you, which of their internal software systems do you have access to now, Mark?"

"There's three separate software programs that Brandson uses in their sales, service, parts and management. I don't know what system they use for their accounting department. I have access to contact management, or CM, used by all the sales reps and managers. That's where all the thirty or so screen shots that I emailed to you came from."

"Okay, go on." John was patiently taking notes.

"The second system is called AX, and it's used exclusively by managers. I don't have access to it. Then you have the DOS-based ERA system used by service and parts, but also by the F&I guys on the lender and backroom files. I don't have access to that system either, but once in awhile the F&I guys will show me specific screens in their ERA system when I have questions about deals. Stop me if I'm going too fast."

"I'm with you so far. Sounds like a hodge-podge of software they compiled over the years." John was eager to continue.

"Let me clarify something. From internal files, I'm certain that Tony Grimes is Anthony Richard Grimes, not the Anthony P. Grimes in Ocala that you referenced in your email. This is the used car manager that we call 'The Village Idiot' who lives in Jax, commutes almost everyday, DOB 3/19/1963, and drives the late-model grey Camry SE that you already have the VIN on. This is the same Tony Grimes who bragged to our new recruit class a few months ago about his purchase of forty new Toyotas. How the hell does a manager buy forty new Toyotas unless fraud is involved?"

"Rhetorical question."

"Right. Also, the transaction figures that they used on those deals make no sense. The Florida Division of Banking and Financing are on this, and I understand from your emails that the Florida Department of Revenue is also investigating, along with the Division of Motor Vehicles because of the unpaid sales taxes and fake title information," said Mark.

"That is correct," confirmed John. "That makes three state law enforcement agencies conducting their own investigations, as well as three Federal agencies, U.S. Attorney General, FBI, and the IRS. From my experience, they'll likely consolidate their investigation with one agency. The Feds have already been to the dealership a few times, studying specific files. And let's not forget the Gainesville

PD and Detective Matt Anderson, who has original jurisdiction on many of the crimes. I heard that GPD is now coordinating their investigations with the Feds."

"I just hope that they're really sharing info with each other," Mark said. "Think of the lives that could have been saved on 9/11 if they'd done that."

"Don't worry. I see them cooperating, but I can't give you specifics."

"Understood," said Mark. "If we can get some media coverage, the investigation would accelerate and this whole thing would snowball. Law enforcement would feel some pressure from the public and maybe charges would be filed sooner. Just as important, the media could help us warn other potential victims about buying at Brandson *before* they become victims of fraud. Seems like we're moving at the speed of molasses in winter on this stuff."

"Try to be patient," said John. "These economic crimes take time to investigate and prosecute. I'd like to see some help from the media, too. I don't know if I've mentioned this, but the Feds are also looking into your idea to use the RICO Act to prosecute the money laundering and offshore wire transfers, and their use of funds to buy exotic cars. If the money trail can be traced. Their intent to conceal their unlawful gain is also relevant in using RICO."

"Sounds like law enforcement has plenty of tools. I just hope they use them. RICO has some teeth in it. These guys belong in jail. You mentioned in one of your emails that the business editor at the paper wanted to talk to me. I would be willing to do so as long as he will accept the condition of my anonymity. Would he agree to that?" He was convinced reporters were primarily interested in grabbing the spotlight by sensationalizing the facts to increase their market share to boost ad revenue. If there was an opportunity for them to turn the tables and use the media to advance the investigation, he was willing to take the risk of direct contact with reporters.

"I'm fairly certain that he would agree to respecting your anonymity," said John. "Remind him of your option to recant everything if they attempt to blow your cover. Also, you could threaten to take the story to one of their competitors. You actually have more leverage than you think."

"Okay, good points. I'm new at this, can you tell?"

"Yeah, well, no one is born a whistle-blower," said John. "Employer crimes can escalate and cause the employees to reach such a level of discomfort that they're forced to take action. It takes a lot of guts to do what you're doing, KG. Most just walk away."

"I appreciate your support," said Mark. "I might be willing to stick my neck out a little further if I wasn't working with a bunch of drug-crazed, drunk psychos obsessed with automatic weapons. The last thing I want to do is paint a big red bull's eye on my back, or expose my family to retribution."

"Like I said, your anonymity is understandable," said John. "I've just emailed you all the media contact info for Andrew Tarr at the paper, and Jennifer Treadstone at WUFZ. Both of them are working on stories about Brandson. I would recommend that you use your throwaway cell phone only for these conversations. Be careful what you say. Let me know how it goes, okay? Maybe we can get them to work for us."

"Thanks again, John." As he hung up with John Dunne, Mark knew he had to be careful. Reporters were like piranhas devouring a carcass and would do almost anything to uncover a big story, including putting other people's lives in jeopardy. He remembered being chased in his car at high speed through a parking garage in Manhattan two days after 9/11 because the lunatic reporter was convinced Mark had a great story about the death of his five friends at Cantor Fitzgerald.

He checked his watch. It was eleven twenty. Time to ring up Jennifer Treadstone at WUFZ/NPR. As he walked to the kitchen to pour himself a third cup of coffee, he dialed Jennifer's number on his throw away phone. After ringing five times, it rolled to voice, so he left the reporter a message. As he left his VM, he wrapped his shirt over the phone to make his voice less recognizable.

"Hi, Jennifer, this is KG. I've been working with law enforcement and John Dunne at CVC to expose the crimes at Brandson. I understand you're working on a story and I'd like to talk with you about some additional information that you may want to include in your story. It's crucial that I remain anonymous. I can't leave you my number, but I'll try you again later tonight."

As he sat in front of his computer and sipped his coffee, he read the rest of the email from Dunne. Mark dialed the second cell phone number on his list, hoping to have better luck reaching Andrew Tarr. It rang three times before he heard the reporter's voice.

"This is Andrew." On his way to interview a victim of Brandson's fraud, Andrew slowed his Honda Civic down as he noticed the caller ID flashing "Private."

"Is this Andrew Tarr of the *Banner?*" asked Mark.

"Yes. Who's this? There's no number on my caller ID." Andrew had almost decided not to answer the phone out of fear of being punked again.

"This phone isn't traceable. You can call me KG, Andrew. I've been working with John Dunne at CVC and the FBI on uncovering the crimes at Brandson. Before we continue, I need to have your agreement that you'll respect my need to remain anonymous, otherwise, I have to end this conversation right now." There was a long pause while the reporter thought about this.

"Yeah, sure. I can reference an anonymous source. How do you fit into all this, KG?" Andrew pulled his car over to the side of the road, almost spilling his coffee. He laid his notepad on the center armrest and grabbed his pen, setting his Starbucks coffee in the side cup holder.

"I'm the confidential informant that's exposing these crimes. John told me I can trust you. How much of a story do you have prepared?"

"Well, I've been working on it for a couple of months. It's a full page now, if my editor runs the whole thing. Before I tell you anymore, KG, I'd like to ask you a question to verify who you are. I get a lot of crank calls. I'm sure you understand."

"Sure. What's your question?"

"What's the name of the most recent alleged fraud victim who is a Dean at the Law School?" Andrew knew if his caller could answer the question, he had the right guy.

"Dr. Michelle Ross, Dean of the College of Law." Mark couldn't forget her.

"That's correct. Just wanted to be sure of who I'm talking to."

"Totally understand. When is your story on Brandson scheduled to run?" Mark wanted to do a little digging, not knowing how much Andrew was willing to tell him. He sensed a slight air of mistrust between them, and Mark knew he might have to throw him a bone or two to keep him in the game.

"Well, it was scheduled to run in Sunday's edition, but my editor told me it's on hold until we can get more corroboration. I've got all the complainants in there, interviews, even some photos of the victims. I get the feeling that there's a lot more going on."

"What makes you say that?" Mark went a little deeper, wanting to know how much Andrew knew about the drugs and money laundering.

"I've been hearing rumors of a large-scale criminal investigation, but no one will go on record until charges are filed. You know, we might be able to help each other out here." There was a pause as he waited to hear Mark's reaction.

"In order to help put a stop to these crimes, we need your help, Andrew. What can I do to convince your boss to print that story?"

"Well, for one thing, would you be willing to call and talk to my editor?" Mark thought about Andrew's idea for a moment as he weighed the pros and cons of having direct contact with the editor-in-chief of the local newspaper.

"If he will respect my anonymity, then yes," said Mark. "I'll talk with him. What's his cell number?"

"352.213.6397. Just remember 213.N-E-W-S. His name's Doug. Doug Grayson."

"Got it. What's the best time to call your editor-in-chief?"

"How about right after lunch today? I think I can persuade him to talk with you, even though you're an anonymous source."

"Done," said Mark. He wanted to seal the deal before Andrew changed his mind.

"You might be able to tip the scale and get him to give us the green light to run the full page. He's worried about getting sued by Brandson. Tell me. From what you know, how big is this story?" asked Andrew. Mark was thinking that now is the time to throw him that bone.

"Okay. Just so you have an idea, this could be the biggest story of your career, maybe in the history of your paper." Mark was hoping that might be enough to appease him. It wasn't. Andrew wanted more details.

"Why do you say that?" Andrew asked. "Can you be a little more specific?"

"The kind of story that topples corrupt state attorneys and wins Pulitzers. Of the hundreds of victims, the biggest is Toyota. It's a forty to seventy million dollar scam, with six different law enforcement agencies investigating Brandson right now. How's that for a story?"

"Help me break it. If I help you, will you promise to deal with me exclusively?"

"You help me put these criminals away, Andrew, and I'll give you an exclusive on all of it. The Pulitzer's up to you. Now, I need to feel I can trust you. Are we a team?" Mark listened carefully to the non-verbals as well as what he said.

"We are. Call my boss in about an hour. To make sure he takes your call, I'll let him know to expect an anonymous call from KG on a private line. You're all set. Just make the call. I want this story, too."

After hanging up, Mark was now convinced Andrew was firmly on board. He was hungry, and he wanted that Pulitzer. Mark was counting on his greed for fame and fortune. Now, all he had to do was convince the editor to run the story.

An hour and a half later, Mark dialed 352.213.N-E-W-S. Grayson answered the phone on the fourth ring.

"Doug Grayson."

"Mr. Grayson. I'm KG. Did Andrew tell you I'd be calling?" Mark eased himself into the conversation, not knowing what to expect from the man who ran the *Gainesville Banner.*

"Yes, he did. I understand you're the source of much of the evidence concerning the alleged frauds at Brandson. And you wish to remain anonymous, is that right?"

"Yes, sir. I gave some additional information to Andrew, which I will share with you. The civil complaints filed with GPD through CVC are just the tip if the iceberg. I have documentation that Toyota has been defrauded of between forty and seventy million dollars, and the rest of the hundreds, maybe thousands, of frauds could easily top another thirty million. And growing everyday."

"Yes, I'm aware of these alleged activities," said Grayson. "Andrew has written a masterful story about it. I appreciate the risks that you've taken to shed light on the corruption there. However, let me get right to the point. I have two problems with publishing the story."

"If you can tell me what they are, I may be able to help you," said Mark.

"Sure. One issue I have is that you're an anonymous source—"

Mark interrupted him, saying, "Yes, but you have twenty to twenty-five other witnesses and complainants to corroborate these crimes, as well as internal documents proving the frauds—"

"Which we have referenced, but the chain of custody of those documents is something we need to corroborate by someone willing to go on record. Will you go on record?"

"Chain of custody?" asked Mark. "I'm confused. Law enforcement has accepted their authenticity. Why can't the local newspaper?"

Grayson responded, saying, "The police don't have to worry about a multi-million dollar lawsuit. We do. Will you go on record?"

Mark had anticipated some pressure on this point. He knew if he revealed his identity that it would make the editor's job a lot less risky, but his own life could be in serious danger. "At some point, I may, but not yet. I can do more for the investigation if I stay anonymous. Look. We both know that you'd sell a lot more newspapers with this story. I'm asking you to recognize there are larger issues at stake here. What else is holding you back?"

Grayson answered, "As much as I would like to run this story now, and it is a helluva story, our parent company, Media Springs, has been threatened with an eleven million dollar loss of annual ad revenue from Brandson Enterprises with their southwest Florida dealerships if we proceed. The decision to publish is being made at Media Springs. I'd like to help by printing it, but it's no longer my decision."

There was a long pause before Mark answered. "Well, from what you've said, it looks like you're letting Brandson bribe your parent company into suppressing a very important news—"

Grayson interrupted. "Whoa! I didn't say that, GK, or KG, whatever your name is. As a matter of fact, I've already said too much. I'd appreciate it if we can agree that we never had this conversation." He sounded angry, and Mark feared he was about to hang up. Realizing he'd hit a nerve, he bit his tongue, avoiding any further mention of bribery. Another long pause followed, and Mark was purposely quiet, intent on waiting to hear what the editor might let slip out next.

Realizing that he'd made a mistake in admitting that his parent company had been bribed, Grayson was flustered and embarrassed. Now, he was suddenly cautious and looked for a polite way to end their conversation.

"I guess that's it, KG. I've got a meeting starting here. I'd like to do more to help, but, like I said, my hands are tied. Call me in a week, and I'll let you know of any changes on that story. Good luck with everything." With that, Grayson hung up.

It was clear to Mark that he'd heard more than the newspaper editor had intended to say. Not only was the conversation a dead end, it had ended awkwardly, and his thoughts turned to WUFZ now. He wondered if the radio station would also be subjected to the heavy boot of Brandson's bribery.

As he finished the last bite of his egg McMuffin, Raj Patel studied the roster board from his seat in the meeting room. It was the third Friday in August, and the board showed that he was in third place with fifteen sales, behind McCreedy with sixteen, and Brent with seventeen. He was gloating, knowing that as soon as Larry updated the sales board, he would be in first place and ahead of his internet boss, Brent Bell. His watch indicated eight fifty-eight, two minutes to go before missing reps were declared late and subject to Larry's fearsome temper and five dollar fine.

"Raj, nice job, buddy. Heard you had seven deals this week. Is that right?" Dennis Testi sat down one seat over, offering a fist bump to the man often referred to as Jabba the Hutt.

"Thanks, Dennis. Yeah, had a couple of referrals come through this week."

"Heard you had a twenty pounder," said Raj. "Was that the cheese deal that Larry gave you with the older couple who were hooked up to that green oxygen tank?"

"Yeah. I thought that old geezer was going to croak before he signed off," said Testi. "They were giving me a hard time about the mark-up, so Larry said I should turn off the valve to his oxygen tank to persuade them to sign. I wasn't sure if he was serious. Ya never know with Larry. Got their lame asses for a twenty thousand dollar commission! Crushed 'em. How 'bout them apples?" They shared another fist bump.

"All right, ladies. Nine o'clock. Let's see who's not here!" Larry marched into the room like he was commander-in-chief of the Allied Forces on D-Day and surveyed the seats in the meeting room. He wore his signature Louis Vuitton ostrich loafers and matching belt with Dockers and black Toyota polo that looked like he'd taken it off a kid on the playground.

"Tony, let's update the board," said Larry.

Tony Grimes jumped up, black marker in hand. Other than some bruised knuckles, he showed no visible signs of his collection duties from the night before.

"Brent! How many you got out, man?"

"Uh, let's see . . . " Without looking up, Brent was focused on his cell phone, checking his text messages, "Uh, I got twenty."

"Fantastic! You the man! Paul?"

"I got nineteen."

Larry interrupted, "Damn, Paul! Why can't you ever remember to wear your name badge? Five dollar fine, right now, cough it up." Larry stepped forward, angry that one of his buddies was so ill-prepared. He held out his hand to Paul.

"It's in the armrest in my truck," said Paul. "You want me to go get it?"

"Right now! And bring me five bucks!" Larry was unyielding, annoyed with having to continually remind his top producers to wear their name badges. McGreedy obediently made his way out the rear door toward the parking lot to retrieve his name badge and cash for his master. Tony continued going down the list of names.

"Raj?"

"Twenty-two." It was Raj's turn to gloat, and he was better at it than anyone. Whenever he gloated, usually over stealing a deal or sticking it to a customer, he squinted his eyes. With his eyes squinted, it was uncanny how closely he resembled his namesake, Jabba the Hutt.

"Raj, you rock! Seven deals. Great! You're leading the board." Tony was busy placing the seven Xs for each of his new deals next to Raj's name. The man from Pakistan was pumping his fist up and down in celebration of his first-place triumph.

Tony continued down the sales board. "Dennis?"

"I've got fourteen."

Larry interrupted, "Our new crusher!" Larry watched Juicifer look down at the floor when he made the pronouncement, embarrassed to have lost the dubious honor of being the "Top Crusher." "Dennis got a twenty pounder yesterday, everybody. He absolutely *crushed* a little old lady and her husband. Actually forced them to clean out their savings to make the deal! Fantastic! Give it up for Dennis!"

At Larry's command, all twenty-nine reps, sales, and F&I managers present applauded Dennis's performance. The three exceptions were Rich, who was at a DCF hearing downtown at the courthouse, Brent, who had just left the meeting to meet a customer, and Mark, who was still at home recuperating from surgery.

Everyone else bowed to the Devil's handywork.

NINETEEN

It was warm in his office, and the elected state attorney in north central Florida tilted the bottle of lemon-flavored Perrier, draining the last few gulps. It was unusually hot for September, and the heat from the sun was only a problem between nine and ten thirty in the morning. After midmorning, the roof overhang shaded his second floor office window from direct sunlight. Thomas Lewis tossed the empty bottle into his trash can beside his desk and focused his attention on the file in front of him.

At the age of fifty-six, losing the battle of the bulge, and nearly bald after thirty years of service, Lewis was now in his third term as state attorney for the Eighth Judicial Circuit serving Alachua, Baker, Bradford, Levy, Union, and Gilchrist counties. After graduating from the University of Florida Law School, he was hired as an assistant state attorney. He was promoted to a felony prosecution position after four years prosecuting juvenile court cases. Deft at political maneuvering and caseload management, he never failed to select the criminal cases that would best thrust him into the spotlight as he climbed the proverbial ladder of success. After serving as chief assistant state attorney for seven years, Mr. Lewis was elected state attorney twelve years ago, gradually discarding the lowly misdemeanors and gravitating to cases involving the most serious of capital murders. Cases that got the most publicity for himself and his entourage.

For three decades, Thomas Lewis slowly built an organization that would be loyal to him. His office had become the largest law firm in the Circuit, with over a hundred assistant attorneys, paralegals, and staff assistants under his command, all paid for by the State of Florida. Now at the top of the food chain, he could focus on the important matter of campaign contributions and the funding that would best serve to perpetuate his legacy.

He stared out his office window at the cars coming and going from the parking below. "Vivian, bring me another Perrier, will you?" He could hear the refrigerator door open in the adjoining room and the clanking of bottles. His executive assistant entered his office holding a cold bottle of lemon-flavored Perrier wrapped in a napkin. Married with a family, she was used to catering to the men in her life.

"Here you are, Tom." She pushed aside a stack of files and set the bottle on his desk beside him. "Kinda warm in here, isn't it?" She brushed her hair back and straightened herself up, noticing the strong morning sun streaming through the office window. "Maybe you should take your coat off."

"As much as I'd like to, Vivian, I've got Jim Brandson's general manager stopping by in a few minutes," he explained. "Tommy something or other. When you get caught up, check on our request for that window tint, will you? That would sure help with this heat."

"I sure will. By the way, Tommy Catatonia *did* call. He's running fifteen minutes behind schedule for your ten o'clock with him." She peered at him over the top of her reading glasses which she wore pushed out to the tip of her nose, waiting patiently for her boss's response. In her forties and younger than Lewis, Vivian was quick to defend him, loyal to her man and his mission, convinced he had a great future ahead.

"Okay, thanks, Viv. That'll give me time to call Detective Anderson at GPD on this Brandson file. Lotta loose ends, here." Detective Anderson, who headed up the Economic Crimes Division, was in charge of the local investigation and often served as his liaison with GPD.

"Yes, sir. I'll let you know when Mr. Catatonia gets here." She exited his office, heading back to her desk around the corner from his. Spinning her old-school Rolodex, she found Bob Powell's number at Custom Glass Tinting and gave him a call to see if he'd received their purchase order.

Lewis dialed Detective Anderson's desk phone. After ringing ten times, there was no answer. Next, he dialed the detective's cell phone. After ringing twice, the detective answered.

"Lieutenant Anderson."

"Matt, Tom Lewis. Got a minute?"

"For you, Tom, absolutely. What's up?"

"Got a coupla questions on this Brandson investigation."

"Shoot."

"I've read the Brandson file and your reports. Who, exactly, has spoken with this confidential informant who's been feeding us these documents?" Although Anderson was not a big fan of relying on information supplied by CIs, he had started to wonder if Lewis was undermining the situation to denigrate the evidence and drag his feet on the investigation. It wouldn't be the first time he'd seen the state attorney go easy on one of his larger campaign contributors.

Anderson answered, "John Dunne, the director at Seniors Against Crimes, has spoken with him several times. The CI uses an untraceable cell phone for these conversations and John claims he doesn't know the CI's identity."

"You know anyone else who's spoken to this character?"

"My gut tells me the FBI has, but they refuse to say for sure." Like John Dunne and the FBI, Anderson knew the CI had a greater value in providing more evidence for them if he could remain anonymous.

Lewis continued. "And you think he's an employee at the dealership?"

"Yes, he has stated that to Dunne."

"What's keeping him from coming forward?"

"Fear for his safety. He says the managers are a bunch of drunks and drug-crazed, trigger-happy gun freaks."

"Do we have any evidence of these allegations," asked the state attorney.

"Yes we do." From their rap sheets, Anderson knew this to be true.

"Are the Feds sharing with us?"

"As a matter of fact, Tom, they are. I think they realize that with seven separate agencies conducting their own investigations, it's in the public interest to do so," said Detective Anderson.

"Well, here's what I'm wrestling with," said Lewis. "I know Agent Danley thinks we have enough evidence to meet the probable cause threshold, but I'm not so—"

Anderson interrupted. "Tom, they'll serve their subpoenas if we don't serve ours. We would lose control and, possibly, original jurisdiction."

Lewis responded, "Granted, but I'd hate to be the one responsible for putting over a hundred people at Brandson out of work unnecessarily. What about this Jack Gates character. What do we have on him?" Lewis was leafing through the seven files totaling three hundred eighty-three pages that laid on his desk, trying to keep track of all the low-rent characters at Brandson. Some of the information in the reports was just unbelievable.

"Well, Brandson's attorneys are still running interference for him," said Anderson. "Gates has two prior fraud convictions and one felony conviction for narcotics with intent to distribute, a coupla bad checks, and a few misdemeanors. Oh, and two DUIs."

"What else? What about the CVC complaints?"

"That's the crazy part with Gates. Brandson's already paid out a hundred and nine thousand dollars in civil settlements on his behalf. Apparently, he's made them so much money that they're not quite ready to let go of him. With just a little more evidence, we'll have enough to bring him in for questioning. Then, maybe he rolls, if we offer him a deal."

Lewis continued. "Why would they hang onto Gates? Unless he knows so much they're afraid of him?"

"Probably. I think you're right. I think they're afraid to cut him loose, a little victimless extortion goin' on there."

"Very likely. Did you pull jackets on Catatonia, Wells, Pfister, Grimes, and Shifter?"

Anderson had done his homework. "Yes. Multiple felony convictions for drugs, aggravated assault, and fraud on Wells, Shifter, and Grimes. Wells is also the subject of a current Federal investigation for tax fraud and has been charged by the IRS. Catatonia and Pfister are relatively clean, only a couple of misdemeanor battery and gambling charges."

"How do guys with jackets like this even get hired?" Lewis had a hard time wrapping his head around this. He would definitely think twice before recommending that particular dealership.

"Wells did the hiring. I'm thinking maybe he smudged a few applications for his buddies. What do you think, Tom?"

"Obviously. Some of this stuff is just hard to believe. Whatever happened to background checks?"

Lewis intended the question to be rhetorical, but Anderson answered it anyway. "I guess this is what happens when you put a convicted felon in charge of hiring."

Lewis continued. "More important, where does Toyota corporate stand in all this? Who have you spoken with at Toyota USA or Toyota Motors?" The state attorney wrestled with all the moving parts of the case, but never stopped looking for the best headline.

"I spoke to a couple of senior vice presidents. I get the feeling they're stalling. They say they're looking into it. Obviously, if they were to claim to be a victim of a seventy million dollar criminal fraud, it would be a public relations catastrophe for them. Of global proportions. Probably cheaper for them to eat the seventy million."

There was a long pause and Lewis took a sip of his Perrier. Then he said, "I see two references to a second CI who is former law enforcement. What do we know about him?"

"There are three possibilities, but nothing has been confirmed." Lewis was running out of questions to ask. Deep down, Anderson was still not convinced that Lewis had any real desire to prosecute the case. The reason for his reluctance to prosecute was still a mystery.

"All right, there, detective. Carry on. Appreciate the update. How 'bout we talk again in a few days?" Lewis mindlessly brushed some lint off his coat sleeve.

"Sure, Tom. Look forward to it." For the sake of his career, there could be no other viable answer for the young lieutenant of detectives.

As he hung up the phone with Detective Anderson, Lewis heard his assistant say, "Ask him to take a seat. I'll be right up." She then stepped around the corner and knocked on his opened door.

"Mr. Catatonia is here to see you, Tom. Shall I bring him up from the lobby?" The state attorney was looking off in the distance, lost in thought about his conversation with the GPD detective. After a moment, he looked up at his assistant and smiled smugly.

"Sure, Vivian, bring him up." Lewis folded his hands together, elbows up on his desk, thinking. He needed to figure out a way to get the FBI on the same page with his political agenda. A few minutes of self-indulgence slipped by before the balding, portly man wearing a tailored, black Brioni suit came into view through the doorway. Lewis stood up to greet his guest, and Vivian did the introductions.

"Mr. Lewis, this is Mr. Catatonia."

"Mr. Catatonia, a pleasure, sir." They shook hands. Lewis added, "Please have a seat." Lewis waved his hand at the two overstuffed leather chairs.

"Shall I close your door, Tom?"

"That would be fine, Vivian." She dismissed herself and closed the door behind her, giving the two men some privacy.

As he took a seat, Catatonia said, "Please, call me Tommy."

"Okay, Tommy. Call me Tom." As he took his seat, he added, "I want to thank you and your organization once again for the generous support that you gave to my re-election campaign four years ago." Both men were both quite practiced at putting on their best public relations facades as they exchanged pleasantries.

"Well, Tom, that's why I'm here today. Mr. Brandson sent me to personally thank you for all the fine work you're doing in our community, and the support you've given to our sixteen dealerships as we've grown over the years." Catatonia pulled an envelope from his finely-tailored Italian suit and placed it in his lap. The GM continued.

"To ensure full compliance with the new campaign regulations, Mr. Brandson has had this year's five campaign contribution checks for twenty thousand dollars each drawn on five separate accounts in the names of his three nephews and two nieces. In doing so, it was our thinking that this would help to keep a lower profile and yet provide you with the funding we think you deserve for your upcoming campaign." Catatonia smiled again, and Lewis smiled back, nodding appreciatively.

As he laid the five checks on the State Attorney's desk in front of him, Catatonia added, "There are, of course, no strings. We just wanted to express our appreciation for your support in advance, whenever our interests can be considered to be in alignment."

"That's very generous of your boss, Tommy. Please express my sincere thanks. We can do a lot of good with your contributions. Everything from hiring new staff to fixing leaks in our buildings. You might want to check for leaks where you are. They can really run your bills up!" He paused for a moment, waiting for agreement from his guest with what he thought had been an artistic double entendre.

Catatonia hesitated for a moment, searching for the right response. Then he said, "Good idea, Tom. You know we like a tight ship, free of leaks. We look forward to many years of smooth sailing ahead." The GM paused, adding, "Be great if we knew more about where they came from." Catatonia eyed the checks on the desk again as he trained his gaze back on the state attorney.

Lewis met his gaze and said, "Ya might want to call KG Plumbing. KG's been a good source. That's all *I* know."

Catatonia nodded emphatically and said, "I appreciate your seeing me today, Tom. I know you're a busy man. I'd like to stay longer and chat with you about our growing family of dealerships, but I've got an appointment at my office in twenty minutes. And, gotta check that plumbing for leaks. Thanks again."

They stood and shook hands enthusiastically, mutually agreeing to their tacit understanding. Tommy Catatonia, general manager of Brandson Toyota, turned and exited the office of the state attorney, feeling good about successfully fulfilling his boss's directive.

It was Wednesday, September 5th, five weeks since his surgery. He no longer needed his arm sling, brace or splint. Slowly, his wounds were healing and sutures disappearing. So far, he had resisted Tommy Catatonia's pressure to return to work before he was ready. He brought up the Danziger disaster more than once as a reminder of what happens when injured employees still heavily medicated were pressured to return to work prematurely. That event had cost Brandson more than ninety thousand dollars in surgical, prescription, and physical rehabilitation expenses, as well as increased insurance premiums. It had also cost one of their top salesmen quite a bit of pain and lost wages.

This morning, Mark sat at his desk in front of his home PC trying to decide which of his sixteen emails to read first. There was one was from Dr. Sandra McGowan, the pretty green-eyed redhead whom he'd helped in service before his surgery, and another from Rich at the dealership.

Figuring he had the doctor in the bag and could call her later, he was more intrigued with the one from Rich. He opened it first. As he read Rich's wishes for a speedy recovery, along with his suggestions on how to get a free month's supply of Viagra, something else caught his attention. Buried in the body of the email was the question, "Why is Rocky Gambrone going through boxes of our customer files in the private conference room?" *Brother, I don't know,* he thought, *but that's a real good question.* He reached for his phone and dialed Rich's number. On the fifth ring, he heard Rich's voice.

"Hey, Marky-Mark." He sounded out of breath and could hear him walking quickly, probably heading outside for more privacy. "Hang on a sec. I need to get further away from the building."

"Sure. Can you pick up the pace a little, I got a very pretty doctor waiting."

Huffing and puffing, Rich said, "That's a switch. A doctor's waiting for you, huh?"

"Why, is that so hard to believe?"

"It's definitely a change from what *I'm* used to."

Rich was almost far enough away from prying ears to ensure their privacy. Mark asked, "So, what would you do for a good cardio workout if it wasn't for these phone conversations on the grassy knoll?"

"Whatever," said Rich. "Hey, listen to this. They got Rocky going through our deal jackets in the executive conference room. Earlier, I saw him in Tricky Ricky's office going through our customer files in the ERA system."

"How do you know he was in the ERA system?" Mark asked.

"The screen was that deep blue color, you know, like when we clock in and out on ERA. I only had a quick peek from about ten feet, but they were definitely lender deal screens he was working on." He could hear Rich saying hello to someone walking by on.

Mark knew Rocky Gambrone was Brandson's under-the-table IT guy and a master of manipulating information on the web. Larry hired him several years ago when Rocky had first demonstrated his unique set of computer skills by hiding financial assets for him, manipulating the bank accounts and altering lenders' loan files. He could do this by making unauthorized changes to internet data, websites, and by using backdoors that very few IT professionals even knew about. He knew code and he knew how to cover his tracks. It was rumored that he used to launder money for a major drug cartel and that he still maintained those underworld contacts.

Mark was concerned. "This is bad news, Rich. You know this guy's capable of deleting key files without leaving a trace. How long has he been there?"

"About an hour," said Rich.

"I can't believe that they've got him doing that stuff in broad daylight," said Mark. "If they don't care about the staff seeing him do this, then Larry and Tommy C. must be desperate to hide evidence."

"I think you need to let 'those guys' know about this."

"Don't worry. 'Those guys' and CVC will be my next phone calls. While I've got you on the phone, what else is going on there today?"

"Funny you should ask. Earlier this morning, Tommy C., Larry, and Bryan all got into a major argument in the private conference room. They were screaming at each other at the tops of their lungs. I've never seen them that violent. The whole dealership heard them."

"What was it about? Could you hear anything specific?" asked Mark, wanting as much detail as Rich could give him.

"Mostly pointing the finger at each other, accusing each other of defrauding everyone. Ironic, huh? Major, major blow-out."

Mark said, "They're hearing the rumors, feeling the heat. Now, the wheels are starting to come off their dirty little wagon. Sounds like they're starting to turn on each other like the rabid, junkyard dogs that they are. Law enforcement was hoping for this."

"Yeah. There will be a day of reckoning for these guys. 'Til then, I've got to earn a living. I've got a daughter to raise and bills to pay."

Mark said, "You and me both. In spite of the rumors, I'm not made out of money either, bro. What's cookin' with Carla's stuff?"

"I swear, my wife's a nut job. It almost seems like she's got a death wish. She got out on a four hundred dollar bail then got arrested again for stealing a bottle of rum from a liquor store. So, the Marion County Sheriff's Office arrested her for the fourth time, and now she's back in jail 'cause she can't come up with the thousand dollar bond. Can you believe that?"

Mark said, "I don't get it. She's already been arrested three times, now four times in three months? How come they keep letting her post a low bond? All she does is go out and do stupid stuff, score drugs, get high, and commit more crimes." Mark remembered they set his bond for his DUI crash at twenty thousand dollars, which seemed excessive, even to the prosecutor. There didn't seem to be any rhyme or reason to this bond-setting business.

Rich said, "I didn't know this until lately, but every time she gets arrested and bonds out, the county makes money. Is that nuts?"

"And this is the mother of your child?" asked Mark.

"Yup. I guess the maternity thing didn't take with her."

"Guess not," agreed Mark. He knew Rich's wife was wacked.

"Oh, almost forgot the weirdest part of all this," said Rich. "You remember the coked-out stripper that Carla was staying with that was busted for felony gun possession and intent to distribute cocaine?"

"Yeah." Mark was paying attention. He had a feeling that a strange story was about to get even stranger.

"Well, after three days in jail, the Marion County Sheriff's Office released her on her own recognizance."

"Wait. Hold the phone. You're saying a stripper with a felony conviction of dealing cocaine, who was caught with a firearm and drugs in her house while she was on parole from another felony, was released on her own recognizance? Seriously?"

Rich answered, "That's right. Her name is Lucille Cranston. Go online to MCSO Mugshots. You'll see her there. I found out later that the MCSO let her out by design."

"What do you mean?"

"The US Marshall's office suspected her of illegally selling assault rifles, but they didn't have the weapons as proof. They couldn't bust her without more evidence. So, they hatched this plan to let her out, thinking she'd go for them. Two hours later, they pull her over with seventeen assault rifles, AK-47s, and a thousand rounds of ammo in her trunk and back seat."

"You've got to be kidding me. In Ocala?"

"Yep. It's all true. When they searched her house, they found eleven more AR-15s and AK-47s equipped with forty round banana clips in her attic, sixteen grand in cash, and another fifteen hundred rounds."

"And this is the stripper your wife's shacking up with, what's she got in mind, a revolution for God's sake? I mean, you can't make this stuff up!" said Mark.

"She is done, brother! Felony gun and drug dealing in unlicensed automatic assault rifles while on parole? She'll probably get fifteen or twenty years."

Mark switched gears and did his best gay doctor impression, saying, "Well looky here, Richie, when Carla gets out of rehab, guess she'll need a new place to stay. Ya know, I got a lot of room over here—"

"Ha! You'd last about two seconds before she'd have your nuts in a vise!" Mark knew Rich's wife was about as useful as learning to speak Klingon.

Mark continued with his gay doctor impression. "Well, funny you should say that, 'cuz I actually do use my vise to crack nuts around Christmas—"

"Yeah, right! You're the nut job!"

"Yeah, well you've burned through so many local girls you're gonna hafta move to Pennsylvania and date Amish chicks," joked Mark.

Rich changed the subject. "Oh, by the way, I sold two more deals for us since we spoke Monday. Patricia Rhoads asked for you when she came in and bought herself a four cylinder Tacoma low-boy. That was a fifteen hundred front. And Chris Duer, you remember him?"

"Sure do. I had him pegged for a looky-loo." Mark did his best to side-step the tire kickers and looky-loos, but sometimes you just couldn't gauge their motivation until after you'd spent some time with them.

Rich continued. "Chris said he's been by to see you twice. Well, I finally sold him a used Venza. Took me three hours. I thought he'd never sign."

Mark asked, "What'd we make on that?"

"You mean, including the fake certification that we charged him for? Duer was a twenty-three hundred dollar front, so we did okay. If we get paid for it. The Venza only had twelve thousand miles on it. The mechanic never did the hundred-and-sixty-point inspection for the certification."

"What makes you so certain that they faked the mechanic's certification on the Venza?" asked Mark.

"Because I saw the used car porter sitting in the car, filling it out and signing it when I was on the lot with another customer yesterday. I watched him fold it and stick it in the glove box."

"I can't believe how blatant the managers are with some of these frauds," said Mark. "They act like they've got diplomatic immunity from the law, for God's sake."

"Well, guess what? I made an extra copy of it. Ha! Like I said, there will be a day of reckoning. Hey, let me run, I think I see a customer."

"Wait," said Mark. "Do me a favor when you get home tonight. Scan that forged certification and email it to me, will you? That's an important piece of evidence."

"You got it, bro. Gotta run, can't let this customer get away."

"Go get 'um, tiger!" Mark had a feeling that Rich was getting off on being a cop once again, and he was glad they were on the same team.

He turned his attention to alerting the FBI and CVC about Rocky Gambrone's destruction of evidence. While he wasn't sure if this new development would accelerate their investigations, he was certain that they needed to know about the customer file deletions immediately.

Deeming this new information as urgent, he decided not to wait for Rich's email of the forged certification later in the evening. From his anonymous address, he labeled the emails to Special Agents Brad Danley, Frank Moser, and Economic Crimes Agent James Costello as Urgent, and copied John Dunne, who would forward it to Detective Anderson at GPD and his contacts at the Florida Attorney General's office in Tallahassee.

In the email, he described all the new developments that he was aware of. He included likely computer file deletions at the dealership, hard-copy document alterations, as well as a description of Rocky Gambrone's IT capabilities and known criminal background and associations. He urged the authorities to do whatever they could to preserve as much evidence as possible, before it was too late and the evidence disappeared into cyberspace forever.

TWENTY

It was Saturday morning, and Mark sat at his desk daydreaming about tonight's date with sexy Sandra McGowan. They had exchanged phone calls and emails for the past few months, testing the water, flirting on the phone whenever they could find the time. Now that he'd been back at work for three weeks and was no longer encumbered with his arm sling, he welcomed whatever physical demands she might subject him to tonight. He was guessing that it would likely become a contest of who was the better tease. Either way, he was primed and ready.

"Penny for your thoughts, there, Marky-Mark." Scott Pruden had jolted him back to reality with his jovial exuberance.

"Oh, I was just thinking about this girl—"

"That's dangerous ground. I thought you were in a safe place there, in between wives and boats."

"Just like you, Scott, I'm trying to figure out which is more expensive-wives, or boats. Guess more research is required, huh?" Mark thought for a moment, adding "You think you might have room aboard your floating palace for a gorgeous bikini?"

"I like you, Marky-Mark, but not in a bikini," joked Scott.

Mark went with the flow, doing his gay doctor with a limp wrist routine, which had become much easier after having recently broken it in three places. "No, you silly. I mean a girl."

"Okay, so this time it's a girl, huh? Ha! Describe."

"About five-foot sex, a hundred eighteen—"

"What? Did you say five foot sex?" asked Scott.

"Uh, Freudian slip, maybe . . . "

"And, I don't want to see you in any slips, either. Way too much visual information there, Marky-Mark."

Mark continued his description of Sandy. "Green eyes, strawberry blonde cut in a page boy, athletic, perfect body, some really cute freckles on her—"

"Whoa. Let me stop you right there, before you embarrass yourself," said Scott. "What's she do for a living?"

"Sandy's a trauma surgeon." Mark could almost hear the 'ching-ching' of the cash register going off in Scott's head as his eyes lit up like a pinball machine.

Scott leaned forward, stroked his bald head feigning indecision, and asked, "You got any pictures?"

"Not yet. Working on it." Mark tried to think of a video that would help describe her. "You remember that Rod Stewart video called 'This Old Heart of Mine' from the 90s, with that really hot blonde dancer—"

"We're talking of a girl here?"

"Stop it, you homo. Yes, a girl. Anyway, the girl in the video is that really hot-lookin' blonde, page-boy cut, very short green vinyl dress—"

"I know exactly which girl you're talking about. Your girl looks like her?" Scott was getting excited.

"Almost identical," said Mark, "except Sandy has a strawberry blonde pageboy, green eyes, and a few more freckles on her face. I have a date with her tonight."

Scott cocked his head and pressed his hand down on Mark's desk top for emphasis. "Okay, here's the deal. All seriousness aside. You get her in a bikini, on my boat, and I'll spring for the drinks, food, gas-everything. Even the bait. No-wait. You're bringing the bait, right? Her! You could just drop her off at my boat, if you wanted—"

"Keep dreamin', baldy. Hey, you've got a nice-lookin' wife, and she's twenty years younger than you, you old fart. Sandy's my date. You can look, but not touch. We got a deal?"

Scott said, "Deal. Can I drool?"

"If you must, but bring a bib." They did the fist bump to seal the deal. Then, Scott slid his chair in a little closer and lowered his voice, and Mark braced himself for what he was about to say next.

"Hey, let me run something by you", said Scott. Mark sensed it was something more serious. "I've been hearing rumors about a police investigation here. You heard anything like that?"

Sensing a possible set-up, Mark sat back in his chair, deciding how to respond. He was uncertain of where Scott's loyalties lay. Scott was often opportunistic and had aided Larry in rewording the addendum portion of the new car sales stickers a month earlier. He did it in in a way that effectively circumvented the law. As his reward, Scott was given a cheese deal. Mark decided to be cautious and guarded with his answer.

"Yeah, I heard those rumors, too," said Mark. "Are you really surprised? You've seen the fraud here. It's blatant. Am I right?" Scott slid back in his chair. He said, "Yeah, but c'mon.Welcome to the car business, right? Aren't they all a bunch of shysters?"

Mark smiled. He liked his friend, but he sensed that Scott couldn't be trusted with confidential information. His moral compass seemed just a little off, and he could be playing for the other team. But he'd still take that boat ride on Scott's new Sea Ray. Sandy would love it.

Suddenly, Larry appeared behind them. "All right, ladies. Let's get back to work. Mark, stop wasting Scott's time. We need to sell some cars today! C'mon." Larry stood over Mark's desk and clapped his hands together loudly. Scott went back to his desk. "Mark, get on the phone." The self-proclaimed Devil hadn't taken his nice pill today.

"Sure thing, Larry," said Mark. He paused then asked, "By the way, do you have anymore of those phone leads that I could call?"

As he headed back to the sales tower, Larry responded gruffly over his shoulder, "I gave them all to Paul and Juicifer. Now, get on the phone before I hurt your other arm."

Before Mark could respond, his desk phone rang. As he picked it up, he could see that Jo had guests at her reception desk in the front of the showroom. She said, "Hey, Mark, I have some customers here for you. You want to come up and say hello?"

"Be right up, Jo." He hung up and prepped his desk.

The Shaws had phoned Brandson earlier this morning. Mark had taken the call and found out that they received a letter from Brandson offering them over seventeen thousand dollars for their five year old Rav 4. Although this sounded like a lot more than their trade was really worth, he'd closed them for an appointment. He headed to the front desk to introduce himself. Reaching to shake Bob's hand, he said, "Hi, I'm Mark McAllister. We spoke on the phone. Nice to meet you both."

"It's a pleasure to meet you, too," said Bob. He held the letter up to Mark, pointing at the wording. "Says here, Brandson'll give me almost eighteen thousand for my Rav 4. That's why we're here." He paused to hear Mark's response, expecting confirmation on the offer price.

"C'mon over to my desk," said Mark. "We'll get started on the appraisal. Can I offer you some bottled water?"

Janice said, "Sure. That sounds good." They seemed like friendly, good-natured people, raising Mark's hopes for a deal.

As they talked more and strolled toward his desk, Mark found out that they were interested in another Rav 4. They sat down together to work out the details. Their trade was paid for, and they wanted to use their trade plus some cash for the new Rav 4 upgrade.

"Before we get too far into this, Mark, I want to make sure that the offer from Brandson to buy our Rav 4 is solid. We're limited to a down payment of eight thousand cash, plus our trade. We don't want to make payments."

"I understand, Bob. If you have a key to your Rav 4, I'll have our appraiser take a look at it, and we can start from there." Even though they had bought it from Brandson originally, Mark wanted to verify the VIN and the actual mileage. He took the key from Bob and headed outside. After his inspection of their Rav 4 Limited, he took the key, appraisal form and blue sheet, and headed into the sales tower.

"Whatcha got there, Marky-Mark?"

Mark showed Kirk all the data on the blue sheet and said, "The Shaws came in on the upgrade letter. They're nice folks and repeat customers of Brandson. They bought it here five years ago. I just verified the VIN and miles. Here's the appraisal sheet and key." Mark put them on the desk in front of Kirk. "They're looking to pay the cash difference, no financing. They're firm on wanting to confirm their trade-in allowance before they look at a new one. You have time to take a look at it?"

Kirk looked up at Mark and scowled, not wanting to get out of his chair. He studied the information on the blue sheet and asked, "What do they want for their trade?" Mark looked at him and tried to ignore the bruise under his eye.

"Well, the letter they brought in from us says seventeen thousand plus, so that's kinda what they have in mind. They're working with eight thousand in cash to put toward their new Rav 4."

Kirk looked at him and said, "They want us to pay them seventeen grand on an older Rav 4 with seventy-six thousand miles on it? Really? Let's go take a look at this gold-plated Rav."

As he stood up, Kirk farted loudly, surprising everyone in the room. Larry looked up from his desk two seats down and said, "Jeez, Kirk, couldn't you wait 'til you got outside, man?" Larry pinched his nose and added, "Really, bro, you gotta lay off those dead possums."

Kirk ignored the razzing from his boss, and Mark followed the used-car manager out to the Rav 4, keeping a safe distance. They found the SUV parked in front, baking in the hot Florida sun.

"Another black Rav 4?" asked Kirk. "We've still got two of them out on the lot. They know that black's not a real popular color in ninety-five degree weather?"

"This one's a Limited with four-wheel drive. Aren't those features that our buyers like these days?" Mark knew he had to build more value for their trade in Kirk's mind if he was going to pull this deal off.

Ignoring Mark's question, Kirk sat down inside and started the engine. He confirmed the odometer reading at seventy-six thousand, two hundred five miles, checked the shift mechanism, and turned on the air conditioning. Kirk switched off the engine and they walked back inside.

Kirk sat back down at his desk and did some figuring on his computer, then handed Mark the appraisal form with a four-figure number circled in black. Kirk said, "Tell them that the reason we can only give them seventy-five hundred for their trade is because of the high mileage. Got it?"

Mark answered his boss by saying, "I will do that in the most positive way possible, Kirk, but you know they're not going to be happy with this. That's about ten grand under what they're expecting."

"Just do it," commanded Kirk.

Mark walked out of the sales tower feeling like a condemned man on his way to the electric chair. As he sat down with the Shaws, he smiled, trying to put a positive spin on the numbers. They leaned in closer to get a better look at the figures on the appraisal.

"Bob and Janice, your Rav is in good shape, but it's five years old and has a lot of mileage on it," said Mark. "Our used car manager can only give you seventy-five hundred for it. I wish we could do better for you, but my manager says the age and mileage on your trade are holding down the value." He looked at them apologetically, hoping they would be flexible and still interested in a good deal on a new one. Bob picked up the appraisal and looked at it like it was covered in horse manure.

"Are you kidding me?" asked Bob. "This is a joke." He looked up at Mark, adding, "We thought we could count on what your dealership offered us in the letter. You know, Janice and I went online to Kelley Blue Book, and even they said our Rav 4 is worth around seventeen thousand. What kind of rip-off dealership are you running here?"

"Hey, I'm sorry," Mark said. He could see Bob and Janice were really upset with the offer. "If it was up to me, I would give you more."

Bob said, "Unless we can get something close to the seventeen grand that's promised to us right here in this letter, we're leaving. This is starting to look like a waste of our time."

The Shaws stood up, preparing to leave. "Wait one minute," said Mark. "If I could get you more for your trade, and discount the price on a new Rav 4, would you be interested?"

"We're not even on the same page, Mark. He'd have to come up at least another nine thousand dollars." He looked at his wife, who was clearly as upset as he was. "What do you think, honey?"

Janice slung her purse strap over her shoulder, turned, and faced away from Mark, looking out toward the front door. She frowned disapprovingly and said, "You don't want to know what I think!"

Mark said, "Wait one second. I have an idea." He headed into the sales tower to see if Kirk would help him resurrect the deal.

"Kirk, we're about nine thousand dollars apart on the trade-in price. What's the best we could offer them for their Rav 4?" asked Mark.

Kirk made a face at him. He said, "I told you what to tell them! Did you screw it up?" Mark waited for an answer to the question he asked. After a moment, Kirk finally gave him a figure. "I'll go eighty-five hundred, but that's it!"

Mark ran out the door to his customers who were still standing at his desk. "Bob and Janice, my used car manager said he'd go up to eighty-five hundred. What do you think?" Mark knew they were still miles apart, but he wasn't giving up.

"We think you're a nice guy, Mark," said Bob. "And we're not mad at you. But we don't like the way they do business here. If they send out a letter offering us a certain amount of money for our car, then, by God, they ought to honor it! Not some bait and switch bull! C'mon, honey, let's get outta here." They headed for the door.

Hungry and thirsty after his ordeal with the bait-and-switch letter, Mark headed back to the cafeteria for some lunch. As he walked down the hallway toward the back of the dealership, he passed Tricky Ricky on his cell phone.

"That's right, Jim, the new Mercedes SLS AMG on your website," said Tricky Ricky. "I'm only interested in the signature model-S you have listed for two hundred six thousand. Yeah, the white one. Is that one still available?" After Rick stopped a few feet down the hallway, Rick added "No . . . not interested in any financing, all cash deal . . . yeah, I know it's a collectible, but I'm not going over two hundred. Period. That's my out-the-door offer. Oh well, let me know if you change your mind."

As Mark turned the corner, he thought about this. So, that's what the F&I guys were doing with their ill-gotten gains. Buying collectibles. He heard that Rick already owned a new Aston Martin, a vintage gull-wing Mercedes, and a brand new Audi R8. And they were all white. Whoever said crime doesn't pay obviously hadn't met these guys.

"Gary, it's seven o'clock, Saturday night. Go home. Spend some time with your family." Gronske's sergeant, George Acevello, was a family man and a republican with conservative values. He encouraged his detectives to maintain healthy relationships with their families, but he knew Gronske was a workaholic.

"I will, George," responded Gronske. "Just tying up some loose ends here." He had pages from several active files spread out over his desk and his computer. The detective was slowly piecing together evidence from three recent drug busts. One of the drug deals resulted in a victim being severely beaten behind a downtown nightclub called Club Liquid. He recalled the case from a few months ago.

"Okay, Gary, have a good night," said Sergeant Acevello. "Say hi to Carla. Maria has dinner waiting for me. See you later."

The file read that the beating victim from the Club Liquid bust was serving a one year sentence at Raiford State Prison for his third conviction for drug possession. The victim had no memory of the assault. Tyrone Davis had suffered permanent brain damage from the attack that had left him unconscious and slumped against a dumpster. The injuries were so severe he couldn't remember anything that happened that night. Having his victim unable to identify his attacker frustrated Gronske, but he was getting closer to figuring it out.

There were a lot of similarities in the three case files he was reviewing. In each one, there were several references to a muscular white guy named Tony, who they figured to be the main supplier. Tony's name first came up in Gronske's questioning of a homeless man who overheard the argument preceding the assault behind Club Liquid. All three cases involved the same type of uncut cocaine, meth and vials of HGH. All three crime scenes involved downtown nightclubs, and he and his partner had recovered over sixty thousand dollars worth of illegal drugs from the busts. They knew there were a lot more drugs out there connected to these cases, and Gronske intended to find the perps responsible for causing so much misery in his community.

Tonight, the most popular Izakaya-style sushi restaurant in Gainesville bustled with food, drinks, and customers hungry for Japanese cuisine. The neon-lit bar at the entrance to Club Liquid was full of thirsty party animals in a festive mood and cruising for action. The Florida Gators had beaten their archrival Florida State this afternoon, and on a night like this, everybody got lucky. The sound of laughter and people having a good time reverberated from every corner of the restaurant. With perfect weather and the temperature in the sixties, it was a gorgeous Saturday night. The majority of the customers streaming in were young couples in their twenties, wearing their most provocative outfits, as they made their entrances through the brass-plated double doors.

Mark and Sandy sat patiently on the leather couch in the customer waiting area, completely entertained by each other and the continuous fashion parade streaming in the front door. Even though most of the guys stepping inside were accompanied by smoking hot dates, they still had a hard time keeping their eyes off Sandy. Anticipating a wait, Mark left his date for a minute to retrieve two glasses of cabernet from the bar.

She was the center of attention in a little black dress that was a carbon copy of the black, cross-strapped backless dress worn by Demi Moore in the movie *Indecent Proposal.* Only it looked even better on Sandy. The dress accentuated her sumptuous cleavage and toned, athletic legs. Rejoining her on the leather couch, Mark got a kick out of noticing that the men in the reception area stopped talking every time she crossed and uncrossed her legs.

Their appreciation for the impromptu fashion parade was interrupted by a man's voice. "Mark, we have your table ready. It's good to see you again." The owner of Club Liquid, Hiro Suzuki, had stopped over to greet them. Mark shook his hand. "I like your silk dress shirt. Brioni, right?" asked Hiro. Without waiting for Mark to answer, he turned to Sandy. "And who is this gorgeous woman with you who graces our décor with her beauty tonight?"

As Sandy extended her hand, Hiro kissed it. "Sandra McGowan. Please call me Sandy."

"You two look great together. Thanks for coming tonight. Let me show you to your table." Hiro turned to Sandy. "This is Mark's favorite table, and you two are perfect for it." Hiro led the way, Sandy followed, and Mark followed her behind. He was mesmerized by the hypnotic sway of her hips as she walked. He was totally entertained by the way she pretended not to notice that so many eyes were entranced by her moves.

"Here you go. The 'goldfish bowl' is all yours. Barbara will be right with you," said Hiro as he seated them and handed them menus. "Enjoy your dining experience." Hiro headed back to the front desk.

Sandy said, "I see why they call it 'the goldfish bowl.' I really like the bay windows, and the feeling that we're dining outside. Pretty cool." Sandy had removed her Gucci heels after Mark had seated her and was now teasing Mark with her foot under the table.

Mark was tempted to return the favor. He saw that the couple nearest them were whispering and watching Sandy's foot in his lap. He said, "You keep that up, and I'm going to have to crawl under the table and find out what brand of panties you have on."

Batting her eyelashes, she said flirtatiously, "Sweetie, I'm not wearing any. How do I know you're not all talk?"

His appetite for sushi took a back seat as he struggled to maintain his dining decorum. "We gonna skip the menu and go straight to dessert?" he asked.

Before she could answer, a pretty, young Asian waitress with exotic features approached their table. Mark was a little embarrassed and grabbed Sandy's foot, holding it away from his crotch. He began giving her a foot massage, hoping the waitress hadn't noticed the effect that Sandy was having on him. The waitress said, "Hi, I'm Barbara. I'll be your server tonight. Hiro said to take real good care of you. Would you care for some cocktails?" She glanced at his crotch, then blushed and quickly looked away.

Mark looked at Sandy, then back at Barbara. He said, "I was just giving Dr. McGowan here some needed physical therapy. Her foot has been in contact with too many hard surfaces lately, and her ligaments need loosening." Mark smiled at both girls, trying to put his own spin on the steamy scene his date was creating.

Sandy said, "Let's have two more glasses of the Meridian Coastal '94 we had earlier. We like that, right sweetie?"

"I think the Meridian sounds great," said Mark calmly. He looked up at their server and smiled. "It would give the doctor something to do with her hands and mouth until I can get her home for more therapy." Cocking his ear toward the far back corner of the restaurant, he thought he heard familiar voices.

Barbara laughed and said, "Yes, sir. Coming right up."

"You have no idea," he said. "Honey, while Barbara is bringing our cabernet, I'm gonna excuse myself and head for the restroom. I've gotta rearrange a few things in my pants. Feels a lot more crowded in there since you danced the 'Nutcracker' on my balls." Sandy smiled seductively at him as he deftly lifted her foot from his lap with a final caress and headed for the rear of the restaurant.

Winding his way through the tables of festive customers eating, drinking and celebrating, Mark found his way to the far back of the restaurant to investigate what he thought he heard earlier. Sitting at a large table around the corner from the men's room alcove, in the furthest darkened recesses of the club, he spotted Tricky Ricky, Larry, Kirk and Tony. They had their backs to him, unaware of his presence, while they watched a waitress in fishnet stockings dancing on a table. A burly bouncer who Mark didn't recognize stood guard over the group of party animals with his arms crossed.

A feeling of fear swept over him as he secretly watched them from the entrance to the alcove. They alternated hunching over and doing lines of coke laid out on their table. He noticed it was stacked with cash. 'The Redneck Mafia' was in full party mode, boisterous and oblivious to anyone else's presence as they drank, exchanged fistbumps and snorted narcotics in the darkest corner of Club Liquid.

His first reaction was to call Agents Danley and Moser. Then he thought about Sandy. Wanting to keep her safe from this group of miscreants, he chose to be discrete and returned to his date at the front of the restaurant. He felt protective as he watched Sandy, unaware of the danger in the back, foot wagging, legs crossed, smiling mischievously up at him. She still had one shoe off.

Demurely she asked, "Darling, did you get all your equipment ready for me?' Her teasing brought him right back to the flirty mood they shared earlier.

As he pulled his chair out, he asked, "You're not taking any heart medications, are you, Sandy? I just want to make sure that your heart is healthy enough to handle four or five days of non-stop strenuous exercise." Mark smiled and sat down, listening to the cacophony of happy celebrants that surrounded them.

"You're the only medicine I need," she said with a steady gaze. He could feel the caress of her foot again.

"Okay. We can skip the meds," he said. "All those nasty side effects they mention in the fine print. The pain and swelling, maybe I can handle. But the vomiting, headaches, bleeding out the eyes, loss of hearing, constipation, uncontrollable flatulence, nosebleeds, diarrhea, loss of muscle control, jaundice, dandruff, incontinence, loss of speech, menstrual cramps in men, labial fatigue, ringing in the ears, chronic ringing of your doorbell, liver failure, bleeding out the rectum, brain damage, kidney disease, intestinal blockage, addiction to trans-fats, blindness, liver failure, heart attacks, coma, and complete loss of blood pressure. . . . well . . . who the hell needs that, right?"

The couples nearby were chuckling. Sandy kept it going. She had the inside track. "I like the part in the commercials where the announcer says, 'and, if you know of anyone who's suffered from these conditions, or even died, have them call us immediately! They may be eligible for a cash settlement.'"

Mark laughed. "Yeah. That's my favorite part," he said. "I write that number down every damn time and drop it off for all the victims at the cemetery!"

The three couples sitting nearest to them were visibly entertained by their satire of big pharma's TV ads. Their foot play was being studied with a great deal of interest by several customers in the restaurant, and their behavior proved contagious. During their dinner, Mark and Sandy kept hearing the sound of shoes dropping under the tables around them.

They managed to finish a tasty dinner of edamame, sushi, and a dish of mango sherbet without attacking each other. They enjoyed the sherbert so much that they made a point to stop by the supermarket on the way home and pick some up for later. With Sandy's tousled hair, bare feet, and dress askew, the looks from the store clerks had been priceless.

She proved to be a delicious diversion from the pressures he was under. Sandy showed him how randy she could be on their way home. Once he had to pull the car to the side of a secluded road to properly address her maternal instincts. He was glad they hadn't been stopped on the way to his house. Trying to explain a beautiful, naked, sex-crazed hottie in the front seat with him, and the undergarments hanging from his rearview mirror, would have been challenging.

She was insatiable. Slowly and ravenously, they spent the next twenty-four hours exploring each other's erogenous zones. He had released a hunger in her that seemed to consume them like the afterglow of an exploding star, eclipsing all of his past experiences.

They flowed together like two rivers, 'til Mark couldn't tell her from him.

TWENTY-ONE

Mark leaned on the parts counter waiting for the color-keyed body side molding that he'd ordered last week. He was flipping through his last few phone calls to see if he'd missed anything important while the parts clerk rummaged around in the back looking for his order.

"Hey, Marky-Mark. Heard about your hot date playin' footsie on Saturday," said Raj. He'd spotted Mark waiting at the counter. "We heard she was a real hottie. How come you didn't invite us?"

Mark looked up from his phone. "Well, I was going to, Raj, but I couldn't find a restaurant that didn't require shoes."

"Funny guy. So, you going to that round robin golf tournament at West Side Country Club on Sunday?" Raj was picking at a pizza stain on the front of his shirt.

"Oh, that thing," said Mark, smiling. "No, I don't think so. Too many people died last year."

Raj chuckled as he picked at his shirt. "Anyone ever tell you that your sense of humor is a little on the dark side."

"Yeah, Stevie Wonder. He told me I had a great face for radio, too." Raj laughed, waved him off, and headed over to schmooze with Gene in service and talk to him about scoring some weed.

Jeremy returned to the counter and dropped a long cardboard box down. He entered the product code off the box into his computer and figured up Mark's bill. "So, let's see . . . including your twenty percent employee discount, that's one hundred nineteen fifty-six. You wanna put it on your tab?"

Mark said, "Sure. They can take it out of my January paycheck. Pre-tax, that saves me another"—Mark did the math on his cell phone calculator—"two dollars and fifty-one cents."

"You the man. Hey, you saved enough to get yourself a Dreamsicle." Jeremy chuckled at his own joke, always trying to one-up the sales guys.

Mark smiled and said, "Yeah, well, I got your Dreamsicle hanging right here." He was still thinking about his two steamy days with Sandy and feeling his oats today. After she was back in town from her trip to the medical convention in New York, he planned to give her a call.

"Hey, thanks, Jeremy." Mark slung the long cardboard box over his shoulder and headed over to his desk to check his voice mail.

The big box caught Rich's attention, and it was his turn to razz him. He swiveled his chair around and said, "So, whatcha got there, Marky-Mark, another steel-belted inflatable doll? Whad'ya do, break the last one?"

"Uh, well, not exactly. Actually, it's a fifty pound supply of fruit-flavored condoms. Got some company coming over this weekend."

"A girl this time?" With Carla in jail for the fourth time in three months, Rich was looking to live vicariously.

"Yeah, a girl this time," said Mark. "By the way, thanks for the email and the attachment. It's in the right hands now." Mark had forwarded the document to law enforcement for their review with a note updating them about the certification fraud that was on the rise at the dealership.

Rich nodded. "So, how many cars you got out this month?"

"I'm doing okay, even though it's only the third day of the month. I sold one Saturday, and I have another deal lined up for tonight. So, how'd your Division of Children and Families hearing go?"

Rich sighed and looked down at the floor. "My wife's a piece of work. I'm convinced she's possessed. She's been arrested and bonded out all four times now. She's pissed off at me 'cause I'm movin' on, telling that bitch in charge at DCF that I'm a drug dealer and an unfit dad. How 'bout them apples?"

Mark said, "Those paper shufflers at DCF must be dumber than a bag of rocks. Carla's been arrested four times this year for nine different crimes, got a history of drug abuse, and shackin' up with Lucile Cranston, the stripper busted for dealing in drugs and assault rifles, *while* she's on parole from her last conviction, and DCF believes you're the bad guy? What's wrong with this picture?"

"Welcome to my world," said Rich. "Hey, how 'bout we trade girls for awhile? I heard about your new hottie."

"As much as you might like that, bro, I can't yet." Mark was smiling, Rich knew a joke was coming. "She says she needs more therapy."

Rich said, "Uh huh. And you da doctor, right?"

Mark said, "Chew got it. Confusing sometimes, though. She's coming over tonight to play doctor. She says she loves the therapy, but she's always screaming. Go figure." Now he was grinning.

"I'll bet." Rich grabbed his new cell phone and walked over to Mark's desk. He pushed the cardboard box to the side. "Hey, check this out." He showed him a photo of a young, beautiful girl with tattoos smiling and posing naked on a bed. "Meet Donna. Picked her up in a club in Daytona Saturday night. Nice, huh?"

Mark looked at the photo on Rich's cell phone. Donna had a tattoo of a large, red rose on her derriere. "You like those girls with the tats, huh?"

"Oh, yeah." He pointed at the rose on her derriere in the photo. "Can you see the bite mark right there on the rose?" Rich was obviously proud of his handiwork.

Before Mark could answer, McGreedy ran over and interrupted them. "Hey, guys, you know we're gonna be on the news tonight?"

"What are you talking about?" asked Rich, swiveling in his chair.

"There's a TV reporter from WJXT filming us from across the street. Check it out." McGreedy was excited, hoping he could get his ugly mug on the evening news.

They headed to the front of the dealership to get a view of the action, joining three more reps who also heard about the news. They could see a man on the sidewalk stooped over a large video camera that displayed the station's call letters WJXT. It was aimed at the front of the dealership from across the street. An overly-animated female reporter was holding a microphone as she spoke into the camera and gestured toward the Brandson dealership behind her.

Larry stormed up to the group of sales reps and unloaded on them. "Ladies, that's just our TV ad they're filming. C'mon. This isn't some fifth-grade field trip! We gotta sell some cars today! Let's go!" He clapped his hands loudly, and the reps scurried in all directions like roaches running from a can of Raid. Mark and Rich may have been the only ones who knew Larry was lying about the film crew.

Bautista watched the traffic on Monroe Street from his office window on the third floor and waited on the call from his boss. Tired of pacing back and forth, the Director of the Consumer Protection Division of the Office of the Attorney General was ready for the conversation that had already been postponed twice. He had exchanged several emails this morning with his boss, the Attorney General of the State of Florida, Patricia Bondini. Bondini was elected to the position two years ago, and Bautista liked her style, choosing to stay on under her leadership. Deciding his chances were better with the new AG, he gave up his part-time gigs modeling men's suits to focus full-time on his law career at the CP Division in Tallahassee.

This morning, his boss was finally set to conduct a conference call with himself, the Assistant Director of the Federal Trade

Commission in Washington, and the Chief of Detectives at the Gainesville Police Department. He waited impatiently on the call. The investigation had reached a critical phase, and they were trying to decide if the evidence and testimony had reached the necessary threshold to issue subpoenas and warrants. And, which of the law enforcement agencies would issue them.

Randy Bautista's office was the enforcement authority for all multi-circuit violations of the Florida Deceptive and Unfair Trade Practices Act. It was also his responsibility to cooperate with the FTC in the investigation of national or global business enterprises. The division protected consumers by investigating companies that employed unfair methods of competition or deceptive and unfair trade practices. Of the twenty-one active current cases that the Florida AG was currently involved with, the one targeting Brandson Enterprises had the full attention of his boss, and he knew why. The Attorney General had a sweet spot for the city where her alma mater was situated. Also, one of the fraud victims, Dr. Michelle Ross, the Dean of the Law School, was a personal friend of Patricia Bondini.

As Bautista focused on the traffic below, there was a gentle knock and the door opened. It was Mary Anne, his assistant, and the only person authorized to enter his office without explicit permission. Bautista always thought that the attractive brunette of twenty-six had a demure, sexy-librarian look. He'd graduated seven years ahead of her at Stetson Law School. Mary Anne often made him wish he wasn't married with a family.

"Have you heard anything from Patricia yet?" Mary Anne set the mail on his desk and walked to the window to stand next to him. She knew how anxious her boss could be when he was waiting for an important call.

"Waiting on the four-way conference call," he said without looking up. "Should have a heads-up in a few minutes."

"What's the FTC doing on this case?" asked Mary Anne.

"The usual. Preparing some routine subpoenas, possibly some warrants."

"For all their dealerships in Florida?"

"Probably for the corporate headquarters in Sarasota and their four dealerships in the Gainesville area. Looks like a lot of innocent people are getting defrauded down there, and we're going to put a stop to it."

Weighing the case against Brandson, they stood in silence for a moment and watched the traffic on the street below. Never had the moving cars gotten less attention. Mary Anne was curious about one more item that might trigger the involvement of the U.S. Attorney General. The scope of their authority would change if the US AG got involved in the prosecution. She looked up at her boss.

"They going to use the RICO Act?" she asked.

Bautista tried not to look at her. "Still deciding. Depends on whether the overseas wire transfers are admissible. And, whether we can prove the gun and drug sales are part of the enterprise. The money trail is gonna be the key to invoking RICO."

Bautista's division was also responsible for the civil provisions of the Racketeer Influence and Corrupt Organization (RICO) Act. The RICO Act had some real teeth. It dealt with continuing patterns of multiple illegal activities including fraud, theft and misleading advertising, and usually involved a conspiracy to conduct such activities on the part of several individuals simultaneously. With the enormity of the alleged criminal activity occurring at Brandson, Bautista had a feeling that there was a good chance the RICO Act was going to be applied.

As Bautista's trusted assistant and junior attorney for the last four years, Mary Anne had also been privy to the reports from both named and anonymous sources of additional felonies at the dealership. With the biggest car company in the world potentially on the hook for the millions in fraudulent unearned bonuses, she knew their case could easily escalate to a high-profile media frenzy. If that happened, she hoped the ensuing drama would catapult them together into the national spotlight.

She settled into one of the high-backed leather chairs facing his desk and crossed her legs in an exaggerated fashion, trying to draw his attention. "What about the bribery and extortion?" she asked, tossing her hair back. "Certainly, if additional evidence of those crimes can be gathered through warrants and testimony, we could show that Brandson's managers are part of a criminal enterprise masquerading as the legitimate business of an auto dealership. Therefore, it seems that RICO would be appropriate here."

Bautista's brow furrowed as he studied his assistant. In the years that they had been a team, he was always surprised at how well she could focus on what was significant. He was impressed with her loyalty as well as her argument. It was an argument that he had already thought about presenting to the AG.

He said, "Good points, counselor. If we could persuade the CI to come forward and go on record, that would certainly strengthen our case, too. Unfortunately, the editor at the *Banner* is also reluctant to go on record about the bribery. He's afraid of losing his job. We may have to subpoena the editor, and that could be tricky."

"We're a good team, Randy," she said. "We win most of the time. Let's look at each problem as a solution in disguise. If we do that, we'll figure it out." She stood up and straightened her back, highlighting the profile of her breasts against her blouse. She caught him starring at her breasts, fueling the feeling of control she had over her boss. She smiled at him and pulled her hair back confidently.

"I'll go check the emails," she said. Sashaying toward the door, she flounced her hips provocatively, stopping at the sound of his voice.

"Leave the door open, Mary Anne. I want you in here when the call comes in."

Feeling his eyes on her derriere, she looked demurely over her shoulder at him as she stood in the doorway with her hand on her hip. "Sure, Randy. Anything you say."

The evening news anchor at WJXT studied the video taken today by his Business News Editor, Jan Barnes. He was pleased with the results. He sat through the video for the third time in the studio's editing booth, looking to cut an additional twenty seconds off the run time. Her interview of John Dunne from CVC needed to fit into a three minute time slot so that the entire story, including the story's lead-in and shots of the front of the dealership, wouldn't exceed five minutes. Five minutes was just about the attention limit of the typical viewer in the Gainesville market for local stories. The five minute allotment would still leave time within the thirty minute broadcast for two other stories, weather, sports, and sponsorship advertising.

"What do you think, Jeff? You like it?" Jan sat next to her boss in the editing booth, eager for his stamp of approval. Jeff Baxter was the number one-rated news anchor in the north central Florida viewing area.

"Well, considering it was a rush job and put together in one day, yeah . . . I do. I wished you'd set up one more lighting array, but I think we can brighten it up with the mixer." He rubbed his chin as he thought about the content. "So, the guy from CVC says there may be another couple hundred victims of fraud out there, and hundreds of thousands of dollars has been already paid out in settlements to victims? Wow. Just when you thought it was safe to go back in to the dealership."

"Right?" As you can see in the video, John also mentioned there was a criminal investigation that was underway at Brandson, but I couldn't get anyone at GPD, ACSO, or the state attorney to comment, confirming or denying. So, probably better that we delete that part."

"Agreed", said Baxter. "When we can get confirmation of the criminal investigation, we can always put that in a follow-up." He thought for a moment then added "So, the general manager said he'd get back to you on the story?"

"Yup."

"How long ago did you speak with him?"

She glanced at her watch. "Three hours ago."

"And you did tell him we were running with it today, right?"

"Sure did. When I asked him to comment, he was kinda short and hung up pretty quick. Said something about running it by their attorney first."

"No wonder its taking them so long to respond." Baxter looked at his watch. "It's almost four o'clock. We're running out of daylight here. Let's give Mr. Catatonia—that's his name, right?"

"Yes. Catatonia."

"Let's give him one more call and see if we can get his comments before the five o'clock deadline."

At that moment, the General Manager of WJXT, Randall Newman, made a surprise entrance to their editing booth. "That won't be necessary, Jeff. We're pulling the story, so . . . put everything you have on disc and bring it to me."

"What's going on, Randall?" asked Baxter. Being the number one-rated news anchor in north Florida, Baxter didn't appreciate having the rug pulled from under him without some discussion from his producer. He often found himself at odds with his manager and often disagreed with his boss's ideas on major stories.

"Are we the only ones in the booth?" asked Newman.

"Yes sir," said Jan. She'd invested a whole day on this exclusive and felt she deserved to know why it was getting pulled.

Newman decided he would tell them the truth. "You two are not to say anything to anyone about what I'm about to tell you, agreed? Heads will roll if you do." Randall's shirt cuffs were rolled up and perspiration was visible on the back of his shirt. He looked like they'd put him through the ringer on this one. He was pinching his upper lip indecisively, as if testing his resolve on whether he should divulge all the details. "I just got off the phone with Eric Berman, the lead corporate attorney for Brandson Enterprises. They threatened to cancel all of their advertising with us, and all future ads, if we run this story. That's about four million in annual revenue."

"You going to let them suppress our lead story using the threat of pulling ad revenue, Randall?" asked Baxter angrily. "That's messed up."

The GM leaned against the edge of the desk and folded his arms. He felt like he was standing on quicksand. "Let's be clear. I don't like prostrating ourselves anymore than you, Jeff, but our holding company needs this revenue. Diversified Media Group made this decision, not me. Sorry guys, but my hands are tied. Bring me the discs, and everything you have on it. I know how disappointed you are, but we can't run this story. Yet."

"What do you mean 'yet', Randall?"

Newman clarified the parent company's requirements for running the story. "If there are charges filed or arrests made, we can certainly report on those events. But those are the conditions that must be met." Baxter folded his arms and looked at his reporter for agreement. Barnes let out a deep sigh and nodded reluctantly, acknowledging that more digging would be needed before they could air the story.

Having explained Media Spring's conditions to broadcast the story, Newman exited the editing booth. As the chief executive of the station, he resented corporate interference with their news coverage just as much as his staff. He just didn't have the luxury of indulging his feelings in the matter.

Deflated by their boss's visit, Baxter and Barnes grudgingly put the story on the back burner, but they had no intention of giving up. Experience told them they were only seeing the tip of the iceberg on the corruption at Brandson.

TWENTY-TWO

It was almost eight o'clock in the morning, and the traffic he passed in West Putnam County was mostly workers from the potato, bean, and melon farms that dotted the countryside. Wells already had ten points on his license and one more ticket could cause him to lose the right to drive in Florida. He took a sip of his triple expresso and thought about the *Girls Gone Wild* scenario that he and Tony Grimes had cooked up for Club Liquid tonight. His cell phone rang. It was his party pal, Tony.

Wells answered, "Hey, big guy. You ready to throw some cash around tonight? Score some poon?" For Tony Grimes, the question was about as rhetorical as they come.

"Yeah, man!" said Tony. "Club Liquid sure beats the hell out of Six Flags, huh? Hey, I got a little of that crystal blue and 'E' from last weekend. Should I bring it with me?"

"Does a bear shit in the woods? We'll be ready to shoot ourselves out of a carnival cannon after some of that stuff, right?" It was four days before Christmas, and they were in full party mode.

"Okay. The party favors are comin'," said Tony. "Should be enough for you, me, Kirk, Juicy, Dennis and ten of our closest lady friends. Hey, how much cash we got saved up from our other deals?"

Wells thought for a moment, temporarily distracted as he passed a slow moving pick-up truck driven by an old man in overalls. "I'm thinking three, maybe four grand worth of Ben Franklins there in the bottom of my drop safe."

"Sounds like a party!" After missing their last night out on the town, Tony was hell-bent on spending every last dime of their party cash this time. An incoming call from Tommy Catatonia appeared on Well's phone. "Hey, big guy, got another call I gotta take. See you at the meeting."

"You got it, boss." As he hung up, 'The Village Idiot' was as giddy as an eighth grade kid with an ice cream cone and his head stuck up his hot teacher's skirt. Wells had it all figured out, and he knew how to keep his partner-in-crime happy. He switched over to his boss's call. "Hey, Tommy, how's it hangin'?"

"Hey, Larry. You on your way in?"

"Yeah, man. Just passed the farmer-in-the-dell. What's up?"

"I need for you to have Rocky fix the rest of those bank lender files. I got corporate and the Florida Department of Motor Vehicles crawling up my ass about it. I can't ask accounting to do it. You know the ones I'm talkin' about, right?" Catatonia avoided mentioning the file names in case anyone was within earshot.

"Yeah, I know. Ricky and Jake's files. A little out of wack, right? Why don't you just have the lenders email me with questions, and I'll be happy to ignore them in the order that they are submitted." Wells was amused by his own humor, but his boss wasn't in the mood.

"Don't mess around with this, Larry. Make them look believable."

"Okay. I'll put Rocky on it after the meeting. Anything else?" Larry thought he could see the silhouette of a cop car up ahead, so he tapped his brakes to slow his Lexus from ninety to the posted limit of sixty-five.

Tommy explained further. "Bob and I are getting tired of writing checks on those CVC cases. Don't forget, all that comes out of your bonus money. I've been meaning to ask you this: are we sure we want to keep Jack and Dennis? They've already cost us over a hundred and twenty grand in settlements this year, plus attorney fees. You ready to cut 'em loose yet?" Tommy always felt like he was tap dancing on Larry's behalf to keep the conservative CFO of Brandson Enterprises happy. Bob Gregory had made it clear he wasn't too pleased about the money they were paying in out-of-court settlements on the frauds and overcharges by Juicifer, Dennis Testi and Raj Patel.

"Tommy, we covered this last month, right? You and I agreed that as long as they weren't arrested for anything work-related, and they're makin' us double what they cost us, that we'd keep them around. Right?" Larry's buddies were fiercely loyal and had his back, knowing his 'Redneck Mafia' would do whatever dirty work he needed to get done.

Catatonia relented. Wells was making them almost a million a month, and it acted like a drug on his common sense. "Okay, Larry, but we're gonna have this conversation again in January. Agreed?"

"Okay. What else ya got there, Tommy?" asked Wells as he passed a Florida Highway Patrol cruiser.

"How's it going with the IRS. You come to terms yet?" Catatonia knew Wells had nothing but contempt for the IRS and resented having to deal with the responsibilities and consequences of his tax fraud. He was concerned about the distraction the legal battle was causing his GSM at work.

It pained him to talk about it, but Wells knew his boss had a right to know if he was going to remain a free man. "Yeah, well, their witch hunt has been going on now for five months," said Wells. "My attorney thinks he can get them to do better than their last offer."

"Which was what?"

Verbalizing the penalties gave him indigestion. "Thirty days in jail, three years probation, and two hundred thousand dollars in fines. John thinks he can talk 'em down."

Catatonia sympathized. "That sucks, bro. I'm rootin' for you." Catatonia thought about the three resumes he had lined up—just in case.

"Thanks. Ya got anything else for me?"

"Well . . . I'm thinking' that we got a leak here somewhere. CVC is latching on to our problem customers way too soon. My sources tell me someone's passing them information. How else could they be moving against us as fast as they are? They're filing complaints within days of our problem deals."

Their conversation was interrupted by a hissing sound. "Wait, Tommy, you were breaking up. Can you say that again?"

"*I think we have a snitch,*" repeated Catatonia.

Wells responded. "You know that consumer watchdog group was on WUFZ radio about their victim program, right? Maybe they're hearing about it from there, or from friends who've heard their show. We're not their only target." With the trooper now out of site in his rearview mirror, Wells accelerated back to ninety and watched the farms fly by. He took another gulp from his triple expresso and thought about the conversation.

Catatonia continued. "Well, we've got Eric Berman working on the leak source, too. Every time he gets into a settlement conversation with that Dunne guy at CVC, he's probing him for clues. So far, the guy's been a stone wall. Eric think's he's protecting someone."

"Like who?"

"I don't know. You're closer to the reps on the floor. You tell me." Catatonia was convinced this was his GSM's problem to solve since Wells did all the hiring.

Wells began to make a mental list of all the disgruntled sales reps for a moment, focusing on the ones they still owed money to. He suspected that the informant had to be a current employee.

Someone who was unhappy with their paycheck shortages and had access to Brandson's files. But that was a long list, since he'd been shorting just about everyone there. Even the F&I guys were forced to pony-up to fund his lavish lifestyle.

"I'll work on it, Tommy. I'll put my spies on it. If it's one of my guys, I promise you, I'll find out, and I'll take care of it. My way." He spotted a gas station ahead and slowed the Lexus. "Hey, I gotta stop here for some gas. See you in about twenty minutes."

He stopped and put the car in park, leaving the engine running so the AC blew cold. Opening the glove box, he removed the black zippered pouch with the syringe, vial of testosterone, rolled up hundred dollar bill, and cocaine. As he held the vial upside down at eye level and penetrated the rubber seal with the needle, he did a quick check around him to make sure no one was watching. Then he injected himself with a massive shot of anabolic steroids that was three times the recommended dosage. He put the cap back over the needle and put it back in the pouch. Next, he poured the cocaine into one long, single line on the top of his leather armrest. He snorted half of it into each nostril, sat back, and waited for the rush.

For three minutes, he did nothing but experience the power of the coke and HGH as it washed over him like a giant tsunami. Then, he was moving again. As the front wheels of the Lexus hit the edge of Highway 20 westbound, he downshifted into second and floored it, leaving smoke and a patch of rubber behind him thirty feet long. He remembered her words clearly. She had shrieked that he had the emotional stability of a bag of rats in a burning meth lab. As he accelerated to over a hundred miles an hour, the countryside turned into one big blur. He left that bitch behind.

Mark slipped into his seat in the second row of the meeting room, sipping his coffee and waiting for another tumultuous day. He was ten minutes early for the Friday morning meeting. Rich sat down one seat over in the row behind him with his can of Red Bull.

"Hey, Marky-Mark. You're here early. We gonna sell some cars today?" Mark turned to look at his friend. Rich was sporting a new shorter haircut, and this time he'd added a spike in the front.

"That's the plan." Mark turned to do a fist bump, then turned his attention back to his cell phone.

"You hear about the pay cut?" asked Rich.

Mark looked up at Rich. "What pay cut? Are you messing with me?"

"Wish I was. Ten percent cut, effective today. The managers were just passing out the new pay schedule at our desks. They put one on yours, too. Here, check it out." Rich handed him the new commission schedule. He scanned the new reduced percentages, shaking his head.

"Did they give a reason?"

Rich shrugged. "Bryan said something about higher expenses. He said they'll explain it in the meeting. Betcha it has something to do with all those settlements they're being forced to pay out."

Mark grimaced at the thought of a shrinking paycheck and leaned closer to Rich, lowering his voice. "I'll bet you're right. On top of the money that they're already not paying us, they're gonna take another ten percent? What's wrong with this picture?"

"Yep. That's the way it looks," said Rich. They both felt powerless to stop the thievery. Rich had a young daughter to support, and was stressed over being able to pay his bills. In the last few months, he had to borrow against his credit cards just to get by.

"If you think about it, we're actually subsidizing Juicifer's, Testi's and Patel's frauds," said Mark, "because the dealership is shifting those expenses to us." He paused, looking at the floor. "Is this the dealership from hell, or what?"

"This is why Bihn, Roy, Pete, and Russell quit," said Rich. "This nightmare keeps getting worse for us, while our managers are making thirty to sixty grand a month and buying Louis Vuitton shoes with matching six-hundred dollar belts."

"You got anything else lined up? Just in case?" asked Mark.

"The Health and Fitness Center has a sales position open. I'm lookin' around, but I'm hopin' we can fix this. I've invested two years learning to how sell Toyotas. I don't want to throw that away." With Rich as fanatical about fitness as Mark was, selling gym memberships sounded like a good fit for him. Before Rich could say anymore, they were interrupted by Mark's cell phone. It was Jo at the front desk.

"Hey, Jo. What's up?"

"Your customers are here about a Prius. Where are you?"

"I'm in the meeting room. I'm on my way. Thanks, Jo." Mark stood up to ask Rich a favor. "Will you tell Larry I'm with a customer? I'll catch ya later." As he walked out of the meeting room, he was thinking how happy he was to skip the meeting and all of Larry's brain damage, but the pay cut weighed on him as he made his way to greet his customer.

His appointment resulted in the sale of a new Prius. Mark made it a point to warn them about Tricky Ricky's flim-flam to keep their payments at the agreed upon figure. The new Prius was delivered by eleven o'clock, and Mark was finishing with the paperwork when Raj walked up.

"So, Marky-Mark, what do ya think about the pay cut?"

Mark looked up and shrugged. "Pretty soon we'll be payin' Brandson to work here."

"You coming out to party with us tonight at Club Liquid? Larry's buying."

Mark looked at him, suspicious of his motives. "Raj, I've officially failed at becoming an alcoholic. God knows I've tried."

"Ha! C'mon, coupla drinks won't hurt ya." Always wary of Raj's schemes, Mark had a feeling that he was only acting as the messenger for someone else. Everyone there knew Raj was Larry's lackey.

If he had his head any further up Larry's keister, they'd have to tie a rope around his feet to pull him out.

"Is it gluten free?" Mark asked. He was hoping that Raj would get the hint and go bother someone else.

"You betcha. They got some hot lookin' babes there wearing nothing but a thong and pasties. Kirk and Larry said they'd pay for everything. C'mon out with us." Seeing Raj push so hard made him wary. His instincts told him Larry hatched this plan to get him drunk and spill his guts, a thinly-veiled attempt to try and ID the CI.

"Sounds tempting, but I've got a different 'thong' in my heart. She's a smoking hot trauma surgeon who wants to play doctor tonight, and she loves my custom vibrating stethoscope." Mark looked up and grinned. "I promised to check her pulse at forty-six different locations on her scantily-clad body tonight. She claims it's an emergency."

Raj continued to stand there with his squinty eyes and a big grin on his face. Jabba the Hutt was living vicariously, and it started to creep him out. Right then he made a decision to stop sharing his experiences with Jabba, especially the personal stuff involving Sandy.

On his way to the sales tower, McGreedy had overheard his plans with the stethoscope. He turned to Mark and said, "You bad boy. Is she the one that likes to play footsie under the table at Club Liquid?"

"I'm wondering if there is anyone in this town who hasn't heard about my date with Sandy," said Mark, looking around the show-room. "Anyone? Please raise your hand."

He spotted a past customer seated in the service lounge, and Mark excused himself. As he stopped in front of her lounge seat, the elderly woman recognized him and put her book and glasses down on the seat next to her.

"Fran, how are you?" said Mark warmly. "Is George here with you today?"

A troubled look came over the older woman's face as she answered. "George is in the hospital again. He's got some problems . . . complications . . . with his heart by-pass from two months ago." She had difficulty speaking the words. Seeing that she was upset, Mark sat down to talk to her.

"We're going through a rough patch is all." She paused, looked down at the book in her lap. Tears welled up in her eyes. "We had to give up our new Corolla last month."

"What? The red one you bought from me last year? What happened?" he asked. Mark remembered the deal. He'd worked hard to get them a great price, surprised to hear that she no longer had the car.

"We have our old Toyota pick-up truck in today for service," she said. "We never told you what happened to our payments on the Corolla . . . 'cause George was so mad about it."

"Was it something that happened in finance? Did Rick jack them up on you, Fran?" He cocked his head as he recalled their conversation. "I think I remember warning you about that before you and George went in there to sign up."

"Yeah, you did. It was our fault. We let him talk us into some kind of, ah, expensive extra warranty or something, and some other stuff that pushed our payment up to over four hundred and fifty dollars a month. I tried to tell George we couldn't afford that . . . payment. He and that guy, they just wouldn't listen to me," said Fran as she dabbed her eyes with her napkin. "We appreciate everything you did for us, Mark. We just didn't expect George to get sick again . . . is all. That put a big dent in our budget, too."

Mark stood up. "I understand. Who's your service writer today? Is he taking good care of you?" Although he felt bad about her situation, he was sorry he'd come over to talk with her.

"Chester, or Chet, or something."

"Chuck," said Mark. "He's a good man. I'll go let him know you're one of our special customers and to take really good care of you. And please tell George I wish him a speedy recovery, okay?"

Mark headed over to service to talk with Chuck. *Damn that Rick Gonzalez*, he thought. He wondered if he'd *ever* see any referrals from his customers after Tricky Ricky got done with them.

Although it offered the best sushi in town, Wells liked Club Liquid for the hot hookers, half-naked table-top dancers, and the free drinks from their regular bartender, Ross. When Ross was working the bar, Wells could throw him a couple of vials of HGH or an eight ball of coke and get free drinks for himself and all his friends all night. Located deep in the heart of old downtown, the bar could be accessed by several dark little alleyways patrons could take in and out without being noticed. The dimly-lit interior was ideal for their drug deals, so he and his "Redneck Mafia" could do a little business while they got toasted and lined up some strippers and hookers for the rest of their weekend.

They sat at one of the large tables in the back corner, giving them a view of the front entrance so they could keep track of who was coming and going. With a twenty thousand dollar deal lined up to unload a kilo of coke, Wells would be cautious. He tossed the vodka and cranberry back and ordered another one as Tony and Kirk walked in, ten minutes late as usual. They crowded him into the corner as they made themselves comfortable at the table.

"Hey, darlin'," said Kirk, waving their server over. "Nice place," he added, starring at her fishnet stockings and thong as she stood ready to take their orders.

"Yeah!" said Tony, eyeing her up and down. Wells looked around for his buddy Ross, but didn't see him at the bar. "Where's Ross tonight, honey?" he asked the waitress.

"Ross is off tonight," she said, balancing her tray and smoothing the front of her thong invitingly. "I'm Amber, and Frank's our new guy working the bar tonight. What can I get you guys?"

"I'll have a Jaeger on the rocks," said Tony. He was watching Kirk starring at Amber's shapely pelvis. "I'm not sure what Kirk wants is even on the menu." He smiled at Amber, trying to score some points.

Turning to Kirk, she smiled and batted her eyelashes. "Honey, anything's available for a price. What can I getcha?"

Kirk leaned forward, laying his thick arms on the table in front of him and looking up at Amber. "For now, bring me a Bushmills, straaaiiight up."

She repeated the order. "Okay. Got a Jaeger, rocks, and a Bushmills, stttrrraaaight up," winking at Kirk. "Larry, you ready for another vodka cranberry, honey?" She sucked on the tip of her pen suggestively.

"Sure, bring me another one," said Wells. He pulled a wad of hundreds out of his pocket and laid them on the table. Amber watched the bills on top curl up like they'd been rolled up recently. She stared at the stack of hundreds on the table, then spun on her heel to retrieve their drinks. She flounced her hips like a shameless Victoria's Secret runway model on her way to the bar. The guys at the nearby tables hooted in approval, one of them aiming his keychain flashlight at her derriere as she pranced toward the bar.

"Work it, girl!" shouted Tony, completely entranced by the exhibition. "Whew! We gonna break the fun meter tonight, boys!"

"What time are Juicy, Dennis, and Raj joining us?" Wells asked.

"They wanted to go home and change. I told 'em to hook up with us here around ten thirty." Kirk waited for his boss's approval.

"Perfect," said Wells. "That'll give us time to do our deal with Rocky's guys at ten. He's still got them comin' for the kilo, right?"

"Yup," said Kirk. He looked at Tony. "You brought it, right?"

He lowered his voice. "Under the front seat of my car," said Tony.

"Okay, we're set then," Wells said.

Behind the bar, Moser was pouring the last of the three drinks ordered by the Brandson managers. He set it on Amber's tray, completing their order. He and Amber stood on opposite sides of the bar at the very end, out of sight of the managers and away from the other customers. The bar that separated them made it easier for Moser to control the strong sexual attraction he had for her as he tried harder to focus on Amber's face.

"One last thing, Amber." Frank grabbed the specially-prepared Heinz ketchup bottle from the shelf behind him and set it on her drink tray, along with the modified salt and pepper shakers. Her hearing on prostitution charges was coming up next week, followed by the DCF hearing that would decide her child custody case.

"When you deliver their drinks, switch the ketchup, salt, and pepper shakers as he's gathering the bills to pay you. He'll be a little distracted. Make it look routine. You've already noticed the bottle on their table is half empty, so he shouldn't say anything about it. Don't get the other shakers from their table mixed up on your tray."

Amber looked worried. "What's in the ketchup and shakers?"

"Just salt, pepper and ketchup. And a coupla tiny microphones so my guys in the alley outside can hear their conversation." Moser was patient with her. "Don't say anything. Just do it. Make it look routine, like I said. Just be your normal, sexy self. Ya got 'em drooling all over ya, Amber. If you want those hearings to go your way, you do this for us." Frank was counting on the fact that she really didn't have much choice.

"Okay," she said hesitantly, adjusting her straps and making sure her breasts weren't fully exposed. "But what if he says something about the ketchup and stuff?"

"He won't. But if he does, just tell him the Health Department requires us to put out fresh bottles every three days. He won't have a problem with it. Trust me."

"Yeah, you're right. That sounds good." She smiled at the FBI agent. Moser was patiently building some confidence in his new recruit. She looked more like a Vegas showgirl than an informant.

"Oh, one last item. Pay attention to who gives you the money. Larry, Tony, or Kirk. Got it? Very important. These guys are hardcore criminals and we've had them under surveillance for some time now. We need to be able to identify the source of the cash. Any questions?"

"Think I got it, Frank. I'm good." Amber smiled. Though she wasn't crazy about working for the FBI, if this is all she had to do to keep custody of her child and avoid jail time, she'd do it.

"Sweetie, you're better than good. You're gorgeous. Go work your magic." Moser shooed her off like this was no big deal and they did this everyday. At least, Special Agent Frank Moser did it everyday.

When she returned to their table with their drinks and special package, they were huddled together, talking secretively. "You guys ready for some fun?" she asked, testing the waters.

"Honey, we were born ready," said Wells looking her up and down like his own personal popsicle. "How much we owe ya?" He had his stack of hundreds at the ready.

"Twenty-six fifty," she said as she did her well-rehearsed 'bunny dip' and set the drinks down. As she bent down, Tony leaned forward and did a pretend bite of the one of the tassels on her outfit nearest his face. Amber laughed, pretending to enjoy his silly gesture.

Tony and Kirk watched her appreciatively as Wells counted out four one hundred dollar bills from the top of the stack on the table. As he did so, she reached across them and switched the ketchup bottle and salt and pepper shakers like it was an after thought. The switch went off without a hitch. Watching from across the bar, Moser was relieved as he waited nervously from where he stood at the kitchen entrance.

As she completed the switch, Kirk looked up. "Amber, you take such good care of us." Secretly, she was repulsed by his looks and the fact that he smelled like a Mexican restaurant.

"You gonna be around a little later, darlin'?" asked Wells as he put the four one hundred dollar bills on her tray. "'Cause there's lots more where this came from." He raised his eyebrows expectantly, adjusting his Louis Vuitton glasses on the bridge of his nose.

"For that amount of cash, I can be available all night." She pushed her chest out and put her hand on her hip suggestively. She had the guys at both tables salivating at her every move.

"That's what I was hopin' you'd say, darlin'." To seal the deal, he added another hundred to her stack, laying it on top of the other bills that had curled up on the table.

Amber feigned a blush. "Thank you so much. You guys are sweet." She took her tray and was about to head back to the bar with her cash when the guy with the keychain flashlight at the next table demanded her attention. The geeky-looking student was waving his hand around like he had to use the bathroom. "Hi, uh . . . Amber . . . could we get another round over here?"

"I'll be right back to get your order, guys," she said. Amber knew she had to get the bills back to Frank, untouched. She walked up to the bar and put her tray down, catching his eye and pointing at the stack of hundreds.

She pulled out her compact to check her lipstick, trying to act non-chalant. "Larry gave me the Franklins. He has about thirty more on his table," she said. "Those guys are loaded. I never realized there was that much money in selling cars." Amber looked at the customers to her right and left at the bar to make sure they couldn't hear her. She lowered her voice and leaned over the bar. "The ketchup bottle and shakers are right where you wanted them, Frank," she said. She straightened up and posed like a showgirl, proud of her work.

"That's my girl. Piece 'a cake, right?" Moser took her tray and squatted under the bar like he was preparing her drinks. He reached for the set of tongs, grasping the five bills and placing them into the evidence bag under the counter. He sealed up the evidence bag and put it into a zippered satchel that had a combination lock. After he removed five fresh hundred dollar bills from the cash box for Amber, he locked the satchel in the cabinet and wrapped the chain with the key around his neck, tucking it under his shirt. Then he stood up to see Amber waiting patiently for her five-hundred-dollar tip.

Moser couldn't help avoiding feeling protective. As he placed the stack of hundreds on her tray, he said, "Look. We both know what they have in mind. I'm not going to tell you what you can or can't do with them, but you do need to be careful with these guys, Amber. These guys are violent convicted felons. You know what I'm saying, sweetie?" Moser's eyes were full of expression.

"Sure, Frank. Whatever." Moser winced at her sarcasm and firmly grasped her forearm to make sure he had her full attention. He tried again.

"I want you to be careful with these guys, Amber."

She looked at his hand on her forearm. "Where was all the fatherly advice when you were telling me to be my 'normal sexy self' a while ago, Frank?" The young man nearest to her on the bar stool downed his last sip of beer and was checking her out. Drawn to their little melodrama, he was just out of earshot but trying hard to tune in.

Moser patted her arm gently and withdrew his hand. He repeated himself. "Be careful with these guys, okay?" Now the young man on the stool was signaling for another beer. Frank nodded at him, holding up an index finger. "Be right with ya, partner." He turned his attention back to Amber.

She eyed the stack of hundreds on her tray. "I did my part. Don't worry about me. Just keep your end of the bargain, Frank." She folded the bills and stuck them into her thong, smoothing them out as Moser watched her touch herself. Knowing she had a lock on the situation, she grabbed her tray and turned on her heel, prancing back to her customers.

Frank poured a beer for the guy at the other end of the bar, then walked back to the opposite end, away from any customers. He hit the redial button on his cell phone and spoke quietly to Agent Danley parked in a van in the alley behind the bar.

"Brad, you and Jim up and ready? We're good to go. We've got enough bugs on their table to make the Orkin man nervous. Copy?"

"Copy that, Frank. We're five by five. Recording starting right . . . now. I think I just heard one of them fart."

TWENTY-THREE

Special Agents Brad Danley, Jim Costello, and Frank Moser sat around the conference table at the FBI field office in Gainesville, unwrapping the sub sandwiches brought in by their assistant. It was half-past noon on Friday, and they were preparing for a lunchtime conference call to hear what the Lab Director at the FBI Regional office in Atlanta had to say about the package of evidence from Gainesville. It had been five days since the agents had sent the evidence gathered at Club Liquid last week.

Agent Danley checked his watch again. He was hungry. "What time did Higgins say he was calling us?" He was ready to take a huge bite of his roast beef sub but wanted to avoid having a mouth full of food when the call from Atlanta came in.

"Five minutes ago." Costello tore open his chips and pushed a handful into his mouth, too famished to wait for the phone to ring. "I'm starving. You want my tomatoes, Frank?"

Before Moser could answer, the LED on the speaker phone lit up and the phone emitted an electronic ring tone. The supervisor reached over and hit the answer button.

"FBI Gainesville. Agent Danley."

"Hey, Brad. Chuck Higgins, Atlanta Bureau. I have the lab results you've been asking about. Who else is on speaker with us?"

Agent Danley looked around the conference table at his two coworkers. "You have Frank Moser and Jim Costello here."

Agent Higgins continued. "Okay, guys. Here's the lab report. There were traces of cocaine on three out of five of the bills we analyzed. Chemical deposits on the bills you collected from the suspect indicates a ninety-nine percent match with the composition of the cocaine seized from the last five interdictions in your area."

"Great work, Chuck," said Danley. "What about the recordings. You've verified voice prints, right?"

"Yeah, there's that, and we've traced the cell numbers," said Higgins. "Now we have a few key members of their network identified. But let me get back to the bills you collected for a second."

"Sure. What else ya got?" asked Agent Moser in between mouthfuls of Black Forest ham and Swiss cheese.

"Well, turns out one of them had traces of blood on it," said Agent Higgins. "We thought it was red ink, at first. Once we identified the substance as blood, we ran a DNA screen and found a match with a Tyrone James Davis. Turns out Davis is a beating victim from last August. We ran him through our files and found out that Mr. Davis has a pretty thick jacket, with three priors, two of them felonies, all drug and weapons related, plus a few misdemeanors."

"Yeah, I think I remember that assault," said Agent Moser. "Right behind Club Liquid. Gotta be a connect there. The case was handled by a GPD Detective . . . I wanna say Gronky. No, it was Gronske."

"That's right," said Higgins. "Good memory, Frank. According to the case file, Davis pled guilty back in August to drug possession and is currently serving a five-year sentence for a third offense. When GPD found him in the alley, he'd been beaten unconscious and later couldn't identify his attacker. File says he suffered a concussion, so it's possible he had amnesia. Now, we have this connection between Davis and our three suspects."

"And, Club Liquid is smack in the middle," said Moser. "We have a few new reasons to continue our undercover ops at that location. Looks like these guys are runnin' drugs outa that place."

"Maybe it's time to talk with Detective Gronske," said Agent Danley. "See if he'll work with us." He looked around the table and got nods of approval from Costello and Moser.

"I would suggest you approach his CO first, a Captain Greg Arnofsky," said Higgins.

"How'd you know who his CO is?" asked Agent Costello, noting the surprised looks from his two partners.

"What, you think you guys are the only ones that do their homework?"

It was around seven on Saturday night as Mark returned to his home office PC, intent on finishing the email updates for the seven law enforcement agencies that were investigating Brandson. He sat at his computer, reflecting for a moment on the streamlined procedures that made this an easier task for him tonight.

Last week, John Dunne volunteered to become the sole recipient for all of KG's emails and documents. Due to the sheer volume and diversity of crimes that were being investigated at Brandson, there was full agreement on the new arrangement by law enforcement. The temporary accord gave Dunne and CVC full responsibility for distributing specific documents for the appropriate law enforcement agencies. The streamlining also helped to reduce KG's exposure to fewer contacts and avoid what he feared most—becoming a target for the media, Brandson's attorneys, or drug-crazed rednecks with assault rifles.

He finished scanning six of the seventeen incriminating documents that he garnished from Brandson printers and faxes during the past week. Now he wanted to send the rest that showed fresh proof of more fake car deals at the dealership while Dunne was still online with him. Severe weather warnings were coming across the TV in his office, and the on-screen radar sweeps indicated the approach of severe lightning. As he sent the last emails and documents to Dunne, he hurried to disconnect all his electronics before the storm hit.

The Business News Editor for the *Gainesville Banner* sipped his morning coffee and scanned the latest newswire stories on his desktop PC. It was eight o'clock on the first Monday morning in March as Andrew Tarr daydreamed about his plans of winning a Pulitzer Prize for his investigative story on the corruption at Brandson. With law enforcement moving at the speed of molasses on a cold morning in Vermont, the risk that another reporter would break the story increased each day, and this bothered him. He remembered the conversation about the exclusivity pact he'd made with KG. He hungered to be the one to break the story wide open and watch it go global. The dozens of business news articles he wrote over the past few months as Business News Editor were artful, often heralded as quintessential examples of investigative journalism. Some of them had earned him professional awards. So far, none of them had made it into the national wire services, but he was certain that the Brandson story would—maybe even go viral on the net. His ringing phone interrupted his thoughts.

"Business News Desk, Andrew speaking."

"Hey, Andrew, how's it going?" He recognized John Dunne's voice. "You have a minute?"

"Absolutely, John. What's new with our story on Brandson?" Andrew was personally committed to developing the story in spite of the hold on it, and Dunne was just the man to help stir the pot. Tarr promised Dunne latitude in prioritizing the interests of his group's victims in exchange for Dunne's exclusive updates on new developments. It was a good arrangement for them both, and it kept Tarr one step ahead of the competition.

"Well, you've heard about the fake car sales there, right?" asked Dunne.

"I've heard the stories, and I got your email of the redacted screen shots. It appears that they document twenty-four of the fake sales from Brandson's own files. Why? What else do you have?"

"We've confirmed that one of the managers is actually bragging about the fraudulent deals in a sales meeting. In front of seventeen people," said Dunne.

"Jeez. Brandson seems to have some incredibly stupid people working there. Love to have a recording of that, right?"

"We may not need a recording. I've already spoken to two witnesses. They say there are three or four more that would be willing to testify, if needed. They were all present in the meeting when Tony Grimes bragged about buying twenty-four new cars. Can you believe that? How dumb can a manager be?"

"That does seem pretty stupid," agreed Tarr. "Those managers must be convinced they're above the law."

"Some of the guys call Tony Grimes 'The Village Idiot'. At least, that's what my CI calls him." There was a pause as Tarr made his notes.

"Hey, what else can you tell me about the CI's motives in all this?" Tarr wanted to work the human-interest angle a bit more.

"KG's committed on cleaning up, in his words, 'the sewer' that he works in everyday. In conversations, he's expressed a strong desire to make car buying at Brandson an honest and victimless activity. Imagine that. Now, that may sound a little Don Quixote-esque, but he's been trying to influence the managers with his ideas. I dunno. Maybe he's being overly idealistic."

"Why won't he come forward and go on record with this stuff?"

"Let me remind you there would be no criminal investigation at all if it weren't for KG's efforts," said Dunne.

"Granted." Tarr was using his technique of sounding hesitant in order to draw out more details from John.

"Also, KG is more valuable to us if he stays undercover. Only as an employee can he continue to give us access to evidence that we wouldn't have without a search warrant."

"Why don't we have enough evidence to get warrants and subpoenas yet?" asked Tarr.

"There's a threshold of evidence that the authorities need, and KG wants to make sure that we exceed it before his cover is blown."

"Maybe KG's smarter than we give him credit for. Does he have any experience with undercover work?" Tarr continued to bait him with questions, jotting down as many of the juicy details as he could squeeze out of him.

"No prior experience that I know of. We can't overlook his concern for his own safety. I've heard these managers hunt with assault rifles when they're drunk."

"With assault rifles? Really?" Assault rifles were a hot topic lately, and Tarr wanted more details.

"Apparently, most of the managers there own AK-47s and AR-15s, some of which have been converted to fully auto-"

"Isn't that illegal?" Andrew interrupted.

"Depends," said Dunne. "We do know that some of them are felons that brag about their guns. I'm also hearing stories of drugging and dealing meth and cocaine."

"How the hell can they be getting away with this stuff? It sounds more like a Martin Scorcese or Quentin Tarantino movie."

"Yeah. The *Pulp Fiction* of car dealerships, right?"

"You said some of these guys are convicted felons, right? How do we know this?" asked Tarr.

"It's all public information. Here's a fun factoid for you. Might even make a good headline. One of KG's favorite sayings is 'you can't make this stuff up.' He's always saying that."

"You can't make this stuff up, huh?" repeated Tarr. "Look John, I've gotta head to a staff meeting that's already started. I appreciate the update. I wish they'd just let me print it!"

"It would certainly help us out if you could. Let me know if they take the shackles off, will ya?"

"Count on it, John." As they ended their phone call, Tarr stepped into the hallway to join the staff meeting already underway in the main conference room.

Mark stood over the red FRS coupe in the showroom, admiring the lines and checking the specs of the new sports car listed on the Monroney sticker. It had been highly touted in the press, a joint marketing venture between Subaru and Toyota. This was the first FRS to arrive at the dealership. Four months of a major ad blitz had preceded the rollout and expectations were high. The hood of the FRS was propped open invitingly to show off the high-performance propulsion system, and the car was polished to a glossy-mirrored sheen. Though his sports car days were over, he could still admire the sleek lines of a beautifully-designed car.

"Did you test drive one yet?" Scott had sidled up to him, and they both stood admiring the first new sports car to be introduced by Toyota since the Solara was discontinued years ago.

"Not yet. I'll leave that to the kids who enjoy tearing around town in a sardine can."

"What do you think? Think it'll sell?"

"Truthfully?" said Mark. "After that huge four-month ad blitz, I half-expected them to announce it had an interstellar drive system, and that they'd discovered life on Europa with it or something. Or a twelfth planet."

"Twelfth planet? You know there's only eleven, right?" Scott was trying to keep from grinning.

"Yeah, well, you just keep smokin' that wacky weed. I hear it's good for follically-challenged senior citizens." Mark patted him on the shoulder.

"So, Marky-Mark, when we gonna head out onto the high seas with your new hottie? I'll bet she'd dress up my boat real nice."

"I'll betcha she'd dress up that old row boat of yours pretty nice, too."

Before Scott could mount a suitable response, Mark's phone rang. He checked the caller ID and recognized the Manhattan number as one of his corporate customers.

"Well, hello there, good lookin'. How's business at Physician's Labs?" he asked. The executive assistant to the senior V.P. of marketing at Physician's Labs in New York was a repeat customer. Mark was looking forward to arranging the purchase of the sixteenth Yaris for Sarah's sales force.

"Hi, Mark. Love what you do for me," she said.

"Oh, what a feeling, Sarah." She liked playing the ad slogan game with him.

"Let's go places," she said, enthusiastically.

"Uh . . . , you win. I can't think of anymore slogans," he said. It was always better for business to let her win.

"That's great. You know how much I like winning, right? I need your help on a three-car deal," she said.

"I'm happy to help you get that corner office you've been dreaming about. You know, the one that overlooks the Statute of Liberty," replied Mark.

"I wish it were that easy, sweetie. Here's what I need. Same features as last time. New three-door Yaris hatchback, automatic, power windows, power door locks, cruise control, can be either silver, black, or white. I need your best cash out-the-door price on a *three*-car package deal. Get me the best price and I'll overnight you a check."

"Got it. Tell me the price we have to beat, and when you want them delivered." He knew Physician's Labs liked their cars delivered to their sales reps, usually somewhere in Florida.

"For you, honey? Sure. I need you to beat it by at least a hundred bucks, okay? Make me look good. So far, the best quote is forty-two thousand, six hundred. Delivered within thirty days. Still wanna play?"

"Absolutely. Thanks for the opportunity to be of service," he said.

"Cut the crap, sugar," said Sarah, ever so sweetly. "Get me the price I need, and let me know when you're comin' to see me. Okay?"

"Call you back in a few minutes. How you know you want me to come see you when you don't even know what I look like, Sarah." She was fun to flirt with.

"Sure I do, honey. Saw your photo on the website."

"And that didn't scare you off?"

"Far from it, dear."

He played into her little fantasy to keep her in a good mood. "Okay. What kind of wine should I bring for us?"

"I like oaky chardonnays. Get back to me as soon as you can, Marky-Mark."

Mark went to his desk, excited about his deal and immediately sat down to create the transaction paperwork in contact management. He hit the print button and headed to the tower to show the deal to Larry or Bryan. He looked for Larry first. Bryan always deferred decisions on losing deals back to his boss.

"Whatcha got there, Marky-Mark. You still a pole smoker?" Mark printed the three deals on the glass in the new car section, ignoring Larry's taunt. He grabbed the print-outs and laid them out in front of his GSM.

"Larry, we've got a shot at making our month here. This is an all-cash corporate deal, best out-the-door price wins. They've bought fifteen cars from me in the past two years, and want to make it eighteen. Can we do this deal?"

Larry looked at Mark for a moment, then scanned the documents. At first, he scowled at the figures. Mark was losing hope for an easy deal. Then, Larry checked with Bryan to see how they were doing on the new car sales month-to-date figures. The sales figures didn't cheer him up, and Mark's hope for a three car deal returned.

After doing several rapid-fire computations on his desk calculator, Larry looked up at Mark. "Yeah, okay. Write 'em up, Marky-Mark. With Juicy's eighteen pounder with the old farts yesterday, we can do the deal. Have Jo at the front desk arrange the deliveries. Good job, Marky-Mark. Now, get outa here, ya pole smoker," he said, smiling demonically.

As he stepped out of the sales tower, he noticed the two well-dressed men in dark suits who just walked in. Thinking they looked like well-to-do customers, Mark quickly walked up to snag them before someone else got there.

"Hi, welcome to Brandson Toyota. Are you here to see anyone in particular?"

The taller of the two men reached into his inside coat pocket and displayed a badge. "I'm agent Velasquez, and this is agent Clark. We're with the IRS Fraud Division. We're here to see Mr. Wells. Can you tell me where I can find him?"

Before Mark could answer him, Jo said, "Mark, you go ahead with your deals. I'll take care of these gentlemen." She picked up the phone and dialed Larry. "Larry, there are two men here from the IRS who'd like a word with you. Can you come up to the front desk, please?"

He was thankful that he'd gotten Larry to approve his deal before the arrival of the IRS agents, figuring Larry's mood was about to go straight down the tubes. He noticed the dark blue storm clouds billowing on the horizon and headed out to find his three new Toyotas before the skies could open up. He dialed Physician's Labs to let Sarah know their three-car deal was done and she could stop shopping. Getting her voice mail, he left her a congratulatory message to seal the deal as he continued to put more distance between himself and the front desk. He was getting caught up in too many beehives lately and wanted no part of the one that was brewing.

As he steered his unmarked Dodge Charger into one of the parking spaces at GPD marked 'Official Business', Moser thought about how he was going to approach Detective Gronske. Local law enforcement was usually paranoid about having the Feds muscle in on their investigations and claiming Federal jurisdiction. Moser found that by using a less heavy-handed approach with briefings, he could be more effective in moving cases forward. He thought about his conversation yesterday with Gronske's CO as he placed his ID chain and badge around his neck and stepped out of his Charger. He was encouraged by Captain Arnofsky's cooperative attitude and had even suggested Gronske would appreciate the opportunity to work with him. Moser was running out of leads and needed a break in the case.

The GPD officer at the front desk looked young enough to be a college student. Eyeing Moser's badge and recognizing his steely glaze and no-nonsense attitude as that of a fellow officer, the young desk attendant became more alert. His name badge read, "Ofc. T. Sapp," and Moser was thinking that he'd probably never seen an FBI agent wearing flannels and jeans before.

"Special Agent Moser here to see Detective Gronske."

"Yes, sir. I'll see if I can locate him for you," said Officer Sapp in an official tone. He dialed the detective's extension. "Okay. I'll send him back," said Officer Sapp into the phone. He hit the electronic release for the security door leading inside to the CID and waived him through. "Just follow the hallway, take your first left, and he's either the third or fourth desk you come to."

Moser headed toward the west side of the police station to hook up with Sgt. Gronske, passing several uniformed GPD officers along the way. When he got to Gronske's desk in the Criminal Investigation Division, they recognized each other and Gronske waived him over. Moser stood and waited for the detective to finish the call he was on. He noticed Gronske was about the same age and build, only the sergeant had more hair.

"Gotta go, Chuck. Got someone here to see me," said Gronske into the receiver. As he ended his call, Gronske stood up to shake hands with his FBI counterpart. "Gary Gronske. Please have a seat, Agent Moser."

"Thanks. Call me Frank. You guys look pretty busy today, so I'll be brief," said Moser, running his hand over his bald head as he took a seat.

"Probably not as busy as you guys downtown," said Gronske.

"Gary, if I can call you Gary . . . "

"Sure." Gronske settled back into his chair as he waited to hear what Moser had to say.

"We respect your jurisdiction, Gary. We're actually working a couple of fraud and heavy drug cases that may be connected to some of your active files. I thought we might be able to help each other out," said Moser.

"Sure. That works, Frank, as long as we're straight up with each other. Nothing held back. Right?" He seemed sincere. Moser began to relax.

"Of course," said Moser as he smiled at his GPD counterpart, intent on forging a cooperative relationship with the detective.

"Our office has been working on a big case involving fraud, forgery, money laundering and illegal drug sales at a local car dealership. We think the dealership is the center of a criminal enterprise that's connected to a number of other cases you've been working," explained Moser.

"Okay. How can I help?" asked Gronske as he leaned back in his chair. He'd already heard about some of the investigations at Brandson.

Moser proceeded to brief the GPD detective on their stakeout at Club Liquid, the lab analysis of the bloodstained bills, and their recordings of planned, large-scale drug deals centered around downtown clubs. At the end of their twenty minute briefing, they both agreed they were probably after the same suspects. They spent another ten minutes discussing some of the case details, including the drug-related beating of Tyrone Davis. Moser agreed to have the recordings and lab results released to Gronske in exchange for sharing the eye witness accounts and field reports held by GPD on the fraud and forgery issues. They made the arrangement subject to the final approval from their COs, not expecting any delays. The two officers had a good feeling about their new partnership, and the beginning of a task force was taking shape.

TWENTY-FOUR

Mark eyed the box of freshly-baked Krispy Kreme donuts Jo held open for him. "Oh, go ahead, Mark. It's Sunday. Take a break from your diet. You'll work those calories off today," she said as she held the box open. Unable to resist the sugar-glazed treats, Mark caved in and reached inside the box with a napkin and snagged one of the the diet-killers.

"Jo, this is so good. Should I ever spot your car in Mexico City, I'll wash your windshield for free. Guaranteed."

"Wise guy. By the way, did you know we hired a second comp-troller?" said Jo.

This bit of corporate news surprised him. "Jo, why would they do that, unless they've lost trust in Kelly Allen. Isn't she still our head of accounting?"

"I guess so. I heard they've asked her to train the new controller. She must be lovin' that." Jo leaned forward, adding in a whisper, "I also heard they've uncovered some, uh, accounting irregularities. But don't tell anyone. You might get a subpoena."

"Whoa, daddy. Accounting irregularities, huh?" They both knew the frauds went far beyond cooking the books.

Mark wiped the last of the donut glaze from around his mouth. "Jo, did you ever find out what those IRS agents wanted with Larry?" Jo leaned forward again and lowered her voice to almost a whisper.

"I heard they served him with a subpoena and a search warrant that was four pages long," she said, looking over her shoulder to see if anyone was standing behind her.

"Unbelievable. I overheard the managers say they charged him with tax fraud."

"That's what I heard too," she said. "They wanted all the information on the last five cars he bought. Rachel in accounting said he paid over seven hundred grand for them. Cash." Ron walked by them with a customer and she stopped talking, settling back in her chair to wait for him to pass. Mark leaned against the reception desk as he thumbed through the calls on his cell phone.

Jo leaned forward once again, whispering more news. "I heard his wife is trying to divorce him, but he—"

"Mark, go sit down and get on the phone! We need some appointments today," shouted Kirk across the showroom from the tower. Mark acknowledged Kirk with a wave. "Jo, I'll catch up with you later," as he headed to his desk to check emails and voicemails.

There were twenty-one new emails and a voicemail from his church accountant. The accountant sent him a referral who was in the market for a nice used car under five grand, and he knew it wouldn't be easy to find. After jotting down the contact information, he went back to his list of new emails, excited by the one from Sandy. She described her date with him Saturday night as "the most incredible physical experience of my life." His mind wandered, visualizing her on his bed wearing only her lingerie. A hot-blooded, thirty-six year old beauty had a lot in common with an experienced carpenter. No good wood gets wasted. A familiar voice behind him brought him back to reality.

"Are you making those calls like I asked you?" Kirk stood at his desk dressed in baggy Bermuda shorts and flip-flops, reeking of booze and burritos. He noticed the bruised knuckles on his right hand, and it didn't take much to figure out what he'd been doing last night.

"Got a referral from a friend I'm getting ready to call right now," said Mark. He looked up at his used car manager. Kirk's eyes were watery and bloodshot from the night before. "Did you hear back from the bank about our Joe Becker deal from last Thursday?" he asked Kirk. "On the used Hyundai Sonata? You said his credit score was workable with his two grand down."

"Nothing yet. I'll let you know," he said curtly. He turned, tripped on his flip-flop, cursed, then steadied himself and walked back toward the service area. Ian was watching from his desk fifteen feet away. Unable to resist the temptation to razz his buddy, he got up and walked over to Mark's desk. Wearing his red Toyota polo shirt and khakis, he looked thin, maybe all of a hundred thirty-five pounds.

"Well, that was a little underwhelming. You think he enjoyed his trip?" joked Ian.

"Looks a tad hungover, huh?"

"Did you ask him if he could spare a pint of Jameson's Irish Whiskey?" asked Ian.

"I think he lost a pint just from evaporation standing here at my desk. Look, my plant's wilted." Mark pointed to the drooping plant beside his desk.

"I heard he moved in with his mother. Can you imagine what he'd be like to have as a roommate?" asked Ian.

"Are you kidding? This squirrel is happy with the nuts he has," said Mark.

"Are you ever serious?" asked Ian.

Mark went into his impression of a philosophy professor he knew. "Herman Hesse once said that seriousness is an accident of time. It consists of putting too much emphasis on the present, or something like that. Benefits of a classical education," said Mark as he bowed to his one-man audience.

"So, Marky-Mark, I never asked you what your degree is in," said Ian.

"Prison architecture, and I sincerely doubt that I could make any improvements on this place," said Mark with a wry smile.

The weather was depressing everyone. It was dark and raining outside, and seemed like a good day to wear a black suit. Tommy Catatonia stood at the front of the meeting room, ready to conduct the Friday morning sales meeting in a black Brioni suit. Mark noticed how much Catatonia resembled the notorious John Gotti.

Most of the reps thought of their general manager as a smart guy. There was no way he could be dumb enough to be unaware of all Larry's scams going on right under his nose. Most of them were convinced that the so-called Customer Service Inquiry, with the five hundred dollar fines, was a scam concocted by Larry and supported by his boss. They found out that those five hundred dollar fines went straight into the managers' pockets as part of their bonus money. The only two salesmen who were stupid enough to have a major confrontation with Larry over the missing commissions were both fired months ago.

This morning, Tommy was filling in for Larry. The demonic GSM was tied up in court with his IRS tax fraud hearing at the Federal Courthouse in Jacksonville. When Tommy stood in for his GSM, it was often to make important announcements that affected the pay of sales reps. Fearing more bad news from their GM, Mark and Rich braced themselves as they waited in the second row of the meeting room.

"Okay, guys, listen up." Tommy looked annoyed. "You may have already heard about the personnel changes we've made. Unfortunately, we had to let go of Jack Gates and Dennis Testi. Jack and Dennis were responsible for the dealership having to shell out over a hundred and nineteen thousand bucks to satisfy claims filed by unhappy customers with those bozos at Consumers Against Crimes. And that doesn't include attorney's fees which were another thirty grand. Mr. Brandson is not too happy about it, and I'm telling you right now, we need to pay attention to this." *The hypocrisy was unbelievable*, thought Mark.

Just then, Brent Bell's phone rang. Tommy glared at him and barked, "Brent, turn off your cell phone. Everybody, check your phones, make sure they're off." He paused and looked around the room to make sure everyone complied.

Tommy continued. "We now have a zero tolerance rule for any sales rep who's involved in a new CVC complaint. Not only will they be terminated, but we're going to take any money used to settle the case in our Customer Satisfaction Program out of their last commission. Any questions?" Tommy looked around the room for takers.

McCreedy's hand went up. Mark had a feeling McGreedy was about to ask some dumb-ass question, and instinctively knew this was the wrong time to do it.

"What's up, Paul?" Tommy looked perturbed. "Tommy, Jack's been calling me from Nissan and wanting me to sign up with him over there. Just thought you should know." A twitter went through the room in response to McGreedy's brown nosing.

"Okay, thanks for the heads-up, there, Paul. If any of the rest of you guys want to go over there and work with Jack selling Nissans, let me know right now."

Rich leaned over and whispered, "Jeez, talk about throwing your buddy under the bus. Is that how he treats his friends?"

"Well, probably too much chlorine in that gene pool," whispered Mark.

"Mark, you got something you want to share?" asked Tommy, annoyed with their second-row conversation. Somewhat embarrassed, Mark offered an explanation and an apology to his boss.

"Sorry, Tommy. We were just noting the genealogy of certain individuals, and how they're prone to erroneous conclusions." Mark tried to keep a straight face, relieved to see that Tommy was amused.

Tommy laughed, and said, "Oh, yeah? You're a geneticist, now?"

"Well, sir, just part-time. But I am opening a drive-thru window for patients in a hurry." Mark had stuck his neck way out, and even his buddy Rich shifted nervously away from him, not sure how Tommy was going to react to his risky attempt at levity.

Tommy chuckled and said, "All right, wise guy." He pointed at Mark, adding, "You, and the rest of you wise guys. Go sell some damn cars!"

Detective Lieutenant Matt Anderson, Economic Crimes Specialist, CID, GPD, and Detective Sergeant Gary Gronske, CID, GPD, huddled around the conference table with their captain and Special Agents Brad Danley, Frank Moser, and Jim Costello of the FBI. The multi-agency task force was laying all their cards on the table as they discussed the crimes at the dealership. As they reviewed the latest intelligence information on their suspects at Brandson, the COs, Arnofsky and Danley, were also assigning tasks and dividing up the caseload. Danley had just summarized their latest findings and reviewed the most recent evidence collected by the task force.

Danley continued. "That's what we've got as of Friday. We will continue to build our cases against Brandson for bank fraud and money laundering. We need to serve our warrants before they can destroy anymore evidence. They've got their IT flunky Gambrone in there deleting key files, so I want you guys to pick him up on the felony weapons charge to take him out of our crime scene. The sooner, the better."

Shifting in his chair, Gronske chimed in. "We can pick him up anytime. We have the affidavit and sworn testimony from the former owner of Gambrone's 9 mm PPK. And we have a certified copy of the New York State Court's stipulation from four years ago that prohibits Gambrone from owning a firearm. We know he carries one in his car, so let's pick him up."

"Okay. With our new forensics software, we can recover and reconstruct the files that Gambrone may have deleted," said Danley. "Let's pick him up on the felony weapons charge and slow them down. That okay with you, Greg?"

The highest-ranking officer in the room, Captain Gregory Arnofsky had listened to his detectives and the FBI agents attentively. Now he leaned forward and shared his strategy. "Yeah, okay, let's serve the warrant on Gambrone. The way I see this shaping up, the Bureau can continue gathering evidence on the bank fraud, forgery, and white-collar cases, while GPD handles the street crimes, drug deals, and investigates the consumer complaints brought by CVC. Let me hear your ideas on the frauds against Toyota."

"Toyota's weighing their options," said Costello. "Technically, until they decide to declare themselves a victim, that's going to be hard to move on. They could use their control of the dealer franchises to recoup their twenty million in lost bonus money. Their executives are stalling us, waiting to see what develops. Toyota has a long history of moving slowly on major decisions."

"Jim's right, Greg," said Danley. "Toyota could still choose to recover the millions they paid in fraudulent bonuses by either a civil action, or by exercising their control over the franchises and forcing Brandson to repay it without ever going to court. My guess is that they exercise franchise control using the fraud clause, because they could do so privately. I'm convinced Toyota will do everything in their power to keep this scandal out of the media." He paused, looking at the three GPD officers to see if they had questions. Anderson and Gronske nodded in approval. So far, they were all on the same page.

Danley continued. "Here's something else. By threatening to pull their franchises from the holding company, it would give them a lot of clout. Jerking their franchises with Brandson Enterprises would be a major setback for five of their seventeen dealerships."

Danley's phone rang. He looked at the caller ID and stood up to take the call. "It's my CI at Brandson." He stepped outside so he wouldn't be interrupted.

Danley listened to his caller. "Brad, it's KG. You asked me to let you know if there was any change in Jack Gate's employment. As of yesterday, he's been fired from Brandson. He's now working at the Nissan dealership on Main Street. I have a manager walking toward me right now, so I gotta run," said Mark.

"Okay. Thanks," said Danley. He stepped back inside Arnofsky's office to share the news with his task force.

"Guys, just got a tip that Gates was fired from Brandson," said Danley with a smirk. "He's out from behind that protective wall that Brandson's attorney was putting up for him. He's over at the Nissan dealership. Let's go pick him up. Maybe we can get him to roll up on Wells. You guys have a Coke machine around here?"

"Down the hallway to your left," said Gronske. "Wait, Brad. Quick question. Who do we grab first? Gates or Gambrone? Who's a bigger flight risk?"

"We know where Gambrone lives in Jax Beach. Gates has three or four different places he stays, and he moves around, so let's grab Gates first. It's Friday afternoon. We know where we can find them both until about seven tonight." Danley looked at Arnofsky for approval.

Captain Arnofsky nodded at his two detectives. "Pick up Gates first, then bring in Gambrone. Make sure you confiscate their cell phones immediately so they don't tip anyone off. Go."

It was after seven thirty. The skies were still dark and it was drizzling outside. From his home PC, Mark read the last few emails from John Dunne. He was particularly impressed with the detailed research Dunne had completed on the Florida statutes involving Florida's Unfair and Deceptive Trade Practices Act. His email also stated that Elizabeth Melmann, Orlando Bureau Chief for the Florida Attorney General's office, had taken the lead role in the investigation of Brandson. It was the Florida AG's responsibility under the state's Deceptive Trade Practices Act. Mark hoped that Brandson's tentacles didn't reach as far as the Orlando AG's office.

He took a sip of his cabernet, settled back in his office chair, and breathed a sigh of relief. The investigation was gaining momentum. Glancing outside to check on the weather, he noticed the silver late model Camry still sitting on the street outside his house. It had been there for about five minutes, and he could see from the exhaust fumes that the engine was running. Concerned, he turned off his computer and switched off the lights in his house. His heart was pounding as he stood in his office in the fading light, trying figure out what the driver was up to. *Was it a shooter or another bomber?* The Camry with the tinted windows and engine running had a sinister air about it.

As his eyes adjusted to the darkened interior, Mark grabbed his binoculars to get a better view of the suspicious car sitting at the stop sign seventy yards from his front door. He pressed the low-light setting on the marine binoculars and peered into the drizzle outside. He could make out a man sitting in the driver's seat behind the half-open window holding what looked like a scanning device with an antenna extending outside the car. Very slowly, he opened the blinds just enough to see the car parked in front of his house. From his new angle, he could read the car's Florida tag number, PA8 39F. He had seen this car before at the dealership, and the man sitting behind the wheel trying to hack into Mark's computer was Rocky Gambrone, Brandson's sleazy underworld IT guy.

Gambrone must have noticed the house going dark and the blinds opening. Within a few seconds, the scanner antenna withdrew back inside the Camry. Then he saw the nickel-plated automatic emerge from the car window and heard the gun shot. Then another shot. Fearing for his life, Mark ducked down and watched the driver's window close, and the car lurched into gear and took off around the corner at high speed. In a panic, he fumbled around for the flashlight he kept nearby and located the detective's card he kept on his desk. The card had the case number from the mailbox IED explosion last year. He dialed 911, and a female officer answered the call.

"911, are you having an emergency?"

"Yes, ma'am, I'd like to report gunshots and a stalking, and I have a prior case number involving an explosive device to cross reference," blurted Mark. His heart was pounding as he tried to stay calm. He gulped down the last few ounces of wine, hoping it would calm him down. Mark gave her the address, tag number, driver's name and car description, along with the prior case number 02-12-009797.

"Ma'am, I need you to notify Detectives Matt Anderson and Detective Gary Gronske, please. They know what's going on," he said.

"Sir, are you okay and in a safe place?" asked the dispatcher.

"Yes, ma'am, and the perp has just fled the scene heading north in the silver Toyota Camry SE, Florida tag number PA8 39F."

"Stay on the line with me, sir. I'm getting something over dispatch," she said. As he was holding with the dispatcher, Mark could hear her on her headset in the background. "Fifty-two, roger your twenty. APB suspect Robert Gambrone heading north from Morningwood Forest in a silver Toyota Camry SE, tag number PA8 39F. Shots fired. Suspect has outstanding felony warrant and is armed. Approach with caution." Mark couldn't make out the response from the officer in pursuit over her radio. The dispatcher came back on his phone.

"Sir, we have dispatched two patrol cars to your home."

"Thank you, ma'am. I'm just going to sit here in the dark and wait for them." He took a long breath and peeked out the blinds again. Seeing nothing moving outside, he retreated back through the darkened house to the kitchen for another glass of wine.

His nerves were shot after the gunshots. Not a believer in owning guns, the only weapon he had in the house was a pneumatic speargun he kept on a shelf in his closet, only good at very close range. He wasn't even sure it still worked. He kept his ear tuned for the sound of breaking glass or screeching tires. Sitting quietly in the darkened office, he was thankful he hadn't been shot. Another five minutes ticked by. It seemed like an eternity. Then, he heard the sound of the patrol cars roll up outside. Relieved, Mark turned the front lights on and greeted the officers at the door.

"Mr. McAllister?" Even though the inside lights were on, the officer stood in his entryway shining his flashlight in Mark's face. Mark could make out sergeant stripes on the young officer's uniform.

"Yessir."

"You all right?"

"Yessir."

"Good. I'm Sergeant Ramos. We're gonna take a look around, see if we can find any shell casings, bullet holes or other evidence. Just sit tight. I'll be right back to take your statement." He went back outside in the light drizzle and joined the other three officers to direct the search. In a few moments, Mark's house was surrounded by the four officers, the light from their flashlights bobbing and peering under hedges, exploring every nook and crevice outside.

Ten minutes later, they found two spent nine millimeter shell casings on the road in front, Gambrone's tire tracks from where he peeled out at the stop sign, but no bullet holes. While Sgt. Ramos was taking his report, Mark learned that there had been a high-speed chase on I-75 ten miles away, and Gambrone had been stopped, handcuffed and taken into custody on multiple felony charges.

Plagued by visions of Gambrone returning with his nine millimeter in the middle of the night, Mark woke up in a sweat after having nightmares about insidious, tentacled monsters chasing him down dark alleys. Unable to sleep, he spent the rest of the night staring out his office window.

TWENTY-FIVE

Mark sat at his desk, pondering his moves in the market, pleased that Tesla was taking orders for an enormous number of their high-performance Model S. He picked up a thousand shares of Yahoo at fourteen bucks. Not really a big fan of Facebook, he did manage to trade a thousand shares of the stock for twenty percent gain over a two month holding period. Without his stock market gains this past year, his income from Brandson would be leading him down Tobacco Road and into the poorhouse.

"I see you're in early for a Monday. What's cookin', Marky-Mark?" asked Rich as he logged onto his system. It was busy at the dealership this Monday morning and he could hear the phone ringing constantly. McGreedy was out front leaning over the back of a Tundra talking with a customer redneck-style with his arms resting on the tailgate.

It was May, and morale at the dealership was at at an all-time low point. Stress seemed to be taking its toll on everyone at Brandson, especially the salesmen. Rich was taking blood pressure meds and looked like he was gaining weight. Mark updated him in a phone call over the weekend on the developments at the Florida Attorney General's office. Elizabeth Melmann, the Bureau Chief at the AG's office in Orlando, was now running the show and had become the proverbial tip of the spear in the intensifying multi-agency investigation of Brandson Enterprises. A few days ago, both Juicifer and Rocky Gambrone were arrested on the same day, and the scandalous news had spread throughout the city like a firestorm.

"Good news is the market's pickin' up steam. Hey, I forgot to ask you how Carla's doing," said Mark. "Did she make bail again?" Saddened by his question, Rich looked at the floor.

In a low, calm voice, he said, "Carla slit her wrists yesterday."

"Jeez. Is she okay?" Mark turned off his monitor and went over to sit with his friend.

"Yeah, she'll be okay. They stitched her up. We're trying to get her Baker Acted so she can't hurt herself anymore. She's depressed over our divorce, trying to get us back together. Romantic, huh?"

"Romance like that, who needs a guillotine," said Mark.

Raj was walking toward them eating a piece of pizza with his shirt hanging out. "Hey, guys, you pick up any hot babes this weekend?" He stood over them like Jabba the Hutt chomping on a live toad, sucking down something disgusting.

Not in the best of moods, Rich answered him "Raj, the only way you'd get picked up would be on a scavenger hunt." Raj never really realized how close he was to the wood chipper with Rich.

Raj stood there, squinty-eyed, munching on his pizza. "There was some pizza left in the back, but I think this is the last slice."

"So, let me guess. You're having pizza because they ran out of toads?" asked Mark. Not feeling gracious toward Raj this morning, Raj had gotten away with snaking him out of a nine-hundred-dollar commission, and the deceit was still an open wound. Ignoring Raj, Mark turned to his trainee.

"How's your blood pressure, Rich?" asked Mark.

"It's normal now. I cut my meds in half. Why, what's your advice, doc?"

"More exercise, less alcohol, less red meat and dairy, more fish, and add some Eleuthero root, spirulina, spinach, fresh produce and omega-three fatty acids," said Mark. "You'll lose weight, have more energy, and live longer. And you won't need a script."

"Serious? Where do I have to go to score all of that? The last health food store I was in was charging double normal prices."

"It's all available at Publix, where shopping is a pleasure," said Mark. "It's the only place I buy my groceries. Great customer service, prices are reasonable, and I, uh . . . kinda have a crush on one of their cashiers," Mark confessed.

"What's his name?"

"Don't be a smart-ass. Her name is Brittany. You should talk. Last time Bryan spotted you puttin' the move on that nineteen-year old at the mall kiosk, he said you looked like a monkey trying to hump a watermelon."

"I happen to like watermelons. Hey, there's a car outside I want you to see."

This was their code for having a private conversation in a secluded area where there was less chance of being overheard. It was a gorgeous, warm spring day outside, and Rich headed out the side service door. They met up on the used car lot a hundred yards from the building and now stood behind a big white Sequoia for cover.

Rich was in full cop mode. He had his black cop boots and Terminator sunglasses on. "My buddy at GPD tells me Rocky hasn't made bail yet. When they arrested him Friday night for illegal possession of a firearm by a convicted felon and aggravated stalking, they found four ounces of coke hidden in the armrest of his Camry."

"Happy days are here again," said Mark. "I had no idea they already had an APB out on him when I called in his gunshots and stalking." They watched an emaciated bag man pushing a shopping cart along the sidewalk that bordered the lot, waiting until he was out of ear shot before continuing.

"Well, I spoke as KG to Agent Danley," said Mark. "Brad told me the state attorney's going to oppose his release on bond. So, they nailed him with three felonies. Put a fork in him. He's done. With his prior felonies, he'll do at least three to five years."

"Congratulations on helping to put a dirtbag like Rocky behind bars where he belongs," said Rich, offering him a fist bump. "I heard Juicifer made bail on his felony fraud charge. Rumor is that Larry posted his hundred thousand dollar bail. Can you believe that? They know he has a serious coke habit, so they're waiting for him to screw up."

"Don't worry, he will. Where do you think his last four hundred grand in commissions went?" asked Mark.

Rich put a finger against his nose and sniffed.

"Exactamundo," said Mark. Most of the reps knew they did their coke snorting in the locked bathroom on the second floor where there wasn't anyone around. "You know," said Mark, "with Juicifer fired and arrested, Dennis Testi fired, and Rocky arrested on three felonies, Larry and Tommy can't be far behind. I have a feeling their days are numbered." Rich kicked at a spot in the asphalt and nodded in agreement.

"We've got a good start on cleanin' this place up," said Rich. "Maybe one day it'll be safe to buy a car again." As they walked toward the entrance, he added, "When I describe what goes on here to my buddies at ATF and GPD, it's like they don't believe me. Like you're always saying, you can't make this stuff up. Have you told Sandy about any of this stuff?"

"I want to keep her out of it. She knows I've butted heads with the managers when they're dishonest. I haven't really told her what's goin' on here. I'm trying to keep her safe. She'd probably want me to quit. Some of her hospital staff have had negative experiences at Brandson."

"Why am I not surprised? I've gotta make some calls," said Rich.

"Okay. You go on ahead. I'm gonna go around back to detail, check on a few things." On his way back to the showroom, Mark took a moment to talk to a couple of service customers in the hallway who were watching their cars being serviced through the window. As he rounded the corner into the customer lounge, he stopped when he saw Special Agents Danley, Moser, and Costello standing at the front reception counter. They were wearing their duty belts and vests as they flashed their badges at Jo. Danley held a handful of documents and Mark guessed they were the search warrants. As he watched the agents from a comfortable distance, he realized that the glass awards case he was standing next to was full of sales plaques that were given to Brandson Toyota over the years. Ironic, he thought, since all the awards given over the last four years were based on fraudulent sales figures.

Looking to avoid any awkward moments with his buddies at the FBI, he did a one-eighty and walked through one of the service writer's offices to the service drive outside. Through the glass partitions, he still had a view of the events unfolding at the front desk as he watched the agents present Wells with the search warrants.

Spotting the FBI's presence at the reception desk, it was Tommy Catatonia's turn to join the group. Catatonia led the agents back toward the accounting offices where the computers and servers were located, planning to offer as much cooperation as necessary to save his shaky position as the general manager at Brandson.

Scott emerged from the showroom onto the service lanes, side-stepping a car that was exiting toward the street. "Hey, Marky-Mark, you see who's here today?"

"Looks like law enforcement's catching up with some of the shenanigans here, huh," answered Mark. "What happened to your customer? The mom with the baby in a stroller?"

"Yeah, well, when she saw the FBI agents at the front desk, she got nervous and suddenly had to run out to an appointment." He lowered his voice. "You, uh, wouldn't know anything about the FBI being here, would you?"

The question made Mark a little testy. "Is that one of Raj's rumors or something? What do you think, Scott? You don't think there's any reason for them to be here?"

Scott studied him for a moment. "Oh, I know there's plenty of reasons for them to be here. I—"

"Well, why don't we just stay out of their way and let them do their job. Who knows, maybe *our* jobs might even get easier." Mark's phone rang, and he could see Rich's number displayed on the caller ID. He stepped away from Scott and walked quickly down the service drive. "Hey, what's up?"

"Guess who's in the accounting offices in the back going through our computers?"

"I know. I saw *those guys* up front a few minutes ago. We gonna go work for Ford now, or you want to hang in there a few more days to watch the fireworks? Where are you now?"

"I'm in the back, grabbin' a snack," said Rich.

"Well, I'd join you, but I think it would be best for me to stay away from the offices in back right now. I don't want any awkward moments with *those guys*, right? Let them do their thing,"

"Good idea. I'll let you know what's goin' on."

"Roger that."

Jennifer Treadstone needed only twenty-two more semester hours to graduate with a Masters degree in Journalism from the University of Florida. For the past two years, she was known in the community as an investigative reporter for WUFZ/NPR radio, a station licensed and operated by UF. The radio station was staffed with mostly graduate students and offered opportunities for future reporters studying at the College of Journalism and Communications.

As a reporter, what gave Jennifer her biggest rush was exposing scams at local businesses on her radio talk show "Consumers Hotline." The popular talk show targeted consumers and working professionals on their way to work. She had followed the developing story at Brandson Toyota for over six months and now had the full support of her general manager in headlining the story for their audience. Following her conversations with John Dunne at Consumers Against Crimes, and interviews with Brandson's victims, she was driven to get the word out about the fraud and overcharging. Jennifer had heard the rumors about the use of bribery by Brandson to suppress the stories. In the absence of any advertising by Brandson at WUFZ, she knew there would be a slim chance of bribery by the dealership over lost ad revenues. WUFZ was their best shot at getting the story out to the public.

It was eight thirty on a Thursday morning. Showtime. Preparing to air her broadcast, Jennifer glanced up at her studio director on the opposite side of the sound-proof glass and took her cue to start her show. She was on the air.

"Shopping for a car is often a stressful, confusing, and sometimes even a high-pressure situation," she began. "But one car dealership here in Gainesville may have gone too far beyond just bait-and-switch advertisements and aggressive sales people. They may be violating state laws designed to prohibit unfair trade practices," said Jennifer into her studio mike.

Jennifer glanced up at her director while she took a quick sip of water. The director nodded for her to continue as Jennifer could see the call lines lighting up. "Over the last three years, the local branch of Consumers Against Crimes, which is a special program of the Florida Attorney General's office, has settled nineteen cases on behalf of car buyer victims against Brandson Toyota. To date, the organization has successfully recovered in excess of a hundred and twenty thousand dollars for Brandson customers, according to John Dunne, manager of the local office at the watchdog group." She took another quick sip of water from the bottle on her desk and saw her director giving two thumbs up as the incoming phone lines continued to light up.

"Case files collected and reviewed by WUFZ News all tell similar stories involving elderly and even handicapped people visiting Brandson and getting sold significantly overpriced cars, as well as unwanted extended warranties and unnecessary service plans."

Now, all the incoming lines were busy with callers. Jennifer continued her broadcast. "This trend has not gone unnoticed by Brandson Enterprises, the parent company of the local dealership. According to Dunne, three salesmen have been fired, and the General Manager and General Sales Manager have been reprimanded and placed on corporate probation. The former salesmen are now reportedly working at a Hyundai dealership in the Atlanta area.

"WUFZ News has reached out to the attorney representing Brandson's parent company several months ago, one month ago, and again this week, and our reporter's calls were not returned. Managers at Brandson did not return our repeated phone calls either, and officials at Brandson Automotive in Sarasota directed our inquiries to the local Brandson general manager, who did not respond to any of our repeated attempts for comment."

"WUFZ News reporters have interviewed several victims of the frauds and overcharges at Brandson in the past few months and have learned that many of them had no intention of buying a car when they visited the dealership. On average, victims have paid from five to twenty thousand dollars over sticker price for their new cars. According to Florida statutes, it's illegal for a dealer to add any costs to a car without properly disclosing the additional costs or profits to the customer." Jennifer took another sip of water as everyone on staff at the studio now held two thumbs up. Jennifer contained her excitement with the success of the broadcast, continuing with a professional, even tone.

"Officials with CVC said they believe there may be hundreds of victims, and many of them may not be aware that they are victims. If you have any information about these practices, whether you're a victim yourself or not, you're encouraged to call us on our consumer hotline at any time. You don't have to give your name. That number is 352.392.4778. We have officials standing by right now to take your call and answer questions."

Pausing briefly, Jennifer continued her broadcast. "After being contacted by the Alachua County chapter of the Consumers Against

Crime office, the Gainesville Police Department launched its own criminal investigation into the activities at Brandson. Officials at GPD have acknowledged an ongoing investigation, but, beyond that, would not comment further."

She could see all five of the volunteers busy taking calls. Now, all thirty incoming lines were blinking with additional callers waiting. Encouraged by the robust response, she continued her broadcast.

"The State of Florida Attorney General's office has confirmed that they are currently investigating several cases of alleged fraud, dishonesty and overcharging at Brandson, but could not comment further about the active investigations. Once again, if you think you have been a victim, or know someone who may be a victim, our hotline number is 352.392.4778. Thanks for listening. This is Jennifer Treadstone, WUFZ News."

TWENTY-SIX

Standing under the portico, he shook the excess rainwater from his umbrella and closed it. The United Methodist Church loomed above him, and the architecture was impressive. He paused to admire the four-story stained glass windows and intricate coffered ceilings five stories above him. It felt cold and damp inside as Mark made his way down the aisle.

Finding himself thousands of miles from Florida, he felt temporarily removed from the crime scene that consumed him at the dealership. The five-day family leave of absence he'd arranged with his bosses to attend his aunt's funeral in upstate Michigan gave him a much needed break from the mounting pressures at Brandson.

The crowd had been respectable, especially for a widow who had outlived so many of her family members. Local politicians, townspeople, poets, and fellow members of the Cadillac Area Artist Association had ventured in to find friends and relatives, and to pay their respects. The remains of his aunt had been tastefully preserved in a porcelain urn sitting on an oak table at the end of the aisle. During the funeral, he noticed that most of the interior of the church had remained unchanged since Mark's last visit twenty-three years ago.

Four hours later, as the Delta flight sat poised to move down the runway, the captain's voice came over the intercom as he cited the weather as the reason for their thirty minute delay and thanked everyone for choosing to fly Delta. Mark took a moment to reflect on the buffet lunch at Bertolini's, one of the best events he'd ever shared with his cousins from the north.

As the plane lifted into the air, he felt the bump as the landing gear retracted on the Boeing 757, and his unexpected trip to Cadillac was over. The engines whined loudly as they ascended, and he watched the countryside fall away beneath the jet. He wished everyone would just quit dying on him.

Special Agent Jim Costello leaned back in his chair and rubbed his eyes, weary from searching through hundreds of Brandson customer files. It was half past six on a Tuesday evening. His desk was surrounded by boxes of files scattered everywhere. In between other active cases, he and Moser had been sifting through the hard-copy and digital files for the past week. Today, they'd consumed three pots of coffee and Costello was leading their search through the files. They had found evidence of seventeen bank and finance frauds in the two weeks of intensive investigation, and their instincts as seasoned FBI agents told them they had only scratched the surface in uncovering more crimes.

The problem they'd run into was the one hundred forty-seven files that were encrypted with a symmetric key cypher using a special encryption system. He and Moser tried using every decryption sytem they could find, without success. Brandson's attorneys were acutely aware of the encrypted files and they were evasive about the existence of a decryption key. In more than ten years of computer forensics, the FBI had yet to encounter encrypted files that defied their decryption talents. They were determined to either locate the cypher key or figure out a way to unlock the files.

Costello settled back in his chair and took another sip of coffee from the styrofoam cup. "Frank, how many Brandson managers would you say had access to the encrypted files?"

Moser looked up from the monitors on his desk and studied his partner. Frustrated, he ran his hands over his head and thought about Costello's question. "Who would Larry Wells trust with his life?" he asked.

Costello was exhausted from hours of digging through files. "Ignoring the fact that you're answering a question with a question, that's still a good question," said Costello. He gulped the last bit of coffee from his cup, crushing it in his hand and tossing it into the trash can. He stood up, stretched, and twisted from side to side, trying to rid the stiffness and tension from his torso. Frustrated, he wiped his glasses with his shirt. "Why the hell don't we have any damned windows in here?"

"We figure this thing out, we get that corner office in Honolulu. Would that make you stop bitchin'?" asked Moser.

Costello ignored the implausibility of a corner office in Hawaii. "I'm thinking Wells trusts no one with this key. From what I know about that slimy cockroach, he keeps it for himself. And only for himself."

"Okay, good point. But where you goin' with this?" asked Moser.

"Wells is too smart to keep the key on him, in case we searched him. He'd have to keep it handy. Somewhere close to where he sits, so he can keep an eye on it," said Costello.

"Jim, remember that dealership you guys busted in Orlando four or five years ago?" asked Moser. "I think it was, uh . . . Arena Automotive, or something like—"

"Yeah, Arena Auto. We found an encryption key taped to a ceiling tile above the managers' desks," said Costello. "My partner,

Beth, found a half-pound of coke in a drawer in their office. We wound up padlocking the whole place."

A quizzical look came over Moser's face. "Whatever happened to your last partner, Beth? She was a looker. You remember those skirts she used to wear? Jeez. She could've been Katy Perry's stunt double." Moser leaned back in his chair and put his feet up. He clasped his hands behind his head as he pictured Beth in her tight skirt sitting at his desk with her gorgeous legs crossed. "Yeah, she was hot," said Costello. "She hooked up with the Northwest Regional Director and transferred out to the Seattle headquarters two years ago. Hell, she's probably runnin' the place by now. She had his balls wrapped around her tongue."

"Yeah. How did you manage to keep your hands off her?"

"Who says I did?" Costello sat there, smiling smugly at his partner, wiping his glasses again. With his iconic GQ-looks and slim build, Costello was often mistaken for a male model, and he took full advantage of it.

"Okay, stud nuts. Back to work," said Moser. "Let's do this. I say we plan an early morning search of Well's office before the managers get there, tomorrow, including the crawl space above his desk. We need that cypher key."

"I'm on board with that. How 'bout six tomorrow morning?"

"You're on. I'll let Brad know. Wells usually takes off Wednesdays, so that works. Meet ya here a little before six." Moser stopped to stifle a yawn. "Would you believe I've been so tired lately that I actually fell asleep last night while I was goin' down on my wife."

"Guess that explains the dream you had when you were kissing Abe Lincoln, right?" joked Costello.

"Smartass. Hey, I just remembered. I got something for you here, stud nuts." Moser leaned forward in his chair and opened his bottom drawer. He rummaged through the contents and found what he was looking for. Pulling out a CD, he pushed it across his desk toward Costello.

"What's that?" asked Costello.

"My daughter's Katy Perry CD. You know, a little bubble-gum music so you can reminisce about your ex-partner, Beth."

Eric Berman watched the traffic on Washington Boulevard and waited on the call from the Orlando Attorney General's office. For the last thirty minutes, he had been pacing back and forth, and checking his watch frequently. He was tired of waiting. Unable to concentrate on returning phone calls, emails or preparing his cases for trial, he couldn't get his mind off his inability to nail down a definite deal on behalf of his client, Brandson Enterprises. Beth Melmann, Bureau Chief at the Florida Attorney General's Consumer Protection Division, had proven to be a little more elusive than he predicted.

Melmann had taken over as the lead investigator on the Brandson investigation a week ago. He had already spent several hours and many phone calls trying to work out a settlement. She was evasive in their last call, saying that she needed to delve into the investigation a little deeper, review documents and interview witnesses before she could talk about a settlement.

Berman's biggest fly in the ointment was this KG person. KG was leaking information and documents to law enforcement for the last eight months. As a result, the investigations kept expanding. They had to find out who he was, which of their dealerships he was working at, and figure out a way to neutralize him if they wanted to stand a chance of avoiding criminal charges.

There was a lot riding on the outcome, and Berman tried to stay focused on the pot of gold at the end of the rainbow. Mr. James Brandson, the sole owner of Brandson Enterprises and the seventeen dealerships controlled by Brandson Automotive, had generously provided Berman and his firm, Grabbot, Strickland, Berman and Runn, with the offer of a half million dollar bonus if he could reach an administrative settlement with Melmann and avoid a criminal prosecution. Mr. Brandson had also provided a budget of up to another half-million dollars for fines and restitution if the civil remedy could be hammered out with the Florida AG's office before everything went to hell in a hand basket.

Berman was under a lot of pressure from his partners, as well as Brandson, to deliver the settlement. He had been the sole bread winner since his wife quit her job at the development firm in Sarasota when the real estate market collapsed. They lived on the water, had a vacation home in the Bahamas, owned four cars, a sixty-foot Hatteras, and enjoyed a luxurious lifestyle. With three kids in private school, failure was not an option. He dug down deep, drawing upon his twenty-four years of experience in business law and commercial litigation. Unless he could stop the leaks and do a deal with Melmann, the damage would just keep getting worse. He would avoid being responsible for losing the firm's biggest client at all costs.

He jumped when his phone rang and unconsciously patted down his thick grey hair as if he were heading into a meeting. Berman read the 407 area code on his cell phone. It was the call from Orlando that he'd been waiting for.

"Eric Berman."

A woman's voice on the phone said, "Please hold for the Attorney General." There were a few moments of silence, followed by a click as his call was switched over. Then, another woman's voice.

"Eric, Beth Melmann. How are you?" The Bureau Chief at the Orlando Florida AG sounded tense. She'd been on the phone and reviewing emails from three different law enforcement agencies for the past four hours, and she had a headache.

"I'm fine, Beth. Thanks for getting back to me."

"Sure. I'm afraid I'm not quite ready to give you what you want, Eric, but maybe we can get a little closer today," she said.

"Okay. So, what have we got?"

"Well, I haven't had a chance yet to review all the evidence against your client yet. We do have a fair number of documents pointing to defrauding Toyota and thirty or so customers. And, it looks like some possible warranty fraud at Brandson in Gainesville."

"Warranty fraud?" Berman put on his best dumb blonde act.

"Yes, and I'll explain in a minute. Also, alleged bank fraud on the part of a . . . uh . . . hang on, let me find that file . . . a Ricky Gonzalez."

"That's a surprise," said Berman.

"Look, Eric, if we're talking a civil fine and settlement here, you've got to cut the crap and work with me. You know damn well Gonzalez has been implicated in at least eight civil fraud complaints filed through CVC," said Melmann. She interpreted the next few moments of silence as complicity on Berman's part and proceeded with her case.

"Now, I have directed GPD and CVC to cease complainant interviews. Our office will now be handling that. In addition, I just wanted you to know that I've issued subpoenas to CVC, and the executives in charge there, for all emails and documents in their possession relating to Brandson. Of course, these documents will be made available to you during discovery." Melmann was very matter-of-fact in summarizing her duties and activities, confident that she now had complete control of the conversation.

"Question for you, Eric. Do you have an employee at Brandson with the initials KG?"

"Why do you ask?" Berman thought he had a great dumb blonde act, but it was wearing thin on the AG.

"We going to play more games, or are we going to put our cards on the table, Eric?" Berman could tell she was getting miffed.

"We don't employ anyone with those initials. We hear rumors—"

"From who?"

"Well, from GPD. And Tom Lewis's office at the state attorney's—"

"Okay. I'll talk with him about that," said Melmann. "Although that is in and of itself inappropriate, this KG thing is one loose end we both want to tie up, right Eric?"

"You better believe it. You don't intend on acting on anonymous tips, do you?"

"Of course not. You know I can't do that. So, Eric, based upon your earlier commitment to clean house over there, you're still willing to do that, right?" She was confidant that this would be a rhetorical question.

"Yes, we know we'll have to make some changes," said Berman.

"Good. We ask that your firm immediately replace Larry Wells, their GSM, Anthony Grimes, the used car manager, and Kelly Allen, the comptroller there at Brandson. Sooner or later, let's say within sixty days, Catatonia, Shehan, and that slime ball Gonzalez, who defrauded my friend, the Dean of the University of Florida Law School. He has to go, too. Agreed?"

"Ah, Beth, that's a lot to ask."

"That's non-negotiable. You want a civil settlement, or criminal charges? You better decide." Melmann sounded firm, and Berman knew he had no choice but to agree to the changes in personnel.

"Okay, done," said Berman. "I'll persuade them to do it."

"I know you will. Now, what do you have for me?" asked Melmann.

"Of course, you have our promise to cooperate fully with your investigation. And, well, we'd like to support you in your re-election bid next year. To the tune of, say, two-hundred fifty grand," he said.

"Eric, are you nuts? We're in the middle of an investigation, here! You know I can't—"

"Cash. No witnesses. No receipts. You can send someone to pick it up." There was a long pause. Berman could hear the sound of her fingers tapping absent-mindedly on her desk.

"Let me think about it."

TWENTY-SEVEN

Moser sipped his coffee in the predawn darkness, moving quietly so he wouldn't wake his wife and kids. After eighteen years as a Special Agent with the FBI, he was used to getting up early for special assignments. It was still dark outside. He pushed the button that lighted the dial on his watch. Five twenty, Wednesday, June 12th. He slipped into his vest, buckled his duty belt and fastened the Velcro thigh strap on his forty caliber Glock holster. In the dim light, he stopped to admire the faces of his three teenage kids in the framed portrait photos sitting on the credenza.

Placing his ID badge and chain around his neck, he thought about the private sector job he was offered two months ago. If he took the job as the executive director of a large Florida-based private security firm, he would be in charge of overseeing security for over sixty condo associations and office buildings throughout the state. He interviewed with the Daytona Beach firm twice, and they made him an attractive offer with a salary well over six figures. The owners had shown him how they planned to market his years of experience at the FBI, and how it would help with the firm's expansion. With the added revenue the owners expected to see, they could afford to make him the six-figure offer.

Moser told them he would kick it around. Sometimes he wished he'd already jumped on it. He enjoyed the restaurants, beaches and night life along Ocean Boulevard on his two trips to Daytona. He was impressed with the strippers, too. When his wife had asked about the charges on their credit card statement, he told her it was part of an assignment in Volusia County, setting aside the dirty little secret as an inconvenient truth. She had her nights out, and he had his diversions. After twenty-three years of marriage, it only seemed fair.

At his current GS-12 level, he still had one more pay grade available to him in a non-supervisory role before he maxed out at GS-13. The job offer was a lot more than he was making, even with availability pay, but he would lose most of his Federal benefits. Achieving the rank of Field Supervisor with the FBI would give him the income and benefits he really wanted. If he could break the Brandson case, he knew Danley would likely recommend him for a supervisory position and he'd have a better shot at moving up the chain of command. So the rest of you out there, just keep taking your psychotropics and eating your teevee dinners. Frank Moser was moving on up the food chain.

Weaving through the early-morning traffic in his Charger, he put these thoughts aside and forced himself to focus on what was on tap for today. Hitting a string of green lights on University Avenue, he was making good time. He checked his watch again. Five minutes ahead of schedule. Moser had a good feeling about their game plan today.

On the first search, their focus had been on retrieving the computer and hard copy customer files. The FBI's proprietary 'ghosting' software had worked well during the searches of Brandson's computers, but they hit a brick wall when they uncovered the one hundred forty-seven encrypted files. They needed to find that key cypher.

Moser's boss had anticipated the possibility of needing to conduct more than one search. In the eleventh hour, Danley came through.

He had secured an extension and modification from District Court Judge Bishop on the warrant and had the cypher key specifically itemized on the paperwork. It was Wednesday, their prime suspect's day off, and by beginning the search three hours before any managers were due to arrive, they anticipated being able to complete their mission without any interference from Wells or his thugs.

Pulling into the bank parking garage, he drove to one of the empty spaces reserved for "Federal Employees" along the far wall. He spotted Costello standing beside his Crown Victoria, sipping on a large Starbucks. Moser pulled into the empty space next to him. As he stepped out of his Charger, he could see Danley standing at the rear of his Ford Escape. The hatch was open, and he was putting his vest and duty belt inside the SUV. Moser watched him slam it shut.

"We going in light, Brad?" asked Moser.

"Yeah," said Danley. "Let's be comfortable for our search today. Just ID badges. I'm not expecting any trouble from these bozos," said Danley.

"Sounds good to me, boss." Moser walked back to his Charger, popped the trunk and pulled off his duty belt and vest, laying it in the trunk. Before he closed the lid, he checked the security mechanism on his AR-15 to make sure it was locked and secure in its cradle. Then he slammed the trunk shut and activated the alarm.

"Frank, I got you your triple expresso latte," said Costello, handing him two large Starbucks to Moser. "Here, give the mocha to Brad. I'm gonna lockup my Glock and vest."

Five minutes later, they were four miles further north on Main Street in Danley's black Ford Escape. Seeing no one on the lot as they approached the dealership, the three FBI agents pulled into the brightly-lit parking lot at Brandson. It was exactly six o'clock. Danley turned off the engine and the three agents pulled out their their latex gloves. As they headed for the main entrance, they could see lights on in the showroom where the janitor was running the polishing machine back and forth over the tile floor. With Moser next to him, Danley pounded loudly on the door and held up the warrant while Costello adjusted the fit of his gloves.

"FBI. Search warrant!" shouted Danley. The janitor looked up and turned off the polishing machine, waving at them from inside. He stepped across the showroom floor to open the door.

"Morning, guys," said the janitor as he let the three men into the dealership. "I wasn't expecting anyone for a couple more hours."

"We're not here to buy a car," said Moser. "I'm Agent Danley. This is Agent Moser, and that's Agent Costello. We have a warrant to search the premises." Danley held up the warrant for him as a matter of routine, unsure if the janitor would understand it. Steve had been the janitor at Brandson for the last four years. He stared blankly at the warrant, clearly intimidated by the document and the three agents.

"I'm Steve, the janitor. What can I do to help?" he asked meekly.

"You can open the sales managers' office right there, straight ahead," said Danley, pointing to the sales tower. With the janitor leading them, the three agents charged into the showroom, stopping to admire the new cars and reaching for their pocket-size LED flashlights

The janitor clutched his broom insecurely, pushing his equipment cart out of the way as the men stepped toward the tower. The FBI agents stood at the office door and waited impatiently for the janitor to input the entry code on the push-button pad.

"Let's see, I think it's, uh, I think it's six-six-six," he said. He entered the numbers. The lock clicked, releasing the latch, and the door opened, releasing the smell of Mexican food.

"What demonic individual came up with that combination," asked Danley.

"Uh, I think Mr. Wells is in charge of all the security codes around here," answered the janitor. "I'm pretty sure he's the one that sets them." He seemed oblivious to the Biblical reference Danley had just made.

Danley lowered his voice. "That's right. I remember our informant saying Wells likes to refer to himself as 'The Devil'"

"I don't remember that," said Costello.

"You were in Jacksonville that day. For your computer training,"
said Moser. "That's the day we had our first briefing with our CI."
They spread out behind the chest-high counter and began to rifle
through piles of papers, throwing them into a big cardboard box on
the credenza next to the printer after they finished inspecting them.

"Okay, guys, listen up," said Danley, taking command of the
operation. "Jim, you take the overhead cabinets to your left. Frank,
take the ones on your right, and I'll start with the cabinets and
drawers under the credenza. Then, we start on the ceiling tiles. Let's
find that cypher key."

"Brad, toss me your keys. I forgot that four-foot stepladder in the
back of your SUV. So we can get up into the ceiling," said Moser.
He caught the set of keys in mid air with one hand and headed to
the parking lot. A couple of minutes later, Moser returned with the
aluminum step ladder and set it up in front of the credenza along
the back wall of the sales tower. They continued to tear the office
apart, examining every document they got their hands on.

After thirty minutes, they'd gone through all the shelves and
every key that hung in the cabinets. Then they started working on
the drawers, pulling them out of the cabinets, turning them upside
down and taking them apart. They scoured every available surface
for the missing cypher.

"Hey, check this out," said Costello. Duct-taped to the under-
side of the last drawer was a white vinyl pouch with three syringes
inside. They were labeled L, K, and T with a black Sharpie marker.

"I'm guessing L for Larry, K for Kirk, and T for Tony," said
Danley. "Put it into evidence and send it to the lab." Costello took
photos with his Canon digital camera and dropped the pouch containing the syringes into an evidence bag that was preaddressed to
the FBI lab in Atlanta.

"They're definitely shootin' something illegal here. The lab guys will tell us what," said Moser. He pulled a handful of change out of his pants pocket. "I'm gonna grab a soda. You guys want one?" Danley shook his head. He was looking through a stack of photos of naked women from one of the drawers. Costello said, "Bring me a Coke, high-test, none of that diet crap." Then he noticed the X-rated photos. "Damn, Brad. Let me take a look at those."

"Okay." Danley looked at Costello. "When you're done gawking at the photos there, Jimbo, let's start on the ceiling tiles," said Danley as he set up the stepladder.

Spotting a tile that showed some signs of dirty fingerprints, Danley climbed up to the top step of the four-foot ladder and slid the soiled tile back. With his head up in the ceiling, he did a slow, 360-degree search with his flashlight. He spotted something that reflected the light about three feet away, something that looked like it didn't belong up there. He repositioned the ladder closer to the spot with the strange reflection, sweeping the area again with his flashlight.

"Jim, hand me those tongs, will you. There's something up here," said Danley. "Get a bag ready." Costello handed him a pair of evidence tongs and opened a plastic bag. Danley used the tongs to grasp the small plastic baggie in the ceiling and pulled it toward him. He brought it down from its hiding place and dropped it into the evidence bag that Costello was holding open.

"Well, will ya look at that," said Costello as Moser returned with their drinks. Moser put the cans on the counter and stepped up to the plastic baggie, scrutinizing it with his co-workers.

"Looks like pure flake cocaine to me. I'd say, maybe three or four grams there. Could be an eight ball," said Moser. "I wonder whose prints are all over that little party favor?"

"It's gonna be interesting to see who cops to it," said Costello.

Moser reached for one of the three cans of soda that he had set on the counter. Moist from the condensation, the can slipped out of his hands, bouncing off the desk and onto the floor.

"Sorry about that, Jim," said Moser. As he got down on all fours and reached under the chair to retrieve the coke, Moser spotted an open seam in the vinyl cover under the bottom of the manager's chair. He grabbed his flashlight to get a better look.

"Hey, hand me some tweezers. I think I got something here," said Moser. Carefully, he separated the partially-opened seam with his fingers. Holding the flashlight in his teeth, he reached inside the pocket with a set of tweezers and extracted a three-by-five card. He pulled the card out of the bottom of the chair and placed it on the desk in front of him.

"Guys, I think we just hit the jackpot," said Moser.

"Let me see," said Costello. He put his reading glasses on and took a closer look at the three-by-five card. On it were combinations of rows of letters on the X-axis, and rows of numbers on the Y-axis, with what appeared to be a repeating keyword. It looked like it was all hand-printed in blue ball-point pen.

"Looks to me like a Vigenere cypher here. No wonder we couldn't decrypt those files. Without this key, those cyphers are almost impossible to decrypt," said Costello. He removed his reading glasses and turned to his boss. "Brad, I'm pretty sure this is our key."

Danley studied the three-by-five card again. Elated by the find, he let out a loud, "Way to go, guys!" and the three shared a celebratory fist bump.

Drawn to the commotion in the sales tower, the janitor stuck his head in the door. "Everything Okay?" Steve couldn't believe what a mess they'd made. He surveyed the office, annoyed that everything was pulled out of the cabinets and strewn on the floor.

"Yup. We're done here. Leave us for a few minutes. Hey, Steve, thank God they have you, right?" said Danley.

Looking confused, the janitor said, "Yeah, I guess so." He shook his head and exited the sales tower as ordered.

"If I wasn't such a klutz, we may never have found it," said Moser. Danley popped the top on his Mountain Dew and clinked soda cans with Moser and Costello in celebration of their find.

"Okay, guys. Let's pack up and head back to the office," said Danley. "Jim, you take charge of the cypher key. I want you to plug in those codes as soon as we get back. Let's find out what's in those files."

TWENTY-EIGHT

Through the fading light he could see the old mustard colored single-story house dated from the early nineteen hundreds, and it needed a good coat of paint. Situated in a rough neighborhood frequented by drug peddlers and hookers a half-block off Main Street, few would have guessed that the house was the law office of Braswell, Lang, and Narino, PA. The faded wooden sign with the firm's name was hard to read, deteriorated by years of sun and half-hidden by the Spanish moss that hung from the giant hundred-year old oaks. The huge oak trees formed a canopy over the house, allowing small patches of shadowy light to peek through on this early summer evening.

Mark was in his third week of family medical leave from Brandson and thinking seriously about heading up a class action suit against his own employer. Sad over the loss of his aunt, and with his mom still weak from the effects of pneumonia, he wasn't sure if he even wanted to return to the hell hole that he'd worked at for the past four years. Wearing both the hats of sales rep and confidential informant weighed on him heavily. He was twisted up over the continuing corruption and slowly losing the will to work in a crime scene. The great man's words, who once said that the truth shall make you free, kept resounding in his head.

He steered his car into the office parking lot, driving over a series of thick tree roots that had buckled the pavement so badly that he hit his head on the ceiling of his Camry. He pulled in next to a black Mercedes and brought the car to a stop near the steps leading to the front door. Rubbing the top of his head from the bump, he looked around the grounds, wondering when the last time the lot had been paved.

Braswell, Lang and Narino was one of the most successful class action law firms in Florida, having won a string of lucrative suits over the last decade. His online research on the firm highlighted one of their latest court victories that involved a group of plaintiffs that were awarded a twelve million dollar settlement from a major cigarette manufacturer.

Two years before that they were victorious with a class action suit against a major drug company. A year prior to that award, they won a six million dollar settlement on behalf of victims who suffered from birth defects caused by prescription anti-depressants. The firm had a solid history of winning consumer law suits, and he wanted them on his side.

As he exited his Camry, he locked it and took a closer look around in the failing light. With at least two multi-million dollar settlements in the bag, maybe the firm could afford to spend a little on sprucing up the place. It looked more like a budget rehab center or a home for wayward women than a law office. Then he noticed the security cameras pointing his way from under the eaves over the entryway. A security guard emerged from the shadows at the edge of the parking lot and walked slowly toward him in the twilight.

"Evening, sir, can I help you?" asked the guard. They stood about ten feet apart, and Mark could see he was a stocky guy that looked a little like O.J. Simpson during his early years as a running back. He wore a tan and brown uniform with black boots and a duty belt that held both a Glock and a taser at his side. The neighborhood didn't look that rough, and he thought the guard was packing a little heavy for a mixed development eight blocks from downtown.

"I'm Mark McAllister, here to see Rick Narino," said Mark. "I have a seven o'clock appointment with him."

"Yes sir," said the guard. "Give me a moment to check with my boss." He pulled out his cell phone and speed dialed a number, announcing Mark to someone inside the office. After a brief conversation, the guard put the phone back into his pocket.

"Yes, sir, you can go on in. Right up the stairs to your left," said the guard, pointing toward the short flight of stairs.

The guard faded back into the dusk under the canopy of trees and Spanish moss as Mark walked up the stairway. He peered into the camera overhead and heard an electronic buzz. The lock released, and he turned the knob and stepped inside. The cramped reception area that was once part of the porch was quiet and empty, devoid of any signs of activity. There was the faint sound of a Mozart violin concerto coming from above. A pass-through window leading to an empty desk sitting on the other side of the wall that separated the reception area greeted him. A small, colonial-style coffee table was surrounded by three chairs and a sofa, and a red, hand-woven Persian carpet covered the dark-brown hardwood floor. There was a varied assortment of magazines displayed on the coffee table. After a few moments, he heard footsteps, and the door to the offices inside opened. A young man in a tie and white dress shirt came out to greet him. He had short brown hair, brown eyes, and really bad teeth.

"Hi, Mark, Rick Narino." They shook hands, and Rick led Mark inside to his office. "Sorry about the security outside. We've had a few incidents with drug dealers and panhandlers lately, so we added more security after hours for the safety of our clients." He motioned toward the two high-back upholstered chairs facing his desk. "Please, have a seat. You brought your files, right?"

"As promised," said Mark. "You think my car'll be safe out there?"

"Of course. Mine's out there, and Lou's on the job. And our motion-activated security lights come on at seven," Rick assured him. He looked at his watch. "Right about now, as a matter of fact."

Mark sat down in the closest chair and put his attaché case in the empty seat next to him. He pulled three thick, legal-size files out and set them on Rick's desk. "Okay if I put these here?"

"Of course," said Rick. "I appreciate your flexibility on the timing of our meeting. It's been a busy week, and I was closing a big commercial deal earlier today, not sure of how long it would take. I wanted to take a look at your case as soon as possible because of the statute of limitations issues with some of them."

"Yes, there's that. Are those limitations for four years, or is it five in Florida for written contracts?" asked Mark. He intended to float this question as a test of Rick's knowledge of pertinent statutes, as well as a test of his ability to think on his feet.

"Actually, it's four years for statutory liability," said Rick. With his correct answer, he had passed one of Mark's hurdles.

"John Dunne at CVC has told me about your help with two victims who had filed complaints against Brandson through his office," said Mark.

"Yes, I remember them," said Rick. "Morris and Jimenez. We settled for over forty-three thousand dollars for the frauds and overcharges on those two. The lion's share went to the victims' reimbursement."

"As it should, right?" This was another little test from Mark, an opportunity to gain an understanding of Narino's sense of fairness.

"Of course," answered Rick.

"Did Brandson's attorney, Berman is his name, I think—"

"You're right. Eric Berman—"

"Did he require your plaintiffs to sign waivers on future liabilities?" asked Mark, as he jockeyed to survey the legal landscape that he was preparing to journey into.

"Yes, Brandson did, as part of the proposed settlement," said Rick. "In consideration of the amounts of the settlements proposed, which was actually more than we expected, I advised the plaintiffs to accept their terms, since neither of the two plaintiffs had any other actionable issues with Brandson."

"Is it your opinion that Brandson was a little generous on the settlements to ensure that the complaints wouldn't find their way into court and, therefore, the public domain?" asked Mark. "So far, they've managed to bribe their way out of any negative publicity."

Rick looked at Mark anew, as if he had just seen him for the first time. "What part of Philadelphia did you receive your law training there, Mark?" asked Rick as he smiled broadly. Confronted with another view of Rick's teeth, Mark tried not to be distracted. There was no shortage of reasons for him to dislike attorneys, even without the lack of cosmetic dentistry.

"Well, due to the crimes at Brandson, I've done a lot of research on the laws that govern business practices. I've also been exchanging strategies with John Dunne for several months," said Mark. "John and I are on the same page here. Investigating economic crimes was his forte when he was a detective."

"That's impressive," said Rick. "You seem educated, articulate, and have a good grasp on the issues. Maybe you missed your true calling. Would you like a soda or glass of water, Mark?" Knowing full well Rick was blowing smoke up his ass, Mark was starting to like this guy anyway and could feel himself becoming more relaxed with him.

"Sure. You have a Coke machine? High test if you have it," said Mark.

"Sure do. You mean caffeinated Coke, right?" Mark nodded, and Rick swiveled in his chair to open a mini-fridge that was built into the credenza behind him. He pulled out two Cokes, and a couple of napkins from the drawer, and set them on his desk next to his banker's lamp. "Here you go. Nice and cold."

Mark grasped the Coke, popped the top and took a sip. "Thanks. By the way, Rick, I'd like to ask that we invoke the attorney/client privilege for confidentiality in everything we discuss. Much of what we're going to talk about is sensitive information, and I haven't made a firm decision on how to proceed. I still feel conflicted about suing my employer, but I'd still like to hear your ideas."

"I understand the conflict that you face," answered Rick. He thought for a moment about what he was about to say. "It's tough to do what you're doing. Without question, your life will get harder as you try to do the right thing. Just so you know, I usually offer confidentiality, regardless of what we talk about. Let me share something with you."

"I'm all ears," said Mark in his best imitation of Ross Perot.

"Ha. Yeah. Given the many statutory violations by the dealership, and the fact that Brandson is now the focus of several criminal investigations by various law enforcement agencies, any class action case could become very significant for future case law," said Rick.

"As well as fame and fortune for the prevailing firm?" asked Mark.

"I hope so. Money can't buy happiness—"

"I wouldn't know. Lately, I feel like I'm lacking both," said Mark.

"Ha! Yeah, well, maybe our firm can help you with both," said Rick.

"I'd be grateful for that. John was complimentary on your ability to bring about a favorable outcome for his victims at CVC," said Mark. "Now I'm wondering if we can be as successful in a class action that could involve scores, maybe even hundreds, of victims of the frauds."

"Are you prepared to resign your position at Brandson if we file this suit with you named as a party to it? It will become public record when we file," said Rick. He sat back in his chair and folded his hands together, tacitly testing Mark's commitment to move forward.

"Either that, or I would offer you my help confidentially in preparing your case. As of right now, as an employee, I still have access to Brandson's internal files. Those files could be as big a help to you as they have been to law enforcement and hundreds of victims. Any good citizen has a responsibility to report serious crimes on the part of their employer to the authorities, right?"

"Yes you do," said Rick. "As long as you don't break any laws, share proprietary secrets with Brandson's competitors, or misappropriate personal info. Reporting crimes is different. You can't be expected to ignore criminal activity." Rick took a sip of his Coke and settled deeper into his chair. They began to feel more comfortable with each other, and Mark could feel an atmosphere of trust begin to develop between them.

"Good, 'cause I hate being arrested," said Mark. "One time, when I was a kid playing on a playground at school one day, I had to pee really bad. So, I relieved myself behind some bushes. What did I know? I was just a kid. Then I heard some girls giggling, and the next thing I know a cop is holding me by the back of my shirt and threatening to arrest me for indecent exposure."

"So, what happened?" asked Rick.

"He had to let me go. He said I had insufficient evidence," said Mark. Rick chuckled politely. Mark continued. "I think it was one of those catch and release programs. You know, when they're too small and you have to throw them back."

"Ha, cute story. Hey, I just remembered something important. As far as how the class of consumers is defined in the statutes, it might be difficult to include you."

"Why?" asked Mark. This confused him. "I'd be heading up the suit."

"From memory, without having the statute in front of me, as an employee of the firm where you bought your four Toyotas, you may be excluded from the class of consumers," said Rick. "It has to do with what the court would consider an 'arms length' transaction."

"So, if what you're saying is correct, because I worked at the dealership, you're saying I may not be able to be included in the class action because I worked there? Am I not a consumer too?" This seemed kind of screwed up, and Mark hadn't just bought one new car from Brandson. He'd been overcharged on four cars over his tenure of employment at the dealership.

"That's how it's written. I mean, I'll review it and look for another angle if you want to be part of the suit, but you might be precluded from joining it," explained Rick.

"What about a separate suit for the overcharges and consequent punitive damages. Would that avenue still open to me?" asked Mark.

"Sure. But based upon prior offers made by Brandson in settlements, they required that all of the complainants sign a waiver of all future suits or actions in order to receive their settlements."

"So, given the likelihood that they would force me to agree to a waiver, signing it would then force me to forego any future actions to recover money illegally withheld, like from my paychecks for the last four years? Is that what we're saying here?"

"That's exactly right, I'm afraid. So, you'd have to pick your battles carefully," Rick explained.

"The employer-employee issues involve about fifty grand that they owe me. Do we have to agree to these restrictions?" Mark asked.

"No, but they'll try to limit their liabilities with you. By the way, are they taking care of all your workmen's comp expenses?" asked Rick.

Mark was beginning to appreciate Rick's ability to see the big picture. "Yeah, they have, but not willingly. I had to threaten the comp carrier a coupla times with legal action. Getting them to pay up and find me a competent team of physicians, instead of their 'Doc-In-The-Box', well, that wasn't easy. Do you know they tried to tell me my accident injuries were from pre-existing conditions?"

"That's actually more common than you might think," said Rick. He reached for some papers on his desk. "We have a number of actionable issues here against Brandson. Shall I prepare a retainer agreement?" he asked. He was casual, but confident, and Mark liked the smooth way he closed him for a commitment.

"Yes. Let's move forward," said Mark.

Following his meeting with Rick Narino, Mark returned home around nine o'clock and checked his emails. There was one from

Sandy inviting him over for a home-cooked dinner Friday night. It was late Monday night. He was craving her feminine charms, not sure he could wait that long to see her. He sent her a return email accepting her invitation, adding that she didn't need to prepare a desert because she was plenty sweet for him. Then his phone rang. It was Sandy.

After a steamy conversation with Sandy, he composed himself and focused on the day's messages, returning to his PC to read John Dunne's latest email. It was a doozy. The Florida AG, Beth Melmann, had subpoenaed all of Consumers Against Crimes' records regarding the issues at Brandson. She was consolidating her lead in the investigation and had requested that Dunne have no further contact with KG 'of a substantive nature'. Dunne's email said the AG had served another search warrant at Brandson today, and also simultaneously at Brandson's corporate headquarters in Sarasota.

Of everything mentioned in Dunne's email to KG, what stood out the most was the series of eight questions asked by the Attorney General about KG that appeared at the end of her email. Instead of questions about the actual crimes being committed at Brandson, she seemed to be more focused on John's relationship to KG. The AG knew that KG had worked at Brandson for four years, yet she'd asked no questions about any of the crimes that he may have witnessed. Odd, he thought. He read the wording in the main body of the email again:

KG:

FYI—All new victims' contact information will be forwarded to the FL AG's office during their ongoing investigation. CVC has been authorized to open new victim's case files and assign a case number for the purpose of documenting the victim, then forward the file as "closed w/referral to FL AG" to law enforcement to make contact.

The above directive is made by the AG's office to avoid conflict of activity on any active case file. If you are unable to get addresses of victims with all contact info, I will create a separate case file for each one w/just the info you have and forward to AG's office. I expect the FL AG will have more luck w/a phone contact than CVC's office in the past as they have personnel trained specifically for interviewing victims of economic crimes.

As always, thanks for your help with these frauds and investigations.

JD

As he read it over again, Mark wondered why the AG wanted the consumer watchdog group out of the way, given all the victims and the body of evidence that the group had assembled to date. Also, Dunne had completed a great deal of statutory research and devised many of the various strategies of how to prosecute the crimes at Brandson. All of this had been handed to law enforcement on a silver platter. Ironically, John was an unpaid volunteer who was doing a better job of investigating and uncovering the crimes than any of the salaried law enforcement personnel that Mark had dealt with. In his estimation, they owed CVC a huge debt of gratitude. It bothered him that an office with a political agenda and an elected official at the top, who was high on campaign contributions and low on motivation, had taken over the investigation. As he thought about this predicament, his phone rang. It was Rich.

"Hey, what's up, buddy? You selling a lot of cars there at Grabbit, Ripitoff and Run?" asked Mark.

"Well, if I was still there I might be," said Warren. "I got into it with Larry yesterday over my paycheck. There was another eighteen hundred bucks missing. All he cares about is the IRS case he's fighting and dodging the search warrants."

"What a bunch of sleazebags we work for, huh?" said Mark.

"Used to work for. I told him I can't live on twenty-five hundred a month and support my daughter," said Warren. "He gave me a bunch of made-up crap and wouldn't pay me my money. So,

I quit and walked out. I'm done with their thievery, Mark. I've had enough."

"For real? What are you gonna do for a job?" asked Mark.

"They offered me my old job back at AT&T with a better pay plan and a management position. They said the economy's pickin' up and business is boomin'. Within a few months, I think I could be making a decent living there," said Warren. "What about you? Are you ever going back? You've been on family medical leave now for what—a month now?"

"Sandy wants me to sell my place and move in with her, and I'm very tempted. When I'm not flying Sandy to the moon, I'm actually making more money in a week trading the markets than I did all month working seven days a week at Brandson."

"I don't know why you even bother with the brain damage at Brandson in your financial situation," said Rich. "How the hell did you last four years there?"

"I've never been a quitter." Mark paused and thought for a moment. "Ya know, I thought you'd be doin' a lot better at Brandson. With all the firings, you have less competition, don't you? They fired Juicifer and Dennis for fraud. Larry fired Eddie, David, and Pete for complaining about money missing from their paychecks. Ian left to start his own internet operation. Plus, I'm not there. You should be tearin' it up, hittin' it outa the park, bro."

"You'd think. Word's gotten out up and down Main Street, and at the other dealerships, about the investigations, the frauds, drug deals, all that. Larry's goin' nuts 'cause he can't find any sales reps that want to work at our store."

"Gee, what a surprise." Mark couldn't control his sarcasm. "Operate a moral sewer, a regular daily crime scene. Rip off every customer ya can, rip off Toyota, rip off all your hard-working sales reps on their paychecks, plus get investigated by seven different law enforcement agencies, all of a sudden no one wants to work there. Gee, what a surprise." Mark heard a big sigh from him, and he knew Warren had heard enough for today.

"Preachin' to the choir, Marky-Mark," said Rich. "If I could get Carla out of my life and get back with AT&T, I think I can make it. I'm like ninety-five percent divorced, and now she's pounding on my door every night after her strip shows. I can't seem to cut loosa this girl."

"You're a cursed, man Rich. And Carla's possessed. What a pair you two are. Why don't you just take her to the beach and throw a stick 'til she get's tired of chasing it? Then drive away," said Mark.

"You're funny. Don't think that'd work. She'd find me."

Mark listened for any sign of humor from his friend, but all he heard was silence. "Look, let me know where you wind up. I wanna make sure you're okay. Let's keep in touch," said Mark.

"You know I will. Later," said Rich. He sounded depressed. He had a feeling they wouldn't be seeing each other at the dealership again. Neither of them had the stomach for it anymore. He'd lost his trainee to the denizens of the sewer.

Mark returned to John's emails trying to figure out what the Florida AG was up to. He was puzzled by her focus on details surrounding KG's relationship to John Dunne, rather than interviewing the victims of the crimes occurring at Brandson.

The most recent events, emails, and questions made Mark suspicious of the AG. Dunne was being pressured to give him up. Mark didn't mind bus rides, but he preferred riding in the bus, not under it. CVC and local authorities began to suspect the likelihood of a hidden agenda at the Florida Attorney General's office. What the hell had he gotten into, he kept asking himself. He felt as if the political subterfuge and rip currents were dragging him out into the open ocean and sucking him under.

TWENTY-NINE

The FedEx guy had just left Wells's private office. Wells had a lot on his plate today. His wife was threatening him with divorce again after she'd intercepted a phone call from one of his *Girls Gone Wild* weekend hotties. The authorities were all over him, and the IRS still hadn't agreed to accept his lawyer's last offer to settle his tax fraud charges. Also, he faced a laundry list of unpleasant tasks that were being forced upon him today by his boss's boss, Bob Gregory, the CFO of Brandson. He felt like his head was being squeezed in a giant steel vise that was slowly and painfully closing.

He checked the return address on the package just delivered to make sure it was the one he'd been waiting for. It was from Zurich Cantonal Bank, and he unzipped it from the top carefully, avoiding any damage to the documents. Inside the pouch was a paper-clipped stack of letter-size papers, written transfer authorizations prepared by the staff at the Swiss depository. The bank in Zurich had offered to fax or email the wire authorization to him, but Wells had declined. He was fearful that the FBI could track any electronically faxed or emailed documents to his home or to the dealership. He now regretted choosing his current offshore bank primarily for its high rate of interest. In selecting a new offshore bank to be the new depository for his untaxed slush funds, he'd focused on what was more important to him now—a staff fluent in English, and hours of operation that were more in line with his own.

It was mid-morning, the second Tuesday in July. Wells had already spent two hours this morning, and part of the previous day, trying to complete the transfer of his one-and-a-half million dollar secret slush fund. The account was so secret his wife had no clue the money even existed, and he wanted to keep it that way. In accordance with their strict privacy rules, Zurich Cantonal Bank had not asked about the origin or source of the funds. The lack of required disclosures made offshore banks the ideal place to hide his drug money, along with the untaxed profits from the sales of his exotic cars, as well as the fraudulent bonuses from the fake car deals that he concocted with Tony Grimes.

With the FBI now in possession of his key cypher, Wells had to protect his cash and prepared to move the funds to the new account he'd set up at Bank of N.T. Butterfield, Ltd. in Bermuda. The other encrypted offshore account files were harder to connect directly to him. Now he wished he'd kept the key cypher hidden in his wallet instead of concealed in the seam of his office chair. He had feared a body search by the FBI on the two days they were tearing through customer files at the dealership. If he could transfer the account quickly, he could still stay a step ahead of the Feds. He signed the transfer authorization with the new account information and placed the papers into the letter-size file folder. Careful not to catch the edges, he stapled the folder shut, slipping it inside the FedEx priority package he'd already prepared.

Wells picked up the office phone and dialed Jo at the front desk. "Jo, will you come in here a second?" he asked the receptionist.

"Sure, Larry. I can't see you. You're in your back office, right?"

"Yup. C'mon back. I need you to do something for me." He felt like he was moving too slowly, falling behind. He needed to pick up the pace today. The hangover was putting a drag on his energy, and his thoughts drifted to the eight-ball of coke in his pants pocket, a sure-fire way to break out of his slow-motion stupor.

Jo opened the door to his office and stepped inside. "Here, take this to Stephanie in accounting," he said, handing her the FedEx pouch. "Tell her it's the priority package we talked about earlier. Make sure she sends it next day air, urgent delivery. Got it?"

"Next day air, urgent delivery. Got it," Jo parroted. As she did an about face and headed toward accounting, Tommy Catatonia was the next face to appear in his doorway.

"I need to talk with you, chief. Got a minute?" Tommy Catatonia looked like he'd been up all night and slept in his shirt and tie. With bags under his eyes and unshaven, he looked sleepless and stressed out.

"Now's not a good time, Tommy," said Wells.

"Why not? It's important," answered Catatonia.

"'Cause you said you need to talk with me." He grinned, but he could tell his boss wasn't in the mood for his jokes.

"Quit messin' with me, Larry. This is serious." Catatonia handed him a copy of the email from Bob Gregory and sat down, trying to look beyond the scrapes and bruises on his GSM's knuckles. He knew better than to even ask. "Bob copied me on this email to you. He wants you to handle the terminations of Kelly Allen and Tony Grimes. He says that's all on you, 'cause you hired them. If you feel like you need me to back you up, we can do them in my office," he said, smirking.

"I'll handle it, Tommy." His arrogance returned as he thought again about the eight-ball in his pocket. He needed a couple of lines right now like the earth needed gravity.

"Next, you're gonna tell me you can parallel park a train. Here's something else that Bob wants us to be aware of," said Catatonia. He handed Wells a copy of the Florida Attorney General's search warrant. "He asked me to remind you that this is the fifth search warrant we've been served with in less than two months. Two from the FBI, two from the IRS, and now one from the Attorney General's office."

Wells got upset and removed his glasses, wanting to make better eye contact with his boss. "What are you saying, Tommy? This is all my fault?"

"You're sayin' it's not?"

"I'm telling' ya right now, if I go down, you go down," said Wells. He stood up, still upset. "I'm gonna hit the can. I don't want to get into another screaming match with you over this stuff."

Tommy stood up and tucked in his shirt. "Look, I know you had a rough night, Larry. So did I. Thanks for asking. But this is a day you need to stay straight. We've got a lot at stake here, and we need to stop messin' around." Wells could see the fear in Catatonia's eyes and knew his boss was serious.

"Okay, Tommy. I'll call you if I need you for back-up."

They exited his office together, Catatonia heading to his office, Wells to the upstairs bathroom to snort a couple of lines. As he waited for the elevator doors to open, the GSM reached into his pocket and checked to make sure the baggie of coke was still there. The doors opened, and he rode the elevator upstairs to the second floor bath that would give him the privacy he needed. Feeling paranoid as he exited the elevator, he checked the hallway in both directions and quickly entered the restroom, locking the door behind him. He dumped out a pile of the white powder on the counter and used his American Express Platinum card to shape the pile into two four inch-long lines. Rolling up a hundred dollar bill from his pocket, he first snorted one line, and then the other. Tilting his head back, he felt the powerful rush as the narcotic hit him like a sledgehammer between the eyes. Sucking it back into his sinuses, he was blown-away with euphoria and the sensation of unlimited power coursing through his veins. In his mind, he was transforming himself from a wimp with a hangover into The Incredible Hulk.

"Oh, hell, yes!" he shouted out loud. "Damn! That's what daddy needed!" Now he was ready to tackle the tasks he was facing. Before he could finish putting the coke away, there was a knock on the door.

"Larry, it's me, Kirk. This daddy needs some party favors too, bro."

Larry unlocked the door for his partner-in-crime and they shared a fist bump in the doorway. "My bitch kept me up all night," said Kirk, apologetically.

"Was your bitch a girl this time?" asked Larry with a big grin, still holding the door halfway open.

"Yeah, and she loves to bury the burrito as much as me. You got a bump for me up here, boss?" Kirk looked as desperate as his boss felt this morning. They were both proud to share a policy of never allowing their jobs to interfere with their nightlife.

"Sure, man, always got a coupla lines for my bros," said Wells as he handed the plastic baggie to his used car manager. "Jeez, Kirk. You look like you've been suckin' on your bloody Marys minus the tomato juice and celery. C'mon in here and do a couple with me." Wells handed him his credit card and rolled up hundred dollar bill.

"Thanks. I need this, boss," said Kirk. He bellied up to the sink and poured a generous pile of the crystalline powder on the counter. Next, he shaped it into two lines with the Platinum American Express card.

"Here we go!" Kirk shouted. He snorted up the cocaine on two passes and tilted his head back, pinching his nose and sucking the coke back into his sinuses. "Damn, Larry! This stuff's rocket fuel! Is this that pure Columbian you've been braggin' about?" They stood next to each other at the bathroom sink, eyeing themselves in the mirror.

"Can ya tell?" he asked, grinning at Kirk's reaction to the potency of the uncut cocaine. He watched the used car manager's pudgy face contort from the raw power of the narcotic as it worked its way into his sinuses.

"Damn, bro," said a surprised Kirk. "I think that's the best stuff I've ever done. I am definitely off to see the wizard!" They shared another fist bump as Kirk farted. Wells found this amusing.

"I can see you like it, there, Fart City. We're flyin' high now, huh?" he said, grinning into the mirror like a Cheshire cat. Wells added, "Hey, by the way, got some news I think you'll like. I've been asked to cut Tony off the desk and send him packin' today. I have mixed feelings about it, but Gregory's not givin' me a choice. You'll have the whole used car shootin' match for yourself. How 'bout them apples?"

"Why?" asked Kirk, apparently surprised by the news. It was no secret that Kirk had always felt his own experience and knowledge of used car sales was vastly superior to Tony's. He was often annoyed that Wells tolerated Tony's lack of management skills for as long as he had. Kirk would often ridicule his co-manager's incompetence, especially when he'd spend thirty minutes pulling a credit report when it ought to take five.

"It's Bob Gregory's idea of cleaning up the mess around here," said Wells. "Tony's my bitch scapegoat." Wells had found his best use ever for 'The Village Idiot' when they convinced him to sign up for the fake car deals, something that none of the other managers had been willing to do. Tony was the only manager they could find that was dumb enough to be a buyer in the frauds.

Kirk laughed. "Yeah, bitch scapegoat. Have you told him yet?" he asked.

"I was gonna wait 'til after lunch," said Wells. "After these party favors, I kinda lost my appetite for lunch. The Beverly Hills diet, imported from Columbia, right?" Wells pinched his nose and snorted hard again to pull the coke deeper into his sinuses. He lifted his black Toyota polo up, exposing his abdomen in the mirror and rubbed his skinny stomach. He enjoyed drawing attention to his lean body, even if it was an all male audience. They acted like two teenage girls at the prom, primping in the bathroom mirror and comparing notes on their dates.

"I'm gonna do another line. How 'bout you, bro?" asked Kirk. Eyeing his boss's flat stomach in the mirror made him feel self-conscious about his size fifty-four waist and massive man boobs. He would need to drop a hundred and seventy pounds to match physiques with his boss.

"Sure. I'll do another bump with ya. Then I gotta head down-stairs and chop some heads off." Kirk poured another pile of the sparkling crystals onto the sink counter, shaping it into two long lines with the card.

"Door's locked, right?" asked Kirk.

"Yeah, it's locked." They took turns snorting another line of the pure Columbian cocaine. The powerful drug caused Kirk to fart again, which entertained Wells to no end.

"You sure are a gassy fella, there, Kirky boy."

"Stuff's so potent its makin' my O-ring spasm," said Kirk. "Ya know, I really can't feel too sorry for Tony getting canned," he said. "I mean, the lights are on, but nobody's home."

"Yeah, well, you're right. He is kinda slow," agreed Wells, still admiring his abs in the bathroom mirror.

"You ever meet his wife?" asked Kirk.

"Never have. Is she hot?"

"Oh, man, is she. Ya know, she's twenty years younger than him, and her family's loaded. Plus, he's hung like a donkey," said Kirk. "I swear, the guy could paint a face on it and ride in the car pool lane."

"Ha! Well, check this out, Kirky." Wells was grinning as he grabbed his whole crotch area with his hand, making it bulge out through his pants in the mirror. "You're good with real estate. Does this look like a lot to you?" Kirk felt like he was watching the theatre of the absurd.

"Big enough to subdivide," said Kirk, humoring his boss. "Those growth hormones kickin' in there for ya?"

"Oh, hell yes! Okay, I'm headin' back downstairs. Give me a two minute lead so we don't look too gay, right?"

"You got it, boss."

"Kirk?"

"Yeah?"

"Can I have my Ben Franklin and my coke back?"

"Sure. Sorry," said Kirk as he handed back the hundred dollar bill and his entertainment package. Wells held it up to the light, noting it was about half gone and stuck the baggie into his pants pocket.

"Force of habit. Whewww, that's good stuff. What'll it cost me for an ounce of that rocket fuel?" asked Kirk.

"An ounce of that stuff'll set ya back thirty-two hundred," said Wells.

"Fifteen hundred for a half ounce?" Kirk countered.

"Plus lunch tomorrow, and we're done." They fist bumped on the deal.

"Can I pay you on delivery?" asked Kirk.

"Sure, bro. Your credit's always good with me. Have your cash ready when I bring it in with me tomorrow."

After Kirk returned to the sales tower, Wells rode the elevator down to the first floor and thought about what he had to do for the rest of the day. The idea of having to fire his bodyguard and partner-in-crime, Tony Grimes, was eating away at him, especially after he'd promised Tony immunity from termination for sticking his neck out on the fake car purchases. He needed to get the firings out of the way so he could focus on transferring his offshore funds and stay ahead of the authorities. There was his one-and-a-half million at stake, and the Feds and Florida Attorney General were closing in on him. Wells needed a scapegoat, and Tony Grimes would do just fine.

He didn't mind as much having to fire Kelly Allen for her role in the fraudulent car sales, and just for being a bitch in general. Kelly's run as the comptroller at Brandson had been coming to an end for some time, and everyone seemed to know it except her. All the girls in the back office were convinced she was a stone-cold 'be-otch', pompous and unforgiving with her subordinates. "The Redneck Mafia" had all grown to dislike her for constantly opposing them on their get-rich-quick schemes. Now that she was a participant in the faked certifications and fraudulent car sales, and in up to her neck, they finally had their chance to get rid of her.

With the cocaine spinning him into a whole new dimension of unchained chaos, Wells returned to the sales tower with a demonic determination to rid himself of the gargoyles that were perched on his shoulders. When he stepped inside the sales tower, Tony Grimes was the only manager on the desk.

"Where's Bryan, Tony?"

"I think he's out. Wait, I think I see him coming back. He was appraising a used car trade-in for a Highlander deal," said Grimes.

"Why didn't you appraise the used car yourself? You're the used car manager, right? Why are we tying up my best closer appraising used cars?" he asked. "You know I need him to handle TOs for the sales reps." Wells was clearly annoyed.

"Bryan said he wanted to handle it. Sorry, Larry. Is there a problem?" asked Grimes. He watched his boss intently, looking for signs of forgiveness. There were none on Well's face, and this bothered him.

Wells studied Grimes, but avoided giving him an answer. Instead, he sat down and printed a copy of the email from Bob Gregory that ordered him to terminate both Allen and Grimes and grabbed it off the printer.

"Need to talk with you, Tony. Come with me. We might as well get this over with." He headed to his private office with Grimes following close behind.

"Sounds serious," said Grimes. Wells ignored his pandering and led him back to the private office behind the sales tower.

The GSM sat down at his desk and put the email in front of him. Grimes stepped halfway inside his office, holding the door open. Unsure of what to expect, he could tell his boss was unstable and out of his gourd on coke. He watched Wells carefully for clues as to what was going on.

"C'mon in and close the door, Tony. Have a seat."

"What's this about, boss?" As he positioned himself in the chair, Grimes was unable to get comfortable.

"Tony, there's no easy way to say this, so I'll just say it. I've got good news and bad news. Good news is I have a manager's position lined up for you at Flagship Toyota in St. Augustine. Bad news is Bob Gregory has made the decision to terminate you. Just so you don't think it was my idea, here's the email. I'm sorry, bro." Well's face was unemotional, as unforgiving as the faces on Mt. Rushmore.

At first, Grimes was confused, thinking that Wells was playing a practical joke on him. After all, they were partners in crime. Seeing that his boss was serious, his face turned beet red. Wells had seen this look on his bodyguard's face before, usually right before he punched someone. As a deep sense of betrayal came over him, Grimes went ballistic, jumping up from his chair.

"You scumbag, you promised me 'immunity from termination' when I signed off on those fake car deals!!" screamed Grimes. "What am I supposed to do now, stay home and count the wrinkles on my dog's balls?" Wells jumped to his feet, their faces now inches apart. The men were so angry that spit flew from their mouths and their eyes bulged out as they screamed at each other.

"I promised you immunity from ME terminating you, bozo! I can't control what Bob Gregory does!" yelled Wells as the veins in his neck and forehead swelled. "It's not right, and it's not wrong! It just is!"

Bryan Pfister heard the yelling from the sales tower. Concerned that a fist fight was about to break out, he sprang into action and ran to his boss's private office. He'd seen Larry and Tony throw punches before at the drop of a hat. Risking injury to himself, he pushed Larry's door open and rushed to get between them, positioning himself as close to the middle as he could get. He was four inches taller than Tony and just as muscular, but still had no desire to have a punch land in his face from either of them. Bryan pleaded with them to calm down.

"Guys, cool down! C'mon! Every customer in the dealership can hear you," he said. He leaned in and put a hand on each of their shoulders. "C'mon. Whad'ya say, guys?"

Grimes turned to Bryan, demanding an explanation. "Did you know anything about this, Bryan?" He was still beet red with anger. Fearing Tony might take a swing at him, Bryan removed his arm from Tony's shoulder.

"Know anything about what?" Bryan asked.

"Larry says Bob Gregory's forcing him to fire me!" yelled Grimes.

"Bryan, go back to your desk. I got this under control," said Wells. "You don't want to get in the middle of this!"

"You sure, Larry? You guys look ready to murder each other." Bryan took a few steps toward the door then looked back toward Tony.

"Tony, to answer your question, I'm just now hearing this." Looking back at Larry, he added, "You sure you got this?"

"Yeah, I got this Bryan. Tony and I'll work it out." Wells looked at Grimes. They'd been through worse situations together. A lot worse than this little fracas.

Tommy Catatonia had heard the ruckus all the way from his own private office where he had just fired Kelly Allen. Worried about a possible brawl breaking out, it was his turn to check in on his GSM. He picked up the phone and dialed Well's office. Thankful for the interruption, Wells picked up the phone on the first ring.

"Larry, what's goin' on back there?" asked the general manager.

"I'm giving the bad news to Tony, as directed. Obviously, he's not taking the news very well. We're working things out." He knew his boss wanted Grimes gone as bad as Gregory did. An idea sprang into his head. "Do we have a severance check I could offer him to ease the pain a little, Tommy?" As he floated this idea on the phone with his boss, he watched Tony Grimes nod favorably to the idea of an additional severance payment.

"Yeah, sure, tell him he can have an extra coupla grand today as a severance bonus," said Catatonia. "Don't bother calling Kelly in accounting to authorize it. I just fired her."

"Hey, I told ya I'd take care of that, Tommy."

"You got your hands full there, Hoss. I decided to take some of the load off you today. Tell Tony we'll throw in an extra two grand and I'll get it cut from accounting and bring it back to you in a coupla minutes." He hung up. To Catatonia, an extra two grand was worth it to help get rid of their biggest potential liability on the fake car deals. It was the one thing the brass was most upset about. Especially the CFO, Bob Gregory. He headed back to accounting to have the check cut.

As Wells hung up the phone, he was feeling sorry for his body-guard. Grimes had stepped in and defended him in many violent bar brawls, and it was hard not to feel a twinge of gratitude for having kept him out of harm's way all those times. He thought about Kirk's reaction to the news in the upstairs bathroom only minutes ago.

Wells reminded himself that Tony's family had money, and he had a pretty, young wife and other sources of income that were still under his control. He thought about some ways they could reorganize their drug dealing business and the huge amounts of cash they were making.

"Tommy says he feels bad about having to cut ya loose, Tony," he said. "He's bringin' you an extra coupla grand right now."

"Appreciate that, Larry, but I think I'm still getting' the shaft here," said Grimes, still angry about being let go. He could see Larry was distraught over having to fire him, and his instincts told him to take advantage of his boss's guilt. He settled back in the chair, waiting expectantly for more concessions.

"By the way, you know we can still do the extracurricular stuff we been doin' at Club Liquid and St. Augustine Brickyard," said Wells. "Hell, we make more money doin' that than we do selling cars anyway, right?" Wells was now dangling the big cash carrot in Tony's face.

Grimes sat there in silence, starring off into space, mulling things over. He was still steamed up about getting the boot so unexpectedly, but he was starting to accept his fate. With all the investigations going on, he knew he was at risk. Bob Gregory was unlikely to change his mind after the dealership had been served with five search warrants in the last two months. He knew it was his turn to be the fall guy.

After a few moments of weighing his options, Grimes finally responded to Wells's last concession. "Yeah, okay. I'll still do the deals with you, Larry. I know this wasn't your idea. How 'bout a fifty-fifty partnership on the nightclub action, and we drop Kirk? That's fair, especially since he gets to keep his job here, and I'm getting the boot. Just you and me on the night club action. You handle the financing and provide the product, and I'll set up the deals and provide protection for you. Deal?" Grimes held out his fist for a bump. Wells hesitated, taking his time with a response. He eyed Tony and sized up the situation, carefully considering his proposal. He knew there was no love lost between Tony and Kirk. Tony was off the managers' desk, and now Tony wanted Kirk out of their cash-rich drug business.

"Since it's my money and my connection, I'll go sixty/forty with you on all deals outside Gainesville that you set up. Deal?" Wells held out his fist for a bump.

"Deal," said Grimes. They did the fist bump to seal the deal.

The men were surprised to see Betsy Wheeler from accounting appear at the door. She knocked politely and pushed the glass door open cautiously. Betsy was a shapely young brunette who used to be a Hooter's girl before being hired for the accounting pool, and most of the girls in the accounting department were consumed with jealousy over the attention she got from the mostly male staff at the dealership.

"Sorry to interrupt, guys," said Betsy. She had a check in her hand as she walked up to Wells at his desk. She wore a pair of black, tight-fitting slacks that accentuated her curves, and a low-cut blue halter top to show off her cleavage. "Larry, our GM asked me to give this to you. It's a check for Tony Grimes for three thousand dollars. Here." She extended it to Wells. He just sat there with Tony, and they both looked her up and down like she was a freshly-grilled T-bone steak.

"Did you say three thousand?" asked Grimes.

Betsy glanced at the check still in her hand as she brushed her brown hair back. "Yeah, that's what it says, three thousand dollars payable to Anthony J. Grimes." She handed it to Wells as she turned and walked back toward the door.

"Thank you, darlin'," said Wells. He turned his attention back to his bodyguard. He re-examined the check he was handing him. "Quickest extra thousand you'll ever make, right big guy?"

Grimes stared at his now former GSM, reminding himself they were still partners-in-crime. "I think this is Tommy C.'s way of saying 'goodbye and don't make a fuss'."

"Maybe," said Wells. "Maybe you should take the money and run."

Taking advantage of his calmer demeanor, Wells leaned closer to him. In a more secretive tone, he said, "We are still going to make a ton of money together, Tony. I want you to call me when you have some deals lined up. Anything up to a kilo. Be careful. It's both our asses if you screw up. I've gotta get back to work." They did one final fist bump and exited the back office. As they walked out into the showroom, a few of the sales reps were relieved to see that they hadn't beaten each others' brains out.

Today, the two went their separate ways. Grimes gathered up his personal belongings, said a few hasty goodbyes, and walked out the front door of the dealership with his box full of belongings and three thousand dollar check. Wells sat down at his desk in the sales tower, relieved that the painful ordeal of having to fire his bodyguard was now behind him. He sat there with a disgusted look on his face and thought about heading upstairs to do a few more lines. Bryan looked over at him from the new car desk, trying to gauge his mood.

"Glad that's over, right?" asked Bryan. He could always tell when his boss had been dipping into the coke. His brain and emotions were fried, and he couldn't stop pinching his nose. "Probably rather have a root canal, right?" Bryan was sympathetic, but he also knew a good house cleaning was long overdue at Brandson.

"Damn Bob Gregory to hell and back," said Wells. "Did you have a chance to put together the August floor schedule?"

"I was waiting on you to tell me what you want to do about Mark. When's he coming back? Is he ever?"

"Don't include him on the schedule. It's been almost two months since he left on family medical leave. His aunt died, and I hear his mom is dying of pneumonia. Human resources says not to fire him. He told Paul and Raj that we owe him forty-five grand in back pay and he's still in pain from his shoulder surgery. Let's not give him anymore reasons to sue us than he already has."

"Sure. We'll do it without him. What about Scott, Robert, Rich and T.J.?" asked Bryan.

"Go ahead and put Robert on it. He's still my favorite monkey. Scott's still playin' with his wife's money, so he's gonna stay out. T.J. and Rich are still mad about their missing money, so I doubt that they're comin' back. Hell with 'em."

"Okay. I'll make the changes. By the way, I forget to mention. Your IRS attorney called. He says you need to look at the attachment he sent you in his email an hour ago," said Bryan. "He says it's urgent."

"Okay. Thanks." Wells stood up. "I'll be back in fifteen. I'll be on my cell if you need help with a deal."

He walked back to the elevator, pushed the call button, and the doors opened immediately. Wells stepped inside. As he rode the elevator up to the second floor bathroom, he pulled what remained of the eight ball out of his pants pocket. About half still remained. As he quickened his pace toward the bathroom, his desire for the drug grew stronger. He stepped inside the bathroom and locked the door, laying out two more lines on the counter. Pulling out his hundred, he rolled it up and snorted the two lines. The rush he'd been craving felt fantastic, raising the level of dopamine in his brain to a new level. A cascade of pleasure rolled over him from the powerful narcotic, and he felt like he was being swept away in a tidal wave of euphoria. His troubles seemed to vanish, replaced by the feeling of invincibility as the familiar warmth of the cocaine surged through his veins. Now, he was ready to read the email from his criminal attorney and find out what kind of garbage deal the IRS had offered him this time around.

He made his way back downstairs to his private office where he busied himself with personal tasks. He moved like a machine now that he had his fix, enjoying the feel of the coke rushing through his body. Next, he opened his emails. He clicked on the email from his attorney, then the attachment describing the latest offer from the IRS to settle his fraud case. Larry was disgusted when he read the offer. Two hundred twenty-five thousand dollars in fines, penalties and back payments, thirty days in jail, three years probation, and two hundred hours of community service is what they were offering. In the email, Brian was recommending that he take the deal. The offer was actually worse than the last one they had made him. He was mad enough to spit nails. He knew he had to cool down. He couldn't afford to risk alienating his criminal attorney because of his anger toward the IRS. His contempt for Federal employees had reached an all-time high.

Then, his cell phone rang. It was a rare call from Bob Gregory, probably checking to see if he completed the two terminations. He wasn't crazy about talking to the CFO after being forced to fire one of his own managers. Under pressure from Wells, Tony Grimes had chosen to be the patsy in the series of frauds that were his boss's creation. Wells knew he had to take the call.

"Hi, Bob. How's *your* day going?" He tried hard to sound cordial, desperate to disguise the dislike he had for Brandson's CFO. Gregory was a college grad, and Wells despised men in the car business who had a college degree. The 'Luis Vuitton Redneck' didn't need an education to make himself eight hundred grand a year, and he did little to hide his contempt for salesmen with an education that went beyond that of his own Palatka High School diploma.

"Not bad, dealing with a lot of legal issues over at your dealership, as you well know. Did you complete the terminations of Kelly Allen and Anthony Grimes like I asked?" asked Gregory.

"Yes, sir. They are gone." Wells was expecting to hear something praiseworthy from Mr. Gregory. It had been a stressful job to have to fire his partner-in-crime, and he was still annoyed about it.

"Okay, then. Pack up your stuff. You're fired too," said Gregory in an even, calm voice. "Tommy will help you with the paperwork. We're being forced to clean things up there at Brandson. Good luck to you. Oh, and Larry?"

"Yeah?"

"Don't forget to take your drugs, porn and under aged girls with you. We're done with that crap, too."

There was a click as Gregory hung up and there was nothing but silence on the phone.

THIRTY

After two hours of searching through files looking for similar MOs in recent unsolved drug cases, Gronske was getting tired. It was after eight on a hot evening late in July. The detective bureau was empty except for himself, the duty officer up front, and a lab tech. He pressed against his eyes with the heels of his hands, bleary-eyed from studying computer screens and forensic documents. Somewhere among the files on his desk were a half-eaten roast beef sub, an empty can of Mountain Dew and two empty bags of Lays potato chips. It was a diet that wasn't helping him win the battle of the bulge. He reached for the bottle of Clear Eyes, tilted his head back and squeezed a few more drops into each eye. He was risking another argument with his wife over missing dinner with his family, but he would deal with that. He had bigger fish to fry. Gronske was convinced that the managers at Brandson accounted for a significant part of the cocaine trafficking in Gainesville, and he was determined to gather enough evidence to prove it.

Lieutenant Anderson and Gronske's captain were just as frustrated with the progress of the investigations. Even with the Club Liquid recordings of the suspects arranging a drug deal, Tom Lewis, the local state attorney, still stubbornly refused to issue any arrest warrants or bring charges. Lewis claimed GPD needed more hard evidence to have cause to arrest Wells, Grimes, Shifter, or Gonzalez. Gronske and the rest of the task force were completely baffled by the headwinds they were running into at the state attorney's office. They questioned Lewis's allegiance, wondering if the state attorney was even on the same team in the pursuit of justice for the fraudsters and drug dealers.

The GPD officers were also at odds with Lewis over his characterization of the evidence as sketchy, inconclusive and circumstantial. The lab techs were able to identify Shifter's and Wells's prints from the dusty baggie of uncut cocaine found in the ceiling of the sales tower, and they were keeping it quiet for now. A lab analysis of the syringes marked "L," "K," and "T" had proven that traces of steroids were present, but no illegal drugs.

A search of the suspect's medical records showed that all three men held prescriptions for anabolic steroids written by a Haitian pain management physician in Hialeah. The Miami Pain Management Center was a known 'pill mill', but the prescriptions were issued legally.

The managers had proven to be more elusive than they imagined. Besides the eight ball in the ceiling, the only hard evidence of drug trafficking at Brandson was the quarter pound of uncut cocaine that came from the arrest of Rocky Gambrone on the illegal weapons and drug possession charges last month. Lab analysis showed that it had the same chemical makeup as the baggie found in the ceiling and likely came from the same source. Gambrone had entered a plea of innocent on the charges of obstruction, stalking and possession with intent to distribute, and a plea of nolo contendere on the illegal weapons charges. Claiming he was a flight risk, the judge had set a one million dollar bond, which no one had yet posted. In view of his previous felony convictions for trafficking, and the evidence they now had, Gronske and his task force were confident they would convict Gambrone on at least two of the felony charges.

Of the five felony drug and assault cases linked to the Brandson managers, there had been four separate eyewitness accounts of the crimes without a positive identification of their suspects. Two weeks ago, Captain Arnofsky had secretly sent in GPD's best undercover narcotics officer to set up a drug deal with the suspects, without success. Gronske was convinced someone on the inside had tipped them off about the sting operation as their suspects managed to successfully sidestep the trap. Only a few officers at GPD and two assistant state attorneys in Lewis's office had known about the planned sting operation. The task force began to suspect a leak from the state attorney's office. Gronske was frustrated, and he needed a break in the case. He decided to phone his buddy, Frank Moser, at the FBI to find out if they'd found anything in the encrypted files that would help them in their prosecution of the street crimes. He dialed Moser on his cell phone. After the fourth ring, a hoarse voice answered.

"Moser."

"Frank, it's Gary Gronske over at GPD."

"Hey, Gary. Thought I recognized your number. I'm sittin' here at my daughter's softball game. What's up?"

"I've kinda hit a wall here on our Brandson suspects. Off the record, our local state attorney is up for re-election this fall, and he doesn't seem interested in helping us move our case forward," said Gronske. "It's like he's afraid to rock the boat or something."

"Off the record, I've heard that about Lewis's office. Makes you wonder where some of his campaign money comes from," said Moser as he watched an attractive brunette take a seat in the front row bleachers.

"Yeah, well, that's a whole 'nother conversation. I'm convinced the term 'elected law enforcement official' is an oxy moron," said Gronske. Out of the corner of his eye, he could see Terri glancing his way in the lab as she worked.

"Yeah, the highest law in the land shouldn't be for sale to the highest bidder," said Moser.

"Amen to that. Hey, I need a favor. I heard your IT guy broke those encryption codes on those files, and I need something to help us move along our street crime cases. You got anything I can use for the drug deals, CVC complaints or weapons violations?" asked Gronske. He could hear the sounds of parents cheering on their kids in the background over Frank's phone.

"Well, let's see. Let me think. Sorry about the noise, here. I remember Jim decrypted one hundred forty-five files. Two were so corrupted we were unable to restore them."

"What about the rest. Anything that would help our investigations?"

"Hang on a sec, Gary. Let me get away from these bleachers and find a quieter spot," said Moser. Gronske could hear moms and dads shouting at the kids on the softball field as Moser put some distance between himself and the rest of the crowd.

"Okay. I found a nice big oak tree to stand under while we talk. Better that we keep it away from the wrong ears." Moser paused as he checked his surroundings. "Okay. Now I can talk. I'll give you a thumbnail sketch of what we found."

"Appreciate it, Frank. We'll keep it just between us," said Gronske.

"There were about forty files that point to bank fraud by Sheahan and Gonzalez, their F&I guys. We already had some evidence of this from the both the civil complainants and from the law school dean. She filed her fraud complaint with Toyota and copied the State Attorney on her letter. Brad's convinced there's enough cause to get a wire tap, but he's not sure if the judge will agree," said Moser.

"Wire taps would help a lot. You going to look at the lenders' files on the other side of those deals?" asked Gronske.

"You betcha," answered Moser. "We already have a subpoena. We'll compare the bankers' credit applications with the customer files at the dealership. It'll make the fabrications stand out like a sore thumb."

"You think the lenders are in on it?"

"Well, we know the in-house lender was participating in the frauds, and we have documents that prove it. We're not sure about the other twenty or thirty lenders," answered Moser.

"Makes sense for their in-house lender to be a partner in the frauds, since they were in on the fake car deals," said Gronske.

"Yup. Then, there's about thirty of the decrypted files that show evidence of large, untaxed offshore accounts, illegal offshore wire transfers, Swiss and Saudi Arabian banks, mostly. We brought the IRS back in on the case with us. They'd already seen the smoking gun with Wells's personal tax fraud."

"Didn't know the IRS had left the case," said Gronske.

"Well, they started out with the individual charges of tax fraud against Wells, and now that's ballooned into a full-blown IRS corporate tax fraud investigation of the dealership," explained Moser.

"Where there's smoke, there's usually fire," said Gronske.

"Exactly. And, there's another twenty or thirty files of exotic cars they bought to hide their untaxed income. More evidence of money laundering."

"What do you think about the possibility of Gambrone rolling over on Wells? Gambrone's facing three felony counts," said Gronske.

"Gambrone knows he won't see his family for twenty years unless he cops to a plea and turns state's evidence against Wells, Shifter, Catatonia and Gonzalez. We'll make him a sweet deal. He knows we want them," said Moser.

"You know that Gates has turned state's evidence, right? He was lookin' at ten years of ass poundings at Federal Corrections in Miami unless he gave up his buddies."

"Yeah, that's what I heard. Let me see if I can guess the names on those decrypted accounts. Wells, Gonzalez, Shifter, Sheahan, Pfister, and, uh, Grimes. And Catatonia."

"Bingo. Except for Pfister. He's the only manager we haven't been able to link with the felonies. We're still digging through the other seventy files. There may be others popping up on that list," said Moser.

"My intuition tells me there's a lot more dirty business there. Anything that could be used to bolster our investigations in there, Hoss?" asked Gronske.

"So far, the only thing I see from the encrypted files that could be used in your cases is if we could make a connection to their drug money, where it was wired into these offshore accounts. That would be the zinger," said Moser. He thought about a way to offer more encouragement to Gronske. "If I come across anything else, I'll call you. Believe me when I say we want these scumbags as bad as you guys do at GPD."

"Appreciate that, Frank. Keep me posted on anything that connects the dots," said Gronske. "For GPD, this case is big. Just so you're aware, we estimate that our suspects account for about half of the cocaine traffic in Gainesville." He paused. "Hope your daughter hits a home run when she gets up to bat."

"It wouldn't be her first time," said Moser with pride in his voice. He could tell Gronske needed encouragement. "Look, these guys have screwed up before, they'll screw up again. By the way, did you know that Wells and Grimes were fired from Brandson a few days ago?"

"No, we didn't know. Who's the hatchet man?"

"We're pretty sure it was Gregory, their CFO. Catatonia's boss."

"How do you keep up on this stuff?" asked Gronske.

"My inside guy, KG. He's given us a lot of help with our investigation. We'd be lost without him. I wish we could put him on our payroll."

"Yeah, you've mentioned your CI before. Does he still work there?"

"Yeah. He's on a family medical leave, but he still has access to their files. After he tried to reason with them, he just got fed up," said Moser. "He says it like workin' in a moral sewer. I think he's ready to walk."

"Your CI's a trooper for staying in the fight this long," said Gronske. "I'm surprised that Brandson didn't dump Wells and

Grimes months ago, right after they dumped Gates. Couldn't happen to nicer guys, right? Any idea what they're planning, or where they're going?"

"You mean besides being responsible for half the cocaine traffic in Gainesville and defrauding just about everyone in the county? We heard they're starting up their dog and pony show all over again at a dealership in Atlanta. They'll be Georgia's headache until we get our warrants. They'll be out of Melman's jurisdiction, but not ours. Kinda makes you sick, doesn't it?" asked Moser.

"Atlanta, huh? It'd be nice if we could get the state attorney on the same page with us," said Gronske. "You got anything else?"

"Yeah, they also axed their comptroller, a lady named Kelly Allen. We think she was complicit in the frauds and had knowledge of the money laundering," said Moser. "She was definitely in a position to see a lot of it. We think she'll roll, too. We're keeping tabs on her. We think Catatonia's next to go."

"Okay. Good stuff, Frank. Thanks for the briefing. I'll keep you up to speed on my end. Let me know what else you guys find. I'm looking for anything we can use to prosecute the street stuff. I don't mind a ride to Atlanta to pick these scumbags up," said Gronske.

"I'm with ya, brother," said Moser. "I see more warrants comin' down the road. I'll let ya know. Eventually, I think they all go down."

After they hung up, Moser headed back to his seat in the bleachers to wait for his daughter's turn at bat. It was the bottom of the seventh inning, two outs, and his daughter was on deck.

Five miles across town, Gronske logged off his computers and looked around the office as he took another bite from his sub sandwich. Lab Tech Terri Bennett was still hard at work on what looked like a DNA screen. Gronske had been intrigued with her from her first day on the job two months ago. He decided to saunter over to see what she was up to.

Officer Bennett was a young, petite single mom in her thirties. While she kept to herself at GPD, she was the object of much attention, especially from the men in the department. She had her headphones on, so Gronske walked around to the glass partition in front of her desk and tapped. She slipped her headphones off and motioned for him to step around the partition.

"Hey, how'd we do with that new nanotech print program with the baggie of coke we found at Club Liquid? Did we get any additional hits?" asked Gronske, as he leaned on the counter.

"You mean that eight ball baggie that was in the men's restroom trash can?" she asked. She removed her protective lab glasses, cocked her head to the side and smiled at him, brushing her hair back around her ears. She seemed to enjoy his attention. An erotic fantasy took shape in Gronske's mind as he pictured her wearing just the white lab coat she wore over her uniform with a pair of black sheer stockings and high heels. He forced himself back to reality. "Yeah. I know the prints were dry, but I read about the new technique of using gold nanoparticles that target amino acids on non-porous surfaces. Supposed to be pretty effective on latent prints."

"Yup. I have an app for that now," she said. "I used the new nano kits we just got in last week and got a partial I.D. from it, and . . . .wait." She reached for a file folder from her shelf and flipped to the third page. Scanning it, she said, "An Anthony J. Grimes. It was an ninety percent match. Here, I knew you'd want one, so I made you a copy of the results." She handed him the extra page from the file.

"Terri, you're a genius," he said. "You got time to grab a beer or something?"

Flattered at the detective's interest, she smiled. "You mean now?" she asked. He nodded. "Thanks, Gary, that's sweet, but I'm in the middle of a DNA match for Detective Garber. I'm gonna be tied up here for another thirty or forty minutes. Take a rain check, though." The additional print match and her rain check were enough to make his day, even without the opportunity to share a beer with the lab tech hottie. He liked the way she wore her smoky eye shadow, and the way it accentuated her blue eyes. As he admired her looks, Gronske thought about how bored he was with his wife of twenty-three years. He hungered for a little extracurricular excitement, and an entertainment itinerary began to unfold in his mind. One that involved naked women.

Not wanting to risk annoying a fellow detective, Gronske let her continue with her lab work for Garber. "Okay, sounds good, Terri. Another night then. Thanks for the print work." He held up his copy of the lab report. "This should help move things along," said Gronske.

"Glad I could help. Let me get back to this DNA match. I don't want to screw it up. Garber'll be pissed at me." She smiled apologetically, slipping her headphones back on. Gronske could hear the faint sounds of a Chopin piano concerto before the ear cups sealed around her earlobes. Classy, he thought. Damn if he wouldn't like to drag her home one night and give her a taste of the dark side.

"Okay. Night, Terri." He waved, not knowing if she could hear him. Gronske made a mental note to review the lab report when he got in tomorrow morning. He placed it on his desk on his way out of CID. He was in no hurry to hear another lecture from his wife about spending more time with the kids. Wrapping up the half-eaten sub sandwich, he stuffed it in his pants pocket. Now that Terri had his juices flowing, he decided to stop by Club Risque Truck Stop for a drink and some topless entertainment on his way home. The girls weren't as hot as the clubs in Daytona, but it was only a mile out of his way. He knew he was already headed for the doghouse tonight, so he figured he might as well make it count for something.

THIRTY-ONE

Mark sat at the upstairs conference room table at the WUFZ broadcasting studio, waiting to meet with the reporter. He'd been sitting alone in the room for the last twenty minutes, watching through the glass partition as studio personnel passed by. He admired the intricate craftsmanship of the long wooden table as he imagined the kind of conversations that took place in the room, wondering if they'd forgotten about him. When he arrived at the studio, he'd stuck to his plan of announcing himself only as "that guy" to the receptionist, and from her casual reaction, he guessed that the practice of confidentiality at the radio station was more common than he anticipated. To better conceal his identity, he wore a baseball cap, sunglasses and light-weight jacket for his meeting with the reporter.

As he waited for Jennifer Treadstone to make her appearance, Mark passed the time by looking through some of the files he held. He shuffled through the thick stack of disgruntled Brandson customers, trying to recall the details of each of the deals. He came across one that stood out. It was a Prius deal from last June. In big black bolded letters, Kirk Shifter had used a black Sharpie to scrawl the words: "THAT'S THE WAY THE COOKIE CRUMBLES" across the customer transaction screen shot printed on the day that Mark discovered the subterfuge. Not only had he been screwed over on the deal, but the customers had been screwed over three ways 'til Sunday.

The summary sheet Mark held showed the sale of a certified late-model Prius to his repeat customer, Janice Satchel. She and her husband were charged more than seven grand over the advertised internet price for the car by McGreedy and Shifter. He massaged his forehead, disgusted over how blatant the fraud had been. The Satchels were also charged sixteen hundred bucks for a certification inspection that Brandson had conveniently skipped and never performed. Anyone who was familiar with hybrids knew that a certified inspection on a pre-owned Prius was particularly important because of the complex electro-mechanical technology. Buying one without the certification was risky.

The day after the deal, Janice's "certified" Prius wouldn't start. When she called the dealership to complain to the general manager, Tommy Catatonia wasn't available and never bothered to return her calls. Suspecting deception, she went online to review the Carfax records that she'd been denied on the day of the deal. The Carfax report on her car stated that the Prius was involved in a serious accident a year earlier and sustained damage to the hybrid drive system. She and her husband were infuriated when they discovered they'd been defrauded not only on the price and the condition of the car, but also on the certified warranty.

It was all coming back to him as he read through the summary sheet. When Janice and her husband returned to the dealership the next day with a copy of the Carfax, they were madder than a hornet's nest. The Satchels had demanded the return of their money and a cancellation of the deal. What a train wreck it was. The files in his hands contained the details on thirty-seven similar defrauded and angry customers.

Two weeks later, after the Satchels had filed a complaint with Consumers Against Crime, GPD investigated the frauds. Wanting to avoid publicity, Brandson Enterprises agreed to settle with the Satchels for the sum of forty-two thousand dollars. The conditions of the settlement included agreeing to drop all charges, signing a waiver and keeping the dispute out of civil court, as well as the 'court of public opinion'. Tired of the lies and weary from the emotional disappointment, the couple eventually agreed to the terms and collected their check, wanting to put the whole mess behind them.

The Satchels were prohibited by the terms of their agreement from going public with their story. Mark figured if the story was somehow leaked to the press, Brandson would have to prove the Satchel's were responsible in order to invalidate their settlement. Since their original complaint with GPD was a matter of public record and the details were fully accessible by news reporters, maybe this cookie wasn't quite done crumbling.

He looked up to see the door at the far end of the conference room swing open, and an attractive blonde reporter wearing glasses and a strapless sundress entered. She had an armful of files. From a distance, she looked almost young enough to be a student. As she walked toward him, he could make out the crow's feet around her eyes and guessed her age to be around thirty-two. He sat his cap on the table and took his sunglasses off so they could make eye contact. She smiled at him and extended her hand to introduce herself.

"Hi, I'm Jennifer Treadstone. Thanks for coming in to share your story." Mark stood up, noticing her sparkling blue eyes and firm handshake. Her shapely figure and beautiful smile reminded him of Brittany Spears.

"For now, you can call me KG."

"Okay," she said. She set her files down on the table beside him and cocked her head to the side as she stood looking at Mark's files spread out on the conference table. She removed her glasses and unconsciously nibbled on the earpiece as she studied Mark and the files.

"Look's like we have a lot to talk about, KG," she said with her alluring smile. After listening to him talk on the phone about his past experiences with the media, she knew he was stressed out about their meeting. She was doing her best to get him to relax and put aside his mistrust of reporters. Jennifer took a seat to his left.

"John Dunne speaks quite highly of you, Jennifer," said Mark. "He's a man I trust. He told me that you and WUFZ have been a big help to the victims and his consumer protection group in exposing the frauds and overcharging at Brandson."

"Thanks for saying so. John is amazing. I've never seen a volunteer so committed to exposing rip-offs and corruption," she said. "He's an ex-New York City detective, right?"

"Over twenty years. We seem to enable each other with our goal to get to the truth. We teamed up about eighteen months ago. As you know from the police investigations, there are a lot of other crimes going on at the dealership."

"Yeah, I've heard about the investigations. At this point, we have to be careful and treat them as *alleged* crimes," said Jennifer. She waved at a co-worker through the glass partition.

"I was impressed with your story about some of the early cases they settled on behalf of the victims. You have a great voice, and sound passionate in your broadcasts about putting a stop to the frauds. John told me the story about how you helped apprehend that bank robber last year. Amazing."

"Well, all I did was trip him when he was running out the door with the cash bag. I had no idea he was gonna hit his head on the getaway car. The ski mask didn't do much to soften the blow, I guess." She smiled and shrugged her shoulders.

"How did you happen to be at the bank that morning?" Mark was digging, wanting to know more about the woman he was about to entrust with his life.

"I was jogging and stopped by the ATM. I like to stay in shape." She straightened up in her chair and pushed her chest out, inviting Mark's evaluation. He guessed that this was part of the seductive allure she relied on as a reporter.

"Well, apparently, it's working. You look very fit." He smiled, pleased to meet a fellow fitness fanatic.

"So do you." She gave him a look that would melt an iceberg.

"Anyone ever tell you that you look like Brittany Spears?"

She rolled her eyes. "Yeah, I do hear that from time to time. Are you a runner, KG?"

"I do five to seven miles at sunrise. On a beach if there's one around." He paused, then explained, "Hooked on the endorphins." He noticed she kept eyeing his lucky tan and fuscia "Bora Bora" cap, with the black manta ray emblazoned on the front.

Curious, she said, "Interesting cap. I'll bet you didn't find it at Walmart. What's with the manta ray?" She traced the manta ray's outline on the cap with the tip of her French-manicured finger.

"A momento from the seven months I spent sailing in French Polynesia. The manta symbolizes strength and intuition in Tahitian folklore." Mark cocked his head, waiting for her response.

"Looks like it's seen a lot of action," she said, raising her eyebrows expectantly.

"Two typhoons and a hurricane. The natives were friendly, and, as you can see, I avoided being eaten." Jennifer laughed, then composed herself.

"Are we ready to get down to business?" she asked, crossing her legs and preparing to take notes. "Gotta question. Is 'KG' spelled C-A-G-E-Y, or with a K and a G?" There was a long pause as they sized each other up. Jennifer was smiling, so he guessed she was messing with him, testing his sense of humor.

"A 'K' and a 'G'. The rest of me is silent." With his equally glib and cryptic answer, he was daring her to match wits.

She laughed. "You're clever. Before we go further, would you like a glass of water or some sweet tea? We've got both in the kitchen behind us."

"Tea sounds good. Hold the hemlock," he said wryly.

She laughed again. "Sure. Let me get my story out of you, first." She disappeared through the double doors. He was impressed with her abstract aqua and orange-patterned sundress, reminding him of the colorful clothing they sold at the *Bon Marché* in Moorea. After a minute clinking around in the kitchen, she returned with two glasses of ice cold sweet tea. Mark sat at the head of the table and Jennifer took her seat to his left. They both took a sip of tea, and Mark let her take the lead in the interview.

She stretched out her arms, laying them on the conference room table to dramatize the point she was about to make. "Well, KG, the truth is our news studio would prefer to know who you are. Your story would carry more weight if we could quote you as the source. Is there a reason you want to remain confidential?" Jennifer was putting on her best demure 'dumb blonde' look.

"Several," he said flatly. He looked around the studio through the glass enclosure to make sure there was no one listening outside. "The biggest reason is that my confidentiality continues to aid the authorities in their investigations. If my cover is blown, I would be far less useful. I hope you and your radio station will respect that." He paused, and Jennifer nodded. "Where do you think the information that CVC used to file the complaints on behalf of their victims came from?"

"The other reason is my safety. We are dealing with a bunch of psychopathic, drug-crazed criminals with lots of priors. Convicted felons with underworld connections. These guys own automatic weapons, and they aren't afraid to use 'em. Even when they're drunk or coked up. I'm a little reluctant to paint a bullseye on my back for these guys."

"Aren't you being a little dramatic?" she asked. "So, what are you gonna do? Live in one of those condos they're building inside those missile silos in Nebraska or something?" He paused for a moment to study her. She was a conniving little hottie. But, she was also an implement of change who needed to understand the importance of the role she was about to play. He was impressed with how perceptive and attentive she had been, so he continued to set the stage, knowing that he couldn't draw a woman using straight lines.

"Not quite ready to join the doomsday preppers yet, Jennifer, but you do realize there's sixty or seventy million dollars at stake here . . . and potential felony convictions for the perps. The walls of my house aren't built to stop a bullet from an AR-15 or AK-47. I hope this doesn't come as a surprise to you, but I'm not too crazy about the sight of my own blood." He smiled at her, looking for agreement.

"You paint a pretty crazy picture," she said. She shifted her position in the chair, propping her elbow up on the table, leaning her head in her hand and waited expectantly for more narrative. She continued to challenge him, testing his resolve, daring him to tell all of his story.

"Crazy is definitely the price of admission with these guys. Have you ever met or interviewed any of them?" he asked.

"No, and, from what I've heard about them, I'm not sure if I want to."

Mark continued with his story. "I've worked with these guys for four years. I've seen them do some crazy, psychotic, violent things. I don't want to debate my confidential status with you." He paused for a moment. Jennifer continued to listen attentively. "Now, I think we can both agree there are some good reasons that go beyond my own safety for continuing to remain confidential until I'm ready for that to change. I do want the truth to come out about all this, and I will help you with your story any way I can. Confidentially, of course."

She was beginning to buy into his plan. She reached for her phone, pushed the power button and took a more serious tone. "I'm turning my phone off so we won't be interrupted." She put the tip of her pen to the corner of her mouth, and he knew a question was coming. "Why me? Why WUFZ?"

"Does Brandson do any advertising with WUFZ?" he asked.

"Not that I'm aware of."

"So, when you call them for their side of the story, which you're obligated to do, Brandson can't threaten your station with restricting WUFZ's revenues by cancelling their advertising in an effort to suppress the story, right?"

"I hadn't even thought about that angle."

"Well, I got news for you, Jennifer. They have."

She was amused by this. "Did you say 'I got news for you'? Ha! You're a stitch." She wrinkled her nose in appreciation of his dry sense of humor. Then, she got serious again. "Okay, tell me why you're bringing this up."

"Sure. Because they've already arranged to have stories buried at both WJXT and the *Gainesville Banner* where Brandson has done a lot of advertising. And they have suppressed stories at both of these media groups using the threat of withdrawing ad revenues. To the tune of about a million dollars a year in each case."

"And you know this how?" She tapped her pen on her pad, waiting for his answer, pressing her cleavage against the conference table. Her body was hard to ignore, and Mark struggled to stay focused on the goals he set for himself in the interview. He wasn't sure how she'd react to his story about the paper's editor. He would stick with the truth. It always seemed to work the best.

"I had an anonymous one-on-one phone call with Doug Grayson, editor of the *Banner*," said Mark.

"I know who he is," she said as she wrote the details on her pad.

"He told me his parent company was threatened with the withdrawal of eleven million dollars worth of advertising if the story on Brandson was published. So, he was forced to bury it."

"By who?" she asked, leaning in closer so he could get a better view.

"His boss. The guy that runs Media Springs, the holding company."

"You're kidding me. Why would the editor tell that to an anonymous caller? That sounds totally whacked." She was incredulous.

"I thought so, too, but I know what I heard him say. Obviously, he slipped up. Life is a game of chess, and he's playing video games. Go figure."

"I hear ya," she said, making more notes. "And the TV station, WJXT? Who'd you talk with over there?"

"Jan Barnes, their business news reporter."

"I know her."

"Off the record, she told me Brandson threatened to cancel over a million bucks in current ad contracts and give the business to their competitor, WGNT, if they ran a negative story about Brandson. She said she overheard that in a phone conversation between her boss, Randall Newman, and their holding company's CEO. By the way, WGNT handles about a million bucks a year in advertising for Brandson, so I didn't bother to call them. I'm sure Brandson would figure out a way to bribe them, too. They've bribed just about everyone else." Jennifer wrote quickly, trying to get it all down. She looked up from her notes.

"Incredible," said Jennifer. He paused to allow her to get caught up. Very focused, she held her hair back behind her ear as she wrote. A young lady walked by the glass partition outside the conference room, speaking excitedly on her phone, oblivious to their presence.

Mark continued with his story. "They've been suppressing the media for months using these advertising bribes. Kind of a story in itself, wouldn't you say, Jennifer?"

She hesitated before answering him, sensing that his question may be intended to put reporters in a bad light. "Let's stick with the story itself," she said. "I can't vouch for the motives of other news organizations." That was the answer Mark wanted to hear. She was doing well with earning his trust, and he was starting to feel more comfortable with her.

She looked up, ready to hear more. "Tell me about the customer file you were reading when I walked in. You looked really sad," she said.

"Sure. The Satchel file is one of about forty defrauded customers that I brought with me. I'm going to let you copy all of them before I leave. And all of the fake car deal screen shots. They've all been redacted."

"That sounds good. I need all the corroboration you have," said Jennifer. "So, everything you're going to give me has been redacted?"

"You can double check. A forensic computer expert showed me how to do it." He paused for a moment and studied the pretty reporter as he weighed his options. "I'd like to tell you about a conversation I had about two weeks ago with Beth Melmann. She's the acting attorney general heading the Orlando office of the Florida Division of Consumer Affairs."

"Why?" She lowered her glasses to rest on the tip of her nose. The call to the Florida AG's office seemed to interest her. 'Why' was such a simple word. Mark thought it was the ultimate 'dumb blonde' question. He drove his parents crazy with it when he was a kid.

"Because, she's been put in charge of the state's investigation of Brandson. When you hear what she was focused on in my conversation with her, you're gonna want to highlight it in your story."

"Sounds intriguing. Can't wait to hear what you have to say." Jennifer leaned forward in her chair expectantly, batting her eyelashes and pretending to hike up the top of her dress. Very coquettish, she was really putting the fox on him. He'd have to stay on his toes to avoid her distractions and stay on track.

"Okay. You might find this interesting," said Mark. "On Monday morning, July fifteenth, at about ten thirty, I called her office and spoke to her. I took notes, of course, because John Dunne tipped me off about her hidden agenda, which was to find fault with CVC to push them aside instead of investigating the Brandson crimes. John and I were pretty disappointed with her entire approach. I told her that I've worked at Brandson for four years and had witnessed a lot of fraud there. And, I was also a victim."

"What did she say?" she asked.

"Not only didn't she express any interest in any of the crimes I witnessed, she asked me no questions even related to any criminal activity at Brandson. Instead, she started interrogating me about my relationship with John Dunne and CVC, how long I'd known him, and whether I knew who KG was."

"Whoa. How'd you handle that little zinger?" asked Jennifer.

"Well, I asked her why that was even relevant to our conversation," said Mark. "I mean, here she was speaking with an employee who had the inside track and had witnessed a lot of the fraud and was willing to discuss it with her in real time."

"So, you sidestepped her question and tried to get her to focus on a more productive avenue of investigation? Good redirect, counselor."

"Thanks for showing up. Yeah, there was a river of inside information that was right in front of her. But she wasn't interested in hearing about any crimes. She refused to answer any of my questions about the progress of the investigation, knowing I was a victim too, which kinda makes me her client. I thought this was really strange. She was a little hostile and did her best to intimidate me."

A puzzled look came over her face. Jennifer also found the Florida AG's actions confusing. "That doesn't seem like the kind of conversation I would have expected from someone who was put in charge of a major fraud investigation," she surmised.

"Bingo. Very curious that she didn't seem interested. Why? Oh, and Jennifer, please put this part in your story. It's truly a shame that the prosecution of major criminal activity in our state is taking a back seat to political re-election campaigns."

"Why do you think she acted like that?"

"Off the record, maybe a deal has already been agreed to, but what kind of deal is the question. Could involve a civil fine. Or criminal."

"Can you elaborate on that for me?"

"Sure. It could likely be a housecleaning type of deal, probably followed by a civil fine payable to the State of Florida. But with no criminal prosecution, and little or no restitution for the victims. She could then claim a victory without really having accomplished anything significant." He paused to let her get caught up with her note taking. "Follow me on the timeline here. So far, we know that Larry Wells, Tony Grimes, Rocky Gambrone, and three of their goons were fired about a month ago. Gambrone's in jail, charged with four felonies. Jack Gates has been charged with thirty-one counts of felony fraud. Three weeks ago, the comptroller was fired. Then, two weeks ago, the general manager, Tommy Catatonia, and the rest of the accounting department was fired. Since then, from the last several conversations the

Florida AG has had with other victims, she doesn't seem to want to hear any new evidence that would force her to conduct a real investigation," explained Mark. "Taken as a whole, what does that look like to you?"

Jennifer's eyes opened wide. "You know, you're right. With the timeline of events, it does look like a deal that gets swept under the rug, leaving a lot of questions unanswered. And no charges filed. I will mention that in the story. Maybe the resulting public outcry will build a fire under their butts. So, don't underestimate the power of public opinion. Or the media," said Jennifer. She smiled, confident in the power wielded by those in her profession.

"That's exactly what the victims want to see," said Mark emphatically. "Help me serve them up a nice big slice of justice pie." His mouth was dry from all the talk. He reached for his glass of sweet tea and took several gulps.

After making more notes, she paused, and a puzzled look came over her face. "I'm curious, how did the Florida AG know about KG?"

"Good question. I appreciate your attention to details. About three weeks ago, the AG's office subpoenaed all of CVC's records and emails. There were over two hundred pages of emails from KG to John Dunne over a four month period containing crucial information about the crimes at Brandson. That's what got this whole thing going, like a snowball at the top of a mountain that became an avalanche."

"Interesting. I don't suppose you brought those emails with you?"

He was waiting for an opportunity to make the transition away from KG, and she provided him with the perfect segway. Mark leaned forward to emphasize the point he was about to make. "You don't need them now, Jennifer. You have me, the river of information right in front of you. KG's gone, served his purpose. Let's forget about him. He's like the match you used to start your campfire. Useful, now discarded and no longer important. Can you feel the heat from our fire?" He held out his hands as if fanning them in front of a campfire. "This isn't about KG anymore. Can we agree on that?"

She thought about this for a moment, and realized that what he said made sense. "Okay. So KG's gone, but we have your story, which essentially includes KG's story, and the stories of dozens of former employees." She was working backwards, flipping the pages through her notes. "And . . . all of the testimony from, what, sixty or seventy victims, so far? And their files. And the supporting documents from the fake deals. And, let's not forget, we've witnessed key employee terminations . . . and several felony arrests. Is that about it?" She thought for a moment, adding, "You realize this could go global."

Mark smiled at her. "You know, for a reporter, you're actually pretty damn smart. Will you feed your story into AP, UPI and all the major internet wire services?"

She nodded in agreement. "You better believe it," she said. "So, what makes a guy like you take the hard road up the mountain? What's next for you after the coming firestorm devours Gainesville?"

Mark was thinking. It was a good question. He realized that his mission with the reporter was now complete. He had secured the media commitment he'd been after for over a year after watching Brandson suppress the truth with their bribery for so long. Now, he could relax and play a little. He answered her question. "Maybe the Spartan lifestyle of a man clipping coupons." He grinned at her, waiting for her to come out and play with him. He knew she wanted to.

She removed her glasses and studied him like a forensic sketch artist who was faced with a difficult caricature. She was ready to create a composite drawing of the character who defied description, but she needed his help. As she chewed on the earpiece of her glasses, she said, "Somehow, that doesn't fit your profile. Seems to me you need more adrenaline," she said. "I've got a coupla questions for you."

"I knew you would," he said. They spent another twenty minutes reviewing victims' sales sheets, files on fake car deals, making copies, and discussing car sales lingo. Mark gave her a list he compiled of former sales employees, with their contact information, who had expressed an interest in helping to expose the dealership's crimes.

When they finished, she was exhausted. She looked up from her notes. Her hair was a mess. She said, "We got ourselves one hell of a story here, KG. My editor is gonna go bananas over it." She smiled and laid her pen down, resting her head in her hand. She got quiet, rubbed her temples, and looked for another way in. "You want some more tea?" she asked. He could tell she wanted something else.

"No thanks, Jennifer. Think I'm ready for a margarita. My inside guy used to always say 'You can't make this stuff up.' It's a helluva story, huh?" He grinned. Surrender was so close, he thought.

"You have an 'inside guy'?" Her obsession with the mystery kept growing. Played out from their intense two-hour dialogue, she harbored a burning desire to know his true identity. She wanted to open all the pages from his personal playbook that were stuck together. Finally, she asked, "Are you ever going to tell me who you are?" She was almost begging him, having solved one mystery and now completely wrapped up in another. He knew she couldn't let it go. She was ready. She pressed her cleavage harder against the table in a subconscious display of her desire to know who he was.

"How bad ya wanna know?" he asked. Her Venus was about to come undone.

She studied him for a few moments, drumming her manicured nails on the table in a staccato rhythm. He could almost see the tension moving lower down her torso. Then, she reached into her purse and pulled out her compact case and lipstick. She applied a fresh coat of pink Estee Lauder over her lips, alternating her gaze between Mark and the mirror, trying to make up her mind.

"You like sushi?" she asked, as she continued touching up her lipstick.

"I could eat it for hours," he said with a big grin. She peeked at him from behind her makeup mirror, trying to decide if he was being fresh or not. His ambiguity was artful, and it was driving her crazy.

"You got any ID or credit cards on you?" she asked him.

"Not really. Just two thousand in cash."

Pressing her lips together to smooth her lipstick, she snapped her compact closed with an air of finality, putting it back in her purse. She looked up, refreshed and ravenous. She gave him her sexiest smile.

"Then I'll drive," she said.

THIRTY-TWO

The front page story in the *Gainesville Banner* about Brandson's settlement with the Florida Attorney General was written in its entirety by the business editor, Andrew Tarr. Andrew had written much of it seventeen months ago. The treacherous tentacles of Brandson, laden with lots of cash, had weighed down the story's release for far too long. The headline read: "AG's OFFICE: BRANDSON SETTLES IN INVESTIGATION" and the sub-caption below it read: "Dealership To Pay $395,000 To Affected Customers". The three-page story covered one-third of the entire front page and ran for another two pages. It shocked and surprised the quiet college community of Gainesville on this sunny morning in July.

The story described the details of the arrests of former Brandson employees Jack Gates, charged with thirty-one counts of felony fraud of a senior citizen, and Roberto Gambrone, charged with felony possession of narcotics with intent to distribute, felony aggravated stalking, and illegal possession and discharge of a firearm by a convicted felon. It went on to articulate the terminations of Gates, Gambrone, Thomas Catatonia, general manager, Lawrence Wells, general sales manager, Anthony J. Grimes, manager, Ricardo

Gonzalez, manager, Dennis Testi, Raj Patel and the comptroller, Kelly Allen.

Buried deeper within the article, the AG's office was quoted in the press release as saying, "Purchasing or leasing an automobile is a major investment, and the Office of the Florida Attorney General intends to enforce our state's laws to ensure that our consumers are protected from deceptive and fraudulent sales practices. Our citizens deserve to receive full disclosure and accurate information when purchasing an automobile in the state of Florida."

It was Sunday morning, nine o'clock, exactly two days after Jennifer Treadstone had aired her story on WUFT's "Consumers' Hotline" show Friday morning. For this mid-sized college town, it was undoubtedly the biggest story of the year. All hell was breaking loose at the dealership as the media reporters swarmed like pirhanas on a cow carcass, climbing over each other and groveling for interviews with Brandson employees, the FBI, IRS and local police. Federal authorities had refused to comment on the deal with the Florida AG's office, citing an ongoing investigation. Rumors flew about further arrests and charges pending, but no one would go on record about what was expected to happen next. Scores of citizens who responded to the article at the newspaper's website felt that the AG's deal hadn't gone far enough and called for criminal charges to be filed against the dealership.

After reading the Brandson story in the *Gainesville Banner*, Tom Lewis, state attorney, set the paper down on his patio table to check on an incoming call. He was a little disturbed about all the calls. This was the eighth phone call he'd received in the last hour.

He heard his wife slide the glass door open. "Would you like more coffee, Tom?" Barb had become well-practiced at reading her husband's moods after thirty-six years of marriage. She could tell he was very worried about something this morning.

He turned and smiled at his wife reassuringly. "No thanks, honey. Just need a little privacy." The glass door rolled shut as his phone continued to ring. Lewis glanced over his shoulder to make sure Barb was busy inside. The call was from was Bob Gregory, the CFO at Brandson Enterprises. Lewis was conflicted about taking the call. Not wanting to be blind-sided again like he'd been on the Brandson story in the morning paper, he decided to find out what was on Gregory's mind.

"Bob, what a surprise. Don't tell me, you guys want your campaign donation back?" After the story broke about all the corruption, Lewis was wishing he hadn't accepted the five checks from Brandson Enterprises a few months ago. Now he was worried about the paper trail, and the money began to feel like a sticky commodity.

"No, Tom, you keep it. We need a man like you at the helm in the state attorney's office." Gregory waited for Lewis's reaction to his subtle sarcasm. He was busy watching the topless stripper stretching out on the chaise lounge on the other end of the pool, out of range of his conversation with the state attorney.

Lewis scowled at Gregory's remark. "Let's cut the crap, shall we? I did what I could for you. I warned you guys about KG. The deal with the Florida attorney general is only a slap on the wrist. This *is* a secure line, right?" Lewis was always paranoid about the NSA monitoring his calls, especially after the Snowden fiasco. He looked around his backyard again to make sure no one was listening.

"Of course, Tom. It's my satellite uplink phone." Gregory paused, shifting gears as he lounged beside the pool at his waterfront home in Sanibel Island. "I guess it could'a been a lot worse."

"Four hundred grand plus legal fees is a pretty sweet deal, Bob. C'mon, you guys can handle it. I heard you guys made over a hundred million last year." Lewis picked up the paper again and stared at the headlines, not expecting Gregory to argue his point.

"Easy for you to say. It's not your million, Tom. Cost us six hundred grand in legal fees." In the absence of any sympathy from the state attorney, he went on to the real reason for the phone call.

"Listen, what can you do to help with the Feds? They're pressing pretty hard, and I gotta find out who this KG guy is. You have any pull with the Bureau?"

"They're runnin' their own show, Bob. Completely independent. I heard they even stopped sharing with GPD. Apparently, they got wind of the leaks. I know their guys here in town, Danley and Moser. Costello's their economic crimes specialist, and I even know who their informant is."

Incredulous, Gregory raised his voice. "You *know* who he is? For chrissakes, tell me, Tom! We've been tryin' to figure this out for months!"

Lewis smiled, enjoying Gregory's reaction. "How 'bout this, Bob. I could text you his name and give the Feds a call for you, see what they're up to. For, shall we say, another hundred K?"

Gregory grimaced at Lewis's greed and lowered his voice. "Thievin' horse trader, you."

"Now, now. You guys got yourselves into this mess. You sure as hell can afford to buy your way out of it. This isn't the time to get cheap on me. You wanna fix this or not?" Lewis patiently watched a squirrel chewing on a nut in a tree a few feet away, confident he would get his hundred grand.

Gregory thought for a moment. He was in a tight spot, and Brandson was hemorrhaging money in damage control mode. He needed that name. Reluctantly, he agreed. "Okay. Sure, Tom. What's another hundred K when Toyota's leanin' on us for thirty million? Same drill as before?" he asked as he dipped his free hand in the pool water to check the temperature. It felt warm and inviting. He smiled and waved at Tiffany in her chaise lounge fifty yards away.

"Cash works better."

Gregory clicked off the logistics in his head, knowing Jim Brandson would likely agree to another six-figure 'donation' to fix their leak. "Sure, Tom. You'll have a FedEx package by Tuesday."

"Soon as I get the package, I text you the name and make the call." With the additional cash, Lewis was picturing how much nicer the pool and deck area would look with a new gazebo for his campaign parties.

Gregory's eyes squinted as his mean streak kicked in. Angry about the runaway expenses of cleaning up the mess, he said, "This time I fix the leak *my* way."

In a condescending tone that sounded like a third grade teacher disciplining his class, Lewis said, "Didn't hear that, Bob."

There was a click as Gregory hung up.

Forty minutes later, in the southwest part of town, Frank Moser sat on his screened back porch, lost in thought. He quit cigars two months ago, but after reading the Sunday paper this morning, he felt like celebrating. Pleased with the story, he pulled out a cigar from his secret stash in the garage, sat back down at his porch table and peeled back the wrapper. His wife always told him the cigars made his breath foul. He smiled to himself, thinking about his favorite response. " . . . *well, honey, just kiss me somewhere lower down.*" Clipping the end of the *Cohiba* with his cutter, he licked it and pulled a wooden match from the box, still thinking about the recent events at the dealership. The flame flickered and Moser puffed hard as he leaned back in his padded chair. Opportunities for career advancement raced through his head as he picked up his iPhone and hit the auto dial button for Brad Danley, blowing a smoke ring into the air. He heard his boss answer.

"See you're up. You read the paper yet?" Danley sounded groggy. He was a tournament-level poker player, and Moser knew he liked staying up late playing poker on Saturday nights.

"Yeah, I read it. You make any money last night, Brad, or are you still funding your neighbor's retirement plan?" Moser drew hard on the cigar and blew another smoke ring into the air as the paper's headlines stared up at him from the glass patio table.

"Two hundred bucks." As he voiced his response, Danley could feel a pain behind his eyes from all the vodka he drank the night before, and his head was throbbing. He was trying to remember where he put that bottle of Party Armor as he got the coffee ready.

"Well, you were right, Brad. Florida AG copped out. Now, they're grandstanding with their lame-ass, slap-on-the-wrist settlement with Brandson. Looks like they're not even insisting that Brandson admit to any guilt or wrongdoing. With the mountain of evidence parked under their own asses, can ya believe that?"

Danley shook his head, disgusted with the Florida AG's deal. "Pathetic. I guess it's up to us to carry the ball into the end zone and round these dirtbags up, Frank. We're the only ones left with jurisdiction in Georgia."

"Count me in on that ride. We're bringing Jim, too, right?" Moser could hear the kids next door playing in their yard behind the wooden privacy fence he built last summer.

"Absolutely." Still in his slippers, Danley lumbered down the tiled hall toward the front door. "Frank, gimme a second. I gotta do something. I'll call ya right back." His wife had taken the kids to church, and the the house was quiet except for the sound of the cat scratching in his litterbox. Now, all he had to do was find that little bottle of Party Armor.

"Sure, Brad. Call me back." Moser was enjoying his *Cohiba*, in no hurry to rush the conversation with his boss. Part of his plan was schmoozing Danley and setting the stage to present his agenda.

Danley fumbled with his bathrobe, tied the belt and stepped out into his front yard to retrieve his *Gainesville Banner*. Two kids on bikes rode by and waved at him as he unfolded the paper and read the headlines. He whistled out loud at the news. "Bet they sell out of *this* Sunday edition," he said to himself as he pulled the front door closed behind him. He took his cell phone back out of his bathrobe pocket and scrolled through it for missed calls. He noticed that the last one was from Tom Lewis. He had a contentious relationship with the state attorney, and Danley scowled at the thought of having to return his call.

Then he auto dialed Moser. "Hey. Looks like I got a coupla calls from reporters, and from our buddy the state attorney. You finally convinced me he's the source of those leaks. I got a voicemail from him a half hour ago."

"I'd bet my girl's college tuition fund on it. Whaddya wanna bet he wants to know our itinerary? You're not gonna call him back, are you boss?" Moser flicked a half-inch section of grey ash from his cigar into his coffee cup, squinting painfully at the thought of any more leaks.

"Not until after we make our run tomorrow." Trying to focus beyond his five-star hangover, Danley was starting to lose track of which of Well's thugs were still in Gainesville and which ones were in Atlanta. "So, how many does that make that he's lured over to the Hyundai place in Georgia?"

Moser tallied them up."Well, I found out yesterday from one of our sources that Tommy Catatonia, Ricky Gonzalez and Kirk Shifter all joined up with Well's new dog and pony show at the Hyundai dealer in Marietta. Looks like our boy's settin' back up with the whole motley crew at his new dealership. They're starting tomorrow. Pretty convenient, huh? You ready to take a ride?" Moser smirked at his rhetorical question.

"Yup. That makes six to bring back. With our crew of three plus Gronske, we're gonna have to take both SUVs for this haul. I've arranged for four agents from the Atlanta field office for back up."

"Sounds like a plan. We gotta bring Gary. He's been chasing down these scumbags for eighteen months, now. We owe him a shot at the action. Without his help, we wouldn't have our warrants yet." Moser thought for a moment as he blew another set of smoke rings into the air. In all the hoopla over the story in the paper, he forgot to mention something he'd come across this morning on the NCIC link on his home PC.

"Oh, you ready for this? Guess who Jacksonville Beach Police snagged last night in a drug sting operation at Mulligan's On The Beach?"

"Justin Bieber?"

Moser chuckled. "Funny, Brad. Close. None other than our very own 'Village Idiot', Anthony J. Grimes. They charged him with felony intent to distribute. I'll bet he's pissing in his pants in that half-assed cage they call a jail over on A1A."

Hearing this, Danley sat down in his leather recliner with his paper and phone. "No shit. I thought for sure he was gonna be our collar. Let's set up an interrogation and custody run for Wednesday. Maybe he rolls up and gives us more on Wells, Catatonia and Gonzalez."

"Sounds like a plan." Moser got serious. "Something I've been meaning to ask you about, Brad." Moser took a deep breath, ready to pop his question.

"Sounds serious. Shoot, Frank."

"We've worked together for five years, and you've been a great boss, but I'm ready to move up. There's a field office supervisory position that just opened up in Orlando. How would you feel about putting in a recommendation for me?"

Moser's request caught Danley off guard, and he was concerned about losing his best man. Every frayed nerve ending in his brain was craving caffeine, and he headed to the kitchen to pour himself a cup. Somberly, he said, "Well, Frank, you've done a great job for me and the Bureau in Gainesville. You're certainly qualified for it. I'd hate to lose you, but, yeah, I can help you with a recommendation. Let's round up these Brandson dirtbags first, and I'll put in the paperwork as soon as the District office can line up a replacement." He poured himself a cup of hazelnut-flavored Dunkin Donuts.

"Appreciate it, Brad. I am focused on our trip tomorrow. You know I'll always have your back." Moser surprised himself, getting emotional over the thought of leaving his buddies in the Gainesville field office. "By the way, when were you gonna tell KG about the two men Wells and Catatonia hired?"

"It's only a rumor, Frank." Danley took a greedy sip of his coffee and sank back into his leather recliner, hoping Moser would let it go.

"From a source we've trusted for a long time. KG's gone to the mat for us and had his neck in a noose for two years. We need to warn him. I don't want to be responsible for him getting hurt." Moser stood up. With a determined air of finality, he crushed what remained of his cigar into the bottom of his coffee cup and pushed his boss harder on the issue. "C'mon, Brad, you know these guys mean business. He's our best CI ever. I think we oughta offer him a deal."

Danley was thinking as he sipped his coffee. "Not sure it's in the budget, but you think he'd work with us on a WP deal?"

"He's got his own money. Plus, he handles himself well and loves chasin' down bad guys. No family in the area to hold him here. Just a girlfriend. And a house that's way too big for him. Let's ask him."

Danley's gut told him Moser was right. It was a good fit, and they owed him. They couldn't just standby and watch him get shot in the head. "Allright. I'll talk to District about it. Talk to Costello and get things ready for our roadtrip. These guys may be packin' AKs and ARs, so we're goin' in heavy."

O'Leary Hyundai and Kia was a modest family-owned dealership tucked into the hilly outskirts of Marietta, ten minutes from the bigger hills of upscale Lost Mountain and thirty minutes from downtown Atlanta. They prided themselves on being large enough to offer competitive prices and services comparable to the big-city dealerhips, but small enough to offer the personal care and attention you'd expect from a family-owned business in rural Georgia. With about two hundred cars sold a month, there were nine acres of new Hyundais and Kias at their two locations, and all makes and models of used cars, trucks, SUVs and vans. The hilly clay terrain made four-wheel drive pick up trucks especially popular with the locals.

It was a sunny morning in late July as the sun shone in the glass-enclosed showroom in front of O'Leary's office. An assortment of new Hyundai sedans and SUVs sparkled in the morning sun, carefully displayed on the tiled showroom floor. Kevin O'Leary, the sixty year old, grey-haired general manager sat at his desk reviewing the dealership's second quarter financials on his PC. Amazed, he ran his hand over his head as he stared at the figures. From what the big man could tell, their sales and profits were up a whopping hundred and fifteen percent since they hired that new fast-talking general sales manager from St. Augustine.

As part owner and general manager of their two dealerships in the Atlanta area, O'Leary had started out sixteen years ago with only ten thousand dollars and two cars on his lot. Several years ago, when the recession ended, he brought his brother into the business, expanded with the additional Kia franchise, and remodeled the two dealerships they ran today. As he prepared to get on his phone, the GM grabbed his styrofoam spitting cup from the desk top and deposited a healthy mixture of saliva and Skoal into the bottom. Now, he was ready for some coffee and conversation.

On the other side of O'Leary Hyundai, the dealership's conservative comptroller, Anita Whitten was at her desk, busy preparing the latest profit and loss statements. Her calculations showed holdbacks, incentives, spiffs, and rebates were increasing as their dealership's turnover accelerated, but she was alarmed by the longer extensions and ballooning total debt. Dealer profits were soaring, but what really had her worried were the deceptions and overcharges that she'd been inundated with. Long term goals were being sacrificed for short term gains by their new GSM. She took a big swig from her Coke, adjusted her glasses, and dug deeper. There were another sixteen misappropriations and accounting entries that weren't adding up. Scrutinizing the figures, she tapped on her computer screen with her fingernail as if the numbers were stuck, testing the accuracy of what she saw. Anita set her glasses down and rubbed her forehead to relieve the tension building in her face. She didn't relish another argument with their new GSM, but she didn't want to lose her CPA license because of his dishonesty. Then there were the complaints.

Printing the troublesome files, she placed all of the allegations of wrongdoing she'd received in a special file marked "NEW COMPLAINTS." The dealership had never had to do this before. There were forty-six emails, letters and phone calls from customers who claimed they'd been defrauded or overcharged by either Larry Wells, Ricky Gonzalez, their new F&I manager, Kirk Shifter, their new used car manager, or Dennis Testi and Raj Patel. Many of the lenders and local banks were complaining about 'alterations and fabrications' in the credit applications. Three Georgia-based banks had even refused to do any more business with O'Leary Hyundai, and Anita was concerned about their reputation.

It was ten forty-five. As she continued to scroll through the computer screens one by one, her cell phone rang. The number read "PRIVATE." Anita was apprehensive about taking the call, but her curiosity and fiduciary duty as corporate comptroller drove her to answer.

"This is Anita. Who's this, please?" She listened intently, trying to recognize the voice on the phone with her.

A man's voice answered, "A friend, Anita. I'm on your side. Do you have a man named Larry Wells working there?" His voice was even and calm, and had a soothing quality to it. It wasn't recognizable to her.

"He's our general sales manager. Who are you?" The man could tell her nerves were frayed and she sounded like she might hang up the phone any second.

The caller paused, and Anita adjusted her phone so she could hear him better. "I'm associated with a group called Consumers Against Crime in Florida, where Mr. Wells last worked. I want to tell you my name, but I can't." The man paused again, very measured in what he had to say.

"Why can't you tell me your name?" She was distraught over the mystery she was being dragged into, wondering if she or her family were in any danger. A myriad of scenarios flashed through her mind.

"It would be better for both of us if I didn't. I'm risking a lot just to call and warn you."

"Risking what?" She could tell the man wanted to say more, but something was holding him back. Was it fear?

"Please, Anita, just listen to what I have to say. You'll be glad you did."

"Wait." She got up, waved at a co-worker sitting at her desk in accounting, and closed her office door. "Okay, I'm listening."

"Good. By now, you're probably aware of certain accounting irregularities, overcharges, dishonesty, maybe even some fraud and forgery on the part of Mr. Wells and his clan. Wells and his 'Redneck Mafia' have been the subjects of a criminal investigation-"

"Criminal investigation?" she asked.

"Yes. Criminal, by the FBI and IRS for more than two years. They have underworld connections." When she heard this, he heard her take a sharp, deep breath. He stopped, not wanting to frighten her, now wishing he hadn't mentioned that part.

"How do you know this?" She pressed the phone tighter against her ear.

"Doesn't matter. Let's just say I know this guy pretty well, and he'll line his pockets, rip everyone off, and take your dealership down. Guaranteed. You can put a stop to it"

"His job application said nothing about-"

"About fraud, forgery, money laundering and extortion? Does that surprise you, Anita?" The truth has a certain ring to it, and Anita knew she was hearing the truth. "Go on."

"If you want to keep your job and get rid of this swindler, tell O'Leary about our conversation and the accounting issues you've uncovered. As soon as you can. Maybe O'Leary mans up and cans him."

"This guy scares me . . . whatever your name is." Her voice trailed off as she pictured her son and daughter in daycare. "I love my kids . . . I don't want to . . . "

"I know. Just tell O'Leary about our conversation." She heard a click as the man hung up. Very distraught, she sat in silence, wringing her hands over what to do. She thought about her kids, and then she took a deep breath, deciding to confront her GSM about the anonymous caller and accounting issues. Maybe she could make a deal and get him to straighten up and fly right. She couldn't quite bring herself to put her entire future in the hands of an anonymous caller. She dialed Well's extension.

"Larry Wells."

"Larry, its Anita. I got something I need to talk with you about. You have five minutes for me?"

"For you, Anita. Sure. C'mon over. You can meet Tommy Catatonia, my buddy from Florida. He's gonna be the new GSM over at our other location."

"Well, it's kinda private—"

"Tommy and I have no secrets. C'mon over, let's talk." Wells hung up. Anita grabbed her file and headed across the showroom toward Well's office, hoping he would understand that it was her duty to question the numbers. Wells had the corner office, and it was the largest and most luxurious of all the offices at O'Leary Hyundai. It was even larger than O'Leary's. Catatonia was seated in one of the leather upholstered chairs when Anita arrived.

"Hi. Just need five minutes." She glanced over at Catatonia, who wore a tailored black Italian suit. It looked expensive. She took the open seat and was struck by how much Catatonia looked like John Gotti, the mob boss. Nervous, she said "Hi, I'm Anita, the comptroller for Mr. O'Leary's dealerships."

"Nice to meet you, Anita." Catatonia seemed pleasant, but aloof. She noticed that Catatonia had not stood to be introduced.

"So what's up, Anita." Impatient with her niceties, Wells wanted to take control and get down to business. The Devil would give her no quarter today.

Flustered, she clutched her files closer to her. "Well, I've been coming across a lot of overcharges—"

Wells interrupted her. "Stop. We're here to make money, Anita. We're gonna sell cars, and we don't care how we do it! That's what Kevin hired me to do! What else ya got?" Wells glared at the comptroller, his patience wearing thin from two other similar arguments with her over the last three weeks.

Annoyed with his rudeness, she continued, nervously smoothing her slacks with her free hand while she continued to clutch her file with the other. "Larry, it's my job to report fraud and uncover-"

Wells raised his voice to intimidate her. "Your job is what I tell you it is. Now, what else ya got?" He was getting nasty, like last time, and Anita was getting more upset. Catatonia said nothing, almost like he expected the conversation.

"We've been getting a lot of complaints, and some of them are serious—"

Wells frowned, leaned forward, and clasped his hands on his desktop. "You're not listening to me, Anita. I was hoping we could work as a team here, but I see it's just not gonna work with you and me. You're fired! Pack up your stuff. I want you out of here by noon today. Got it?" The veins on his face bulged out in anger while Catatonia sat there, pokerfaced. Her mouth dropped open, speechless. She stood up, angry, her voice trembling. "You can't just fire me! I've been working for Kevin five years! I have a family to support! And I gotta call telling me you're being investigated by the FBI! Is that-"

Wells jumped to his feet, yelling, "You say anything to anybody about that and you'll wish you hadn't. You take your kids to Kindercare PreSchool, right?" Anita was horrified at his thinly-veiled threat to harm her kids if she spoke up. Now, she knew for sure Wells was downright evil.

Anita was scared and speechless. This time she was gripped with fear for her kids. Her maternal instincts took over, and she stormed out of his office. Catatonia just sat there without saying a word. Sobbing, she ran to Kevin O'Leary's office, passing co-workers in the hallway who stopped to stare, confused by their comptroller's erratic behavior.

It was eleven-fifteen. O'Leary was in his office studying the floorplan that their new GSM had worked up while he watched Raj Patel in the showroom trying to close a bean farmer he knew. O'Leary thought Well's floorplan was pretty ambitious and would require a bank loan extension from Hyundai, which made him uncomfortable.

"Kevin, I need to talk with you. It's important!" O'Leary looked up to see his comptroller standing in his doorway with tears streaming down her cheeks and holding a thick file folder. Surprised at the sight of her tears, he stood up.

She blurted, "Larry just fired me. Kevin, I can't work with him. He's a monster!"

"What's the *problem*, Anita? Hey, c'mon in, sweetie. Have a seat." He gestured at the leather chairs sitting in front of his desk. For five years, Anita had been his trusty comptroller for both dealerships. He had full confidence in her skills, knowing she had a degree in accounting and finance from the University of Georgia and kept him out of hot water on more than a few occasions.

Regaining some of her composure, she reluctantly complied with his request. "Okay." She turned and closed the door. As she dropped herself into the chair, she handed O'Leary the half-inch thick manila folder marked "NEW COMPLAINTS."

"*That's* the problem, Kev." She pulled on her long brown hair back, wiping tears from her face, waiting expectantly for his response. Almost apologetically, she raised her palms. "You asked me to keep you informed on this stuff. So, I am."

He laid the folder on his desk, sat down and began reading the letters and emails. One after another, there were customers complaining of everything from certification frauds, deception, overcharging, and even forgery. Some of the letters were from local banks and lenders, claiming that documents and loan applications were being altered by someone at the dealership.

"Jeez, Anita, why didn't you say something sooner about this stuff?" He leaned back in his chair waiting for her explanation, confused about how to handle the situation.

"Larry threatened to fire me if I said anything." Her hands were trembling and her voice was uneven. She lowered her gaze as if she were partially to blame. She sensed that O'Leary was conflicted about what to do.

The home-grown Georgia boy leaned forward to make a point. "Anita, this guy's makin' me sixty thousand a month. I can't just fire him."

"Kevin, *he's* making *seventy* thousand a month. That's more than all the other sales reps and managers combined!" She was frustrated, wringing her hands. "Kev, I can't deal with him. He's scary. He's threatened me *and* my kids. I don't want to lose my license or, worse, wind up in jail. It's just not worth it to me. I'm leaving." Anita stood and stepped toward the door. "I'm gonna go pick up my kids."

O'Leary held up his hand but said nothing, convinced she would call him later to say she'd changed her mind. He continued to sit at his desk for several more minutes reading the complaints in the file, finding some of them hard to believe.

At exactly eleven twenty-five, Vernon, his youngest salesman and a senior lineman for the Bulldogs until his graduation last year, came running across the showroom into his office. "Mr. O'Leary, ya gotta see this. There's two big black SUVs fulla SWAT guys pullin' up out front. I think they're FBI agents!"

O'Leary stood up in time to see the first two black SUVs joined by a third that pulled up behind the first two with military-style precision. The doors opened and seven FBI agents and a GPD detective wearing SWAT gear were climbing out, checking their weapons and equipment. As if choreographed, they turned in unison and headed for the front door of the dealership.

"Holy shit, Mr. O'Leary, they're comin' in the showroom!" Vernon stared in awe, only having seen this kind of action in movies and video games.

Holding seven warrants, Danley was the first one through the door, followed closely behind by Moser, Costello and Gronske. This was the day they'd all been waiting for. Backed up by four agents from the Atlanta field office, they looked fierce in their Kevlar vests and duty belts, wearing M-16s strapped to their backs and Sig Sauer P226s drawn and pointing down at the floor. Danley yelled, "FBI! Everyone, stay where you are!"

Danley confronted O'Leary in the middle of the showroom. The general manager still couldn't believe what was happening. "You Kevin O'Leary?"

"Yes, sir. What's this all about?" O'Leary looked them up and down, confused and clearly intimidated by their weapons. Several staff and salesmen stood motionless watching the drama unfold. Danley held the warrants up as Moser, Costello, and Gronske encircled O'Leary and kept a sharp eye out for their perps.

"I'm Special Agent Danley. Sir, we have Federal warrants for the arrest of Lawrence Wells, Thomas Catatonia, Ricardo Gonzalez, Kirk Shifter, Rajaman Patel and Dennis Testi, and we have a Federal search warrant for the premises. Where are these men now?" Briefed from the files and photos of the perps on their way in, three of the eight agents fanned out toward the offices to search for their quarry while two agents holding M-16s positioned themselves beside the side entrances.

Shocked by the presence of the FBI in full SWAT gear occupying his dealership, O'Leary pointed toward the service area to his left. "Patel was standing over there a minute ago, Testi's around here somewhere, and the other four are in their offices in the back. Whad'they do?"

Moser glanced at Gronske with a quizzical expression and took a step closer to O'Leary, still gripping his Sig Sauer pointed at the floor. He got right in O'Leary's face. "What *didn't* they do?" he asked. With his free hand, he waved his group toward the offices in the back. "C'mon, guys, let's round'em up!"

When he heard his name called out, Testi, who had been hiding in the rear corner of the showroom, began to casually meander toward the side entrance where he parked his Mercedes. He held his car keys tightly. Only moments from a clean getaway, he pushed the remote button, and the car chirped as the doors unlocked. With his hand on the handle, he opened his car door, preparing to get in.

"*Freeze!*" Testi spun around to see the agent position the muzzle of his M-16 inches from his face. "Hands behind your head, on your knees *now!*" The agent glanced at the photo on his briefing page to confirm Testi's identity. As his partner clasped Testi's wrists in handcuffs, the agent with the M-16 barked, "Dennis Testi, you are under arrest for conspiracy to use an IED, defrauding senior citizens, forgery and racketeering. Anything you say can and will be used against you in a court of law. Nod if you understand your rights." Handcuffed, head lowered in shame, Testi nodded as he knelt beside the open door of his new Mercedes SLS AMG.

In the same instant, Costello was handcuffing Patel inside the showroom. Sniveling like a third grader, Jabba the Hutt was just too fat to mount a successful escape attempt, and he was read his rights and taken into custody without incident, charged with forgery and multiple counts of defrauding senior citizens. "Cuffs too tight?" he asked Patel. Tears were running down his cheeks as Costello sat him inside his SUV for the long ride back.

"Yeah, too tight," he sniveled. "Could you loosen them, officer?"

"Soon as we get back to Gainesville." Light on sympathy for all the despicable crimes the group had commited against handicapped and senior citizens, Costello checked to make sure Patel was secure inside the SUV and slammed the door. He ran back inside to catch up with Moser and Gronske, stopping to watch two agents taking

Shifter into custody. Costello heard later that Shifter gave up without incident, except for for thirty seconds of uncontrolled flatulence. Moser, Gronske and Costello continued with their room-to-room search for Wells, Catatonia and Gonzalez.

The agents had cleared the dealership of all other personnel and checked the lot to make sure Wells's McLaren P-10, Catatonia's Bugatti Veyron and Gonzalez's Audi R-8 were still parked outside. They had to be hiding somewhere in the building, and they were closing in while Danley stood in the center of the dealership, coordinating the raid with his shoulder microphone and watching the perimeter for perps on the loose. With their Sig P226s drawn and pointing straight ahead, the three agents moved slowly and silently down a narrow hallway toward voices they were hearing all the way at the rear of the building.

Moser had the lead, whispering over his shoulder, "I think I heard them talking inside this storage room." They heard the voices again. Ten feet from the door, Moser yelled, "FBI! Come out with your hands up or we'll use a stun grenade!"

Catatonia yelled back, "Okay, okay, we're coming out! Don't shoot! We're not armed!" As the storage room door opened, Moser yelled, "Step out backwards, hands behind your heads! *Now!*"

Catatonia was the first to emerge, followed by Wells and Gonzalez. "Don't shoot, we're comin' out," pleaded Wells as he walked backwards with his hands behind his head, still holding his cell phone, followed by Tricky Ricky Gonzalez.

"On your knees *now!*" yelled Gronske. As the trio dropped to their knees, the agents rushed them, grabbed their hands, and cuffed them. As Moser restrained Wells, he grabbed the cell phone Wells was holding and put it to his ear. "Who's this?" he demanded.

A voice answered, "Billy Stanger, Larry's criminal attorney. We were arranging his bond—"

"This is Special Agent Frank Moser of the FBI. Wells is under arrest for twenty-seven felony counts. You don't need to worry about his bail bond, Billy. I will guaran-dam-tee-ya the Federal judge in Jacksonville will deny him bond, and we're confiscating this phone." Moser pushed the talk button and hung up, securing the phone in his vest pocket to be tagged and bagged. He looked at Gronske. "Ya ready to do this?'

"I'll flip ya for the honors," said Gronske as he pulled a quarter out of his vest pocket. He tossed it into the air with a flick of his thumb, and Moser called heads as the coin landed in Gronske's palm. Gronske flipped it over onto his forearm, removed his hand, exclaiming, "Heads it is!"

Moser smiled. "On your feet!" The last of the 'Redneck Mafia' stood up, ready to hear their rights. Moser continued. "Lawrence Wells, Thomas Catatonia, Ricardo Gonzalez, you are hereby under arrest, charged with extortion, racketeering, money laundering, conspiracy to distribute cocaine, possession of automatic firearms by a convicted felon . . . ." Moser stepped forward, facing off with Wells, inches from his face, looking straight into his eyes. " . . . and conspiracy to commit first degree murder. Anything you say can and will be used against you in a court of law."

Wells sneered at Moser with unmitigated contempt, the veins on his forehead bulging, unable to control his temper. "You'll never see your snitch again, dumbass!"

Catatonia snapped at Wells over his shoulder. "Larry, shut the hell up! Haven't ya got us into enough damn trouble? Shut up!" Gonzalez chimed in, "Yeah, Larry, shut up for God's sake, man!"

Wells had harbored a deep hatred for law enforcement since he was ten years old. He was unable to control the contempt welling up from deep inside him. Still only inches from Moser's face, he reared his head back and hurled a wad of spit in his face. Shocked, Moser wiped the spit off his face, instinctively drawing back his arm to throw a punch at the undisputed leader of the "Redneck Mafia." Gronske grabbed his arm in the nick of time.

"Frank, he's not worth it." Moser glared at Wells, still struggling to control himself. To the list of charges, he added " . . . and assaulting a Federal agent."

One agent paired up with each of the men, holding them firmly as they were led toward the SUVs to join the other three for the long ride south. The denizens of the sewer were being led back to their cages, where they would remain for a long time.

As Moser put Wells in the back seat of his SUV, he followed procedure and placed his hand on Wells's head to make sure he didn't hit the roof of his vehicle.

The FBI agent turned his prisoner's head toward his own, looked him in the eyes and said, "Look at me, dick head. You charged my aunt seven grand over sticker. She said to say hi."

EPILOGUE

Fedora-topped, tanned and toned, the silver-haired blue blood stopped at the end of the long sandy road that led to the water's edge. Straddling his two-tone Nel Lusso designer beach cruiser at the edge of the ocean, he was thirty feet from the surf as he looked back over his shoulder down the sand road just traveled. He walked the bike a few feet forward to give him a better view of the vast empty shoreline stretching north and south. The sensation of balmy breeze mingling with the warmth from the sunrise penetrated the skin on his face. Not a soul could be seen in either direction. He thought about Sandy.

He was cruising among the blue bloods way down low under the radar, luxuriating in the charming sights and tropical scents of ten million dollar beachfront mansions shaded under green canopies of three and four-hundred year old live oaks on the barrier island.

He stayed small, off the grid, blending in, paid cash for everything, often wishing he could stay, forever and safely, on the reef seventy feet down. He embraced the beauty of the tropical landscape and turquoise surf like it was his birthright. This was his ticket to life. He anguished over whether it offered him enough camouflage to stay concealed from the gunmen who searched for him.

POSTCRIPT

After serving twelve years of a fifteen year sentence for defrauding senior citizens, JACK ARMSTRONG GATES relocated to San Francisco and became a hairdresser. He is currently awaiting approval of his Medicare application for a sex change operation.

Following his termination during the Brandson investigations, PAUL VERNON MCCREEDY opened a carpet cleaning business in Newberry, Florida and married an eighteen-year-old African American girl named Boanmi. They have seven kids of their own, and three more by her ex, who is serving thirty years at Raiford.

ELIZABETH MATILDE MELMANN joined a criminal law practice in Boca Raton after her demotion for failure to discharge fiduciary duties at the Florida Attorney General's office in Orlando. Melman currently lives in West Boca with her mother, who suffers from Alzheimer's and often refers to her daughter as "Sally."

RICARDO MANUEL GONZALEZ served sixteen years of a twenty year sentence for fraud, forgery, money laundering and conspiracy to commit murder. After his release, he relocated to San Juan, Puerto Rico, opening a home for wayward women until his license was revoked for child molestation.

ROBERT FRANKLIN DANZIGER quit the car business and relocated to Erie, Pennsylvania to open a scrap metal yard and canning factory, which he says he needs " . . . like a hole in the head."

KIRK ADOLPH SHIFTER served eight years of a twelve-year sentence for fraud and conspiracy to distribute narcotics and relocated to Schenectady, New York where he owns and operates a small burrito factory powered entirely by natural gas.

Former editor of the *Gainesville Banner*, DOUGLAS HENRY GRAYSON, retired a year after publishing the first of a five-part series on the corruption at Brandson Enterprises. He draws a modest pension and now publishes a local senior citizen guide for television called "TV Facts" in Gainesville, Florida where the magazine enjoys a circulation of seven thousand.

JAMES FRANCIS COSTELLO left the FBI a year after the Brandson raids and is now employed at the NSA where he is a specialist in electronic eavesdropping. He is currently under indictment by the DOJ following the Snowden disclosures.

ANDREW WINSTON TARR and JENNIFER ABIGAIL TREADSTONE married six months after Andrew received a Pulitzer Prize for his series of stories on the Brandson corruption. They have a child named "KG" and own and operate the most successfull independent magazine in Alachua County, Florida, called *32607*.

RICHARD MICHAEL DEVERAUX divorced his wife Carla and left AT&T after three years as a District Manager. He opened a successful chain of strip clubs in South Florida and added DriveUp Bail Bonds at five of the locations last year.

One year after the Brandson investigations, GARY WAYNE GRONSKE was promoted to Lietenant of Detectives at GPD, divorced his wife, and is now part-owner of two all-nude nightclubs in Micanopy, Florida.

ROBERTO HECTOR GAMBRONE served eighteen years for his convictions on conspiracy to distribute narcotics, aggravated stalking, racketeering, and illegal possession of a firearm by a convicted felon. Upon his release, he started a porn website catering to shemales.

The former GM of Brandson, THOMAS RUDOLPH CATATONIA, succumbed to angina while serving a thirty year sentence for conspiracy to commit murder, fraud, extortion, racketeering and money laundering. After his funeral, his widow donated thirty-two Brioni suits to Goodwill.

LAWRENCE KEVIN WELLS is serving a thirty-five year sentence for conspiracy to commit murder, extortion, fraud, embezzlement, forgery, conspiracy to distribute narcotics, money laundering and racketeering. He is currently hospitalized in a high-security Federal penitentiary suffering from "rectal dysfunction" and "complications of pneumonia."

Leaving the FBI one year after the Brandson raids, FRANK PAUL MOSER and BRADLEY SINCLAIR DANLEY became partners, opening their own successful security firm headquartered in Orlando, Florida. Their firm, which manages security for golf course communities, is called "Wackenputt."